COLLECTIONS

OF THE

NEW JERSEY

HISTORICAL SOCIETY.

VOLUME VI.

NEWARK, N. J.

1864.

RECORDS

OF THE

TOWN OF NEWARK,

NEW JERSEY,

FROM ITS SETTLEMENT IN 1666, TO ITS INCORPORATION
AS A CITY IN 1836.

NEWARK, N. J

1864.

INTRODUCTION.

Early in the month of May, 1666, a few small vessels entered the Passaic River and steered their course towards the uplands that loomed in the distance towards the west. The low meadows, through which the river winds its way to its confluence with the Hackensack, must have possessed then, as now, little that was picturesque or attractive, although those on board the vessels referred to may have estimated the "plains of good Hay of 50 acres of Ground, with hardly one tree to be seen upon the whole Spot—and several Places so," as highly as did the early settlers elsewhere in New Jersey, who pointedly alluded to them as among the natural objects that wooed them hither. But the higher land beyond, to which the voyagers were destined, then lying in all its original beauty, varied with hill and dale, plain and forest, must have presented so many unmistakable advantages for the location of a town, that it is not remarkable they should have looked towards it with bright anticipations; although we cannot reasonably suppose that the most sanguine among them, when their thoughts rested upon the probabilities of the future, ever fancied results so great as have flowed from the settlement they were about to make—for these vessels bore to New Jersey the pioneers of those who founded NEWARK.

Since then, while Time has been unrolling his eventful scroll of nearly two hundred years, the successors of the first-comers have diligently labored to cover the site selected for their "town upon the Passaic River" with all the utilitarian adjuncts and appliances which the world's progress has rendered essential to the comfort and happiness, physically and mentally, of a population of 80,000 souls. Success has crowned their labors, and the New Jersey Historical Society present in this volume, the official record of the public measures by which the first adventurous spirits and those who came after them, secured good order, peace and prosperity from the settlement of the town until its incorporation as a City in 1836; confident that the duty thus performed cannot but prove serviceable to the people of the State through all time.

In the month of August, 1665, PHILIP CARTERET—the commissioned governor of his brother Sir George Carteret and Lord John Berkley, the first proprietors of New Jersey under the grant from the Duke of York—arrived in the Province on board the "Ship Philip," bringing with him "about thirty people," who, with four families who had arrived a short time previously, formed the nucleus of the settlement at Elizabethtown. Immediately after his arrival, the governor despatched messengers into New England to publish "the Concessions," so called, of the Lords Proprietors—being the terms upon which settlers would be admitted—and to invite emigrants to the rich and virgin soil of New Jersey.

The propositions of the governor appear to have received immediate attention from the people of Milford, Connecticut, and ROBERT TREAT, a prominent man among them, and subsequently governor of that province, was delegated, in conjunction with others from adjoining plantations, to visit New Jersey and examine into its actual and prospective advantages. Their first intention was to settle on the Delaware river, near the present site of Burlington, but not being favorably impressed with that location they returned to Elizabethtown, and were induced by Gov. Carteret to select lands lying north of that place. Some negotiations had already taken place with the aboriginal owners looking to the acquisition of the tract, and the governor furnished Mr. Treat with a letter to their chiefs, requesting them to perfect the sale directly to him.

These arrangements must have been made in the autumn of 1665, but no interview with the Indians seems to have taken place at that time. The following Spring, as we have seen, the vessels bearing the first company of settlers, arrived in the Passaic. "But," said Mr. Treat, twenty-three years thereafter, "no sooner was the company present got on the Place and landed some of their goods, than I with some others was by some of the Hackensack Indians warned off the Ground, and [they] seemed troubled and angry that we landed any of our goods there, tho' first we told them we had the governor's order; but they replied the land was theirs, and it was unpurchased; and therefore we put our Goods on board the vessels again and acquainted the Governor with the matter."* This conference with the governor, and subsequent negotiations with the Indians, led to the purchase and quiet possession of the lands; although in after years a disinclination on the part of many of the settlers to obtain from the Proprietors the confirmation of their titles by Patents for the property, was the occasion of many disorderly acts and harrassing legal proceedings.

It was while these preliminary measures were being taken that the meeting was held, either on board of one of their vessels, or on the land "near to Elizabethtown," on 21st May, 1666, the result of which may be seen in the opening document of the records, providing for the common occupancy of the new tract by the people from Milford, Guilford and Brandford, should the latter so determine before the ensuing November. It is thought that the first party consisted of about thirty families, but it is probable that only a few remained on the ground the first summer.

On the 30th October of the same year, 1666, the inhabitants

* Elizabethtown Bill in Chancery, p. 118.

of Brandford, previous to embarking, formally acceded to the propositions for a common interest in the new "Town upon Passaic River," and those already on the ground subsequently joined in committing themselves to the "Fundamental agreements," which are on the second and subsequent pages of the book.

As yet the name of the new settlement does not appear in any of the documents, but it seems from "Scot's Model of the Government of East Jersey" (p. 274) that it was probably at first known as "*Milford;*" but on the arrival of the people of Brandford, bringing with them their Church organization, such pre-eminence in the councils of the new settlement was secured, that the name of Milford was dropped and that of NEWARK conferred upon the town, in honor of the Rev. Abraham Pierson, their pastor, who had officiated, or been ordained, at Newark, in England.

To Robert Treat, the first Recorder or Town Clerk, we are probably indebted for the preservation of the documents relating to the settlement from its commencement until 1672, when he returned to Connecticut; and the Treasurer, as ordered by the Town in 1669, provided a Book, which is still extant, in which Mr. Treat commenced the "Record of Lands." The irregularity observable in entering the proceedings of several Town Meetings in the Town Book is probably attributable to the inadvertence of Mr. Treat's successor on copying his papers.

In 1775, Joseph Hedden, Jun'r, agreed with the Town to purchase a Bound Book in folio, and to "transcribe the old Town Book into the new one," in a legible fair hand. This volume contains the Minutes of Town Meetings in Newark from 1667 to 1775, as found in that book, with the exception of the Meetings from April 12th, 1714, to March 8th, 1714–15, which are omitted in that transcript. These are from the original record made by John Cooper, Town Clerk, of which a few leaves relating to the following year are lost. The Town Patent of 1713, and also the Survey given in the Appendix, are printed as recorded by him.

From 1775 to 1832 we have the books as written up by the several Town Clerks, and it has been thought proper to follow the originals as nearly as possible in orthography, abbreviations, capitals, and punctuation, except in the transcript from the old book, in which some additional pointing seemed necessary. In a few instances, an explanatory word or name has been introduced in brackets. The first part of the transcript, or about six pages of this volume, was printed in November, 1834, in the Newark Daily Advertiser, at which time the first leaf containing the names of the signers of the fundamental agreement was mislaid. In the substituted one, the name of Zachariah Burwell is omitted. It is now restored to its place as then printed, and as the Indian and the English Proprietors' Deeds, given in the Appendix, have been carefully compared with the record in the office of the Secretary of State, it is believed they are as near correct as they can be made, as the depositories of the originals, if they are yet in existence, are unknown.

This brief introduction to the contents of the volume is all that has been deemed necessary. It would have been rendered of more interest to the general reader, and more useful in some respects, had it been accompanied by notes and explanations, but it was thought more consistent with the objects of the Society, to place the Records in the hands of the people of the State in their original form, leaving to individual enquirers the developement of obscure events or contemporaneous matter. The Genealogical and local information it contains must render the volume exceedingly acceptable, not only to all in any way connected now with the city to whose history it particularly refers, but also to the inhabitants of a large portion of the State of which Newark is the centre, whose population and business relations, whose customs and manners, as well as their political and religious opinions, have been in a great degree drawn from it, or been framed in accordance with the influences it may have exerted in the past.

The labor and responsibility of superintending the passage of the work through the press devolved upon Mr. WILLIAM A. WHITEHEAD, the Society's Corresponding Secretary, and Mr. SAMUEL H. CONGAR, its Librarian. The Table of Officers in the Appendix, and the Index to the Contents were contributed by the former, and to the latter was deputed the difficult task of reading the proof sheets. It is due to Mr. Congar to say that by no other person could the duty have been so faithfully and intelligently performed, his intimate acquaintance with names, localities and circumstances connected with the town and its history, enabling him to solve doubts and correct errors, where another person would have been entirely at fault.

The Map appended to the volume shows the extent of the town at two periods, being lithographed from a photographically reduced copy of one published in 1806, from surveys made by C. Basham, then principal of the Newark Academy, with additional lines, showing the first home-lots of the settlers.

RECORDS OF NEWARK.

1666.

IMPRIMIS, In the Province of New Jersey, near to Elizabeth Town, and the Town Plotts on Passaic River, made choice of by friends from Milford and other neighboring plantations, thereabouts from New England, on the twenty first day of May, one thousand six hundred and sixty-six, the above mentioned persons had a meeting, together with the agents sent from Guilford and Brandford to ask on behalf of their undertakers and selves with reference to a township or allottments, together with friends from Milford; at this meeting it was agreed upon mutually that the aforesaid persons from Milford, Guilford, and Brandford, together with their associates, being now accepted of, do make one township, provided they send word so to be any time between this and the last of October next ensuing, and according to fundamentals mutually agreed upon, do desire to be of one heart and consent, through Gods blessing with one hand they may endeavor the carrying on of spiritual concernments as also civil and town affairs according to God and a Godly government; there to be settled by them and their associates. They then mutually chose eleven empowered for a committee, viz: Capt. Robert Treatt, Lieut. Samuel Swain, Mr. Samuel Kitchell, Michal Tompkins, Mr. Morris, Sergt. Richard Beckly, Richard Harrison, Thomas Blatchly, Edward Riggs, Stephen Freeman, and Thomas Johnson for the speedier and better expedition of things then emergent to be done; then also six or more, at the least five of the committee who might remain or be in the place, were mutually chosen and appointed to order and settle the concernments and people of the place, till another committee be chosen and settled; all of the eleven above said, do in the name and behalf of the inhabitants there being, or to come, do mutually covenant and agree, that the agents from Guilford and Branford do take up and hold till June in the year one thousand six hundred and sixty seven, and fully to dispose of, provided it be possessed, built upon, and settled according to order, for their associates, for themselves, theirs and such as they shall send, provided that these last bring due testimonials to the committee there for the town, and they approve of them lots, allottments in every division equally privileged as far as may be with the rest of the planters then being or to be; as also the aforesaid agents, and their associates shall be respectively equalized in all privileges whatsoever; the town or limits thereof according to their fundamentals agreed upon with the place may at any time afford or be capable for a mutual benefit. To the true intention and performance hereof, we whose names are underwritten, do subscribe or sign in the behalf of the persons above mentioned in the year one thousand six hundred and sixty six, the twenty fourth of May.

Signed

Copy enrolled per me
ROBERT TREATT, Recorder.

ROBERT TREATT,
SAMUEL SWAIN.

OCTOBER 30th, 1666.

At a meeting Touching the Intended design of many of the inhabitants of Branford, the following was subscribed:

1st. That none shall be admitted freemen or free Burgesses within our Town upon Passaick River in the Province
Deut. 1—13. Exod. 18—21. Deut. 17—15. of New Jersey, but such Planters as are members of some or other of the Congregational Churches nor shall any but such be chosen to Magistracy or to Carry on any part of Civil Judicature, or as deputies or assistants, to have power to Vote In establishing Laws, and making
Jerem. 30—21. or Repealing them or to any Chief Military Trust or Office. Nor shall any But such Church Members have any Vote in any such elections; Tho' all others admitted to Be planters have Right to their proper Inheritance, and do and shall enjoy all other Civil Liberties and Privileges, According to all Laws, Orders, Grants which are, or hereafter shall be made for this Town.

2nd. We shall with Care and Diligence provide for the maintenance of the purity of Religion professed in the Congregational Churches. Whereunto subscribed the Inhabitants from Branford.

Jasper Crane	Ebenezer Camfield
Abra Peirson	John Ward, Senior
Saml Swaine	Ed. Ball
Laurance Ward	John Harrison
Thomas Blacthly	John Crane

Samuel Plum	Thomas Huntington
Josiah Ward	Delivered Crane
Sam'uel Rose	Aaron Blacthly
Thomas Peirson	Richard Laurance
John Warde	John Johnson
John Catling	Thomas his L mark Lyon
Richard Harrison	

And upon the Reception of their Letters and Subscriptions, the present Inhabitants in November following declared their consents and readiness to do likewise; and at a meeting the twenty fourth of the next June following in 1667, they also subscribed with their own Hands unto the two fundamental agreements Expressed on the other side their names, as follows:

Robert Treatt	Francis his F mark Linle	Robert Daglesh
Obadiah Bruen	Daniel Tichenor	Hauns. Albers
Matthew Camfield	John Bauldwin, Sen.	Thom. Morris
Samuel Kitchell	John Bauldwin, Junr.	Hugh Roberts
Jeremiah Pecke	Jona. Tomkins	Eph'm Pennington
Michael Tompkins	Geo. Day	Martin Tichenor
Stephen Freeman	Thomas Johnson	John Browne, Jr
Henry Lyon	John Curtis	Jona. Seargeant
John Browne	Ephram Burwell	Azariah Crane
John Rogers	Robert his R mark Denison	Samuel Lyon
Stephen Davis	Nathaniel Wheeler	Joseph Riggs
Edward Rigs	Zachariah Burwell	Stephen Bond
Robert Kitchell	William Campe	
J his × mark B Brooks	Joseph Walters	
Robert his v mark Lymens		

Fundamental Agreement.

Item, it is fully agreed upon that every Man that comes to be admitted an Inhabitant with us, shall first produce and bring a certificate from the Chief of the Place from whence he comes unless the Town be upon their Knowledge satisfied in and about the Good Carriage and Behaviour of them otherwise: then it is agreed upon by a full Vote of the Town assembled, that all and every Man that comes to be received . . an Inhabitant in our Town on Passaick River, shall first subscribe his Name and declare his assent with the rest of the Town, to all and every one of our fundamental agreements on the other side recorded and here following agreed upon, viz: That it is fully and unanimously agreed upon, as a Condition upon the which every one doth reckon and hold his Lands and accommodations in the Town, viz: that they will from Time to Time pay or cause to be paid yearly in their full

Proportions equally, to the Maintainance & allowance agreed upon for the upholding of the settled Ministry and preaching of the word in our Town, and that was agreed upon before any Division of Land was laid out except Home Lotts—and Eighty Pounds per the year was agreed on and allowed for the present Minister.

Item, it is agreed upon, that in case any shall come into us or arise up amongst us that shall willingly or wilfully disturb us in our Peace and Settlements, and especially that would subvert us from the true Religion and worship of God, and cannot or will not keep their opinions to themselves or be reclaimed after due Time and means of Conviction and reclaiming hath been used; it is unanimously agreed upon and Consented unto as a fundamental Agreement and Order, that all and Persons so ill disposed and affected shall after Notice given them from the Town quietly depart the Place Seasonably, the Town allowing them valuable Considerations for their Lands or Houses as Indifferent Men shall price them, or else leave them to make the best of them to any Man the Town shall approve of.

Item, it was ordered and agreed upon, in Case of changes of Lands or any kind of obligation whatsoever by Gift, Sale, Exchange or otherwise that any new Inhabitant shall arrive or come into Town to inhabit with us; it is agreed and ordered that he or they from Time to Time shall in all Respects subscribe and enter into the same engagements as his Predecessors or the rest of the Town have done, before he or they can or shall be accounted Legal Inhabitants in our Town, or have . . . . . Title to their Lands or Possession therein.

Submit to law amongst ourselves.

Item, it is solemnly consented unto and agreed by all the Planters & Inhabitants of the Town of Newark from their settling together at first, and again publickly renewed as their joint Covenant one with another, that they will from Time to Time all submit one to another to be lead, ruled and governed by such Magistrates and Rulers in the Town, as shall be annually chosen by the Friends from among themselves, with such orders and Law whilst they are settled here by themselves as they had in the Place from whence they came, under such Penalties as the Magistrates upon the Nature of the offence shall determine.

Law settled in the Province.

Item, the present Inhabitants of the Place for their better security & Neighbourhood, desired Liberty to set down and take up their Lotts in a Quarter together, which Motion of theirs was consented unto; and after the Line was run in the Center or Middle Street of the Town by the Surveyor General, and the several Ranges of Lotts agreed upon, and the Middle Highways both in the Length and Breadth of the Town to be Eight Rods wide and the Rest four, with a full Power and Liberty to appoint and agree upon and set out High ways in the most conveni-

Highways.

Water Passages. ent Places necessary for the publick uses and Benefits of the Town, with the like Liberty for Passages for Drains, Gripes, or Water Courses where they were needful; yea though it should fall out to be across or within any Mans Lands or Meadows what and wheresoever for the present untill the Town shall see Cause to repeal this order: the Intent whereof was not but that every Particular Person or Persons should have full satisfaction otherwise for every such High way or Water Passage that shall be taken from him; which was consented unto by the Inhabitants then present that had full Power to order matters for the Good of the Town.

Home Lotts. Item, it was by a full consent agreed upon, that the Neighbourhood of Milford and New Haven should take up their Home Lotts and Quarters in that Part of the Town where now they are, and the Neighbours from Branford and Guilford then present, in Places where now they are; and the Neighbours from Milford and New Haven freely gave way that Captain Robert Treat should chuse his Lotts, and they agreed amongst themselves to go over and fix the Lotts, which was before by the whole Committee agreed upon to be Six acres, according to their Pattent [pattern] of the Surveyors Line, for the General . . the Town: only Captain Robert Treat was allowed to have Eight Acres to his Home Lott; which being done, they belonging to Milford Quarter cast Lotts for the Places where they should have their Home Lotts to settle upon; and after the Lotts prepared, and how they should begin and Succeed, the matter was solemnly submitted to the Lord for his Guidance: and the first Lott next the Captain's fell to . . . Gregory, upon Considerations that he come with his Family to build, and inhabit the same about two Years, which was the Condition of his Entertainment with us in our Town; the Second Lott to the Wife of Robert Denison, the Third to Thomas Johnson, the fourth to George Day, the Fifth to Nath Wheeler, the Sixth to Edward Rigs, the Seventh to John Plum now William Camps, the Eighth to Stephen Freeman, the Ninth to John Curtis, the Tenth to Senior Baldwin, the Eleventh to Mr. Jeremiah Peck, the Twelfth to John Bauldwin Junr, The Thirteenth to Michael Tompkins.—Item, Jonathan Tompkins had the Grant of his Lott, next beyond his Father's; and Martin Tichenor had the Grant of his Lott, next beyond that was John Plum's.—Item, it was agreed that those of Brandford that were present, should agree upon their own places and Way of dividing their Home Lotts, provided they took them together.

Milford Quarter.

Item, it is fully consented unto and agreed upon, that the Range of Home Lotts butting and rearing upon the Wet Swamp, called the Cedar Swamp, between the Neck and the Town; that

Swamp lotts fence their own Rears.

all and every of those Home Lotts butting upon the Neck or Common Line, that they shall make and maintain from Time to Time, at their own proper Charge, the whole fence or Fences at the Rears of their Lotts, and not Expect any Easment, from the Neck Lands being but a Common Burden with all Home Lotts, and the condition upon which those Lotts were given out.—Item, it is agreed that all Home Lotts lying in a Quarter together, shall bear equal Burden in fencing, both inside and outside Lotts, and Lines thereof, provided they be of like Quantity, and the whole Quarter have not universally and voluntarily agreed otherwise.

Fencing.

Item—it is ordered, that any Man that takes up Allotment and Accommodations of Lands in our Town upon Passaic River, he or they shall come with the greatest Part of their family to Build upon the Same, and possess it for the space of Two Years at Least, before they shall have any Liberty or Power to dispose or Sell his Accommodations; and then he or they Shall first Make a Tender of his Sale to the Town in General, and upon Their Refusal he may Sell it to any whom the Town shall Approve of; and that all such sales or Alienations Whatsoever, either to Non residents or such as the Town Allow not of, all such Sales shall be Void and not accounted Legal, and the same to Return into the Town's Hands, they Paying the owner or possessor of it Valuable Considerations as Indifferent Men shall apprize it at; provided that this Order Reach Not to Widows, or the Relict of Persons, or Inheritance to Heirs remote upon the Deceasing of their friends and relation by the Over Ruling providence of God; provided that in all such Sales the Town may have the Tender of it. Note—the Intent of this Order is Not to Hinder Sale of a Small parcell, Before that Time.

Building and dwelling two Years before Sale of Lands.

Item—the Town agreed, that any Man that would take Pains to kill Wolves, he or they for their Encouragement should have 15s. for every grown Wolf that they kill, and this to be paid by the Town Treasury.

Wolves.

Item—Thomas Richards had granted him, that his Lott by the Landing place should be made up Six Acres, if it may be there had without Prejudice to the Town.

Thomas Richards.

Item—it was agreed upon, that Michael Tompkins should have an Acre of Land in his Division of Land, upon the Consideration of the Remoteness . . . and Amends for his Home Lott.

Michael Tompkins.

Item—it is ordered and agreed, that according to the Town's Order for the present about fencing, that Every Man shall set up and make a sufficient Fence in the

Fencing.

Common Line, both at the Rears of the Lotts and elsewhere, between this and the last of March 1667–1668, and maintain the same untill it shall be otherwise disposed of; and is to be set up by the Time, under the Penalty of Two Shillings and Six Pence, for every Rod that is Defective by the Day, and Twelve Pence by the Rod Every Day after till it be sufficiently made; besides all Damages that it may be liable to be charged with; which for the present the Town, by way of Order, sees cause to declare, that where the Fence is insufficient and apparently defective, all Damages shall lye upon the defective Fence or Fences, unless the Cattle be Known or can be proved to be unruly, and then the Damage is to lye on the Cattle.

Item—the Town agreed, that the Way and Rule of proportioning Men's Fence or Fences, should be according to their Lands.

Item—the Town agreed that a rate should be made, for Payment of every Man's Share of the Purchase, and that they would referr the Matter to Seven Men, that should have full Power to hear, examine, and judge of every Man's Estate and Persons, as their Rule, by which they will proceed in Time Convenient to pay for their Lands bought of the Natives, with the necessary Charges of setling the Place, and Mr. Peirson's Transport, and the Divi–sions and Subdivi–sions of all their Lands and Meadows belonging to the same—And the Men so Chosen were Mr. Robert Treatt, Deacon Ward, Samuel Swaine, Mr. Camfield, Michael Tompkins, Richard Laurance, and Joseph Walters, any five of whom shall have full Power to act herein; and for their Direction herein, the Town saw cause to allow and pass upon every Head of a Family, or that takes up Allotment in the Town, to be valued at £50, and for every Child or Servant in the Family besides, Ten Pounds by the Head, which shall be allowed as good Estate; and for all other kinds of Goods and Estates, Real and visible, that Men intend, God willing, to transport on the Place, the Town wholly referrs themselves and the sole Determination into their Hands, according to whose Judgment it shall stand—Which being done, the Town saw Cause that One Third Part of every Man's Estate in generall thorough the whole Town should be deducted, and according to the Remainder both the Charges and Divisions of Land should be proportionated and borne, for this year.

Gates disposed of.

(Note here—the first common Gate next the Great River, is disposed of to make and maintain as their Division of Fences, to Aaron Blacthly and John Harrison; the Second to Mr. Bruen in like Manner, and the Third Gate in like manner to John . . . ., John Bauldwin, Junior for their Fence, and the first Division of Fences.)

And the Same, with a Sure List of Every Man's Estate approved by the Sale Men, are Here set down with their Deductions—as Followeth:

John Browne	308	205
Mr. Matthew Camfield	500	333
Stephen Davies	289	192
Nathaniel Wheeler	186	124
Thomas Luddington	122	81
Thomas Richards	110	73
Thomas Lyon	570	380
William Camp	220	184
Robert Denison	300	200
Thomas Johnson	420	280
Martin Tichenor	169	113
John Catling	315	205
John Bostick	160	120
John Ward, Jun	250	167
Deliverance Crane. 100	150	18
John Curtis	190	127
John Baldwin, Sen	187	91
Joseph Walters	180	120
Micah Tompkins	260	173
Jonathan Tompkins	166	111
Ephraim Pennington	150	104
John Crane	250	167
Edward Ball	160	104
Ser. Richard Harrison	400	267
Edward Riggs	320	213
Zachariah Burwell	160	104
Ephraim Burwell	150	100
George Day	120	80
John Brooks	80	53
John Harrison	120	80
John Rogers	350	233
Mr. Jeremiah Peck	200	134
Mr. Robert Kitchell / Mr. Samuel	750	500

Richard Laurance	273	182
John Ward	360	240
added	50	50
John Baldwin, Junr	145	97
Hauns Albers	100	67
Samuel Camfield	174	116
Samuel Rose	250	167
Mr. Obadiah Bruen	200	133
Mr. Morrish	385	257
Robert Dalglesh	167	111
Aaron Blatchly	80	120
Stephen Freeman	440	293
Thomas Staples	150	100
Lieut. Samuel Swain	550	367
Laurance Ward	370	247
Francis Linle	210	140
Mr. Jasper Crane	570	380
Mr. Abraham Peirson, Sen	644	429
Hugh Roberts	446	297
Josiah Ward	210	140
Thomas Peirson	200	133
Mr. Robert Treatt	660	440
Robert Limon	285	190
Samnel Plum	500	333
Thomas Huntington	350	233
Stephen Bond	140	94
Benjamin Baldwin	120	80
Alexander Munrow	100	67
John Browne, Junr	250	150
Mr. Abraham Pierson, Junr	380	250
Daniel Dod	150	100
Jonathan Sargant	150	100
Samuel Lyon		150

Item—it was again Declared and Agreed upon, that all Lands should Be disposed of with the Consent of all the freeholders of the Town, or the Major part of them that were the purchasers there—Untill it Be orderly Agreed upon Otherwise.

Item—it was by the General Vote and Consent of the Town agreed, that they would lay out and Divide the Land in Our Town by Persons, Estates, and other Condign Qualifications, if any such should appear in any, With The Before Mentioned Allowance to every Child and Head of a Family. And Concerning the Divisions of their upland in the Neck, the Town Agreed to divide or Lay a Division of three Acres of Sized Land to Every Hundred Pound Estate; which after the High ways Agreed upon, Viz, One by the Great River Side and along by the Meadow at Beef Point; and another highway in the Middle of the Little Neck; and another Highway Between The two furthermost Share of Lots in the Little Neck, and from thence to Whelers Point; and So Another down between the Middle Share of Lots down the Great Neck; and another to the Great Swamp; and the Land fixed, the Town by their most General Vote agreed to divide it by Lot, and To begin at Mr. Bruen's Home Lot in the River Spot; only Mr. Robert Treatt had his division Granted to him according to his desire, Unanimously, to Lye in the first spot of Lots Next the River, Adjoining to the Little Cove of Meadow, which he Motion'd To the Town that he Might have all that Lay on this Side the Creek, Against his Land Near Home, which was Granted fully unto Him.

Town Meeting the 6th of *February* 1667—after due preparation and Solemnization for it, the Town Agreed to draw their Lots, which fell with their Numbers & places as Follows.

Mr. Obadiah Bruen	21	Thomas Luddington	60
John Rogers	9	Eleazer Rogers	23
Mr. Robert Kitchel	12	John Bostick	19
Mr. Jer. Peck	16	John Gregory	41
Stephen Freeman	39	Henry Lyon	1
John Curtes	58	Joseph Walters	7
John Baldwin, Sen	6	Robert Dalglish	43
Benjamin Fen	29	Francis Linle	44
John Baldwin, Jun	8	Mr. Jasper Crane	49
Benjamin Baldwin	47	Mr. Leet	48
Martin Tichenor	20	Mr. Mathew Canfeild	59
William Camp	34	Thomas Peirson	10
Edward Riggs	18	Saml. Plum	30
Nathaniel Wheeler	26	Elders Lot	4
Thomas Johnson	2	John Ward, Turner	51
Robert Denison	17	Richd. Lawrance	25
Mr. Abraham Peirson	56	Hauns Albers	24
Laurance Ward	42	Deliverance Crane	40
John Catling	52	Samuel Ross	46
Mr. Samuel Kitchel	15	Thomas Huntington	32
Josiah Ward	3	John Crane	62
Sergt. John Ward	28	Rockwell	27
Mr. Morrish	31	Stephen Davis	53
Edward Ball	37	Aaron Blacthly	11
Sergt. Rich'd Harrison	45	John Harrison	14
Lieut. Samuel Swaine	55	Thomas Richards	13
John Browne, Sen'r	54	Seamans Lot	36
Stephen Bond	22	Taylors Lot	57

Thomas Harrison, Mr. Webster, Goodman Cole, and Joseph Horton having deserted their Lots Before the Recording of them, so they were not Entered in this Table.

Note Here—that Micah Tompkins, Jonathan Tompkins, Ephram Penington, Zachariah Burwell, Ephraim Burwell, John Brooks and George Day desired and had Liberty to Take up their first Division of upland, if it be there to be had, in the Little Neck by Goodman Tompkins; and Hugh Roberts his division at the Rear of his Home Lot; and Mr. Person and Mr. Camfield a part of their Divisions in the Neck on this side Goodman Roberts; Viz, Mr. Person for One Hundred, and Mr. Camfeild for Two Hundred pound.

These may Certify and Declare, that we Whose Names are hereunto Subscribed, being Chosen and Commissionated with full power from Elizabeth Town, and Newark plantation upon Passaick River, to agree upon and fully Issue the Divident Line and Bounds Between the forenamed Elizabeth Town and Newark Town, which is as followeth, Viz; That it is Consented unto that the Center, or place agreed upon by the said Agents of the Towns for to Begin the Dividing bounds, is from of the Top of a Little round hill, named divident hill; and from Thence to run upon a North West Line, Into the Country. And for the Ratification of our Agreements, the Said Agents of Elizabeth Town have marked an Oak Tree with an E, Next them; And the Said Agents of Newark Town have marked the same Tree with N, on that side Next them and Their Town; and to the said Agreement we have this Twentieth day of May in the year 1668, set to our hands Enterchangably.

Truly Copied out of the Original agreement by Me— Robt. Treatt	Agents of Newark Town.		Elizabeth Town Agents.	
		Jasper Crane		John Ogden
		Robt Treatt		Luke Watson
		Mathew Camfeild		Robt. Bond
		Saml. Swain		Jeffery Joanes
		Richd. Harrison		
		Thos. Jonson		

Town Meeting, 10 *Sept*. '68.—The Town freely Consented, by their Jointly Voteing to Give freely to Mr. Parson, the Charges off diging and Finishing his well Hitherto; with the Rest of his Transportation Charges. Item—the Town Consented to pay Mr. Parson Eighty pounds for the first Year, Which is to Be Laid out in Building his House at Moderate prises for their Labour; which Year began the first of Oct'br Last in the Year 1667, and To the Last of October 1668, and so to Stand from Year to Year.

Provision for the Ministry.

And it is Further agreed unanimously, that Mr, Parson shall have allowed Eighty pounds by the Year, for his Carrying on of the Work of the Ministry, which is to Be paid Yearly at Two Several Times, Viz: at October and March, in all several kinds of paym'ts to Be made at price Current; and they do agree to pay Him Yearly, a pound of Butter for every milk's Cow in the Town, in part of his pay.

Item—it is Agreed that Mr. Parson shall be Free From all Com'on Rates, during the Time of his Carrying on the Work of the Ministry in this Place. (Note—his heirs) and Lands After him, The Lords Half Penny, and the Charges of Ways and Drainings in the Meadows, is exempted in this Vote.

Item—it is ordered and Agreed to Build a Meeting House as soon as May be; of Four or Six and Twenty Foot wide, and thirty four Foot Long, and Ten Foot Between Joints: which for the Better Carrying it an end, the Town hath made Choice of Five Men, Viz: Deacon Ward, Sarg. Harrison and his Son John, Sarg. Obdh. [Edw'd] Rigs, and Michael Thompkins, Into whose hands the Town Hath referred Full power for the Managing of the Building; and declared Themselves by their Joint Vote, to Be Willing to Lend their Best help as they shall be Call'd for, upon any Seasonable Warning, According to Proportions; and no Man If Call'd out But must Worke Two days Value, . . . he Satisfies Them with his or Their Grounds otherwise. And For the Better Regulating the Same, the Town Hath Agreed to Leviee a Rate of Thirty Pounds for the Carying on of the same; which Meeting House is 26 Feet wide and a Lenter to It, and Thirty Six Feet Long, and 13 foot Between Joints.

Item—the Town Agreed That Thomas Johnson shall have Eight shillings, for his Son's beating the drum this Year, and Repairing the remainder of the Year; And in Case his Son's shall Be Appointed to Beat it any time Morning and Evening, after This Time; they shall be allowed after the rate of Five Shillings the Month.

It was agreed that Henry Lyon, Sargaent John Ward, and Jno. Brown shall have the sole Power to hear every man's reason of his or Their Absence, Late Coming, or disorderly departing or withdrawing, from any of our Town Meetings, having Legall Warning thereto; and Thereupon to Acquit them, or Return the names of them that they release not, but are by the order Signed unto the Constable or such other Officer as the Town shall appoint to receive them, for the use of said Town.

Henry Lyons Lott Bo't of the Town.

Item—the Town hath sold to Henry Lyon that Home Lott that was Formerly John Gregory's by exchange, that Lyeth next his own, Consisting of Seven Acres, for Ten Pounds; Seven Pounds whereof he is to pay by discharging the Town of their Country Rate, and three pound he is to procure shingle Nails for as soon as he can, or to do his True Endeavour to get them.

Mr. Pearson's Rate.

Item—the Town Agreed for the present that Mr. Pearson's rate and the Town rate, should be made according to the Estates Men Gave in for their Lands; and that a Rate of £80 should be made for the Minister Forthwith, for the Year past, by Deacon Ward and Mr. Sam'l Kitchel; And for the Town, a Rate of One Hundred and Sixty Pounds they are to prepare as soon as they Can; and for every Home Lott that is Granted to the Young Men,

Town Rate.

they are to pay to the Town Rate Twelve Shillings, and for any Stock of Cattle, they are to pay to the Town rate for them besides; and to the Minister's Rate, the Men appointed to make it are to speak with the Young Men in our Town that are for Themselves, and to See what they will Voluntarily pay to the Minister.

Collector. Item—the Town hath made choice of Thomas Johnson to Collect and Gather up the Town Rate: the One Half of it that is to Be paid between this and the first of January next, and the other Half Between this and the Last of March Next, in any Current pay that will pass and is Accepted Between Man and Man upon the place: and the Town hath made choice of Henry Lyon to Be their Town Treasurer for the Year Insueing, or until the first of Next January Come Twelve Months. Treasurer.

Mr. Seth Thompkins' Exchange. Item—the Town hath Granted to Seth Thompkins, Liberty to Lay downe his Own Home Lott, and take up that which was Formerly Granted to Benjamin Baldwin.

Accounts of purchased Lands. Item—the Town hath Chosen Deacon Laurance Ward and Mr. Samuel Kitchell to Take and Keep, and account what the Charges of Our Land Comes to by the hundred, or the acre; and Likewise, what the Charges is about the Building of the Meeting House; and to bring it to the Town, that it may be entered on the Records of sd Town.

Purchase money brought in with other Town Rates. Item—the Town hath voted and agreed, that the charges about the purchasing of our Lands of the Indians, setling the Place, with Mr. Pearson's Transportation, shall be all Brought to the rest of our Town Charges and made up, and . . . by the Town Treasurer with other disbursments of our Town.

Surveyors. Item—the Town hath made Choice of Sarjeant Ward, and John Curtes, for to be their Surveyors of their Highways, for the Year Insueing or until New be Chosen; And full power is put into their hands to Call forth Men to work, when and Where, they in their best discretion shall Think most Needful.

Agreements to Build a Meeting House. Item—the Town hath Bargained with Deacon Ward, Sarj Richard Harrison, and Sarj. Edwd Rigs, for the sum of seventeen Pounds to Build the Same Meeting House, according to the Dementions agreed upon, with a Lenter to it all the Length which will make it Thirty Six foot Square, with the doors, and Windows, and Flue Boards at the Gable ends; only the Town is to Hew and Bring all the rest of the Timber upon the place, which is Agreed upon to be done as soon as they Conveniently Can: With whom the Town

Confided in to have it well done, and Some Abatement in the price if they can afford It.

TOWN MEETING, *Jan.* 1668, Mr. Crane and Mr. Treatt are Chosen Magistrates for the Year Insueing, for our Town of Newark.

Officers chosen. Item—Mr. Crane and Mr. Treatt are Chosen deputies or Burgesses for the General Assembly, for the Year Insueing; and Lieut. Sam'l Swain is Chosen a Third man, in Case of either the other Failing.

Item—Lieut. Sam'l Swain and Mr. Camfield are Chosen deputies, to assist the Magistrates in the Town Courts.

Item—Henry Lyon is Chosen Treasurer for the Year Insuing, as above said.

Ordinary keeper chosen. Item—the Town hath Chosen the sd Henry Lyon, to keep an Ordinary for the Entertainment of Travellers and Strangers, and desired him to prepare for it as soon as he Can.

Constable. Item— the Town hath Chosen Thomas Johnson, to Beare the Office of a Constable in our Town, for the Year Insuing.

Recorder chosen, his Salary. Item—Mr. Robert Treatt is Chosen Recorder or Town Clark in our Town, for this Year Insueing; and he is to have Forty Shillings for his Salary.

Stephen Bond, Pounder. Item—Stephen Bond is Chosen Common Brander in our Town for all Horses, according to our Law for Branding Settled in our Province; and also to keep the Records of the Same for this Year Insuing.

Pounding of Cattle. Item—John Ward is Chosen the Common Brander, and Recorder, of all Neat Cattle in our Town, for this Year Insueing, according to our Country Law.

Item—The Town agreed with Henry Lyon, to Make a Sufficient pound for four Shillings the Rod, unless any will within a Week undertake it of him for Less Money by the Rod; and it is to be Made with Six Good Rails, Six foot High, the Rails Not above Ten foot Long, and the upper Rails to be all Pin'd Together: and for the Bigness of it, it's to be four Lengths in a Side for Two Sides, and Three Lengths and a Gateway of Six foot Long, for Each of the other Two Sides; and the Gate is to Be well Hanged with Iron Hooks and Hinges Below, at the Town Charge: which Pound is to be Set up at the First Opportunity that the Weather will permit; and for the place where it Shall be Set up that is most Convenient by the Frog pond side, is to be as Serj. Rigs, Thomas Johnson, with Henry Lyon shall Judge Best; and the said Edw'd Rigs and Thomas Johnson are to See that it be Sufficiently done.

Viewers of Fences. Michael Tompkins and Serj. Ed'd Rigs are Chosen, to be Viewers of Fences in Our Town for this Year Insueing.

Warners of the Town Meetings. Nathaniel Wheeler and Aaron Blatchley are Chosen, to Warn the Town Meetings for this Year, as oft as occasion shall Require them Thereto: and it is order'd that every man shall provide a Good Ladder, between this and the First of March next Insueing the date, under the Penalty of Five Shillings, and so maintain the same under the Penalty of 1s. by the Month.

Committee for Accounts. Item—the Town hath Chosen Mr. Camfield and Thomas Johnson to be a Committee Adjoined to the Treasurer, to heare and determine what and how Much shall pass, upon account of Mens demands for this Year past; and its agreed that all accounts before that hath not been allowed allready, shall not be admitted to account from hence Forth.

Set Courts. Item—The Town hath Agreed, that there Shall be Two Courts in our Town Yearly, to hear and try all Causes and actions that shall be Necessary and desired within our Compass and according to Our Articles; and that the same shall pass by the Verdict of a Jury of Six men: And one of the Times is to be the Last Fourth day of the week, Commonly Called Wednesday, in the Month of February; and the other, is the Second Wednesday of the Next Following Month of September.

COURT [TOWN MEETING] the 5th *March*, 1668-9, of all the Freeholders of Newark:

John Brown Junior, was by a full vote of the Town admitted and received a planter, and hath the Grant of an Accommodations, Both of uplands and Meadows, According to his Estate that he does Give in, and is truly possessed of; he paying his proportion of the Charges Laid out for it, and do Seasonably Come to possess The Same Some Time this Spring.

Eleazer Rogers also, hath his Former Accommodation Confer'd and Renewed upon him; provided that he do defray all the Charges and Come upon the place to Inhabit, some Time Between this and the Last of May Next; and Transplant his Family Hither, as soon as he Can be prepared and accomplish the same.

Young Mens Lotts Rated. Item, The Court fully Agreed, that the Young Mens Lotts should pay, for each one of them Twelve Shillings, for their Rate this Year to the Towne and for the Ministry.

The motion of Jonathan Sargant and Danl Dod, to have an Acre or two of Land a piece of them Exchanged or Given them to Build on, at the end of the Town near Hauns's, or the Milner's [Millers] Lott, was left to Consideration: and Serg't Ward and Stephen Davis are Chosen by the Town, to Take a View of the Land and Make a True Report of the Nature, Quality, and how much may be spared without prejudice to the Highways or Milners Lott, if any be found there . . . . . . upon such an Account.

MEETING adjourned to the 9th of *March* 68–69.

John Bruen. Mr. Obadiah Bruen's Motion in the Behalf of his Son Jno. Bruen, was taken into Consideration and Granted, that he should have Six Acres of Upland, Somewhere in the Neck adjoining to his Fathers second division; he Taking of his share of Fence, and paying in to The Treasury Sixteen Shillings, for all Charges past To This day.

Viewers and Sizears of the Meadow. Item, The Town for the Better Satisfaction of themselves in General, about the sizeing and Equalizing of Mens first division of Meadow already Laid out, with the due care of Making Drains, and Highways into their Meadows; they have again renewed the Choice of Four of the Former Committee, viz: Lieut. Saml. Swain, Mr. Samuel Kitchel, Serj Edw'd Rigs, and Thomas Johnson, and Added Four more to Them, viz: Serj. Rich'd Harrison, Henry Lyon, John Catling, and Mr. Robt. Treatt as their Co'mitte: fully Impowered by them To finish and perfect the first division of Meadow, in the most Just and Equal way they Can in their Best Skill and ability attain unto, as may Tend to the most hopefull Satisfaction of all it may be, and to Relieve and Supply any that want Meadow for their Inheritance; and To do their Indeavour to Supply any with Grass for the present, that Have their proportion of Good Meadow, and for the want of drains, or highways, Cannot for the present Come at it; and also, to Take a Thorough and Effectual View of the several places in the s^d Meadow, where and how many drains, with the Length of them Needful; and also To View and Survey all the Boggy Fresh Meadow that are in Common, Undivided, adjoining to our Meadows.

Item, they have full power to set out the Highways Laid out a Cross any Mans Meadows, and any Four of the Com'itte have full Power to Act herein, to the Alienating and disposing of any Meadow Lott Lying Vacant; Except the Elders Lott, Seamans and Boatmans Lott, Mr. Websters, Goodman Cole, and The Taylors Lott.

Land Marks. Item—The Town Agreed and Order'd, that every Man shall se that Their be sufficient Stakes and Land Marks, both to Their upland and Meadow Lotts for the present; and that every man that hath a division or divisions of Either Meadow or upland, shall be Injoined by Virtue thereof, within One Year after the date hereof, on perfecting their Lotts to set up and Maintain, under the Penalty of Five Shillings for every default, Two, or More if their needs, Sufficient stone Land

Marks, to every Parcell of upland and meadow that he or they stand possessed of; with the Two Letters of Men's Names Legaly Engraven thereon, about a foot Above the Ground—To be set at each End of Their Lotts.

Burning the Woods. Item—The Town hath Chosen and deputed Nath'l Wheeler and John Curtis, to Take the Care of Burning the Meadows and upland for this Year, and to take pay for it out of the Town Treasury.

D. Wards Exchange. Item—Liberty was Granted to Deacon Ward, to Lay downe his own division of Land in the Neck, and to take up that was Formerly Given to John Wilford.

De Cram. Item—Deliver'd Crane hath Granted to him, an Acre of Land Lying on the Hill, adjoining his Home Lott.

Jonathan Sergant and D. Dodd's Lott. Jonathan Sergant and Dan[l] Dod, have Each of them Granted an Acre and Half of Land to Build upon, near Hauns Albers Lott, where Serj. John Ward and Stephen Davis shall appoint; who are impowered by the Town to set out the same.

Hauns. Item—Hauns Albers hath Granted him, a Little knoll of Land against the middle of his Lott to Build upon, about a rod wide to a Black Oak and so to run of to Nothing, the Corner of his Lott.

Motion about a Mill. Item—The Town saw Cause, for the Incouragement of any amongst them that would Build and Maintain a Good Mill, for the supply of the Town with Good Grinding, To offer and Tender freely the Timber Prepared for that use, Twenty Pounds Current Pay, and the Accommodations Formerly Granted Belonging to the Mill, viz: 18 Acres of upland and 6 of meadow, with the only Liberty and privilege of Building a Mill on y[t] Brook; which Motion was Left to the Consideration of the Town Betwixt this and the 12th of this M[o] Current at Even, and the Meeting is adjourned to that Time: And in Case any desire sooner or in the mean Time, to have any further Treaty or Discourse, about his or their Undertaking of the Mill, they may repair to Mr. Treat, Deacon Ward, and Lieutenant Swain, to prepare any Agreement between the Town and them.

TOWN MEETING, 12th *March*, 1668–69.

None appearing to accept of the Town's Motion and Encouragement to build and maintain the Mill, they agreed to set upon it in a general way, and moving to Lieut. Swain about the matter, he made some propositions to the Town, Order about the Mill. and at Length the Town agreed with him for 20s. by the week or 6 working days, and three Pounds over for his skill, unless he shall see cause to abate it, which if he shall see Cause to do the Town will take it thankfully; for the which he engaged to improve his Time and skill, for the best Advantage and carrying on to an End the whole Work, with all that shall be implied by him, so far as belongeth to his Art and Trade of a Millwright; as also to give his best advice about the Dam, or levelling the Ground, as the Town shall need him, and this to be done as soon as conveniently he can: and the Town promiseth to help him with Work in part of his pay as he needs it, so many Days Work as he works at the Mill; common Labourers at two shillings by the Day, and Carpenters at 2s. 6d. the Day. And for the carrying on of the rest of the Work about the Mill, for making the Dam, with other Necessaries, the Town hath made Choice of a Committee, to be with Lieut. Swain improved for the carrying on of the Work, viz: Mr. Robert Treat, Henry Lyon, John Brown, Stephen Davis, who are to appoint and oversee the Work, and that as near as they can in an equal and proportionate Way, and to keep a clear and distinct account of every mans work and Layings out about the Work. And the Town hath chose Thomas Pierson and George Day, to call men forth to Labour as the Committee shall agree upon; and the Town hath agreed with Zachariah Burwell and John Baldwin, to saw about half the Timber that's to be cut, and for the . . . . Boards they are to have 6s p the Hundred foot, and for the Two inche Plank they are to have 6d more in the Hundred. Item, the Town agreed to send some men forth upon the Discovery, to see if they can find any sutable Stones for Milstones.

TOWN MEETING, the 30th *March*, 1668–69.

Bollens Letter. At which meeting it was agreed, that the matter of Capt. Bollens Demands in his Letter, should be wholly refferred and left with Mr. Camfield, Lieut. Swain, Henry Lyon, and Thomas Johnson, to act and do in it as they shall see cause.

Meeting House raising and standing. Item, the Town Agreed with Thomas Luddington and Thomas Johnson, to raise the Meeting House for five Pounds; the Town having shewed their willingness to be helpfull upon moderate Terms, and to lend them Things as they needed that was within their Compass, to carry it on: and for the Place where it should stand, it was agreed to be set up in the Place where it now lies, and to stand near fronting on a square with the Street; which for the verry Place and more direct manner of standing, it was left to the advice of Mr. Pierson, Deacon Ward, and Mr. Treat.

John Rockwell's admittance. Item, the Motion of John Rockwell was fully consented unto, that upon Consideration that he doth this very Spring Season, come and Settle here in our Town and maintain this or such like sufficient Boat for the use of the Town, or particular Persons in the Town on . . . .

Considerations for his Boat and Time in going with her as he or they . . . . agree, so long as the Lord shall enable him thereto. The Town hath . . . . . declared their renewed Acceptance and Admittance of him into our Town, with the Gift of his former accommodations to him, upon the Conditions aforesaid; as also that they will forbear him for some Time, the present Rate of his Purchase money.

TOWN MEETING, the 17th *April*, 1669, when they agreed to provide Nails, for the closing the Meeting House, in a voluntary Way, to see what every man would do in a voluntarily; and they chose Brother Tompkins and Good'n Johnson to . . . . and know, what the Rest of the Town would ingage upon such Accounts, for such an End; and they are all to be paid out of the Town Treasury—all which Nails are to be paid into Broth. John Brownes, as soon as they can.

Viewing of Fences. Item, the Town agreed, that the common fence that lies down should be mended up speedily, and that the Third Day the next week, the Viewers of the Common Fences should go forth, and view the Fence; and then every man that is found defective is liable to pay his Penalty, and they are to give every man Notice of his or their defective Fences, and return their Names to the Next Town Meeting.

Clearing of the Necks from Cattle. Item—they agreed that all Cattle whatsoever that lye in the Neck, should be fetched out between this and the fourth Day of the next week, by the owners of them: and that all Cattle of what Sort or Kind soever, that shall after that Day be found in any Part of the Neck or Necks, within the common Fence, without a sufficient Keeper, they shall be liable to pay Poundage and Damage; with such Penalty for their leaving the Cattle in the said Neck, according to Order, if any shall prosecute against them for the same.

Item—the Town agreed with John Catling, to hang out and sufficiently fasten some Poles or Young Trees in the River, at the end of or adjoining to our common Fence, and to turn them out and up the River about a Rod or two, and some what back again, after the manner of a Pound, to prevent Hogs swiming round the Fence into the Neck; and upon his so doing that they stand for this summer, he is to be allowed Ten Shillings out of the Treasury for his Pains.

TOWN MEETING the twenty fourth of *May* 1669—The Matter begun the last Meeting, about a voluntary Collection of Nails for the closing the Meeting House was again propounded, and issued as on the Day Book the Particulars thereof may appear—and it was agreed that they should be paid for them, out of the Town Treasury.

Item, it was agreed that Mr. Samuel Kitchell should send, and answer to the Widow Doud of Guilford, about her demands of fifty Shillings from the Town.

Doud's Letter.

Item, the Town agreed unto and chose five Townsmen, for the Remainder of this Year, or untill the first of January next ensuing. And the Men chose were Mr. Camfield, Sarj. John Ward, Sarj. Richard Harrison, Sarj. Edward Riggs, and Robert Denison, who are impowered and betrusted with the Care of finishing of the Meeting House, all the Matters about the common fence or fences in the General Line, ordering or setting out of High ways in the fields or elsewhere expedient, and about the Hearding of Cows, or driving out of the dry Cattle in the Town—and what they shall agree upon herein, the Town will Act accordingly.

Townsmen.

Item, The Town agreed, that Their shou'd be a High-way of two rods wide at Least, Quite a Cross the Great Neck from Meadow to Meadow, in the most Convenient place the Town Men shall Agree upon; and what land they make use of for that End which Belongeth to particular men, they are to be allowed for it Again so Much Land else where, as the Town or Town Men and they shall agree upon.

High Way a Cross the Neck.

Item—Robert Denison is Chosen pound keeper, and he is to have a penny by the Head for Turning the key, or Reception of any Cattle Trespasing, into The said Pound.

Item—The Town Ordered and Agreed, that for all unruly Cattle, or Horses, Oxen, and Cows that are turned in or voluntarily Left in the Neck, or Com'on Field, they shall pay Five Shillings by the head Poundage; halfe to the pounder and half to the Town, besides all damages that they shall do to any Man in his Corn, Grass or Hay, or Otherwise: and for all Cattle that are not unruly, Horses, Oxen, or Cows, Four Pence by the Head Poundage, Besides any damage.

5s. poundage for unruly Cattle.

Item, its Ordered, that for all Hogs that shall be pounded out of the Com'on Fields, shall pay six pence the Head Poundage, Besides Damages; and Calves four Pence, and Sheep at a penny the Head.

Hogs and Calves Poundage.

Item—the Town agreed that Azariah Bush [Beech] should be admitted a Planter, as others have been, and to be accommodated according to his Estate, upon Condition of his maintaining a good sufficient Boat or bigger Vessel, for the Use and Commodity of the Town as they may need, and can agree with him for the Use thereof. And he is granted to have three Acres, or four, for a Home Lott, if the Place will afford it, by the Side of the Miller's Lott.

Azariah Bush Lott.

John Rogers had Liberty granted him, to lay his own Lott in the Meadow, and to take up that which was granted to his Son Eleazer Rogers.

Rogers' Change.

Camp's Change.

Item—William Camp hath Liberty given him, to Lay down his Upland Lott in the Great Neck, and to take it up in the Point of Goodman Roberts Neck, near Sarj. Riggs his Wolfe Pit, if it be there to be had.

Town Meeting 10th June.

TOWN MEETING, 10th *June*, 1669—It is ordered and agreed upon, that the High Way through the Great Swamp shall be mended, and that those that have given in their Names to work at it shall work a Day for a £100. Item, it is further agreed on, that every one shall speedily, either in the said Swamp, or in Ditching the Meadow into the Creek at Maple Island, and on the further side of the Great Swamp where the Surveyor and those . . . begin shall agree upon, shall Work a Day for £200; and that for every two Rod of Ditching that any Man doth according to Order, viz: 2 foot broad and so much in Depth, and near a foot Wide in the Bottom, he shall be allowed a Days Work, and so in Proportion for half Days or other Quantities, as Men's Estates given in amounts unto: and they are to begin this Work at two Places, and carry it so on successively as they shall be warned, or called forth by the Surveyor, or he that is to give Notice; and over Night for the next Day, is looked upon sufficient time of Notice. And in Case any Man or Men shall refuse to go when warned, without satisfying Reasons to the Surveyor, he or they shall have full Power to hire others in their room, though it be for double or treeble Wages, if they cannot obtain it other wise; which shall be paid by he, or they, that are the Refusants to work when called. And Sarj. Ed. Rigs is to begin the work at Maple Island Creek, and Sarj. Rich. Harrison at the other Place. The one part of the Town where the said Sarj. Rigs dwells, is to take it by Succession, or . , ... to the Captains, and from him to Good. Freemans and so to Good. Tompkins, and so round to the other Side of the Street, where Good. Brown and every Man is to warn his next Neighbor, passing by them that have done their Share at the Swamp; and so in like manner for those or that part of the Town where Sarj. Harrison dwells, from his House round, according to order.

High Way Work or order for Ditching.

And the High Way across the town, from the Capt. to Mr. Crane's is that way where it's agreed for parting.

And it's further agreed, that every one shall inform himself from the Rate, or any other perfect list of their Estates, what their share of work or Ditching comes to: and every one that ditches is to set up a stake, marked with the two first letters of his Name legally set on, at the End of his Work or Ditch, so that the Surveyor may view whether every Man hath done his Share, according to Order or no; who are to keep a true account of the

Work that every one hath done, that every Thing may be reduced to a Rate and Rule of Proportion, in Time convenient when it shall be thought meet.

Sizers of Meadows. Item—The Men appointed for the Sizing or Resurveying of the Meadow of such as complains of the badness of their Meadow, or for Grass for their present supply, gave public Notice; that those that desired Consideration from them in the Premises that would make their case known to them, and attend as they need upon the next Second Day come Seven night, which is the Time appointed by them to set upon that Work: or else, if they attend not, or be not supplied, it will be their own Default.

Men that desire boggy Meadow for Amends. TOWN MEETING 23rd *June* 1669.—It was agreed, that in Case any Man shall desire to take his Amends for the first Division of Meadow, out of the boggy Meadow against the front of his own Meadow; the Men deputed for the perfecting the Sizure of the Meadow, (to wit): the Division; they have full Power to lay out to them what they Judge meet of it—they sitting down and resting satisfied in what they do.

Item, the Town by their Vote declared their willingness to receive Eleazer Rogers, and John Bostick; and to possess their accommodation with them in the Town; in case they do come to the actual Possession of them and so remain according to Order; at any time between this and the first of October next—but not afterwards.

dispose of Vacant Lotts Item—it was consented and agreed, that if Need did require and no other way did appear more Likely, that Then the Sizers of Meadow shou'd have full Power, to dispose of all, or any of the Vacant Lotts of Meadow to those that are in want, Either of their division of Meadow, or Amens to that they have; except That which was Mr. Leet's, Mr. Webster's and that set apart for an Elder.

Jno Brown Item—allowance was made that John Brown Jun'r., should without deduction be accommodated, after the Proportion of an Hundred and Fifty Pound Estate. Item, Azariah Beech hath Given His Estate, to Have accomodations for a Hundred Pound Estate.

TOWN MEETING, 28th *July* 1669—the Town made Choice of Mr. Crane and Mr. Treat, to take the first opportunity to Goe over to York, to advise with Col Lovelace Concerning our Standing, Whether we are designed to be Part of the Duke's Colony, or Not; and about the Neck, and Liberty of purchasing Lands up the River, that the Town Wou'd Petition for.

Item—the Town by their unanimous Vote, declared their Free-

Mr. Abraham Pierson desired to help his Father

ness to desire and call upon Mr. Abraham Pierson Junior to be helpful to his Father, in the exercising his Gifts in the Ministry for the space of a Year; and for his Encouragement they are willing to allow him Thirty Pounds, for this Year.

Item—the Town declared their Confirmation of what the sizers of the Meadow had done, in laying out of the Bogs; and saw not cause to alter it.

TOWN MEETING the Third of *December* 1669—The Town assembled, agreed that the Letter prepared should be coppyed out, and sent to Col. Nicholls in the Town's Behalf—and signed by Mr. Treat in the Name of the Town.

Mr Crane's Grant and Exchange

Mr. Jasper Crane hath confirmed and granted to him, all the Land in his Home Lott that is within Fence, to him and his Heirs forever, viz: his own 8 acres and two acres that he took in of Mr. Leet's Lott, and the addition to the Front, of the same Measure that it was laid out by at the First.

D. Crane's Lott

Item—Mr. Crane hath granted him, full Liberty to lay down to the Town his Upland Lott in the Neck, and to take it up partly where late Deacon Ward hath laid down, and to be made up of that was formerly laid out for John Gregory, if he had come to our Town. Item, Delivered Crane was willing to take up his Upland Lott of Gregory's, next his Father.

Freeman's Grant

Item—Liberty is granted to Stephen Freeman, to remove his Lott nearer homeward out of Gregory's, so much of it as is left; provided he lays down of his own to the Town lands, so much as he takes up.

Item—Henry Lyon had confirmed again, all the Land that was formerly laid to Greg.... Lott, and that he hath now within Fence.

Record of Lands

Item—The whole Meeting jointly agreed, that there should be a Record made in our Town by Mr. Robert Treat, of all the Lands laid out in our Town, of what sort soever; beginning first with the Home Lotts, as soon as may be. And the Treasurer is forthwith ordered to do his best Endeavor, to procure a Book for the Records of the Lands.

Way of rating for the Minister

Item—it is agreed upon, that Mr. Pierson's Rate for the Year past, shall be levied and raised as in Manner following—for every Male Person, not freed or disabled to a single Rate 1s. 4d. by the Head, that is 16 years and upwards; for every Acre of Land lying in the Home Lotts under Fence, 3d. by the Acre; and for all other upland and Meadow, lotted out and enclosed, 1d. by the Acre; And for all Horses and Mares of three Years old and upward, 3d. by the Head; and so for all two Year old Horses and Mares 2d. by the Head; and for all Yearling Horses 1d.; And for all Oxen of five Years old and upward at 6d. the Head; and for all four Year old

Steers at 5d. the Head; and for all Three Year old Steers and Heffiers at 3d. the Head; and Two Year olds at 2d. the Head; and Yearlings at 1d.; and for all Cows of four Year old and upward at 3½d. by the Head; and for all Swine of a Year old and upward at 1d; and for all vacant or deserted Lotts or Lands . . . appropriated to the owners dwell in another Town, they shall pay to Mr. Pierson's Rate one Third as much as they did for the purchase, by their Lands one third . . . .

No Farm to be set up near our Bounds.

Item—The Court ordered and desired Mr. Robert Treat, to write to Mr. Ogden and Mr. Bond about our Bounds, and signify to them that it is the Town's Mind fully, to have no Farm settled near our Line or Bounds, if their Town will do the like—whereto our Town consented unto long Since.

Magistrates chosen.

TOWN MEETING, the first of *January*, 1669.—Mr. Jasper Crane, Mr. Robert Treat, and Mr. Matthew Camfield, are chosen Magistrates for our Town, for the ensuing Year. Item—the said Mr. Crane and Mr. Treat are chosen Deputies for the General Assembly, if there shall be any; and Lieut. Sam'l Swain is chosen Deputy, to assist the Magistrates in our Town Courts.

Officers chosen.

Item, Mr. Robert Treat is chosen Recorder in our Town, for the Year ensuing, and the Salary is the same as it was last Year.

Item—Thomas Johnson is again chosen Constable in our Town, for the Year ensuing. Item, Henry Lyon is also chosen Treasurer for the Year ensuing. Item—Sarjeant John Ward, Sarj. Richard Harrison, Lieut. Swain, and Stephen Davis, are chosen Surveyors of the High Ways for a Year.

William Camp and Nathaniel Wheeler are chosen, for to view the fences in our Town, for the Year ensuing.

Item—Josiah Ward and George Day are chosen, to warn the Town Meetings appointed by any of our Magistrates in our Town, for the Year ensuing.

Thomas Johnson or one of his Sons for him, is chosen to be Pounder of any Cattle trespassing, according to Order, any where within our common Fence, for the Year ensuing.

Bruen's Grant.

John Bruen hath given and granted to him upon his Father's Motion, the five acres of Upland next Mr. Bruen's Lott that was formerly laid out as Part of Mr. Leet's Lott, and the other are promised to him; he is to take it up with his Father Bruen's next Division of upland.

Thomas Johnson's Grant of Bostick's Lott.

Thomas Johnson hath given and granted to him by the Court, for one of his Sons, the Lott and whole accommodations of Upland as well as Meadows, that was formerly granted to John Bostick; he paying all just charges for it.

William Camp hath Liberty granted him, to lay down his own Lott of Meadow, and to take up that Lott of Meadow with all the Amends laid to it, for his own Meadow and Propriety, that was formerly given to, and again laid down by John Rogers into the Town's Hand.

Sarj. John Ward's Grant

Item—Sarj. John Ward hath upon his Motion, given and fully granted to him by the Court, that Parcel of upland that was formerly granted to the Boatman, which lies adjoining to his own Division of Land in the Great Neck.

Division of Meadow.

Item—they agreed that the Division of Meadow, entered in Part Page the 6th, be by Lott, and Micah Tompkins was to draw the Lott for those absent; and Mr. Bruen, and so onward was to draw first. And the Lotts as they fell were as followeth:

The Number and Places of the Lotts.

Mr. Obadiah Bruen	42	John Curtis	24
John Rogers	64	John Baldwin, Sen'r.	54
Mr. Robert and...		Thomas Staples	56
Mr. Samuel Kitchel together	66	John Baldwin	14
Mr. Peck	59	Micah Tompkins	57
Stephen Freeman	43	Jonathan Tompkins	40
Ephraim Penington	70	Samuel Rose	49
Benjamin Baldwin	15	Thomas Huntington	23
Martin Tichenor	19	Mill Lot	35
William Camp	46	Robert Limon	26
Edward Riggs	45	Boatman	1
Thomas Pierson	32	John Crane	60
Samuel Plum	25	Zachariah Burwell	29
Elder's Lott	50	Ephraim Burwell	28
John Ward, Turner	55	Thomas Luddington	31
Richard Lawrence	4	John Brook	13
Hauns Albers	69	Hugh Roberts	3.
Nath'l Wheeler	71	Eleazer Rogers	20
George Day	7	John Bostick	21
Thomas Johnson	72	Henry Lyon	41
Robert Denison	38	Joseph Walter	8.
Mr. Abr'm Pierson	51	Sam'l Camfield	52
Mr. Robert Treat	5	Robert Daglesh	58
Lawrence Ward	53	Francis Linle	27
John Catling	67	Mr. Webster	16
Josiah Ward	39	Mr. Jasper Crane	48
Sarj. John Ward	62	Mr. Leete	61
Mr. Morrish	68	Matthew Camfield	6
Edward Ball	9	Stephen Davis	2
Sarj. Rich'd Harrison	47	Aaron Blatchly	33
Lieut. Sam'l Swain	36	John Harrison	24
John Brown	11	Thomas Richards	18
Stephen Bond	65	Taylor's Lott	17
Deliverance Crane	37	Seaman's Lott	12

Note, there are some deserted Lotts that are given to others for Amends, are omitted here.

Dalghesh

Camfield

Robert Dalghesh, hath bought of the Town a little Land in the Front of his Lott, for £1—provided it hinder not the coming at the Brook, watering of Cattle, or High ways. And likewise a little Slip in the Front of Samuel Camfield's was given to him, for that which was wanting to his Lott.

Mr. Robert Treat hath given him, the Meadow on this side of the Creek in the Cove, next Home, all along against his own Land.

Lieut. Swain's Cove.

Item—Lieut. Samuel Swain hath given him, in Lieu of the Slip he parted with of his Home Lott, to Take up four Acres of his Division of Meadow if it be there to be had for him, in the further side of the Creek in the first Cove of Meadow commonly called by the Name of the Captain's Cove; according to his own Motion and Desire.

Mr. Pierson's Pasture.

Item—the Town gave Mr. Abraham Pierson four Acres of the Cove of Meadow beyond Martin Tichenors, with so much Upland on this Side of it as can be spared for the High Ways, to be joined to his own Upland on the other side against it, for a Pasture according to his Desire.

River Bound Creek.

TOWN MEETING, *May* the 7th, 1668. It was then agreed that the Great River and the Bound Creek, shall be accounted in all Respects for a sufficient Fence; and any Hogs or Cattle that takes to swim over it, are liable to be proceeded against as Trespassers.

Item—Samuel Rose engaged to make and maintain a sufficient Cart Way over the Dirty Place near Hauns and by his own Lott, upon the Town's Grant to him to exchange a Little Part of his Lott; which was consented unto.

Item—the Town agreed, that the Common Fence should be proportioned according to Men's Estates and Lands within the same, which was committed to Mr. Samuel Kitchel and Lawrence Ward to be justly shared out—and then the Town agreed to divide the Common Fence by Lott; only that which was casual by Reason of Tide or Floods was to be made and maintained by the Town, and the Lotts are as followeth.

The Common Lifts lye two for one.

4

Lifts. Rods	Lifts. Feet			Lifts. Rods	Lifts. Feet		
5	9	John Rogers	1.	5	0	John Brown, Sen'r	15.16
12		Both. Mr. Kitchels	2.	2	3	Stephen Bond	21.22
3	3	Mr. Jeremiah Peck	42.45	2	8	Zachariah Burwell	17.18
7	0	Stephen Freeman	38.39	2	7	Ephraim Burwell	20.21
3	9	Thomas Staples	9.	2	0	Thom. Laddington	11.
2	3	Jo. Baldwin, Jun'r	13.14	1	5	John Brooks	41.43
4	1	Micah Thompkins	50.52	7	0	Hugh Roberts	16.17
2	8	Ephraim Pennington	25.26	2	15	John Bostick	3.
2	12	Martin Tichenor	7.	9	2	Henry Lyon	29.30
2	14	William Camp	12.13	2	15	Joseph Waters	31.32
8	0	Jonathan Tompkins	4. 5	2	13	Matthew Camfield & Son	5.
5	2	Edward Riggs	49.51	2	11	Robert Dalglesh	46.47
2	14	Nath. Wheeler	32.33	2	13	Francis Linle	37.38
2	0	George Day	48.49	2	14	Thomas Pierson	45.46
6	12	Thomas Johnson	43.44	9	3	Jasper Crane	18.19
4	13	Robert Denison	35.36	8	1	Samuel Plum	12.
10	5	Mr. Abraham Pierson	10.	4	2	John Ward, Turner	26.27
10	10	Mr. Robert Treat	14.15	4	7	Richard Lawrence	27.28
5	14	Lawrence Ward	6. 0	1	11	Hanns Albers	34.35
5	0	John Catling	36.37	2	14	Deliver Crane	8.
3	14	Josiah Ward	22.23	4	9	Robert Limon	44.
5	13	Sarj. John Ward	49.50	4	2	Sam Rose	19.20
6	4	Mr. Morrish	46.47	4	2	John Crane	33.3 .
2	8	Edward Ball	39.40	4	10	Stephen Davis	28.29
6	9	Sarj. Rich'd Harrison	24.25	1	8	Thomas Richards	23.24
3	9	Lieut. Samuel Swain	30.31			Mill Lott	39.40

Note here, the Common fence is lotted in two Divisions, and the Fences are most . . . . .

At a General Meeting of the Town upon the Twenty Fifth and Twenty Sixth of *January*, 1669. Its agreed, that Mr. Crane and Captain Robert Treat should be the Moderators at our Town Meetings, for the Year ensuing.

Lands within the Town not to be given away.

Item, it's by a full consent of all agreed upon, that none of the Common Lands lying within our Town, or High Ways, so far as our Articles will allow of, shall at any Time be given or disposed of to any Man's Propriety, without the Consent of every Freeholder or received Inhabitant of the Town; as the Land about the Frog Pond or Training Place; the Land before William Camp's toward the End, in the Front of those Lotts; as also that at the Rear of them; together with that which lyeth in the Middle Street towards the Landing Place; and that which lyes against Aaron Blatchley's and John Ward's; and Robert Dalglesh's; which is to be and remain as Town Commons.

Mr. Abraham Pierson's Lott

Item—Mr. Abraham Pierson hath the Grant of that Home Lott that was formerly Mr. Leet's, upon Condition that he pay for the Purchase Twenty four Shillings, and for the Fence belonging to it as Sarj. John Ward, and John Brown Sen'r, that are chosen mutually to be Prisers of it according to the State they find it in: and in Case Mr. Abraham Pierson settles not in the Town but shall remove elsewhere, he is to resign it up to them again; they paying him or his Assigns for all his

Charges expended upon it, as Indifferent Men shall value or apprise the same, when he leaves it.

Articles. Item, it was agreed that the Articles should be copied out, at a Town Charge.

A Division of Upland of 6 Acres to the £100. Item—the Meeting in general all agreed to have a Division of Land, viz: Upland to be laid out as soon as can be, of Six Acres to every Hundred Pound Estate. And they chose five Men whom they impowered, and would confide in their Faithfullness and Discretion, to make as just a Sizure and measuring out of the said Division as they can; and wholly to order the Manner of the Lying of the Several Ranges and Shots of Lotts in each Place respectively, with all necessary High Ways, and Passages for Carts and Cattle, commodiously as the Places will afford and do call for, every where. And this Division is to be partly in the Neck to begin there, and to accommodate so many as there will be found Land suitable and com'odious for them. And those that by the Allotment are put by their Desires of having their Divisions of Lands there, they are to . . supplied and fall in their Places upon the Hills, with others of their Neighbours. And for the order of the Lotts and Places where Men are to have their Land in the Neck to lie, was agreed on as followeth. After the vacant Lotts of the first Division are taken up and orderly disposed off, the first Lott next is to begin next Home in that Range of Lotts that lies next Beef Point Meadow, and so to run downward; and the next Tier of Lotts, begining at the End of the other next the Pond ward, to be second; and so onward successively till all be laid out on this side the great Swamp. And then that which is on the other side, begining at the End next the River first, and to end with that Part next Wheeler's Point. And for the Land at Wheeler's Point or near adjacent, it's left at the Sizers Discretion where to lay out any there or no. And the Names of the Sizers are Mr. Robert Treat, Mr. Samuel Kitchell, Henry Lyon, Thomas Johnson, and Sarj. John Ward; and any three of them agreeing, have Power to issue any Matter under Hand about the same.

Order and Place or Mens Land by the Lott.

Sizers chosen and their Power.

And for the Rest of the Land to make up the Division, it's to lie partly within the Common Fence and the lands on this Side of the Two Mile Brook next the Town, if that will reach it, beginning at the River, and so to come South-westward; and in like Manner it's agreed to begin with Limon's Lott, and so along with that Range of Houses next the River, and so one after another as they lye quite across the Town untill they come to Hugh Roberts, for all such as are not supplied with Land or their whole Division in the Neck, or within the Fence by the Two Mile Brook; for which Land it was agreed it should be decided who should have it by the Lott—and that the order of the Lotts were first to begin next Hugh Roberts, and so onward toward the Two Mile Brook; for which Lands, Ten Persons desiring it—Ten Lotts were drawn—Imprimis, Zachariah Burwell had the Tenth Lott, John Brown Senr. the 1st. John Brown Junr. the 4th, William Camp the 5th, Thomas Johnson the 3d, Ephraim Burwell the 9th, George Day the 8th, Henry Lyon the 6th, Widow Elizabeth Riggs the 7th, and Nathaniel Wheeler the 2d.

And concerning 31 Lotts drawn for Lands in the great neck, either in Part or in whole of their Divisions, to lye there, the Lotts fell as followeth.

The Lots of them that have Lands in the Neck:

Imprimis, Aaron Blatchly, for his whole Divison....... 4
Stephen Davis, for his 4 acres.......... 17
Sam'l. Plum, for ⅛ part of his Division.......... 29
Richard Lawrence, for half his.......... 20
John Rogers, for half his.......... 23
John Harrison, for his Division.......... 21
Thomas Richards, for his Division.......... 18
Obadiah Bruen, for half his.......... 9
Sarj. John Ward, for half his.......... 2
John Ward, Turner, for half his.......... 7
De. Crane, for half his.......... 5
Thomas Huntington, for half his.......... 14
Alexander Munrow, for his Division.......... 1
Josiah Ward's, whole Division.......... 28
Mr. Sam'l Kitchell, for half his.......... 15
John Catling, for half his.......... 25
Mr. Robert Kitchell, for half his.......... 26
Edward Ball, for half his Division.......... 30
Sarj. Richard Harrison, for his half.......... 13
Widow Ward, for her half.......... 10
Lieut. Sam'l. Swain, for his half.......... 31
Jasper Crane, for his half.......... 27
Francis Linle, for his half.......... 8
Rob't. Dalglish, for his Division.......... 19
Rob't. Treat, for his half.......... 24
Stephen Freeman, for his half.......... 16
John Curtis, for his Division.......... 6
Abr'm. Pierson, for his Thirds.......... 3
John Brown for his half.......... 22
John Baldwin Jun'r.......... 12
Ephraim Pennington.......... 11

Hans Alberts

Hans Alberts had liberty granted to him, with his first Division, to take up both his Divisions together in the Lott by it that is vacant, that was formerly Eleazer Rogers's.

Jonathan Sargeant's Grant.

Item—Jonathan Sargeant had the Grant or Liberty, to change his Home Lott, for that which was formerly granted to Rockwell the Boatman, lying next beyond John Crane.

—

Item—Accommodations was Granted to him, according to his Estate that he shall Make Appear to any three of the Sizars, if he will Abide in the Town and follow his Trade; Provided he pay his Shear to the purchase for what he hath, as others Have Done.

Answer to the Governors Writing.

TOWN MEETING, the 3d *February*, 1669, the Governors Writing was read, and After some debate upon it they by their Votes agreed as Follows: After all due Sallutations to be presented by the Constable to Our Worshipfull Governor, we, the Inhabitants or freeholders of the Town of New Ark, do by him make Return to the said Governors Writing, as followeth, Viz: That they do Hold and Possess their Lands and Rights in the said Town, Both By Civil and Divine Right, as by their Legall purchase and Articles doth and May Shew. And as for the payment of the Half Penny per Acre for all our Allotted Lands, According to our Articles and Interpretations of them, You assuring them to us, We are ready when the Time Comes, to perform our Duty to the Lords or their Assigns.

Item—the Court Agreed that all that are excluded from Having their divisions of Land or part of them, in the Great Neck, or within the Common fence, or elsewhere—In Case that the Place where their Lotts shall fall to Be, the Sizars doe Not Judge the one half of every Mans Lott to be Good Land, then they shall have Liberty to take up the Half of their Division in some other place, where such Land is to be had, Provided it Be Not in such places as shall be Eminently prejudiciall to the Town: but the other Half is to Be Laid out in its Course, as it fall's By The Houses Successively.

Item—the Court agreed to have the remainder of the Meadow, Both of Boggs and Salt Marsh, So much of it as may Be useful to the Town, for to be Divided or Laid out: and that part of it Above and Beneath Maple Island, toward the Mouth of the Bound Creek, is referred to John Brown Junr., George Day, and William Camp, to Be done by the first opportunity; and for the Next part of the Boggs and other Meadows not already Allotted out, Towards Wheelers Point and that way Toward the Bay, is Committed to Ephraim Pennington, John Catling, and Aaron Blacthly; and from the uppermost Great Pond, for all the Meadow Undivided, upward the Bay and River, that is Worth Laying out is to be Survayed by John Curtis, Stephen Davis and Sam'l Rose, who are Chosen and Impowred respecting to Dispart the Same and to make as full and Exact Return to the Town, Both of the Quality and Quantity thereof as they Can.

John Crane's Exchange.

John Crane had Liberty from the Court, to lay down his own Division of Meadow all but 2 Acres that was

Given him for Amens: and In Lieu thereof to Take up that parcell that was formerly allotted to and Laid down by Wm. Camp, provided that for So Much as is More than his proportion, He will set it of on his Second Division.

Dan'l Dod. Item—Dan'l Dod had Given him that Acre and Half of upland above Hauns Albers' Lott, that Jonathan Sergant Laid Down, he paying for it. Item—Liberty was Granted him to Bring in his Estate, and to have some Meadow in his Second Division accordingly, But Not in the first.

Rob't Denison. Item—Rob't Denison had the Liberty Granted, to Take up that piece or Parcell of Land in the Little Neck that Edw'd Riggs, Deac'd, Laid Down to the Town, upon Account of his Second Division, so far as it will reach Therein.

Martin Tichenor. Item—Martin Tichenor had Liberty Granted him, to Lay Down His first division of upland in the Neck, and to Take it up in the Little Neck as it's their Sized, at the Rear of Dan'l Dod's Home Lott.

Order About Pipe Staves. Item, the Court saw Cause to order and agree, that no Timber shall be Sold or made use of for pipe Staves or Heading but what shall be for the use of the Town, under the Penalty of Loosing all their Labour for any Timber so Sold in the Town after this day, Within four Miles of the Town any where.

Mr. Abra'm Pierson. Item—Mr. Abr'm Pierson hath the Grant for accomodations of £250, without any deduction; to be Laid out to his Home Lott, as a planter in the Town.

Burning Woods. Item—the Town hath made Choice of Stephen Davis and Nath. Wheeler, to take the Care of Burning the Woods and Common Meadows Belonging to the Town Needfull of Fireing.

Town Meeting, 24th *March*, 1669, it was by their Joint Vote agreed, that Henry Lyon and Ths. Johnson should Take and receive every Mans Just Share and Proportion of Wheat for his Land; the Summer Wheat at 4s. pr Bus'l and Winter Wheat at 5s. according to the order and Time perfixed to them to Bring it to Johnson's House Before the day be over, or else if they fail they are to Double the Quantity: which Corn the said Lyon & Johnson is to Morrow to Carry to Elizabeth Town, and Make a Tender Thereof to the Gouvernor upon the account of the Lords Proprietors rent for the Land we make use of, according to Articles 25th March 1670.

Town Meeting, the 24th *Aug.* 1670, the motion of setting upon the Building of a Mill in our Town of Newark: the Town at length Made a full agreement with Mr. Robt. Treat and Serj't

Rich'd Harrison, about the Building and Maintaining of a Sufficient Corn Mill, to be set upon the Little Brook Called the Mill Brook, with suitable Necessary's, and Making the Damns, and all other Provisions Needfull for and Belonging to the sd Mill, and furnishing the same with a Good Miller, and to keep it in Good repair; to Grind all the Town Grist's into Good Meal, Giveing Such due Attendance thereto as the Town being the one Party and the owners of sd Mill the other Party shall from Time to Time and at all Times Agree upon, for the Twelfth Part of Indian Corn and the Sixteenth of all other Grain. And for their Encouragement to set upon the Work with as Speed as they Can, and upon their Efecting and Maintaining thereof, the sd Town doth promise and agree to and with the sd Treat and Harrison, that they shall have the sole privilege of the sd Brook, Not prejudicing Common Highways; with all the Town Grist's from Time to Time, all Stones Capable of Millstones in the Town's utmost Limits and Bounds, with all the Timber that was prepared for it by Jos. Horton, with 2 days work of every Man and Woman that Holds an Allottment in the Town; with all the Lands formerly Granted to Jos. Horton, Entailed to the Mill in all respects as their own Lands During the Time and Term of their Having and Upholding the sd Mill; they being Not to be Alienated or disposed from the Mill without the Consent of the Town; and also Thirty Pounds to be Paid to the sd Crane & Harrison, their Heirs or Assigns at or Before the 1st of March Next, in Good Wheat, Pork, Beef, or one Fourth in Good Indian Corn, at such Prices as may be Like to procure Iron, Millstones, or the Work mens Wages, viz: Winter Wheat at 5s. pr Bus'l, Summer do. at 4s. 5d., Pork 3d pr lb, Beef a 2d, and Indian Corn a 2s. 6d. Bus'l: and upon these Conditions the said Town with their Two Inhabitants aforesaid, have Mutually Bargained and agreed for the Carrying on this Work.

Town Meeting, 5th *Dec'r*, 1670, it was Agreed, that Stephen Bond should have the remainder of p's of Land that is Near or Adjoining to his own, which Hauns Albers Leaves of his Piece, that he hath by Exchange with the Town, in the Neck; for and Consideration of his Home Lott, to Make it as Good as his Neighbours.

Robt. Denison, John Brown, Mr. Peck and Stephen Davis.

Item—it was Voted, that the Present Sizars of the Second Division of Land should Take a View of Robt. Denison's first Division of upland in the Neck, and of Mr. Peck's, John Brown's, and Stephen Davis propounded, and it Appeared his Case was one and the Same; and they are to Give such Allowance and Amendment to any of them in Their Divisions as they find to be Just and Equal.

Jonathan Sargant.

Jonathan Sergant for his Encouragment to settle in the Town, follow his Trade, and to help Mend his

Home Lott, they Gave Him that piece of Meadow that Lies at Beef Point, which was formerly Granted to John Rockwell the Boat Man.

Item—it was declared, that John Brown, Sen'r, was to Have But Half his Division of Land in the Neck on this Side the Two Mile Brook, and Henry Lyon one third; But the Rest Stood for their Whole Shares of their Division Their.

A Rate for the Ministry.

Item—it was Agreed at our Meeting, to raise the Ministers Mantainence for the Year past in the same way that they did the Last Year, and it's their desire they would Accept the same Allowance as was then Agreed upon, and Goe on this Year also: and for the More Speedy Effecting of the rate Granted for the Aforesaid Ends, they Agreed that every Man should Bring a List of his Estate, Between this day Sen'-night at farthest, to the Deacon's, as they were Ordered formerly; and Mr. Sam'l Kitchell and Mr. Obadiah Bruen are Appointed to Join with Them, and to be Helpfull therein for to Make the Rate.

Lotts Cast Jno. Baldwin, Jno. Brown, J'r, Abr'm Pierson, Jun'r.

TOWN MEETING, 12th *Decm'r*, 1670, it was Agreed, that the Land that is Left unlaid out, shall Be Laid out to them to whome it falls By Lott; and the first Lott fell to John Baldwin, Sen'r, to have His whole Second Division of Upland, and One Acre for his staying on the place the first Summer; Second Lott fell to John Brown on this Side the Great Swamp; and the Third Lott fell to Mr. Abr'm Pierson, for his first division.

Item—Micah Thompkens had the Grant of a Little piece of Land, on the Account of his Second division of Land, at his Point.

Recording of Lands.

Item—it was agreed by Vote, that Mr. Robt. Treat shou'd Record and Enter Both the First and Second of Land, into the Book of records.

Serj't Ward's £50 added.

Item—it was Agreed that Serj't John Ward should be Allowed to Have Fifty Pounds to his Estate added, and to Take up Land for it; and that piece of Land in the Neck of the Boatmans, is to Goe on upon the Account which was Before Given Him.

TOWN MEETING, 29th *Dec'r*, 1670, Mr. Jasper Crane Had Given Him, a Little piece of Land Adjacent to his Home Lott, upon the Acc't of His Second Division of Land.

Goeing out of the House row or any where in the Woods.

Item—Liberty was Granted to any that will Now Enter their Minds, to Goe out of the Range and turn for Either a part, or the whole of Their Second division of Land, according as it falls by the Order of House rowe. They have all Liberty for Either the Part or the Whole, Besides the one Half of their Division yt by Lott were Excluded out of the Neck, which Abides the same as in the Former Grant.

Land at Wheelers Point. Item—the Town at this Meeting Took the Matter of Laying out the Land at Wheelers Point into further Consideration, and Gave their full Consent that these Six Men Annexed, shall have it in Equal Parts unless they shall Agree otherwise; and the Men Are Mr. Abr'm Pierson, Henry Lyon, Mr. Camfield, Serj't Harrison, Stephen Freeman, Widow Riggs.

And Those that Entered their Names, to take up the remainder or a part of their division of Lands as they do Make an Entry of, in some other place where they shall pitch upon, according as it shall be Sized; and in Case they agree Not upon their places, it's Agreed that they issue it by Lott. Imprimis, Mr. Crane, Jos. Walters, Henry Lyon, Francis Linle, Mr. Robt. Treat a part.

Frank Linle. Item—Francis Linle had Granted him, the Little Corner of Land for his Yard on the side the Brook Next his Lott, by Estimation About Twelve Rod of Ground; Provided he makes the High Way and Passage for Cattle as Good as it was in the other place.

Hen Lyon. Item—Henry Lyon hath the Grant of that piece of Land at the Rear of Gregories Lott (that was), to range even with the Rear of his other Lott, Next Linle's Lott, upon the Acc't of his Division, so far as the rear of Frank Linle's Line unless the Sizars see Good Cause to the Contrary; but he is not to Come over or Worse the Highways.

Lieut. Sam'l Swain. Item—Lieut. Sam'l Swain hath the Grant of a Little Corner of Island, that lies within his Meadow or the most of it, at the Hither Corner to Make it Straight from one Corner to the other.

Baldwin Jun'r. Item—Jno. Baldwin, Jun'r, had Granted him, a little Slip of Land at the front of his Home Lott, in Lieu of Fifty Pole of Ground that He wanted of his Second Division in his piece in the Neck; and it's to range with Deacon Tompkins his Front at one End, and Come of to Nothing at the other End.

Camp. Item—Wm. Camp hath the Grant of a Little piece of Land, about Twelve Pole, that lies at the Front of his Home Lott at the Hither Corner, for a Yard; upon Conditions his Two Neighbours Give their Consent, and he does not Hurt the Highway.

Submit. TOWN MEETING, 2nd *Jan'y*, 1670, the renewall of our Solemn Agreement to submit to Law and Authority among our Selves, Till it Be settled in the Province, its record fol. 3rd.

Mr. Jasper Crane is chosen Magistrate in our Town

Officers Chosen. for the Year Insuing. Mr. Camfield and Lieut. Swain are Chosen Deputies, to assist the Magistrate in our Town for the Year Insuing. Mr. Crane and Mr. Treat are Chosen deputies for the Generall Assembly, and Lieut. Swain is the Third Man.

Item—Henry Lyon is Chosen Treasurer Again this Year, Mr. Treat, Secretary, and Thos. Johnson, Constable, and Robt. Denison and Jno. Catling are Chosen Haywards for the Town. Jno. Crane and Sam'l Rose are Chosen Viewers of the Fences. Ths. Richards and the Widow Riggs Her Son, are Chosen To Warn the Town Meetings, each of them his Part as they did the Last Year. Serj't Ward and Wm. Camp are Chosen Surveyors for the Ways of Meadows and Upland, Towards Maple Island and the Two Mile Brook; and Deacon Lawrence and Step'n Davis the Highways towards Beef Point and that way; Mr. Kitchell and Josiah Ward for the Highways Down Middle of the Neck, Towards the Great Swamp and that Way.

Item—the Town Choose Jos. Johnson for Drummer as before, upon Condition that he Beats the first Drum at Least up as far as the Saw Pitt, or the Corner of Serj't Harrison's Lott.

Ordinary Chosen. Item—the Town Choose Thomas Johnson to keep an Ordinary in the Town for the Entertainment of Strangers; and Prohibited all others from Selling any Strong Liquors by Retail under a Gallon, unless in Case of Necessity, and that by Licence from the Magistrate.

Mr. Leete. Item—the Town Agreed to Allow Mr. Leete, towards his Disbursments on his place the Sum of Three Pounds, besides what his fence shall Be Apprised At.

A Rate for Highways. Item—it was Agreed upon, that the Charge of the Highways and the Surveying the Land shall be Levied by a Rate, According to Lands only.

Meeting House Floar. Item—the Town Agreed with Thos. Johnson About his Floaring Half the Meeting House for Four Pounds, of Good Chesnut or Oak, of 2 Inches and a Half Plank, and they are to find and do all, to Edge and Lay down the floar on Seven Good Sleepers; and in like Manner they Have Bargain'd with Jno. Brown, Mr. Burwell, Jno. Baldwin, and Jos. Riggs to do the other Half.

Mr. Peirson. TOWN MEETING, 20th *March*, 1670. Mr. Abr'm Peirson hath the Liberty Granted Him, to Take up the Remainder of His First division of Land, in the Little Neck that Jonathan Sergant Laid down Lying on the other side of the Highway, Against His Pasture, According as the Sizars shall Determine.

Item—it was Agreed that Henry Lyon and Thos. Johnson shall Goe to our Governor, in Behalf of the Town make a Tender to Him in Good Wheat for the Payment of their Half Penny pr Acre to Him for the Lords Proprietors, in Like Manner as they did the Last Year at the Day Appointed; in Case that he will Accept of the Same, That then they are fully Impowered to Give Notice by the Warners of the Town, for every one to Bring in his Proportion of Corn to the Constable's House, the Morning of the day appointed, by 7 or 8 O'Clk, that they may send it to their Governor, and take a Discharge of Him for the same; and they are at Least to Bring as Much as they did the Last Year, and More if they see Cause.

Half Penny.

Item—its Agreed that the fence in the Common Line shall be again Proportioned and Laid out a New to every in his Just Share, According to the Number of his Acres within the same; Beginning at or near the First Common Gate Next the Fence, and so to run on Successively According to the Order of Men's Lotts in their First division of fence, untill they Come to the fence at Bound Creek, and thence to Come to the side of Seaman's Lott, Runing up by the side thereof untill they Come to the River at or Near the Middle Landing Place: and for the Whole Enter Thereof, to be Order'd, Appris'd, and set out to Each Man his Just Proportion, it's Wholly Left to the Judgment of Robert Denison, Mr. Stephen Davis, Jno. Catling, Jno. Curtis, and Jno. Brown Junior, to regulate, Value and Lay out every Man his Just Proportion of fence.

Dividing Common fence.

And every Man hath Engaged to set down, According to Their Determination.

Item—its Agreed that a rate of £30 shall be made for the Mill Forthwith; to be raised According to Estates and Lands, in like Manner as the Rate for Mr. Abr'm Peirson the Last Year.

Mill Rate.

At a Town Meeting, 20th *Feb'y*, 1670, it was Agreed by Vote, that Thos. Johnson and Nath'l Wheeler shall Give Notice when to Burn About the Fences, by the Beating of a Drum Early in the Morning, from His House as far as Serj't Jno. Wards.

Item—that Henry Lyon and Thos. Johnson shall in the Town's Name, request the Governor to Confirm Mr. Jasper Crane and Mr. Robt. Treat Magistrates or Justices of the Peace, Which Were Again Chosen the 2nd Jan'y, 1670.

Commissions.

Item—that Jno. Brown, Jun'r, shall Have first Division of Meadow, or as Much of it as the Place will Afford as it shall Be Sized, Lying on Both sides of the 2 Mile Brook.

Jno. Brown's Meadow.

Item—that the Middle of the Town shall have the Bogs or Boggie Meadow, to divide among Themselves without Charge to the Town, from the Widow Ward's Meadow to Jno. Curtes's Creek Meadow.

Boggie Meadow.

Item—those whose Names are under Written, Shall Have Liberty to Take up their divisions of Bogs, from Hugh Roberts stakes to the Widow Wards Meadow; and Agree among themselves to Lay them out, and Make their Highways without any Charge to the Town.

Hugh Roberts,	George Day,	Stephen Bond,
Jno. Brown, Jun'r,	Ths. Johnson,	Robt. Denison,
Wm. Camp,	Zachariah Burwell,	Mr. Canfield,
Widow Rigs,	Ephraim Burwell,	Deacon Thompkens,
Nath'l Wheeler,	Thomas Staples,	Jonathan Thompkens,
Ephraim Pennington,	Eliafaph Preston,	Abr'm Peirson, Sen'r.
Robt. Dalglish,		

Item—Those Whose Names are Here under Written, shall Have Liberty to take their division of Bogs, Each one Against His Lott the Breadth of his Lott, and Agree Among Themselves, without any Charge of their Highways or to Lay them out to the Town. Beginning at Joseph Walters and Ending at John Curtes's Lott, and the Names are as followeth—

Joseph Walters,	John Brown, Sen'r,	Mr. Morris,
Edw'd Ball,	John Catling,	Martin Tichenor,
Josiah Ward,	John Brooks,	Thos. Richards,
Stephen Freeman,	John Baldwin, Jun'r,	John Rogers,
Wid. Ward,	Benj'm Baldwin,	Thos. Johnson,
John Harrison,	Thos. Huntington,	Rich'd Harrison,
John Ward, Turner,	Mr. Peck,	John Crane.
Serj't John Ward,		

Sargents Grant. TOWN MEETING, 21st *Feb'y*, 1670, it was Agreed, That Jonathan Sargent shall have Liberty to Take up his first division of Land, in the Neck, Where he Can find It.

Fence to the River. Item—that the fence Next the River, shall Be made upon the Top of the hill Till it Comes Near the Landing Place; and then down to the River in the most Convenient Place, as far into the River as Low Water Mark.

Item—that Mr. Abr'm Peirson shall Have his first division of Meadow, in that which was Mr. Webster's Lott.

Item—Mr. Abr'm Peirson, Sen'r, Hath the Grant, to have his Second division of Meadow at the rear of his own Lott, the East Side of the Creek.

Item—that a Division of Salt Meadow shall be Laid out, three Acres to a Hundred Pound.

Item—that the Layers out of this Meadow shall begin at the Bound Creek for their Front, and flank upon the rear of Mr. Kitchell, Jno. Catling, and Mr. Morris's Lotts, and end where the Small Hay Cocks Where When the Viewers Viewed; and so to return by Maple Island Creek Till they Come at Mr. Canfields Lott; and so over the Creek at Mr. Canfields Lott; and so Goe down the Creek Till they Come round to Mr. Person's Lott; and so Take; in Mr. Leete's Lott with a Little which Lyeth by it; and So over the Creek Betwixt the Creek and the Pond, till the Pond Comes to the Creek or the Creek to It; and so by Sam'l Rose's Lott, and By the rear of the Lotts; and so round by the Bay to the other Creek. And this Second division of Meadow is to be Be Ordered according to Mens Lotts, or the place where they shall Lye.

The order, Number, and Places of Mens Lotts, for the Second division of Salt Meadow, are as followeth—

Jasper Crane	49	Rich'd Harrison	45
Robt. Treat	42	Sam'l Swain	48
Obadiah Bruen	37	Jno. Brown, Sen'r	16
Jno. Rogers	50	Stephen Bond	11
Robt. Kitchel	57	Zachar. Burwell	15
Stephen Freeman	66	Ephraim Burwell	63
Jno. Curtice	41	Thos. Luddington	25
Mr. Peck	34	Jno. Brooks	23
John Baldwin, Sen'r	47	Hugh Roberts	5
Thos. Staples	65	Henry Lyon	35
Jno. Baldwin, Jun'r	40	Joseph Walters	28
Micah Tompkins	7	Fran. Linle	18
Jonathan Tompkins	44	Robert Dalglish	43
Ephraim Pennington	20	Mr. Camfield	55
Martin Tichenor	13	Sam'l Camfield	22
Wm. Camp	9	Thos. Person	62
Widow Rigs	12	Jno. Ward, Jun'r	64
Nath'l Wheeler	53	Alex'r Munrow	19
George Day	21	Rich'd Lawrence	4
Thos. Johnson	54	Hauns Albers	10
Robt. Denison	33	Deliverence Crane	36
Widow Ward	27	Robt. Lymon	29
Jno. Catling	51	John Crane	3
Sam'l Kitchell	39	Sam'l Plum	38
Josiah Ward	6	Stephen Davis	52
Jno. Ward	46	Aaron Blatchly	59
Mr. Morris	58	Jno. Harrison	17
Edw'd Ball	8	Jonathan Sergant	2
Thos Richards	31	Ab'm Pierson, Jun'r	60
Benj'm Baldwin	32	Eliafaph Preston	.
Thos. Huntington	14	Dan'l Dod	5
Sam'l Rose	24	John Bostick	3
Jno. Brown, Sen'r	26		

Change Lotts of Med'w.

Item—it was Agreed, that any Man may have Liberty to Change His Meadow Lott with his Neighbour, Before it Be Laid out; Provided they Exchange not Above £30 in Estate, one More than the other.

Item—its Agreed that Serj't Jno. Ward, Henry Lyon, Ths. Johnson, Stephen Davis, Jno. Catling, Jno. Curtes, Jno. Brown, Jun'r and Wm. Camp, are Chosen to Lay out this Second division of Salt Meadows. Any Two of these, with one of the Old Ones shall have Power to act.

TOWN MEETING, 2d *April*, 1671, the return of the Men Appointed for the Laying out of the Fence in the Common Line, was Published and declared to the Meeting; and notwithstanding some Difficulties and Intricacies Alledged, they saw Cause to pass a full Vote, ordering every Man to make up his share of Fence, According as it is Given In and Awarded by the Men formerly Chosen and Recorded for that Work; only Stephen Freeman was Promist Full Consideration Afterwards, if he would do up his in the 2 Mile Brook, of Abat'mt; and Agreed that it should be done by the 10th April Next, under the Penalty of 4d. the Rod for every Days Defect, in Not Sufficiently Making, or Maintaining the Same Afterwards, and All the damages that may Come Thereby.

TOWN MEETING, 23rd *May*, 1671, it was fully agreed and Order'd, that Twenty Four Hours Time of Notice to the Warners or freeholders in Our Town, to Them or the People of Houses Where they dwell, shall be accounted upon any Ordinary Occasion of a Town Meeting Legal Warning; not with standing, they do Leave as formerly, full Power in the Magistrates to Call a Town Meeting at any Shorter Time of Warning, upon Extraodinary Business when the Case Requires it and Cannot admit of a further Delay Therein.

Legall Warning for Town Meetings.

Item, at a Meeting of About 40 freeholders being Legally Warned, it was by their Vote fully Ordered and Agreed, that from Henceforth or Untill further Order, any Twenty of the freeholders, the Clerk and one the Magistrates being Present; Provided the said Twenty having Legall Notice Given them; which said Twenty Freeholders of our Town shall have full power, to Order, Act and doe, or Cause to be done, all or any business belonging to the Whole Town or any particular Therein, as fully and Legally as if they were all Present, Might, or Could doe: excepting the admission of Inhabitants, and the Alteration of our Fundamental Agreement; Whereupon we all Came Hither and have subscribed unto and all shall Be obliged to Submit to what shall Be in such wise Agreed upon.

Item—its Agreed upon, that the 5th June Next shall Be forthwith Published, for every Soldier that day to appear at the beat of the drnm, to shew his Arms and Ammunition, and to spend that day in the Exercising their

Training.

Arms, as they shall Agree among Themselves; under the Penalty of 2s. 6d. for Absence, and all former Penalty's Agreed upon for being defective in their Arms—and they so met shall have full power to Appoint an other day of Meeting—and to order the Matter of the Squadrons for the Carrying of Arms to Meeting, and Warding on the Lords days During the Time of Publick exercise; which is the Town's mind and order, that it should be Strikly Observ'd and Attended.

Carrying Arms on the Sabbath.

Item—it's ageeed, that every Man that's Land in any fields Butting on any Highway, wherein he Hath Laid or Cause to be fell or Laid any Wood or Trees, he or they shall remove the same again, between this and the Sixteenth of June Next, and Clear the said way or ways, under the penalty of 1s. for every Days Neglect after the Day aforesaid; and under the same Penalty, to keep Clear the One Half of the Highways that Butts upon his Land. And also it's ordered, that every Man shall Clear away the wind falls and wood, that he found in the one Half of the Highway next his Land, and so keep it Clear; under the same penalty for Neglect, upon Complaint: and for his Clearing the under falls, he shall be paid for his Pains out of the Treasury.

Clearing of Highways.

and Wind Falls.

Item—it's Agreed that the 2nd day of the week and the 6th day of the same week and the Next Days if the Town Need, and the Work Cannot be well done on those days that are appointed and agreed upon by The Town Meeting and the Owners of the Mill to be their Grinding days, upon which days the Miller is to attend his Grinding, and the Town are to bring their Grists, and the Miller Promiseth to do his . . . . as for Himself secure the same untill it Be enclosed, and under Lock and Key.

Grinding Days.

Richard . . . . . is admitted a freeholder, upon Condition of his setting his Name to our Agreements, and Hath the Priviledge of Commonage for Fifty Pound Estate, without Deduction; and He Hath Promised to set About Learning to read—Which was an Encouragement unto Them Herein.

Freeholder.

Ths. Huntington hath Granted to him and them, their Shares of the Highway formerly taken out of their Lotts which Hath Been laid down Again; and the remainder undisposed of the Land Lying At his and their Rears of their Home Lotts, which was formerly Appointed to Them in lieu of the Land Taken out of their Lotts for the said Highway, is Confirmed upon them.

Aaron Blacthly, Promising to uphold his Common Fence without Charge to the Town, untill they Can Dispose of the Land and fence without Loss in the Neck; they Granted him liberty to Lay down some Part of his said division

Exchange.

of Land, viz: that Part lying by Mr. Crane's Flank; and to Take up so much Sized Land for it in the Woods, as upon a Due View of Sizure it Being not prejudiciall to the Town; which so Appearing, they are willing to Accommodate him With.

Highway Exchanged.

Ephraim Burwell, with his Neighbours having their Lands Lying Together, desiring liberty to have a Highway Exchanged or removed, that leads to their lands in the Little Neck by Deacon Tompkens's, from the outside of his Lott one way that Now is, to Almost the out side of his Own Lott, on the other side of his Lott; and he wou'd Be Content to take up some Amens for his Land and Charges in Sub duing it, at the End of his own land; as also the Remainder of His Amens due to him for his Home Lott, which was Granted to him for Amens, if it be there to Be had: and free and full Liberty was Granted Them to place the Highways anew for their Best Convenience Among Themselves, as they shall Agree, they Not annoying any other Mans Land by their alterations: and Likewise liberty was Granted to all them that have their lands on that side of the Highway, to have their Lotts run to the Swamp for their Preservation of the Corn by Fencing or otherwise; the additions of Land Being Inconsiderable as it's presented to the Town which is Given to them, and they have sustained Great loss for want of such Liberty of Fencing, as they say—which moved the Town to Comply with Them.

Lotts run out to the Swamp

Town Meeting, 29th *Sept'r*, 1671. Mr. Jasper Crane and Robt. Treat are Again Chosen Deputies in our Town, for the Service of the Assembly in 3d Oct'r Insuing the date, According to the Governors Warrant.

About Buying the Neck.

Item—free Liberty was by a full Vote Given to any Amongst us, of Freeholders of our Town, to enter on Treaty of Sale, and to Buy the Neck of Capt. Wm. Sandford, or his Uncle, or Both if they Could Agree for it, and pay what they shall engage; and the sd Town wou'd expect Nothing of them, But to pay their Shares to the Minister in New ark, unless they would freely of Themselves Give and Grant some further Priviledge to The Town, where to they May Not be Compelled. And it's Agreed that None shall be exempted from liberty of Purchasing, that doe Now Desire It; and that he shall have and Enjoy his Share and Proportion of what he Purchaseth, according to his adventures and Monies Expended About the same: and there presently appeared so many Volunteers, as to make Tender to Capt. Sandford or such as had the Right of Dispose, the sum of Eight Hundred Pounds In Cattle and Provision, pay hear, with some Pipe Staves, within Four Year Next Insueing: and they refered the Matter to Mr. Pierson, Sen'r, to draw up the Letter, with the Names and Shares that they Propounded to Expend for the Procuring of the same; and to keep a Copy of Mens Names and Shares Adventuring, and what is Committed to the sd Sandford under their hands, for the Buying the sd Neck Aforesaid.

TOWN MEETING, 14th *Nov'r*, 1671, which Meeting adjourned to the 26th Inst. to finish what they Cou'd Not due this day; and Concerning rates it was agreed that all rates that shall be levied this Present Year, (Except the Lord rent and Surveying of Land,) should be made and Levied by Persons Valued at 1s. 4d. pr Head, by Lands the Home Lotts rateable at three half Pence pr Acre, and for the First division of Upland and Meadow to Goe at 1d pr Acre, and for the Second of land Not to be rated this Year; also Cattle to be rated as they were last Year: and Concerning the Lords rent and Surveying of Land, the Charges thereof to be levied by Lands only, which rates was Ordered as follows, viz: a Rate of £50 was Granted to be Levied forthwith, to answer the Occasions of the Town . . . . and where to any unto whom they are Indebted. Item, a rate of £20 was ordered to be made, to pay the Charges of Surveying Lands; which Monies are to be paid into the Treasurer's Hand.

Rates.

Item, its agreed, that a List of every Mans Estate Shall be Brought in to the men apointed, Between this and the 2nd Decem'r Next, and Every one that dwells in the North End of the Town to Serj't Jno. Ward, and those of the South End to Thos. Johnson, under the Penalty of 6d., to be charged to the rates of any that are defective, having Had Notice of this order; which 6d. Shall be Taken out of the Rates of Those Men that are put upon The Trouble to Get it: and the Men Appointed to make the rates are, Mr. Obadiah Bruen, Serj't Jno. Ward, Thos. Johnson, Jno. Curtes, and Jno. Brown, Jun'r, who are desired to attend the work and Issue It as soon as they Can: the Prizes of Corn, and flesh, are the same as it's Expressed in the Country Laws.

Rates.

Item, the Motion of Mr. Abr'm Pierson's to the Town, that he might have his first division of upland According to the Proportion of his Estate, laid out in the Hither side Next the Lott reserv'd for the Elders Lott in the Neck; which was Granted him on Condition that he settles and Abides with us a Considerable Time, Carrying on the work of the Ministry: which if he should not do, but in a few years remove away, then he is to leave the land to the Town for the end Afs'd; he Shall be paid for Layings out About it, if the Improvements of the land hath Not done it before. Item, on the same Conditions afs'd, they are willing to and agree to add Ten Pounds

Abr'm Pierson.

Grants of Lands and adding £10 a Year More.

Yearly More for his Maintenance, for the Time to Come—he shall Also be free from all Rates, Except the Charge of Purchasing and Setling the Place, as others have done.

Item, the Town again Choose Robt. Treat to Record all their Lands and Meadows which are Laid out in our Town, for 2d. a parcell; and every Man is to bring in his parcells of Land to him—with The Number of Acres; and if any Allowance for Sizure they was to make It known how much, and how its Bounded on Each side Thereof: and this they Agreed to do, as soon as they could.

For Record's Lands.

TOWN MEETING, 1st *Jan'y*, 1671—Mr. J. Crane and Mr. Robt. Treatt, are again Chosen to the place of Magistrates for the Year Insewing.

Item—they are Chosen Deputies for the General Assembly, for the Year, and Sam'l Swain is Chose the Third Man. Mr. Treat is chosen Secretary for Next Year. Henry Lyon, Treasurer. Ths. Johnson, Constable. Jno. Harrison and Wm. Camp are to Warn the Town Meetings in their part of the Town; the old Surveyors to Stand Again. Wm. Camp and Jabez Rogers, Haywards for this Year; George Day and Zachariah Burwell Viewers of Fences, who are to Attend it once a Month: they are to Mark the defective Places and Give the Owners Notice Thereof, and allow them 16 Hours to amend it; and then they are again to view it, and for every defect after, He or they shall pay to the Viewers 1s. a Day for every day it lies defective, Besides all damages in the Mean Time; and in Case the owners of The Defective Fences will not pay their penalties, the said Viewers shall have full Power, by Warrant to Distraint.

Viewers of Fences.

Penalty's on defective Fences.

Serj't Rich'd Harrison and Stephen Davis are Chosen, to range the Middle Highway in the Neck, Ag't Francis Linle's and Jno. Catlings Lott.

Item, Mr. Pierson hath the Consent of the Town Given Him, to Buy the House, and any Part of the Lott that Belongs to Widow Elizabeth Ward.

The Rates made for the Town were read and Published, and its agreed that every Man should pay in his proportion to the Treasurer, between this and the 10th Feb'y Next, or else the Constable by order Must destrain for it.

Item, it's Order'd, that No Goats at any Time of the Year shall be kept any where in the Neck, or Common Fence.

Item, Wm. Camp hath Granted him, upon Acc't of That Acre of Land, that the Townsmen in the Time that Home Lott he now dwells on was Vacant in a Common, disposed of to Edw'd Riggs, Deac'd, a Point of Up Land Beyond Martin Tichenor's Land Towards the Point, on

Camp's Grant.

the left Hand of the Highway as they Goe to Maple Island—deemed About 3 Acres.

Colours. Item, it was declar'd by Many, that in Case those that Would have their right in the Colours to Themselves, they should have It, rather than to make any Trouble About It.

TOWN MEETING 22d *Jan'y*, 1671. Mr. Treat and Lieut. Swain are deputed, to Take the first oportunity to Advise with Mr. Ogden, or any other they see Cause, what may be the Safest and Best Course to be taken for the Town, about our Lands and Settlements here.

Sealers of Measures. Item—it's ordered and Agreed, that every Man Shall bring in his or their Half Bush'l. to Henry Lyon and Joseph Waters to have them Tryed, and sealed when made fit with Mr. Crane's; which for the present is the Standard—they shall have 2d. pr. piece for Sealing with the small Town Brand, or **N**.

Mr. Ab'm Pierson, Jun'r. TOWN MEETING, 4th *March*, 1671, it's Order'd for the Church to Call Mr. Abr'm Pierson, Jun'r, to be Joined with his Father in Time Convenient for the orderly efecting It; and they have Agreed upon his Taking Office he shall have and enjoy his Accommodations Granted him, upon the same Tenor and Terms that other Men In our Town Generally hold the Same.

10th March. Item, its agreed, that after the 10th Inst. March, every Man shall secure his Wood, Timber, Corne, and Hay, which is Abroad, or Beare the loss of them with his fences also.

Burning Woods. Item, its Order'd that Mr. Crane, Good'n Davis, and Nath'l Wheeler, shall Take Care for to Burn the Woods this present Year.

TOWN MEETING, 22 *March*, 1671–2. John Brown, Jun'r, is Chosen Recorder for the Town, and to have in Custody all the Town's Writings After Mr. Treats leaving the Town, 'Till Jan'y, 1772.

Widow Denison hath Granted to her, 1 Acre of land and Meadow Adjoining her other land and Meadow—for her staying on the place so Long when the Town was first settled.

Wm. Camp had Granted to him, of his piece of Land in the Point Lately Given him of Four Acres and Half, he shall have 2 Acres of it free from all Charges, in lieu of what was wanting in his Home Lott; the rest on account of his Division.

Martin Tichenor hath 1½ Acre of Land Granted Him, Adjoining his own division in the point, partly for the accommodations of the highway that he made of his Land, and for his Staying so much on his place when the Town was first Settled.

Jonathan Tompkens hath Granted him, a piece of land Lying before the front of his Home Lott, on Consideration of his Home Lotts Being so poor and Scanty.

John Curtis Also hath a Grant of an Acre of Land, for His Staying on the place at the first settling Thereof.

Survey's Chosen. Item, Sam'l Plum and Stephen Davis are Added to the rest, to Finish the Laying out of Lands in that Division Already Begun.

TOWN MEETING, 10th *April*, 1672, Francis Linly is Chosen to Sweep the Meeting House this year, for doing which he is to Have 20s.

Item, it's order'd that No Cows, Calves, Goats, or Sheep, shall Be kept within the Com'on fence, under the penalty of 6d. pr. head; Working Oxen and Horses hath Liberty, with a sufficient keeper.

Order'd, that the Treasurer shall pay Mrs. Kitchel 27s. upon Mr. Leet's Acc't—she Giveing a Rec't for the same.

TOWN MEETING, 13th *May*, 1672. Jno. Catlin and Edw'd Ball have undertaken to Make the Common fence by Thos. Richards's, to keep out all Cattle and Sheep this Year, for 12s.

Mr. Crane and Lieut. Swain that were Chosen representatives for the Town, are desir'd by the Town to Consult with the rest of the representatives of the Country, to order Matters for the safety of the Country.

Jno. Curtes and Jno. Brown, Jun'r, are to have 4s. ap's, for Making the rates the Year Past.

Stephen Freeman is Chosen in Thos. Johnson's room, to lay out the Second Division of Meadow, Till Thos. Johnson is fit to Goe.

It's order'd, that those which want of their first division of Meadow, shall have it made up in their Second.

Henry Lyon's Grant. Henry Lyon hath the Grant, to lay down his first division of Meadow, only that as was for his amends; and to Take up as much as his amends wants of his first division where he Can find It, when the Second division is Lay'd out.

The Tailor's Lott is to be Lay'd out by a Hundred and fifty Pound Estate.

Dan'l Dod is to have his Meadow Lay'd out, by a £100 Estate.

Martin Tichenor and Thos. Ludinton hath Each allow'd them, 1½ Acre in their Second division, for Staying on their place the first Summer.

TOWN MEETING, 17th *June*, 1672. Mr. Crane, Mr. Canfield,

and Lieut. Swain, are Chosen Magistrates for tho Year Insueing. Thos. Johnson, Constable.

Quarterly Courts. Item—there is to be a Quarterly Court held in this Town, Beginning the First Tuesday in September Next.

Item—Mr. Crane is Chosen President of said Court.

Jno. Browne, Jun'r, is Chosen Recorder of said Court.

Court Fees

Item—the Court is to have for Every Action		1s. 6d.
Recorder, entering for	do, -	6d.
Constable, for Serving every Warrant	- -	6d.
Serving an Attachment	- - -	8d.
Jury Men - - - - - -		6d Every Action.

Serj't Ward, Sam'l Kitchel, Henry Lyon, and Thos. Johnson, are Chosen to end the Difference Betwixt Deacon Lawrence and Robt. Dalglish, About their Second Division.

Sam'l Plum and Aaron Blachly are Chosen, to Goe over to Mr. Sandfords about Swine, the Town to Pay Them.

There was a full vote Past Aug. 10th, 1672, that is Not Here Recorded—But is Recorded Folio 36.—[Ordered obliterated, Feb. 25, 1675-6.]

Town Meeting, 14th *Nov'r*, 1672, it was Agreed to have a Rate made, for Defraying the Ministry, and other Publick Charge.

All Lands Alike rated. It's Agreed that all lands shall be a Like Rated Now and Hereafter, upon Condition there be no more disturbance in Town about the way of Rateing; Lands at 1d pr Acre, Cattle of all kinds as formerly.

Item, all Swine and Cattle that are Rateable which are now a Live, or hath been killed since August, shall Be Rated.

Every Man to Bring in his List. Item, it's Agreed that every Man shall Bring in a List of their Estates, to Jno. Curtis, and Jno. Brown Jun'r, Next day after this Meeting; and if it's known they Leave out any of their Estates, they shall forfeit 5s. in the pound; and if any Do not Bring in their Estates Timely, the said John's shall have 1s. for every one they Fetch.

Jno. Curtes and Jno. Browne are to have 5s. each, for Making the rates this Year.

Sam'l Lyon. Sam'l Lyon is admitted a Planter in our Town, and hath the Taylor's Allotment Granted him.

Town Meeting, 28 *Nov'r*, 1672, it was agreed, that the former order that Twenty men should carry on Town Business shall now be repealed; and if any Man doth not Come Timely (After 24 Hours Warning) he shall be fined 6d, Half a day's Absence 15d, and Whole day's Absence 2s 6d, Except he Give a Sufficient Reason of his Absence; if

Order About Town Meetings.

any Goe away Before the Meeting Brake up, without leave, 2s: these fine shall be carried into Treasurer and Pay'd as a Due Debt. If the Defect be in the Warner's, they Shall pay these fines.

TOWN MEETING, 9th *Dec'r*, 1672. Mr. Treat, Deacon Tompkins, Serj't Ward, and Henry Lyon, are Desired to return an answer to Mr. Peck's Letter, Either in Writing or By Word of Mouth.

Item, Mr. Kitchel and Jno. Brown, Jun'r, is to Dictate the Acc'ts of the Town.

Item, the Town agreed to have a Rate of £20 made, for the Town.

Its agreed, that the fence upon the Hill, by the River, shall Be Removed to Stephen Freeman's Corner, and so to the Brow of the Hill at the Towns Charge: the owners of the Fence is to Maintain it there, and Thos. Huntington is to Make the fence from the Hill to Low Water Mark, to secure the Neck; and he is to have No other fence In the Common fence, and for Maintaining that fence, He Hath Granted to Him that Marsh under the Hill.

Stephen Davis and Jos. Walters are Chosen, to look after Clearing of our Highways within the Common Fence, as in folio 26 [39]: and every Man is to have that as Lieth by his Land Cleared by the 12th of this Month; and they Two are to set a Prise upon the Windfalls; and if it be not done by the Time appointed they are To Hire Men to do It, and those that shou'd have done it shall pay them for it.

Item, Mr. Kitchel and Josiah Ward are Impowred, to Call out Men to Work at the Highways.

Magistrate and Assistants chosen. TOWN MEETING, 1st *Jan'y*, 1672—Mr. Jasper Crane is Magistrate for the Year Insewing. Mr. Bond and Mr. Canfield, is Chosen Assistants. Lieut. Swain is Chosen the Third Man.

Item, Mr. Crane and Mr. Bond are chosen Deputies for the General Assembly, for the Year ensuing, and Lieut. Swain the Third Man.

Constable chosen. Thomas Johnson is chosen Constable, for the Year ensuing.

Henry Lyon is chosen Treasurer, for the Year ensuing.

Item, John Brown, Jun'r, is chosen Recorder, for the Year ensuing.

Warners of Town Meetings. Item, Stephen Davis and Martin Tichenor are chosen, in their Parts of the Town to warn our Town Meetings, for the Year ensuing.

Item, John Brown, Sen'r, and Stephen Davis, are chosen fence viewers for the Year ensuing. Item, Joseph Walters hath Liberty to make a Bridge over Maple Island Creek, provided he wrong not his Neighbours by it.

TOWN MEETING, the 31st of *January*, 1672. It was agreed and voted, that the Rate for the half penny an Acre, shall be brought into the Constable's House by the Third day of February next; and in Case it be not brought in by or on that Day, the Constable shall have Liberty to distrain for it; and those that are the occasion of it shall bear all the Charges about it.

The Half penny Rate.

Item, it is voted, that Mr. Peck shall have his Rates that are behind upon the Town's Account, given him.

Mr. Peck and Francis Lindsly have their Town Rates given them.

Item, Francis Lindly hath his Rate that is behind on the Town's account, given him

TOWN MEETING, *February* 15th, 1672. Stephen Freeman and Stephen Davis are chosen, to measure the fence upon the Hill by Thomas Richards's, and after the Convenientest Place from Stephen Freeman's Corner to the Hill; also Sarj't Ward and Henry Lyon are joined with them, and they were to bring the Report of it to the Town; and they were also appointed to settle the Places for the Gates—which accordingly they did.

Item, it was agreed by Vote, that those that set up their Fence in the Swamp shall have Six Pence for each Rod; and those that set it upon Dry Ground, should have five Pence for each Rod.

The Price of removing the Fence.

Item, it is agreed by Vote, that every Man shall have at both Ends of his Fence one Stake, with the Two first Letters of his Name upon them, by the Twelfth Day of this Instant February, upon the Penalty of Two Shillings for every such Defect; the one half thereof the Viewers are to have, and the other half is to be carried in to the Treasurer.

Penalty of not Staking the Fence.

TOWN MEETING, *February* 28th, 1672. Sarj't Ward and Stephen Davis for their end of the Town—Lieut. Swain and Stephen Freeman for the Middle of the Town—Henry Lyon and Thomas Johnson for their End of the Town, are chosen to appoint a fit Season to burn the Woods. Also it is agreed, that every Male from Sixty Years to Sixteen, shall go out one Day to burn Woods. Also it is agreed, that whosoever doth not attend that day (which is to be in May) if they do not go before, he or they shall forfeit his or their Day's work upon the Proof thereof, and pay it to the Treasurer.

Burning Woods.

Penalty for setting the Meadows on Fire.

Item, if any Man shall set fire on the Meadow before the Tenth of March, by Gunning or any other ways, he shall be fined Ten Shillings; Half to the Informer and Half to the Town.

Mr. Crane's Grant.

Item, Mr Crane hath Granted to him upon his Request, that Piece of Meadow containing about 3 or 4 acres, between his first division of Meadow and the Pond, which was laid for a Highway—and he doth promise to drain it, and to let the Highway go through his Meadow any where as they can.

Altering the Highways.

Item, the Town hath left the Matter in Controversy about the Highway at the front of Goodman Johnson's Lott in the Range, to the Judgment of the Men that are appointed to lay out Land; to lay out that, in the convenientest place for the Good of the Town.

Mr. Crane's Grant.

Item, Mr. Crane, having Liquors for Six Shillings a Gallon, and One Shilling and Six Pence a Quart, they paying Wheat for it, hath Liberty to sell Liquors in the Town, till the Country Order alter it.

John Harrison's Release.

Item, John Harrison and Edward Ball hath all their Fine about the Resque released, only they are to pay the Court Charges.

Town Meeting, *April* the 18th, 1673. Mr. Swain and Goodman Freeman have promised to find Iron for the Stakes.

Item, it is agreed, that the Dry Cattle shall be kept beyond the Mountain this . . . and every one that hath dry Cattle shall put them to that Herd.

The Young Men's Grant of Lands.

Town Meeting, *May* the 26th, 1673. It was agreed upon, that the Young Men which have Home Lotts in the Town, shall have Liberty to take up Land in this Division that is now to be laid out, according to an Hundred Pounds Estate; provided they pay to the Purchase as other Planters have Done, according to their Proportions.

Item, that the Young Men shall have Liberty to take half their Division, next after those as have their Second Division (in Part or in whole) yet to lay out.

How much land shall be patented.

Item, it is agreed, that the Highest Estate in our Town is to patten but one Hundred Acres, within that Compass as is already purchased; and so every one accordingly, proportionable to his Estate. And if any desire, he may have his Lott in two Parts.

Item, it is agreed that we should all draw a Lott, and that the first Lott shall chuse, and so to proceed successively according to the Number of their Lotts; and those as will have half or Part of their Proportion but in one Place, they shall stay for the other Part till all the Lotts are out, and then to begin again and proceed as formerly.

The Maner of taking this Division of Land.

Item, it is agreed that the Want of a Lott, or if any Mistake happen about drawing of the Lotts any way, that it shall not breed any Confusion nor alter any Thing.

Item—after due Preparation and Solemnization for it, the Town agreed to draw their Lotts, which fell with their Numbers and Places as followeth—

Jasper Crane	10	Zachariah Burwell	69
Abraham Pierson, Sen'r.	46	Ephraim Burwell	66
Matthew Candfield	18	Thomas Luddington	12
Robert Bond	43	John Brown, Jun'r	52
Lieut. Sam'l Swain	55	Henry Lyon	36
Obadiah Bruen	57	Joseph Walters	47
Jabez Rogers	4	Robert Dalglish	42
Stephen Freeman	13	Francis Lindly	68
John Curtice	1	Thomas Pierson, Sen'r	67
John Baldwin, Sen'r.	14	Benj'n Baldwin	41
Jno. Baldwin, Jun'r	9	Thomas Huntinton	45
Deacon Tompkins	50	Alexander Munrow	15
Jonathan Tompkins	64	John Ward, Turner	3
Ephraim Peninton	38	Richard Lawrence	27
Martin Tichenor	35	Hauns Albers	51
William Camp	19	Delivered Crane	32
Joseph Riggs	53	Sam'l Rose	17
Nath'l Wheeler	56	Jonathan Sargent	59
George Day	48	John Crane	61
Thos. Johnson	16	Sam'l Plum	65
Robt. Denison	58	Stephen Davis	28
Mr. Robt. Treat	63	Aaron Blachly	11
Mr. Abraham Pierson, Jun'r	20	John Harrison	40
John Catlen	39	Thomas Richards	24
Sam'l Kitchell	33	Azariah Crane	21
Mrs. Kitchell	23	Robert Limen	31
Mr. Peck	30	John Treat	62
Josiah Ward	7	Sam'l Lyon	44
Sarj't John Ward	49	Dan'l Dodd	29
John Morris	26	Thom's Pierson, Jun'r	25
Edward Ball	6	Edward Riggs	37
Sarj. Rich'd Harrison	34	Sam'l Harrison	2
Jno. Brown, Sen'r	60	Barth'w Goodrich	22
Stephen Bond	8	Seth Tompkins	54
		Thom's Staples	5

Agreement to send a Petition to our Lords Proprietors.

At a TOWN MEETING, *July* 1st 1673, It was Voted, and agreed by the General and universal Consent and Vote of all our People, that there should be an Address by way of Petition, sent to the Lords Proprietors of this Province, for the removing of the Greviances incumbent, and obtaining of what may be necessary for the Good of the Province, and of this Plantation—in testimony of our Consent hereto, and of our agreement; what necessary Charge shall arise hereupon we will defray by way of rate, proportionably to the number of those who join in the sd. Petition.

Mr. Crane, Mr. Bond, Mr. Swain, Mr. Kitchell, and Henry Lyon, are Chosen a Committee, to consider with the messengers from the other Towns, about sending a Petition to England.

TOWN MEETING, *July* the 5th, 1673.—Mr. Crane, Mr. Bond, Mr. Kitchell, Henry Lyon, and John Ward, Turner, are chosen to agree with Mr. Delevall about Money to send a Messenger to England; and as they did agree with him, it should be paid by the Town.

A Priviledged County is Desired.

TOWN MEETING, *August* 4th, 1673.—It was agreed that we should join with the rest of the Province, to agree with the Generals at N. Orange, to have a priviledged County between the Two Rivers Passaick and Araritine, or with as many as will join with us; and if none will join with us upon that account, then to desire what may be necessary for us in our Town. Mr. Crane, Mr. Bond, Lieut. Swain, and Sarjent John Ward, are Chosen Deputies to treat with the Generals about this Business.

Magistrates Nominated.

TOWN MEETING, *August* 12, 1673.—Mr. Crane, Mr. Bond, Sarj't. John Ward, Mr. Bruen, Stephen Freeman, & John Curtis, are nominated for Magistrates.

Item—Deacon Lawrence, and Sarj't. Harrison, are chosen Deputies to go to Woodbridge.

Military Officers nominated.

TOWN MEETING, *August* 30, 1673.—Lieut. Samuel Swain and Thomas Johnson, are nominated for Captains, Sarj't. John Ward and Josiah Ward are nominated for Lieutenants, Sarj't. Richard Harrison and Mr. Samuel Harrison are nominated for Ensigns.

A Petition sent to Orange.

TOWN MEETING, *September* 6, 1673.—It was thought fit and agreed upon, that a Petition should be sent to the Generals at Orange, that if it might be, We might have the Neck.

Item, Mr. Crane and Mr. Johnson are chosen to carry this Petition, and treat with the Generals about the Neck.

Town Meeting, *September* 16, 1673.—It was agreed by Vote, that what necessary change is laid out at Orarge by the Town's Messengers in the Town's Business, shall be discharged by the Town.

Item, Mr. Crane, Mr. Bond, and Mr. Ward, are chosen to treat with the Generals about Terms for the Neck, and if they can to buy it.

Town Meeting, *September* 24, 1673.—It is Voted, that if we are desired to join with other Towns to send Men to the Indians to demand the Robbers, that we should send Men with them.

Shewing of Arms published. Item.—It was also by the Magistrate's order published, that in consideration of the present Danger, and fear of what may further ensue, We do therefore require that every Man in our Town under Sixty and above Sixteen Years of age, shall meet together with their arms well fixed, upon Eight of the Clock on the first day of October which is this day Senight, upon the Penalty of five Shillings. The Ammunition for each Man to bring with him being half a Pound of Powder, and Twelve Bullets fit for his gun, or Two Pounds of Pistol Bullets, and upon that Day the Soldiers shall chuse the rest of their Officers.

Town Meeting, *October* the 1st, 1673.—It was agreed that a Rate of Thirty Pounds should be levied, to defray publick Charges; and the way of rating should be as formerly, and as it was last year, as fol. 15 and 31, [see pages 41 and 45.]

Orders about Rating.

Item, if any Man loose any of his Cattle betwixt this and Winter, they have Liberty to deduct or keep so much Estate the next Year from being rated.

Item, John Curtis and John Brown Junior, are chosen to make the Rates this year; and every Man is to bring a List of his Estate to them, by the next fourth day.

Treasurer chosen. Item, Thomas Johnson is chosen Treasurer, for the Year ensuing.

Town Meeting, *October* 13, 1673.—Stephen Davis and Martin Tichenor, are chosen Heywards in our Town, for this Year.

Item—John Ward, Turner, and John Catlin, are chosen to go to New Orange to buy Kingsland's Part of the Neck, as Cheap as they can.

Town Meeting, *October* 25, 1673.—It is unanimously voted and agreed by the Town, that every Individual Man or Planter in the Town, shall by Way of Proportion in a Rate be engaged for the Purchase of that Part of the Neck, which formerly belonged to Major Kingsland.

Item—Mr. Crane, Mr. Molyns, and Mr. Hopkins, are chosen to see after Confirmation of the Neck, and to sue for further Easment in Respect of Pay.

Item—Mr. John Ogden, Mr. Jasper Crane, Mr. Jacob Molynes, Mr. Samuel Hopkins, Mr. John Ward, Mr. Abraham Pierson, Senior, and Stephen Freeman, are chosen to take the Pattent in their Names in the Town's Behalf, and to give Security for the Payment of the Purchase.

Item—Stephen Freeman, Thomas Johnson, Stephen Davis, John Ward, Turner, and John Catlin, are impowered to Order every Thing to the best Advantage they can, as belongs to our Part of the Neck as is purchased.

Town Meeting, *November* 17*th*, 1673.—It is voted and agreed, that this Day Fortnight every Man shall bring a List of their Estate to the Meeting as is then appointed for that End, and there be read.

Item—Captain Swain is chosen to be joined with Mr. Crane, to sue for Easment in Respect of Payment for the Neck, and what is else needful concerning that Matter.

Town Meeting, *December* 1, 1673.—John Curtis is chosen, to gather up and carry in to the Treasurer all the fines about being defective in not attending Town Meetings, according as it is written in Folio 31 [see page 45]—and for his Pains he is to have half the Fines.

Warners of Town Meetings and Fence Viewers chosen.

Town Meeting, *January* 7*th*, 1673.—Thomas Ludinton is chosen to warn the Town Meetings for this Year, at his End of the Town—Item, Samuel Plum is chosen to warn the Town Meetings for this Year, at his End of the Town. Item, Joseph Walters and Jonathan Sargeant are chosen for Fence Viewers, for the Year ensuing.

Highways to be made by next October.

Town Meeting, *January* 8.—It is Voted, that the Highways that stand upon Record to the Upland, shall be carried on as men are most concerned; and they shall be called out by the Surveyors to do this Work; and according to the Judgment of the Surveyors it shall be let out by the great, or done by Day's Works; and the Surveyors shall keep an exact account of every Man's Work and bring it to a Rate, which rate is to be made according to the Proportion of Lands as Men possess: those ways are to be done by next October, or sooner if the Surveyors shall see cause.

Surveyors Power.

Item—the Surveyors for these Highways shall have power to call out Men when they see occasion; and every Man is to attend their Call at two days Warning, upon the Penalty of Two Shillings a Day for neglecting coming to attend the Work.

Surveyors chosen.

Item—Richard Lawrence and Stephen Davis are chosen for the River Highway; Mr. Kitchell and Edward Ball for the Great Swamp; these four are to join together, to see after the mending of the Middle Highway that goes down the Great Neck.

Item—Thomas Johnson and George Day are chosen, to be Surveyors of the Highways as belong to that End of the Town as they live at.

Ways on the Meadow to be made by those they most concern.

Item—all particular Ways in the Meadow any where. every Man as is concerned shall be compelled to bear his Proportion according to the Benefit or Use he makes of it; and to agree amongst themselves for the doing of it without Trouble to the Town.

Stubbing the Highways.

Item—it is voted that two Days Work is to be bestowed in stubbing the Highways in the Town; one of the Two is to be bestowed about the Frog Pond, and thereabouts.

Item.—Stephen Davis and John Catlin for their End of the Town, and John Brown Sen'r, and John Baldwin Jun'r., for their End of the Town, are to call out Men to do this Work; and all are to do this Work from Sixteen Years of age to Sixty, upon the Forfeit of two Shillings and six Pence a Day for neglecting.

Ebenezer Dod.

Item.—Ebenezer Dod hath granted to him the Seaman's Lot, lying over the way against Thomas Richards.

Old Trees to be fallen & When.

Item.—It is voted, that every Man is to fall all the Old Trees that stand on his Land within forty Rods of any House or Barn, within Two Years Time, upon the Penalty of five Shillings a Tree.

Robert Dalglish's Grant.

Item.—Robert Dalglish hath Liberty to lay down his Second Division of Meadow, and take up that Piece of Meadow, which was formerly John Crane's first Division.

John Bruen's Grant.

Item.—John Bruen hath Granted to him, that Piece of Meadow which was formerly Robert Dalglish's Second Division.

Item.—Stephen Davis hath Granted to him, a little Piece of Land lying between the Mill Brook and the Mill Lot.

Town Meeting, *January* 31, 1673.—It is voted, that by this day Senight every man shall recon with the Treasurer.

The Rate to buy the Neck.

Item.—It is voted, that according to the list as Men took up Land by at the first, shall this Rate be made by, to pay for the purchasing of the Neck.

Item.—The Magistrates appoint this pay to be made, within three weeks from this meeting.

Item.—Mr. Crane, Mr. Ward, Captain Swain, Stephen Davis, and Thomas Richards, are chosen to compleat this Business about the Neck, with John Catlin and Edw'd Ball.

Item.—Mr. Ward, Stephen Davis, and John Treat, are chosen to go over with these Men to see the Neck, and bring Information about the same.

The Magistrate's Order.

TOWN MEETING, *February* 4, 1673.—It is ordered by the Magistrates, that every Man shall recon with the Treasurer by or before the Seventh Day of this Instant Month, and bring in their pay by or before that Day, upon the Forfeiture of five Shillings.

The Neck sold to John Catlin and Edward Ball.

TOWN MEETING, *February* 24, 1663-74.—It is voted, that the Bargain is confirmed between the Town and John Catlin and Edward . . . . according as is expressed in the Writing of Agreement made between them.

Item.—It is voted, that the Town is willing that Nathaniel Wheeler and John Baldwin shall be their associates.

Item—John Catlin and Edward Ball have also accepted the Bargain from the Town, according as is expressed in the writing of agreements made between them (to this all of them set to their Hands) Viz. John Catlin, Edward Ball, Nathaniel Wheeler, and John Baldwin.

Item—It is voted that John Catlin and Edward Ball shall pay at three equal Payments.

Town Men chosen and their Power.

TOWN MEETING, *March* 19, 1673-74.—It is voted and agreed that there shall be Towns Men chosen, to carry on such work for the Good of the Town as the Town shall think fit to betrust them with, for the Year ensuing.

Item—the Men that are chosen by vote to be Towns Men, are Capt. Swain, Sarj't. Harrison, Stephen Freeman, Stephen Davis, Thomas Johnson, John Brown Sen'r. and John Curtis.

Item—It is voted, that these seven Towns Men are to carry all Town Business, according to the best of their Judgments for the Good of the Town, for the Year ensuing; except disposing of Land, admitting Inhabitants, and the way of levying Rates.

Ebenezer Dod. his Grant.

Item—Ebenezer Dod hath liberty by vote, to buy Edward Balls accommodations, provided he subscribe to the fundamental agreements as other Inhabitants have done.

Richard Fletcher—his Grant.

Item—Upon a motion of Richard Fletcher to . . . . his Land laid together—it is voted that Mr. Ward, Joseph Walters, and Thomas Ludenton, shall view whether it be convenient or not, and according as they find it is left to them to lay out if not prejudicial to the Town; provided he make a way over the Swamp, where they appoint him.

Item—it is voted, that upon the View of Stephen Davis and Samuel Rose, Sarjant Harrison shall have liberty to change two acres of land in the Mill Home Lott (by Samuel Rose's Flanck) for two acres of his own Land on the other side of the Mill Brook, near the Mill.

Item—it is also agreed that the Weavers Thomas Pierson and Benjamin Baldwin, shall be considered by the Surveyors, (Mr. Crane, Capt. Swain, and Robert Dalglesh being joined with them) to make their out lotts on the Hill shorter.

Town Meeting, *June* 29, 1674—It is voted, that there shall be a Petition sent to the Governor (and Council) for the obtaining a Confirmation of our bought and paid for Lands, according to the General's promise.

Item—Mr. Crane and Mr. Pierson Jun'. is chosen to carry this Petition, and present it to the Governor and Council at N. Orange, in order to the obtaining a Confirmation as above said.

Town Meeting, *July* the 3, 1674—John Brown Jun'r. is chosen, to present this Petition to the Court again at New Orange.

Town Meeting *August* 10, 1674—Mr. Crane, Mr. Ward, Mr. Bond, Captain Swain, Stephen Freeman, and Mr. Kitchell, are nominated for Magistrates.

Item—it is voted, that there shall be a Treaty with the Indians, in refference to the purchasing of That Tract of Land as lieth above our Town, by the River.

Item—Sarjant Harrison, Stephen Freeman, Stephen Davis, Thomas Johnson, Thomas Richards, Samuel Harrison, and Hance Albers, are chosen to treat with the Indians about it, and if they find them reasonable in their Price to buy it, and make Return of their Answer to the Town.

Town Meeting, *October* 31, 1674—Mr. Ward, Mr. Kitchell, Mr. Freeman, Mr. Pierson, Deacon Tompkins, Deacon Lawrence, Sarjeant Harrison, Stephen Davis, and Thomas Richards, are chosen a Committee to consider of such Things as may tend for the Good of the Town; also they have Liberty to debate of such Things with any they shall see Occasion so to do, without calling a Town Meeting.

TOWN MEETING, *December* 11, 1674—Mr. Ward, Mr. Kitchell, Mr. Freeman, Captain Swain, Serj't. Harrison, Thomas Richards, Deacon Lawrence, and Thomas Johnson, are chosen to go down to Elizabeth Town to treat with the Governor upon the particulars written, and if they can agree without, not to deliver that writing; but in Case he will not hear them, then they are to present this Writing to him and leave it with him. Item—John Brown Junior is chosen, to subscribe this Writing in the Inhabitants' Name.

TOWN MEETING, *November* 7, 1674—Mr. Ward and Mr. Kitchell, is chosen as Deputies to go over to Bergen, to hear what the Governor hath to read, according to his Warrant.

TOWN MEETING, *January* 16, 1674—That the way of rating shall be as it was last Year, only some abatement of Heads, Oxen, and Cows.

Item—Heads shall be voted at 14 c a Piece, and Oxen at 5 c a Piece, and Cows at 3 c a Piece; all other Cattle and Lands as they were before.

Item—It is voted, that the Estates shall again be brought in to make the Rates by, as is now living.

Item—the Estates is to be brought in, between this and the fourth Day at Night.

Warners Chosen. Item—John Crane for that End of the Town, and Ephraim Burwell for the other End of the Town, are chosen to warn Town Meetings for the Year ensuing.

The Farmer's Bill of Sale. TOWN MEETING, *February* 20, 1674.—It is voted, that Edward Ball and his Associates shall have the Bill of Sale which is prepared—drawn out and delivered to them.

Item—John Brown, Jun'r, is chosen to transcribe this Bill and sign it in the Town's Name, and deliver it to them.

Item—it is voted, that the Town will be obliged to buy Salt of Mr. Windor from Time to Time; provided he be also obliged to supply them at all times from Time to Time, for half a Crown a Bushel.

Item—Thomas Johnson and Thomas Richards are chosen, to go to the Governor to declare the Minds of the Town about pattenting; that they see it not their way for the present, to pattent upon the Terms proposed. Agreement not to pattent.

TOWN MEETING, *February* 28, 1674—Mr. Ward is chosen to carry on Town Meetings, till a new one be chosen.

Item—the Town is Agreed, to take some effectual Course to

free Mr. Crane from that £5, which was due to Domine Luke, at New York.

Item—Mr. Wilson is admitted to be a Planter with us if Mr. Peck and he Agree; in Case he subscribe as others have done.

Item—Stephen Freeman, John Ward, and John Catlin, are chosen to go over to New York; and the Town doth impower these Men, upon good Advice to lay an Arrest upon Person and Estate of Nicholas Bayard.

Conditions and Articles of the Bargain between the Town of Newark, and John Catlin and Edward Ball (with whom by the Town's Consent were joined Nathaniel Wheeler and John Baldwin, Senior,) about Part of the Neck that formerly belonged to Major Kingsland, Agreed upon and consented to the Twenty fourth Day of February, One Thousand Six Hundred Seventy and Three.

That in Case their Part shall be lost by any Claim of Kingsland or any in his Right, within the space of Two Years, the Town shall be liable to return them so much of the Money as shall by that Time be paid by them; they themselves bearing their Part together with the Town, unless those who receive it shall repay it them.

That their Part shall be appertaining to this Town of Newark, as a part of it; and that they shall be liable to bear their Part of the Rates to the Ministry and Country according to Proportion, together with the rest of the Town; paying for their Heads, Stocks, and improved Lands such as they till and mow.

That there shall be a sufficient and free Passage, from the wading place by the Mouth of the Second River to the Town's Land.

That there shall be a sufficient and free Passage, from the Town's Land to the Meadow and the Great Creek which is before the Buildings.

That they shall neither for the present or hereafter, they or their Heirs or Assigns, admit of any to be Inhabitants in their Part of the Neck, but such as this Town shall aprove and allow of.

That they shall have no Right to put any of their Creatures into the Town's Land.

That for and in Consideration of their Part of the Neck, they shall pay Three Hundred and Ten Pounds, in such Pay and such Kind, and at such Time and such Prices, to the Vendue Master at York or to whom the Town shall appoint, as the Town was ingaged, free from all Charge, viz: at three equal Payments—And that they shall be liable to bear whatsoever Damage may fall out, by their failing in the Condition of Payment.

That in Case the Town shall improve their Land, they shall be obliged to make half of the Fence cross the Neck, upon the upland.

That they and their Associates, Heirs and Assigns, or any that shall come to have any thing to do in that Part of the Neck by any Right from them, shall be bound to the true and real Performance of the Conditions before expressed, according to the true Intent of them, in each Particular thereof.

That their further Bound or Line on the Upland should be by the Fence, beginning near the Meadow on the further Side of the broken upland, and so to run in the directest Line, from thence unto the old Fence which crosseth the s'd Neck.

Item—Their Line in the Meadow, begining at the upland, rangeth with the Fence on the further side of the broken upland, and runneth to the Midst of a smaller Clump of Cedars—there being two greater Swamps or Clumps of Cedars, one on each side of it, and so is bounded by the first Cedar Swamp, and then by a Point of Brushy Ground unto a Tall Tree standing alone on the said Point, and from thence upon a Square Line to the Creek that buts against the Buildings; only in Case that it prove so as that they have not a Sufficiency of Meadow for their use to mow within their Bounds, they then are to extend their Line on the further side of the Creek unto the Midst, between the aforementioned brushy Point and Tree, and the next Parallel Point that also buts near the Creek, which Creek is their Bound through from thence unto Hackinsack River.

It is also further Agreed upon, that there shall be a Highway from the Town's Land for the Town's Use, by the Meadow Side, of Eight Rods wide, on firm Land unto the Head of the Creek, with Room convenient for the Town's Cattle; which said Highway they have Liberty to improve, so long as their Land and the Town's lieth in Common: but whensoever they with the Town shall agree to fence so as to part their Cattle, they are then forthwith to remove their Fence, and lay open the Highway for the Town's use as above said.

JOHN CATLIN.

Hereto hath John Catlin subscribed in the Presence of us }

JOHN WARD,
JOSEPH HARRISON.

TOWN MEETING, *March* 8, 1674-5.—It is voted that, that writing which is prepared to desire Mr. Jacob Melyne to produce the Bill of Sale, or any other Writing that may be helpfull to John Catlin and Edward Ball, shall be signed and delivered to them by John Brown, Junior.

Debate with the Governor about Pattenting.

Item—Being it is thought fit we should send in Writing our Minds about pattenting to the Governor —Mr. Ward, Deacon Lawrence, and Thomas Johnson are chosen, to go down to Elizabeth Town and present it, and also to debate with him about that Matter. Both Mr. Pierson's are desired, together with Mr. Kitchell, to draw up Matters in Short for that End.

Town Meeting, *March* the 19, 1674–5.—It is agreed, that is done in Referrence to the arresting of Mr. Bayard, the Town doth consent to.

Item—Thomas Richards and Edward Ball are chosen to go over to York, to carry some writings upon that account.

Fence Viewers chosen.

Town Meeting, *March* 30, 1674–5.—Samuel Plum, Sen'r, and John Baldwin, Junior, are chosen for Fence Viewers, for the Year ensuing.

Town's Men Chosen.

Town Meeting, *April* 28, 1675.—Thomas Johnson, Stephen Freeman, John Curtis, Mr. Samuel Kitchell, Thomas Huntington, John Ward, Turner, and Samuel Plum, are chosen Town's Men, for the Year ensuing.

Item—These Town's Men have committed to them the same Power as the Town's Men had the last year.

Town Meeting, *May* the 10, 1675—It was voted, that those as have not yet taken up their Second Division of Land, shall have Liberty to go out of the Range, and take it up on the other Side of the Two Mile Brook.

John Brown his Grant.

Item—John Brown, Junior, hath Liberty to Lay down his first Division of Upland in the Great Neck, by the Great Swamp, and take it up with his Second Division.

Order about laying out the Third Division.

Town Meeting, *May* the 18, 1675—The Town, after much Debate about the Third Division of Land, thought it not fit to lay out an Hundred Acres to the Highest Estate, have now agreed by Vote that the highest Estate shall not exceed above forty Acres, and the lowest not above Twenty, and the others not to exceed above thirty; and that this Land shall all lie common, for Pasture, Timber, and Stone, till it be inclosed by Fence.

Item—It is voted, that all shall proceed in laying out the Division as they have drawn Lotts; and if any shall neglect his Place by not attending the Surveyor, the next Lott shall have his Place.

Item—William Camp is appointed to speak to Mr. Bond, about

his taking up more Land than his Proportion for his Second Division, before the Second Division be perfected, contrary to a Town Order; aud also to declare to him, that if it fall out that any Man shall take it up for his Proportion, he hath Liberty from the Town (he paying the Surveyor) so to do.

TOWN MEETING, *June* 7, 1675—Thomas Johnson and Richard Harrison are appointed, to go down to Elizabeth Town's Men, to desire that our Bounds may be enlarged towards them.

Item—It is also agreed, that a Petition should be drawn up, and presented to the Governor and Council (by our Town's Men) about that Matter; and John Brown, Junior, is appointed to sign it.

The Meeting House Work. TOWN MEETING, *August* 28, 1675—It is agreed, that the Meeting House shall be lathed, and filled up with thin Stone and Mortar below the Girts, and the Charge hereof shall be levied as the Town shall Agree.

Item—It is also agreed, for the better Security of the Town, all the Men above Sixteen Years of Age, shall from Day to Day as their Turns come, attend this Work about the Meeting House till it be finished, and bring their Arms with them. Twelve Men is appointed to appear in a Day.

Item—It is agreed, that two Flanckers shall be made at two Corners of the Meeting House with Palisades or Stockades; and the charge of all this Work to be borne by the Persons and Estates as belongs to the Town.

Order about Watching. Item—it is agreed, that all the Home Lotts as belongs to this Town, shall watch according to their Turn, as well those as are not Inhabited as those that are.

TOWN MEETING, *September* 10, 1675—It is agreed, that two Men of these Twelve which are to come according to their Turns, are chosen to be Overseers to appoint the Work, and to take Notice who is wanting.

The Town's Men agreed, October 9, 1675, That the Necks where any Corn is, shall be cleared from all Cattle on the 11th Day of this Instant October, and the former Town Order to stand in force again.

Item—Two Men shall be sent down to Elizabeth Town, according as is expressed in the Writing now come from the Governor.

Item—Mr. Bond, Deacon Lawrence, and Thomas Richards are chosen, and any two of them to go down.

TOWN MEETING, *October* 26, 1675—Lieut. Ward and Sarjent

Johnson are chosen Deputies, to go down to Elizabeth Town to meet the Governor and Council.

TOWN MEETING, *November* the 22, 1675—Mr. Samuel Kitchell, Sam'l Plum, John Curtis, and John Brown, Junior, are chosen by Vote, to go from House to House, to take an account how much Land and Meadow every Man hath already, or will take up in this Tract of Land already purchased: as also how much every Man will take of that Land which lieth up the River, which is yet unpurchased.

Item—John Baldwin, Junior, and Ephraim Penintou, may change a Piece of Land in the Neck if they please, each with other.

Item—It is voted, that Thomas Staples' Home Lott Shall be cleared, between this and next Spring.

TOWN MEETING, *January the first*, 1675—It is voted, that the Deputies for the General Assembly in April, shall be chosen by Vote with Hands.

Item—Lieut. Ward and Thomas Johnson are chosen, to attend that Business. Capt. Samuel Swain is chosen for the Third Man, in case any of those fail.

Item—Mr. Samuel Kitchell, John Baldwin, Junior, and Stephen Davis are chosen Grand Jury Men for the Year ensuing.

Officers chosen 1st of Jan'y.

It being ordered by the General Assembly, that a Monthly Court shall be, to decide small Matters; it is voted, that the Members of this Monthly Court shall be chosen by Papers

Item—Mr. Bond, Lieut. Ward, and Thomas Johnson are chosen Members thereof, for the Year ensuing.

Item—John Brown, Junior, is chosen Clerk—and Edward Ball is chosen to be Messenger for this Court, for the Year Ensuing.

Item—John Curtis is chosen Constable, for the Year ensuing.

Item—John Brown, Junior, is chosen, to be Clerk for the Town, for the Year ensuing.

Item—Thomas Johnson is chosen, to be Treasurer for the Town, for the Year ensuing.

Item—John Brown, Sen'r, is chosen, to warn Town Meetings for that end of the Town where he lives, for the Year ensuing.

Item—John Ward, Turner, is chosen to Warn Town Meetings for that End where he lives, for this Year.

TOWN MEETING, *January* 10th, 1675—Captain Swain, Sarjent Johnson, and Sarj't. Huntinton are chosen by Vote, to join with the Commission'd Military officers, to consider about and contrive for the Fortifications belonging to our Town.

TOWN MEETING, *January* 21, 1675.—The Town did Voluntarily by Vote, oblige themselves to pay that money demanded upon account of the Neck, in a Rate made according to Proportion, as they put in their Estates at the first to take up Land by.

Order to Sue Bayard.

TOWN MEETING, *February* the 7th, 1675—The Town by Vote hath agreed, that Mr. Bayard should be sued in Respect of recovering the Money which was paid upon Account of ye Neck—Sarjant Thomas Johnson and John Ward, Turner, are chosen to prosecute this Suit upon Mr. Bayard.

Item—In case of Thomas Johnson's absence, Sam'l. Kitchell is chosen in his stead.

Item—Thomas Johnson is chosen to go to Woodbridge, to desire Mr. Moore to come to treat about this matter.

The Way of rating for the Ministers the last Second Day of September every Year.

Item—It is agreed by Vote, that the way of Rating for the Ministers this Year, shall be upon that rateable Estate which is now visible, as it was the last Year, (to wit,) on Heads, Lands, and Cattle, the Prices as they was before, only the Swine as be now fatting shall not be rated—but for the Time to come the Town hath agreed, that the List of Estate to rate by shall be given in the last Second day of September, in every Year.

TOWN MEETING, *February* 25, 1675–6—It is voted, that the vote which was past the 10th of August 1672 and recorded in fol. 36, [see page....] concerning the Government, shall be obliterated by the Clerk.

Item—Michael Tompkins is chosen, to present the Names of the Members of the Town Court to the Governor, to Establish and impower them to that Work.

TOWN MEETING, *March* the 21st, 1675-6—Having had much trouble about disorderly coming to Town Meetings–the Town doth now agree, that Twenty four Hours shall be accorded legal Warning, and if any Man doth not come to the Place of Meeting to answer to his Name at the Second Beat of the Drum, shall be fined 6c. The Drum is to be beaten twice, in fair weather the first Drum is to be beat as far as Sarj't. Harrison's Gate, and the Second at the Meeting House about half an Hour after, at which Time every Planter shall be at the Place of Meeting to answer to his Name, or else to be under the Penalty afr'd., if he give not a satisfying Reason to the Town of his late coming, And for a whole Day's Absence he is to be fined half a Crown, and for half a Day's Absence fifteen Pence, and for going away before the Meeting is dismissed without leave two Shillings, except he give a satisfying reason as afr'd. Also, if any Man be absent Part of the Day, he shall besides his fine loose his Vote, and stand to what the Town hath done or shall do in his Absence.

Item—Lieut. Sam'l Swain is chosen, to assist the Justice of Peace in our Town Courts.

Item—It is also agreed, that the Clerk shall take Notice of these fines, and demand them of those as are defective, and keep them on the file to be disposed of as the Town shall see cause.

Item—Mr. Ward gives Notice to all that are Planters that they have their Names listed, and attend Town Meetings.

A Rate to be made for Powder.

Item—John Ward, Turner, is chosen to procure a Barrel of Powder, and Lead answerable to it, as reasonably as he can, for the Town's use; provided that the Town pay him once within this week in Corn, Fowls, and Eggs, or any Way to satisfy him.

Item—This Money to be raised by the Ordinary Way of rating, by Heads, Flocks, and Lands; Mr. Pierson's Estate paying to this Rate also. Item—the Rate of this Ammunition is to be the sum of Ten Pounds.

Item—John Brown, Junior, is chosen to make this Rate.

Item—It is agreed by Vote that those Estates which are not yet brought in, shall be brought to the Deacons or the Clerks, within Two Days from this Meeting.

Fence Viewers Chosen.

TOWN MEETING, *April* 17, 1676—Seth Tompkins and Daniel Dod are chosen Fence Viewers, for the Year ensuing, or till new ones are chosen.

Item—It is Voted, that John Catlin and Edward Ball shall have the Rate as is made to pay for the Money as was borrowed upon the Neck Account, provided that the Widow Freeman may have the Benefit of it, according to her Proportion. Item—John Brown Jun'r is chosen by Vote, to deliver this Rate to John Catlin and Edward Ball.

A Committee to lay out the Highways & Landing Place.

Item—It is voted that a Committee be chosen, to lay out the Highway and the Landing Place by the River, near Thomas Richards.

Item—Lieut. Sam'l Swaine, Sarj't Thomas Johnson, Sarj't Richard Harrison, and Mr. Samuel Kitchel are chosen a Committee for this purpose, or any three of them.

Packer Chosen.

TOWN MEETING, *June* the 5, 1676—Joseph Walters is chosen the Packer of Meat for the Town, according to the order of the Gen'l Assembly.

Sealer of Leather Chosen.

Item—Deacon Lawrence is chosen to be the Sealer of Leather for this Town, according to the order of the General Assembly.

Item—John Brown Senior, and Joseph Walters are

chosen, to Seal all Measures of all Sorts for the Year ensuing, according to the Order of the General Assembly.

Item—The Grand Jury Men are chosen, to take care that the Governors Arrears of those that have not subscribed be gathered up, according to the Order of the General Assembly.

Richard Fletcher's Grant.

Item—upon the Request of Richard Fletcher to lay his Land together, and lay the Highway on the South Side of it, it is granted to him ; provided that he make and maintain a good sufficient Highway, for Carts or other use, over the Swamp.

Thomas Ludington's Grant.

Item—Thomas Ludington hath granted for amends of his Second Division of Meadow, that sunken Meadow (together with Part of the Pond) between the Homeward Stake of John Brown's black Stake Meadow, and so streight to the Homeward End of the Pond; also, John Brown is to have half the Pond, and from thence to His further Stake by Maple Island Creek.

John Brown Junr's Grant.

Item—John Brown Junior, hath Granted to him, a small Parcell of Land to set his House on, over the Way, partly against his own Lott and partly against the next Lott, not exceeding above half an Acre.

Town's Men established.

TOWN MEETING, *June* 12, 1676—It is Voted, that those Men last chosen for Town's Men shall be in that Place till the first of January, namely: Sam'l Kitchel, John Ward, Turner, Samuel Plum, Thomas Huntington, Joseph Walters, Azariah Crane, and William Camp.

Order Concerning pounding Cattle and giving in Testimony.

Item.—It is voted that every Male Inhabitant in the Town, aged above fourteen Years of Age, hath Liberty to pound any Cattle being found in trespassing, and if the Matter prove actionable afterwards in our Town Courts, his Oath shall be counted legal Testimony. But if any Persons under fourteen Years of Age find any Cattle so trespassing, and bring them to pound, he or they shall produce Testimony where he or they found the Cattle, before it be accounted legal Testimony. But for unruly Cattle, and such Cattle as are voluntarily left in the Neck, as the Law and Town Order provides.

Item—John Brown Sen'r is chosen Pound Keeper, his Fees as specified.

Item—For Cows, Oxen, Horses, and Swine, six pence by the Head Poundage ; besides all Damages.

TOWN MEETING, *September* 25, 1676—Mr. Bruen hath a Grant, to be rate free.

Item—It is voted, that those as are behind of their Third Division which should have been laid out before this time, shall now have Liberty of a Week's Time to perfect the same, (provided they take not up any Land as is sequestered in the Town Book,) before any shall proceed to take up according to Concession.

Sealers of Leather chosen. Item—John Curtis and John Baldwin Sen'r are chosen Sealers of Leather, for this Year.

TOWN MEETING, *November* 21, 1676—William Meeker's Petition to the Governor, Council, and Assembly, was publickly read and upon this Condition following the Inhabitants of Newark have voluntarily contributed to answer his desire therein, (Viz): That he, nor none of his, nor any Person or Persons in his name, nor in his Behalf, shall at any Time or Times, Place or Places, now or hereafter, attempt to trouble or molest any person or persons belonging to our Town of Newark, upon the Account of his Loss sustained by Reason of the Change of Government: unto this Condition, as the Terms upon which I the said William Meeker do accept this Contribution, and hereunto, I have set to my Hand this 19th Day of January 1676—

In the presence of us WILLIAM MEEKER ꝗ his Mark.
THOMAS JOHNSON
JOHN BROWN JUN'R

At the same MEETING, *November* 21, Thomas Johnson and Deacon Tompkins are chosen to acquaint those as are absent what is done for William Meeker, and to compleat the Business with them and with William Meeker, according to the Town's Act.

Item—every Man shall reckon with the Treasurer between this and the last Day of this week; otherwise he shall not be paid this Year.

Item—Thomas Richards is to make, and maintain, a sufficient Cart Gate to the Landing Place.

Item—Edward Ball hath Liberty to take the Elder's Lott, beyond Mr. Ward's Pasture on the Hill, in Lieu of Part of his Land beyond the Second River, Acre for Acre.

Concerning a School Master. Item—the Town's Men have Liberty to see if they can find a competent Number of Schollars, and accomodations for a School Master, within this Town.

TOWN MEETING, *January* 1st, 1676.—Thomas Johnson and Thomas Richards are chosen Deputies for the General Assembly, for the Year ensuing. John Curtis the Third Man, in Case either of these fail.

Item—Lieut. Swain and Thomas Johnson are chosen Assistants, to sit in Town Courts with the Justice, for the Year ensuing. Item—John Brown, Junior, is chosen Clerk for the Town Courts, for the Year ensuing. Item—Edward Ball is chosen Messenger for the Town Courts, for the Year ensuing. Item—Joseph Walters, John Ward, Turner, and Ephraim Peninton, are chosen for Grand Jury Men for the Year Ensuing. Item—John Catlin is chosen for an Attorney for the Town Courts, for the Year ensuing. Item—John Brown Junior is chosen Clerk for the Town, for the Year ensuing. Item—Mr. Samuel Kitchell is chosen Constable, for the Year ensuing. Item—John Curtis is chosen Treasurer, for the Year ensuing.

Item—Stephen Bond and Samuel Rose are chosen, for Warners for the Town Meetings for the Year ensuing. Item—Ephraim Penninton and Hans Albers, are chosen Fence Viewers for the Year ensuing. Item—Richard Fletcher is chosen Pounder, and to keep the Key of the Pound for the Year ensuing. Item—John Baldwin Junior, Thomas Pierson Junior, Thomas Pierson Sen'r, John Catlin, William Camp, Azariah Crane, and George Day, are chosen Towns Men for the Year ensuing—these Towns Men are appointed to meet every Lecture Day, in the afternoon.

Item—it is voted, that the Country Rate shall be made by the List as Men put in to make the other Rates by.

TOWN MEETING, *February* 6, 1676—The Town seeing some Trees spoiled in the streets by barking, or otherwise; The Town hath agreed, that no green Tree within the Town as is marked with N. shall be barked, or felled, or any otherwise killed, under the Penalty of Ten Shillings so killed.

Item—the Towns Men are chosen, to mark such Trees as are convenient for Shade in the Town Streets.

Towns Men to mark Trees.

Item—Stephen Bond is chosen for Brander of Horses and Mares, according as the Law provides.

Item—John Ward, Turner, is chosen Brander of Cattle, according as the Law provides.

WHEREAS, AT A TOWN MEETING *January* 1st, 1676—there was a Committee sent to the Ministers, for the abatement of Twenty Pounds of their Salary, upon the Consideration of the low condition and many Payments the Town hath to defray; To which Motion of the Town the Ministers complied with, upon Condition that We the Inhabitants of Newark, do oblige ourselves each of us severally for our Parts, and as a Town jointly for the whole, to pay or cause to be paid, the full and just sum of One Hundred Pounds by the Year to the Two present Ministers, in Wheat, Pease, Pork, Beef, Indian Corn, Rye, and other passable Current Pay, at Price Current in the Province, at or before the Twentyeth of February; and also we do, each of us that are behind, engage to pay the Rates already levied. Also we do agree and consent, that the said present Ministers shall be free from all Common and Ordinary Rates, both in Town and Country. This is voted in a Town Meeting, to be an Agreement betwixt the Town and the Two Ministers, this 7th of February, 1676.

Town Meeting, *February* 7th, 1676—Mr. Ward and Thomas Johnson are chosen to go to Woodbridge, and inquire whether Mr. Deleplary hath caused what he hath done in Respect to what he surveyed for our Town Bounds, to be recorded in the Secretary's Office; and if not, to go to him, and use Means to have it recorded in the Secretary's Office Speedily.

To see if our Town Bounds be recorded.

Item—they are also to have the Bill of Sale from the Indians recorded there.

Item—it is agreed that there shall be a Commission procured, for our Justice to keep Town Courts.

Item—Joseph Walters is chosen Packer of Meat, for the Year ensuing.

Item—the Town hath consented that the Town's Men should perfect the Bargain with the School Master for this Year, upon Condition that he will come for this Year, and do his faithful, honest, and true Endeavor, to teach the Children or servants of those as have subscribed, the reading and writing of English, and also Arethmetick if they desire it; as much as they are capable to learn and he capable to teach them, within the Compass of this Year—nowise hindring but that he may make what bargain he please, with those as have not subscribed. It is voted, that the Town's Men have Liberty to compleat the Bargain with the School Master, they knowing the Town's Mind.

School Master.

Town Meeting, *February* 26, 1676—It is voted, that Thomas Huntington shall have the Boggs against his Meadow to the Upland, and he doth take it as Satisfaction for what he thinks he is wronged in his Meadow, provided he may have it, without Trouble from any in the Town, upon account of what was granted against the Lotts.

Huntington's Grant.

Item—Richard Fletcher hath Granted to him, One Acre and a half of Meadow for what is wanting in his Second Division.

Fletcher's Grant.

Town Meeting, *June* 18, 1677—The Town's Men are chosen by the Town, to go to John Johnson in the Town's Name, and testify their Dislike of his taking up that Lott by the Frog Pond. And also to see if he will lay

John Johnson.

it down (or a Considerable Part of it) and take a Lott in some other Place.

The way of rating for this year.

TOWN MEETING, *October* 1, 1677—It is voted, that so much of the Third Division as lieth within Fence, shall pay to all Rates this Year, as the first and Second doth.

Item—it is voted, that the first and Second Divisions shall pay Rates this Year, as formerly.

Item—Heads and Cattle as it was the last Year, (viz): Lands penny for Acre, heads 14d., Oxen 5d., Cows above three Year Old 3d., Steers of four Year Old 4d., Steers of year old 3d., Steers and Hieffers of two Year Old 2d., Yearling Steers and Hieffers 1d., Horses and Mares of three Year Old and upwards 3d., Horses and Mares of Two Year old 2d., Yearlings 1d., All Swine of a Year old and upward 1d.

Item—John Curtis and John Brown, Junior, is chosen, to make the Rates for this Year.

TOWN MEETING, *October* 5, 1677—It is voted, for the perfecting of the List of Estates to make the Rates by this Year, that that those as have not brought in their Estates already, a List of them shall be drawn up, they having a Week's time before to perfect the same and bring it to John Curtis or John Brown, Junior; and upon the Failure hereof there shall be a Warrant given to Edward Ball, to go to every one and take their List, and for his so doing he shall have four Pence a Piece; and those Lists brought to the next Meeting and read there, as others have been.

Item—it is voted, that this Money due upon the Neck Account, shall be made into a Rate.

TOWN MEETING, *January* 1st, 1677—Mr. Thomas Johnson and Captain Samuel Swain are chosen Deputies for the General Assembly, for the Year ensuing. Mr. Ward is chosen to be the Third Man.

Item—John Crane, William Camp, and Sarj't Richard Harrison, are chosen Grand Jury Men, for the Year ensuing.

Item—John Brown, Junior, and William Camp, are chosen to see after the procuring the Laws of the Province, or that Part of them as is between our Town and Elizabeth Town.

Item—Mr. Ward, Mr. Johnson, and Mr. Swain, are chosen for the carrying on Town Courts, for the Year ensuing.

Item—John Brown, Junior, is chosen Clerk of the Town Court. Item—David Ogden, is chosen Messenger for the Town Court. John Curtis is chosen Treasurer.

Item—its agreed by the Town, that two next Neighbours at one End of the Town one Year, and the two next Neighbors at the other End of the Town the Next Year, shall be fence Viewers—beginning at the North End of the Town.

Thomas Pierson, Sen'r, and John Ward, Turner, are chosen fence Viewers for this Year.

Zachariah Burwell and Daniel Dod, Warners of Town Meetings, each for the End of the Town where he lives. Azariah Crane, Pounder and Pound Keeper. John Catlin, the Town Attorney. Joseph Walters, Packer of Meat. John Brown, Junior, and Joseph Walters, Scalers of Measures and Weights.

Ephraim Burwell, Stephen Davis, John Baldwin, Junior, Thomas Pierson, Senior, John Catlin, George Day, and Thomas Pierson, Jun'r, Town's Men. Thomas Huntington, Constable. William Camp, Surveyor of the Highways in the Room of Thomas Johnson—the others to remain, and have the same Powers they had before. John Brown, Junior, Town Clerk.

Inhabitants admitted.

John Gardner is admitted a Planter with Us, he submitting to our Town Orders: he hath Granted to him Thirty Acres of Upland lying at the rear of John Ward, Turner's, Lott, and other Lott rears—lying beyond the 2nd River.

Nathaniel Ward hath a Grant from the Town, of that Home Lott lying by his Father's.

Samuel Potter is admitted a Planter, provided he can buy an accommodation or supply himself by a Grant from the Town; he submitting to our Town Orders.

Town's Men to mend the Gate next the River.

Item—The Town Voted, that the Town's Men shall look after the mending or making of the Upper Gate, and shall be paid for it, because Thomas Richards refuseth to make or mend it as Aaron Blatchly's Agent.

John Davis is admitted an Inhabitant.

Town Meeting, *February* 6, 1677.—It is voted, that the vote made 7th February, 1676, concerning the Ministers, shall be now void, and of none effect.

The last Dividing of the fences.

The Town having made an Act, March 20th, 1670, to have the Com'on fence divided, to every Man his just Proportion and Share, according as he hath acres of Land within the same, and also hath chosen Robert Denison, Stephen Davis, John Catlin, John Curtis, and John Brown Junior to Proportion the same, and hath also engaged to sit down satisfied with their Determination. They having therefore measured the Fence, do find that two acres one Rod and Twenty Poles of Land doth require one Rod of Fence, of that

Land which is already laid out. Also they have proceeded to lay the said fence according to the best of their Judgments, the Number of Lotts and Rods to each Man being also here recorded —beginning with the first.

	Lotts	Rods	Feet		Lotts	Rods	Feet
John Rogers..........	1	$9\frac{3}{4}$		Nathaniel Wheeler.....	32	7	4
Both Mr. Kitchels......	2	20	13	John Crane..........	33	4	12
John Bostick..........	3	$3\frac{1}{2}$		Hanse Albers..........	34	3	12
Jonathan Tompkins....	4	3	$4\frac{1}{2}$	Robert Denison........	35	6	
Mr. Candfield..........	5	9	$12\frac{1}{2}$	John Catlin..........	36	8	12
Widdow Ward.........	6	8		Francis Lindly.........	37	5	12
Martin Tichenor.........	7	3	6	Stephen Freeman......	38	15	
Delivered Crane.......	8	3	12	Mr. John Ward.......	39	12	4
Thomas Staples.........	9	3		Edward Ball..........	40	5	12
Mr. Pierson Sen'r.....	10	$18\frac{1}{2}$		John Brooks	41	1	9
Thomas Ludington.....	11	2	7	Mr. Peck....	42	3	4
William Camp.........	12	$4\frac{1}{2}$		Thomas Johnson.......	43	11	
John Baldwin Jun'r...	13	5	14	Robert Limon.........	44	3	3
Mr. Treat.............	14	2	4	Thomas Pierson	45	4	
John Brown Sen'r.....	15	1	4	Mr. Morris...........	46	7	12
Hugh Roberts.........	16	8	10	Robert Dalglish.......	47	$6\frac{1}{2}$	
Zachariah Burwell.....	17	3	3	George Day...........	48	2	12
Mr. Crane............	18	16		Widow Rigs...........	49	6	9
Samuel Rose..........	19	5		Michael Tompkins.....	50	9	11
Ephraim Burwell......	20	3	14	John Brown Jun'r......		4	6
Stephen Bond.........	21	3	3	Mr. Pierson Jun'r......		4	2
Josiah Ward..........	22	8	3	Jonathan Sargant......		3	
Thomas Richards......	23	4	7	Alexander Monrow....		3	12
Sarj't Rich'd Harrison..	24	12	7	Benjamin Baldwin.....		2	6
Ephraim Pennington...	25	5	2	John Harrison.........		4	14
John Ward, Turner	26	7		Thomas Huntington....		0	
Richard Lawrence.....	27	$7\frac{1}{2}$		John Curtis...........		6	12
Stephen Davis.........	28	5	12	John Baldwin Sen'r....		6	6
Henry Lyon...........	29	13		Aaron Blachly.........		7	
Lieut. Sam'l Swaine....	30	15	2	Mr. Bruen & John Bruen.		8	15
Joseph Walters........	31	3	3	Samuel Plum..........		$12\frac{1}{2}$	

Town Meeting, *October* 22, 1677—to prevent the Rate which was agreed upon on the Neck account on the 5 October, 77; there was a List of what Pipe Staves People were willing to give drawn up—which were to be brought to some convenient Landing by the last of next week, after the Date hereof.

Joseph Walters, was chosen Culler for these Staves.

Stephen Davis and John Ward, Dish-Turner, are chosen to join with John Catlin and Edward Ball as a Committee, to make the best of these Staves to defray that Debt.

Appearing at Town Meeting.

TOWN MEETING the 1st of *March*, 1677-8—It is voted as a Town Act, that all and every Man that improves Land in the Town of Newark, shall make their appearance at Town Meetings, and there attend to any Business as shall be proposed as any of the Planters do, and be liable to any Fine as others are in Case of their absence at the Call, or a whole Day, or going away before the Meeting break up—and also that the Clerk is to set their Names in a List, and Call them as others are called.

Buying Land at the Mountain.

Item—there having been much Debate about buying the Land to the Top of the Mountain, parellel with the Two Lines—Mr. Ward, Mr. Johnson, Samuel Harrison, and . . . . . Richards, are chosen to treat with the Indians about the same, and to agree with them as well as they can.

TOWN MEETING, *March* 30, 1677—It was thought needful and agreed upon by Vote, to send a Petition to the Governor and Council for a Charter, with as good Privileges as our Neighbors at Woodbridge have, of all the Lands which is surveyed to us by the Surveyor as our Town Bounds; and those Lands as are not yet purchased, to have Liberty with convenient Time to purchase it, or till the Indians will sell it.

Item—Deacon Tompkins, Mr. Kitchell, and Stephen Davis, are chosen (with Mr. Pierson's Help) to draw up a Petition to the Governor and Council.

Mr. Ward, Mr. Johnson, Deacon Tompkins, and Stephen Davis, or some of them, are chosen to present the Petition to the Governor and Council.

Running the Lines.

John Curtis and John Treat are chosen to run the West Line with the Indians, and to meet with Edward Ball and Daniel Dod, who are also chosen to run the North Line with the Indians, and meet with the others on the Mountain.

Letters to Holland.

AFTER LECTURE, the 1st of *May*, 1678—It was thought meet to send two Letters to Holland, one to Anthony Colve and the other to the Court of Admiralty, to seek for Reparation for our Expence about the Neck; which Letters being prepared were then read—and John Brown Jun'r was chosen to sign them in the Town's Name.

Country Rate.

TOWN MEETING, *June* 17, 1678—It is voted, that the Country Rate should be made by Head and Estate, as other Rates were.

John Curtis and John Brown Jun'r are chosen, to make this Rate.

TOWN MEETING, *September* 30, 1678—It is voted, that all Meadow as first and Second Division which is allotted and laid out according to Town Order, and all Upland as lieth within any Fence, as first Second or Third Divisions, and laid out according to Town Order, shall pay Rates this Year.

All Lands and Meadow shall pay penny for acres, as it was sized by the Town, Heads and Cattle as they was the last Year.

John Curtis and John Brown Jun'r, are chosen to make the Rates this Year.

Voluntary Proportions to Mr. Pierson, Jun'r.

It is fully and unanimously consented to, and agreed upon by every Planter now present, all being called by Name, that they will from Time to Time pay or cause to be payed Yearly, in their full Proportions Equally in a Rate that may be agreed on by the Major Part of the Town, to the Maintainance and allowance now agreed upon for the Upholding and preaching of the Word in our Town; and Eighty Pounds by the Year is agreed upon to be allowed to the present Minister with his Fire wood—and to be Rate free.

TOWN MEETING, *January* 1st, 1678—Mr. Thomas Johnson and John Curtis are chosen Deputies for the Year ensuing, and Sam'l Swain the Third Man. Mr. Ward, Mr. Johnson, and Mr. Swain are chosen for the Town Courts, for the Year ensuing. John Brown Jun'r, Clerk for the Town Court. David Ogden, Messenger for the Town Court. John Brown Jun'r, Town Clerk. John Curtis, Treasurer.

The Town's Men have Power to agree with the Town Treasurer for his Salary, for the time past and for this Year. The Town's Men have Power to agree, and indent, with all Officers as are to have Salaries in the Town.

Ephraim Burwell, Samuel Rose, Edward Ball, John Baldwin Sen'r, John Catlin, Stephen Bond, and Joseph Johnson, are chosen Town's Men for the Year ensuing, having the same Power as other Town's Men have had before.

Samuel Plum, George Day, and Azariah Crane, are chosen Grand Jury Men for the Year ensuing. Edward Ball, Town At torney. David Ogden, Pounder. Nathaniel Wheeler and Thomas Pierson Jun'r, fence Viewers.

Item—it is voted, that the Warners of Town Meetings, when their Year is out, shall each of them from Time to Time nominate two or three to the Town, to serve in warning Town Meetings for that Year; and the Town to chuse one of them as they think most fit, provided they nominate not any Man that hath served in that Place already, till every Inhabitant hath served once.

Hance Albers and Samuel Lyon are chosen Warners of Town Meetings in their respective Places, for the Year ensuing. John Curtis and John Baldwin Sen'r, Sealers of Leather. Joseph Walters, Packer of Meat. Joseph Walters and John Brown Sen'r, Sealer of Weights and Measures. Richard Fletcher and Edward Ball, Grave Diggers. Thomas Pierson Sen'r, Constable.

TOWN MEETING, *February* 12, 1678-9—The Town consented by Vote, not to sow any Pease white or gray this Year, on the Penalty of Five Shillings a Rod, or for the smallest Quantity, as any Person or Persons shall or may sow.

Item—upon a Report that many are sick of the Pox at New York—It is thought fit to prohibit persons from frequent going thither upon every small occasion, as formerly. The Town hath therefore chosen as a Committee, Mr. Ward, Mr. Johnson, Mr. Swain, Deacon Lawrence, and Sarj't Harrison, to whom Persons shall repair for Liberty; and this Committee or any Three of them to consider whether Persons occasions are of urgent Necessity, and as they find, to give Liberty or Prohibit.

Item—If any Person or Persons shall presume to go without approbation from some of these Three, shall forfeit the sum of 20s., to be distrained by the Constable.

Item—it is agreed that the Meeting House shall be seated in Convenient Time, for our Conveniency in Meeting together for God's Worship.

Item—the Town's Men, Thomas Ludington, Capt. Swain, and John Brown Jun'r, are chosen to contrive for the most decent and convenient Way (as they think) to seat it; also, as near as they can give Report what it will Cost.

Item—it is agreed that the last Purchase Rate shall be made in a Town Rate, in the Ordinary way of rating, by Heads and Estates.

TOWN MEETING, *February* 13, 1678-9—Samuel Dod, doth freely resign and lay down to the Town's Disposal, his Right to any Land, Meadow, or Boggs, which he hath illegally taken up contrary to a Town agreement.

Item—it is Agreed, that Samuel Dod is admitted a planter in our Town, and hath Liberty to possess Lands by Gift or Purchase, according to Town Rights as other Planters do.

Item—Samuel Dod hath Granted to him, that Twenty-five Acres laid out already on Watseson; and that Part of Swamp laid out to him by the Surveyor, Containing about Twenty Acres; provided it shall lie Common for Stone and Timber as the Third

Division doth; and that Part of Land belonging to the Town (if any) lying near Hance's; provided it prejudiceth not the Highway. Samuel Plum and Stephen Davis are chosen to lay out a convenient Highway by Hance's.

Stephen Davis, acknowledging he had taken up some Land contrary to a Town agreement, doth freely resign it to the Town's Disposal; doth request it for his Son John Davis.

Item—John Davis hath granted to him, about Twenty Acres of Land up the River; provided he leave a convenient Highway by the River, of four Rods wide.

John Tichenor doth freely lay down and resign to the Town's dispose, his Right to any Land which he hath illegally taken up, contrary to a Town Agreement.

Item—the Town granted that he may have that land before William Camp's, provided he prejudice not the Highway; also, he doth freely leave himself with a Committee to lay it out, and also to lay out the Highway. John Brown, Jun'r, William Camp and Thomas Ludington are chosen to lay it out, and also a convenient Highway.

Item—Anthony Oleff doth confess his Fault, in taking up land and Meadow, contrary to the Town Order; and doth freely submit it to the Town's Dispose. And upon his Desire he is admitted a Planter.

Item—Anthony Oleff hath granted to him forty Acres of Land at the Mountain, which was laid out to him by the Surveyor.

Town Meeting, *February* 19, 1678-9—Edward Ball doth acknowledge he hath taken fifty acres of land, which is contrary to a Town Agreement; and doth freely resign what is more than his Proportion, to the Town's Dispose.

Mr. Crane saith, he will lay down what Land he hath taken up contrary to a Town Agreement, if others will Lay down all they have taken up, contrary to a Town Order.

Item—the Town Agreed by Vote, that the Town Rate for this Year should be paid at Winter Wheat 5s. p. Bus'l, Summer Wheat 4s. 6d. p. Bus'l, Rye 4s. p. Bus'l, Indian Corn 3s. p. Bus'l.

Item—John Johnson proposed to the Town to lay down that Lott he hath surveyed by the Frog Pond for the Town's use; provided he may have so much of the Pond as is already laid out to him, and an Acre of Land about his House, in such form as Sarj't Richard Harrison and John Ward, Turner, have brought Report of the Town (viz); so far as the first Row of Apple Trees are now from his House, and so by the Pond till the Acre be made up; and also Six Acres of that Lott laid out for an Elder's Lott, on that Side of the Lott next to John Ward, Turner's, Lott; likewise he desires to enjoy for his Use, the whole Lott by the

Frog Pond for the Space of Three Years, if the Town need it not before for an Elder; and also he desireth Liberty to drain the Pond thro this land. This was agreed on by Vote, to be an Agreement between the Town and John Johnson.

Item—the Town doth impower the Com'ittee already chosen, to carry on the Seating of the Meeting House, with as good Prudence for the Town as they can.

TOWN MEETING, *March* 10th, 1678-9—It is agreed, that no Person whatsoever, shall at any Time sett or make fire in the Woods or Meadow, to burn the Woods or Meadow, on the Penalty of paying all Damages they do by the Fire so sett, untill after the Town's Men who are appointed by the Town to appoint a Day for that Purpose, when they see the fittest Season, and to give Notice by the Beat of the Drum; at which Time every Planter is to make their Appearance at the Common Place of Meeting, upon the Penalty of 2 s. 6 d.—and then and there to agree in the Manner how to proceed, for the best security of ye Town.

Penalty of setting fire.

Item—Mr. Crane, Robert Dalglesh, and Jasper Crane are chosen, to lay out Samuel Potter's Lott again.

TOWN MEETING, *April* 17th, 1679—It is thought necessary and agreed by Vote, upon the News concerning the Indians rising, that we for our Parts send to desire the Governor to call the General Assembly, to consider what may be meet to secure ourselves, in Case of such Danger—Mr. Ward is chosen, to carry the Town's Message to the Governor.

John Ward, Turner, hath the Grant of the remainder of the Elder's Lott which is more than John Johnson is to have, for one of his Son's to build on.

TOWN MEETING, *June* 10, 1679—for the better Security of the Town, it is agreed to have a Watch kept in the Town, Three in a Night, at some House appointed by the Sarjents, and one of the Three to stand Centry, one at one Time and another at another; and at break of Day or thereabouts all Three of them to be walking, that if there be Danger it may be timely discovered and prevented, and about half an hour after Daybreak to call the Drummer, and he is to beat the Drum. It is also agreed that one fourth Part of the Town at a time, and so taking their Turns, shall carry arms to Meeting on the Lord's Days—and two to Ward, and one to stand Centry.

The way of watching.

Carrying arms.

TOWN MEETING, *September* 29, 1679—It is voted, that all Persons which have taken up Land or Meadow within the limits of our Town of Newark, and still keeps it in their Possession, shall pay Rates for it this Year, together with all other ratable Estate, as Heads, and Cattle—by Lands, we mean all Land and Meadow laid out by the Town's Order, or by Mr. Deleplary, not depriving any Man of his particular Right given him before by the Town. Also it is Agreed, that if any Person have taken up any Land or Meadow infringing upon any Town Priviledge, as Highways, or Waterings, shall be exempted from this Rate so much of it as is for his Use.

Item—It is voted, that the first and Second Division shall be given in as the Town laid it out, and other land and Meadow as Mr. Deleplary laid them out.

Item—It is voted that all Lands shall pay alike to this Rate, and that all Land shall pay Penny p. acre. And all Heads and Cattle as before, viz: Heads 14d., Oxen 5d., Cows 3d., Steers and Hieffers of Two Years old 2d., Steers of four Years Old 4d., Steers of three Years Old 3d., Steers and Hieffers of One Year Old 1d., Horses and Mares of three Years Old and upwards 3d., Horses and Mares of two Years Old 2d, Horses and Mares of one Year Old 1d, and Swine of One Year old and upwards 1d. p. Head.

Item—George Day hath the Grant, to have his Proportion of Meadow which is wanting in his Second Division, lay out to him at Wheeler's Point in that Meadow which was Henry Lyon's.

Mrs. Morris's Grant.

TOWN MEETING, *October* 13, 1679—Mrs. Morris hath Granted Twenty Shillings in the Town Rate, upon account of what she did for Mr. Bruen.

Orders about Wolves.

Item—It is voted that if any Person shall kill any Wolves, and bring the Heads to the Constable, shall have allowed by the Town Ten Shillings per Head.

Order about carrying Mr. Pierson's Wood.

TOWN MEETING, *November* 24, 1679—It is agreed that two in each Quarter shall be appointed, to look after the carrying in Mr. Pierson's Wood for this Year, and take Care that it be done seasonably. And also to see that every one as is yet behind for the last Year, do first carry their Load; and for their Pains and Care shall be exempted from their Load of Wood. Mr. Johnson and George Day for their Quarter, Mr. Kitchel and David Ogden for their Quarter, Deacon Lawrence and John Ward, Turner, for their Quarter, and Joseph Walters and Thomas Pierson, Junior, for their Quarter are chosen—every Quarter to go out when the Men see Cause to call.

Item—There being Complaint that many as are grown Persons,

as well as Boys, do misbehave themselves on the Lord's Day in the time of Public Service, both in the Meeting House and without by the House Sides; also by sleeping, Whispering, or the like. Wherefore, the Town hath chosen Thomas Pierson, Junior, and Samuel Potter, to use their best Care and Endeavors to restrain like Disorder in Time of public Worship, by rebuking such Persons as behave themselves irreverently, within or without the House; and if they are such grown Persons as will not be restrained by their Rebukes, then they are to present them to the Authority.

Town Meeting, *January* 1, 1679—Mr. Johnson and John Curtis, are chosen Deputies for the Year ensuing. Mr. Ward the Third Man.

John Ward, Turner, Constable.

Mr. Ward as President. Mr. Johnson and Lieut. Swain, for Town Courts. John Brown, Junior, Clerk for this Court. Joseph Harrison, Messenger for this Court. Joseph Johnson, Edward Ball, Stephen Davis, David Ogden, and Thomas Ludington, are chosen Town's Men for this Year, having the same Power as others formerly.

John Curtis, Treasurer. John Brown, Junior, Town Clerk. Jonathan Sargeant and Thomas Pierson, Jun'r, Warners of Town Meetings. Thomas Huntington and Benjamin Baldwin, fence Viewers.

William Camp and Edward Riggs are chosen to see if Elizabeth Town will Agree to meet with us in making a Fence in Order to secure our Field; being the Bound Creek is thought to be no sufficient Fence.

Item—The Town saw Cause to choose a Committee to survey the Highways belonging to the Town tending to the Meadow, both for Quantity and Quality; and also to divide the same equally to several Persons, according to their Proportions of land and Meadow within the Neck. Sarj't Richard Harrison, Thomas Huntington, John Curtis, Samuel Plum, and William Camp, are chosen a Committee for this purpose.

Thomas Pierson, Sen'r, Thomas Pierson, Jun'r, and Stephen Bond, are chosen Grand Jury Men. John Curtis and John Baldwin, Sen'r, Sealers of Leather. Joseph Walters, Packer of Meat. Richard Fletcher, Grave Digger—and is to have 3s. for a Man's Grave, 2s. for a Middle Person, and 1s. 6d. for a Child. Edward Ball, Town Attorney.

Town Meeting, *February* 18th, 1679—Concerning seating Persons in the Meeting House, it was agreed that Persons should be placed according to Office, Age, Estate, Infirmity and Desent or Parentage: by Estate is meant that Estate as Persons purchased and took up Land by, together with the present Estate—comparing all these together. Mr. Ward, Mr. Johnson, Deacon Tompkins, Richard Harrison, Stephen Davis, Thomas Huntington, and John Brown, Jun'r, are chosen a Committee to this Work.

TOWN MEETING, *March* 22, 1679-80—It is agreed, that the Drum being begun to be beaten at Joseph Rigg's Gate, and so all the Way up the Street as far as Sam'l Harrison's Gate, and at the Ceasing of the beating of the Drum three Guns being distinctly fired of—it shall be sufficient Warning for all as are in the Military List, forthwith to meet at the Meeting House in their Arms.

Order for an Alarm.

The TOWN being met together the 29th of *March*, 1679-80, and give their positive Answer to the Governor of York's Writ, (viz): That they have taken the Oath of Allegiance to the King and Fidelity to the present Government, and untill they have sufficient Order from his Majesty we will stand by the same.

TOWN MEETING, *May* 3, 1680—It is agreed that there shall be a Committee chosen, to petition the Deputy Governor and Council to enlarge and settle our Town Bounds. And by Reason we have been hindred and deprived of the Neck, and Hockquckanung also; we desire to have it made up in that Land and Meadow called Poquanuck. and to have a Charter for the whole.

Item—the Committee chosen for this purpose are John Ward, Thomas Johnson, Richard Harrison, Thomas Richards, and John Catlin.

Item—it is agreed, that if any Man shall put out any of Land or Swamp to pasture, within the Comon Fence; the Fence about any such Land or Swamp so made Use of with the afs'd Fence shall be liable to a Survey by two Men chosen for that Purpose, and none but such Fence shall be allowed to be sufficient: and if any Man shall put any of his Cattle into such Pasture and the Cattle break out, the Owner shall pay Double Damage, and Poundage also. And if any such Fence or Fences need Surveying, the Owner of such Fence or Fences shall pay for the Surveying.

Order about Pasture fence.

Joseph Walters and Robert Dalglish are chosen Surveyors for such Fences

John Catlin, Ephraim Burwell, and John Brown, Jun'r, are chosen to do what they can to see who is behind about the Neck Money, and also to gess as near as they can how it will rise in another Rate.

Neck Money.

Highways to be mended.

TOWN MEETING, *June* 23, 1680—It is agreed, that one Man in every House shall go out one Day to mend the Highways in the Neck.

Item—it is agreed that Surveyors shall be chosen to appoint when Men shall go out, and have Power to call a Team or Teams if need require. Richard Harrison and Samuel Plum are chosen Surveyors.

TOWN MEETING, *June* 30th, 1680—Mr. Ward, Mr. Johnson, and Mr. Swain, are chosen to carry on Town Courts. Item—It is Agreed to petition to have another Justice—it is also desired that Mr. Johnson should be the Man for this Year.

Item—It is agreed that we should desire the Governor and Council to grant, that our Town Courts may have Liberty to try Actions of Five Pounds, without Appeal; and if need require to have a Jury.

Item—It is Agreed, that the Town is willing Samuel Whitehead should come and Inhabit among us, provided he will supply the Town with Shoes, tho' for the Present we know not of any Place of Land convenient.

Meeting House Seated.

TOWN MEETING, *July* 24, 1680—It is agreed by Vote, that that Middle part of the Meeting House which is yet to be seated, shall have Three Seats of a Side.

Item—It is voted that Henry Lyon hath a Right to, and Shall have a Seat in the Meeting House—paying proportionably with his Neighbours.

TOWN MEETING, *September* 3d, 1680.—The Town hath engaged by Vote, to stand by Goodman Porter [Potter] and keep him harmless from what shall come to him from Peter Jacobs, by Reason of Stephen Freeman's Bond of forty Pounds.

Item—John Curtis, Thomas Richards, and John Brown, Jun'r, are chosen, to do what they can to see what is paid to Peter Jacobs, on acco't of this Bond of Stephen Freeman's.

TOWN MEETING, *September* 27, 1680—It is agreed by Vote, that those Persons as have been admitted Planters in the Town, and have according to a Town Grant taken up Land, and have not paid the Purchase at all, or only to the Home Lotts; shall pay the Purchase for what Land and Meadow they have legally taken up, to the Town Treasurer, some Time between this Day and the Twenty-fifth Day of March next ensuing.

Item—The Town's Men, John Curtis and John Brown, Jun'r, are chosen, to find as near as they can what of Right doth belong to each Person to pay, according to his Land taken up as afs'd.

Item—It is agreed that all improved Lands, that is, such Land as is plowed and used for Pasture in particular by fencing, shall pay One Penny p. Acre. And all other Lands, as Out Lands and other Lands in the Neck not plowed, nor used for Pasture and Meadow, one-half Penny p. Acre. All Lands is to be brought in to Rate by, as they was the last Year: that is, the first and Second Division as the Town laid it out, and all other Land and Meadow as Mr. Deleplary laid them out. Note, all Lands and Meadow as afs'd, together with Heads, and Cattle, to be as they were the last Year.

Item—John Curtis and John Brown, Jun'r, are chosen to make Rates for this Year.

At the same Meeting, 27th of *September*, 1680. It is voted, that those as will set themselves to kill Wolves and Bears, shall have for every grown Wolf's Head Twenty Shillings, and for every grown Bear Ten Shillings, and for Bear Cub five Shillings.

To make up the Neck Account.

Item—John Curtis, Thomas Richards and John Catlin are chosen to go to New York; to make up all Accounts about the Neck, and do what they can to satisfy Peter Jacobs by borrowing Money to pay him, if they judge it the prudentist Way for the Town—and the Town doth engage to stand by them, and repay it again between this and the Twenty-fifth Day of March Next.

Item—Nathaniel Wheeler, Edward Riggs, and Joseph Riggs, have a Grant to take up Land upon the upper Chesnut hill by Raway River near the Stone House; provided they exceed not above fifty Acres a piece.

A Man chosen to look after the Boys.

TOWN MEETING, the 29th of *November*, 1680—It is agreed upon by Vote, that a Man should be chosen to look after and see that the Boys and Youth do carry themselves reverently in the time of public Worship upon the Lord's Day, and other Days and Times of Worship. And if any grown Persons shall carry themselves irreverently, he is to make Complaint to the Authority and present their Names; and his Word shall be accounted Evidence against him or them offending, whether the offence be committed within or without the House. Joseph Walters is chosen to be the Man for the purpose above said.

Planters admitted.

Item—John Johnson, Thomas Lyon, Matthew Williams and John Mekeny are admitted Planters; provided they pay the Purchase for what land they have, as other Planters have done.

Item—It is voted, that those as have not now given in a List of their Estate, shall have one Week's time allowed them to bring them to the Clerk; and if any Person do neglect, the Constable is to fetch it and have six Pence a piece for his pains.

To bring in a List of their Estate.

Item—There having been a Town Meeting legally warned this 29th of November, 1680, and many being absent—It is agreed by those Planters present to remit all those Fines that are already past, and for Time to Come if any Person or Persons that are Planters shall be remiss in coming, according to the Act made the 21st of March, 1675–6, then those Fines then exprest (according to the offence) are strictly to be gathered up by the Constable, for the Town's Use: or if any come not, being warned by the Constable by special Warrant, at a shorter Time, then the Penalty to be exacted as before said.

Order about coming to Town Meetings.

Town Meeting, *January* 4th, 1680—Whereas, there was a vote past the 29th of November, 1680, concerning the Constables gathering up the Fines for remissness in attending Town Meetings; the Town doth now think it more convenient that the Clerk give their Names to the Treasurer, and the Fine be placed to their Rate.

How to dispose of Fines.

Item—It is voted, that this Money due to Peter Jacobs upon account of Goodman Porter, [Potter] shall be raised by the Estate as is now given in to make Rates by this Year.

The way to raise Money to pay Peter Jacobs.

Azariah Crane is chosen Constable for the Year ensuing.

John Curtis, Treasurer.

Stephen Davis, David Ogden, Jasper Crane, William Camp and John Catlin, Town's Men.

Joseph Brown for that end of Town, and Daniel Dod for that End of the Town where they live, Warners of Town Meetings.

Nathaniel Wheeler and Thomas Lyon, fence Viewers.

Item—It is agreed that these fence Viewers shall view the fence as often as there is Occasion for it, and having viewed them, if they find any Defects, they are to give Notice thereof to the Owners of it, who is to repair the Defects within Twenty-four Hours or sooner if they can, upon the Penalty of One Shilling for each Defect; which fine is to be given in to the Treasurer and plac'd to their Rates; half of it is for the viewers, the other half to the Town.

It is also agreed, that every man shall from Time to Time set up and keep up two stakes, at each end of his Fence one, with the two first Letters of his Name on them; upon the Penalty of One Shilling for every Stake's

Penalty of defective Fence.

Want or Defect, which is to be given in to the Treasurer, half for the Viewers and half to the Town. It is also agreed, that the Heighth of the Fence is to be four feet four Inches.

Item—It is agreed that the Common Fence shall be again proportioned, to every Man his just Proportion according to the Number of Acres of Land and Meadow within the same; beginning at the River, and so to go successively as the Lotts lie now as near as they can, untill they come to the Bound Creek. It is also agreed, that each Man shall agree with his Neighbour concerning making his fence as before, or if they cannot agree, then they have Liberty to take it away if he please.

Item—The Town hath chosen George Day and William Camp to take a view of that Land Daniel Tichenor asked for; and if they consent, and it be not prejudicial to the Town, then he is to have it.

Town's Men to proportion the Fence.

Item—At the said Town Meeting, January 4th, 1680—The Town's Men and John Brown, Junior, are chosen, to Proportion to each Man his Proportion of Fence, according to his Number of Acres of Land and Meadow in the same.

Bound Creek Mill.

Item—The Town doth give their free Consent to any Person or Persons among us, to set up a Corn Mill upon the Bound Creek, near the Two Mile Brook.

Item—The Clerk is chosen, to send to Elizabeth Town in the Town's Name, to desire of them the like Liberty also.

Minister's Rate.

Item—It is voted, the Minister's Rate and the Town Rate shall be made in one this Year.

Sizing the Swamp.

TOWN MEETING, *January* 21, 1680—It is voted that this Business of Difference about the Land and Swamp, shall be ended by the Committee already Chosen to lay out the Fence, who are to size such Land and Swamp as hath been taken up in the Neck, since the fence was laid out.

Item—John Ward, Turner, and Thomas Ludington are chosen, to join with the Committee for the sizing of the Land and Swamp.

Jabez Rogers' Grant.

Item—Jabez Rogers hath granted to him, that he may have the Town's Right of so much of the Swamp at the Rear of his Second Division of Land in the Neck as was surveyed to him, to make his Lott square, and he accepts it for the amends of his first Division.

Item—it is agreed, that there shall be Two Town's Men to the other five.

Item—John Treat and Thomas Ludington are chosen to be Town's Men to join with the other.

It is agreed by the Committee chosen by the Town for that

To pay for the Purchase of House Lotts & other Lands.

Purpose, that any Person or Persons which hath taken up Land within the Town for a House Lott, and hath not yet paid the Purchase, shall by the Time the Town appointed pay Two Shillings for each Acre, be it more or less; and for other Lands lying more remote Three Pence for each Acre, and for Meadow four Pence for each Acre, or else let it lie to the Town's Dispose.

TOWN MEETING, *February* 25, 1680—To prevent sundry Inconveniencies which may grow to this Town of Newark, by the inconsiderate receiving and entertaining of Strangers amongst us—It is Voted, That henceforward, no Planter belonging to us or within our Bounds or Limits, receive or entertain any Man or Woman of what Age or Quality soever, coming or resorting to us, to settle upon their Land: nor shall any person that hath been or shall be received as a Planter among us, by Right of Inheritance or otherwise, sell, give, nor any way alienate, or pass over, Lease or Lett, any House or House Lott, or any Part or Parcell of any of them, or any Land of what Kind or Quality soever, to any such Person: nor shall any Planter or Inheritor permit any such Person or Persons so coming and resorting, to stay or abide above one Month, without Licence from those the Town shall appoint for that Purpose, under the Penalty of Five Pounds for every such Defect; besides all Damages that may grow by such Entertainments.

TOWN MEETING, *June* 8, 1681—It is agreed by vote in a full Town Meeting, that what the Major part of the Town shall conceive and act upon any Account for the Good and Safety of the Town, shall stand good and valid to bind every Individual Planter and Inhabitant to the attendance thereof; upon such Penalty as the Town, or a Committee chosen by the Town, shall see Cause to inflict.

Item—it is voted, that forthwith a Watch in the Night, and a Ward on Sabbath Days be observed. Item—Stephen Davis and Joseph Rigs is appointed, to give a Charge to the Watch every Night. Item—it is agreed that every Soldier do bring his Arms every Day of Public Worship, well fixed, and also Am'unition. Captain Swain and Lieut. Curtis are chosen, to give the Charge for the Watch and Warders.

TOWN MEETING, *July* 18, 1681—Thomas Johnson and John Curtis are chosen Deputies, according to the Writ. John Ward the Third Man.

TOWN MEETING, *October* 19th, 1681—It is agreed by vote,

The Way of rating in the Year 1681.

that the way for rating this Year shall be, that all Home Lotts and all improved Lands lying within the Common fence shall pay a Penny p. Acre. All Lands that are unimproved lying within the Com'on fence, be it first, Second or Third Divisions, Meadow, and the Second Division without the Common fence, a half penny p. Acre, and all other out Lands one farthing p. Acre. All Heads, and Cattle, to be rated as they were the Last Year.

This was voted the 25th Feb'y in 1680, though omitted being recorded till now.

To prevent disorderly Meeting of Young People at unseasonable Times, it is voted as a Town Act, that no House-keeper or Master of a Family, shall harbour or entertain any Person or Persons in the Night after Nine o'clock, or at other unseasonable Times, (extraordinary occasions excepted); nor shall they suffer them disorderly to meet at any Place within their Power, to spend their Time, Money, or Provisions inordinately, in drinking, gaming, or such like; nor shall they suffer any Carriage, Conferrence, or Council, which tends to corrupt one another. All such Persons so transgressing, shall be liable to such fines the Authority shall think fit.

The Town having agreed the 4th January 1680, that the Com'n Fence should be again divided, and for that Purpose appointed the Town's Men and John Brown, Jun'r, to proportion the same, which according to the best of their Judgments they have performed; and do find that four Acres of Land and Meadow requireth one Rod of Fence, and have accordingly proceeded, as near as they can to the laying it out as the Lotts was drawn at first, leaving out the Gates and Barrs which are disposed of as followeth, (viz): The first Gate next the River to Aaron Blachly and Samuel Harrison, to be sufficiently made and maintained from Time to Time, instead of Seven Rods of fence. The Second Gate is disposed of to David Ogden, in Stead of his Proportion of fence in the Common Line, to be sufficiently made and maintained from Time to Time. The Third Gate to John Curtis and John Baldwin, Senior, to be sufficiently made and maintained from Time to Time, in Stead of Seven Rods of Fence. The fourth Gate together with the Fence on both sides, the Breadth of the Highway, to Deacon Michael Tompkins for his Proportion of fence, to be sufficiently made & maintained from Time to Time. The fifth Gate to William Camp, to be sufficiently made and maintained from Time to Time, instead of Seven Rods of fence.

The Sixth Gate to John Ward, Jun'r, and Matthew Canfield, to be made and maintained sufficiently from Time to Time, instead of Six Rods of Fence: the Mile Brook hath One Rod of Fence allowed for it.

The Barrs called Wheeler's Barrs to Joseph Riggs, to be sufficiently made and maintained, handily to be put up and down from Time to Time, instead of Three Rods of Fence—there is two Rods of Fence allowed for the Two Mile Brook. The Seventh Gate to Mr. Thomas Johnson, to be sufficiently made and maintained from Time to Time, instead of Seven Rods of Fence. It is always to be understood, that the Rod Pole this Fence was laid out by, was 16 feet and 9 inches in Length. Thomas Huntington hath his Proportion of Fence, according to his Agreement with the Town—beginning at Low Water Mark, and reacheth untill it meets with Jabez Rogers's fence, which is the first Lott in Order.

	Lotts.	Rods.
Jabez Rogers	1	7¼
Being divided by Aaron Blachly and Samuel Harrison's Gate and Fence.		
Mr. Samuel Kitchel	2	5½
Joseph Johnson	3	2½
Jonathan Tompkins	4	3½
Ebenezer and Jonathan Canfield	5	4¼
Martin Tichenor	6	3¾
Jasper Crane	7	4
Thomas Staples	8	3½
Thomas Pierson, Jun'r.	9	11½
Being in two Places, one in the Swamp against Mr. Bruen's, the other Part next Daniel Dod's.		
Thomas Ludington	10	3½
William Camp	11	7½
John Baldwin, Jun'r	12	3½
John Treat	13	12¼
Richard Fletcher	00	2½
Azariah Crane	00	5½
John Brown, Sen'r	14	7½
Mrs. Mary Bond	15	6¾
Zachariah Burwell	16	2½
Mr. Jasper Crane	17	13¾
Samuel Rose	18	4¼
Ephraim Burwell	19	2¾
Stephen Bond	20	3
Thomas Richards	21	5½
Richard Harrison	22	13¼
Ephraim Penninton	23	4½
John Ward, Sen'r, Turner	24	8¾
Richard Lawrence	25	6
Stephen Davis	26	6
Henry Lyon	27	2½

	Lotts.	Rods.
Capt. Sam'l Swain	28	11¾
Joseph Walters	29	3½
Nathaniel Wheeler	30	4¾
John Crane	31	3¾
Hance Albers	32	4½
John Denison	33	6¾
John Catlin	34	8¾
Francis Lindly	35	7¼
Samuel Freeman—being divided by Joseph Rigg's Barrs and fence		5¾
Joseph Brown	36	3½
Thomas Brown		3½
Mr. John Ward	37	10
Edward Ball	38	7¼
Mr. Sam'l Wilson	39	3½
Thomas Pierson, Sen'r	40	4½
Mrs. Eliz'th Morris	41	10
Robert Dalglish	42	3
George Day	43	4¾
Edward Riggs	44	4½
John Brown, Jun'r		4¼
Mr. Abr'm Pierson		7½
Jonathan Sarjant		4½
Benj'n Baldwin		2½
Joseph Riggs—he hath the Barrs and ½ Rod by them.		3½
John Curtis		6¾
John Meckeny		2
John Burwell		2
John Tichenor		2
John Baldwin, Sen'r		6½
John Curtis and John Baldwin, Sen'r, have 3rd Gate and the fence the Breadth of the Highway, and the remainder of their Proportion of fence		

	Lotts.	Rods.		Lotts.	Rods.
lies next to Thos. Pierson, Jun'r, in Tichenor's Lane.			They have both their fence by their Gate.		
Aaron Blachly		3¼	John Gardner		3½
Sam'l Harrison		5¼	Anth'y Oliff		2½
Their Gate and fence lie together.			Mr. Thos. Johnson		10¾
			His fence lies next his own Gate.		
John Bruen		6½	Thos. Lyon		3
Sam'l Plum		19	Daniel Dod		3¾
Seth Tompkins		1½	Sam'l Lyon		2½
John Ward, Jun'r, Turner		2	Matthew Williams		3½
Sam'l Ward		2	Sam'l Potter		1
John Johnson		2½	John Davis		1½
Matthew Canfield		4			
John Ward, Jun'r		3¾	Sam'l Dod		2½

Item—it is ordered by the Town's Men, that if any Person or Persons shall (at any Time) open any Gate, or pull down any approved or allowed Barrs leading into the Common Fields, and leave them so, shall forfeit the sum of 5s. for every Time he or they so transgress; to be paid into the Town Treasurer, half for the Informer and half for the Town's Use, besides all Damages that may be done upon such Neglects; excepting in sliding Times at the Appointment of Two or Three Town's Men, when Frost and Snow lieth upon the Ground. Also it is ordered as afs'd, that any Person or Persons that have their Lands lying adjacent to the Com'on Fence, and do see Cause to make Barrs or Gates, (though not allowed to be such by the Town) yet the same Penalty shall be to them as to the other, in Case they are left down or open and not carefully shut or put up again.

Town Meeting, *December* 12, 1681—It is voted, that there shall be Surveyors chosen to lay out Highways as far as the Mountain if need be, and to lay out the Third Division to all who have a Desire to have it laid out, and Passages to all Lands.

Surveyors for Highways chosen.

Item—William Camp, John Treat, Thomas Ludington, Jasper Crane, Mr. John Catlin, Richard Harrison, and Stephen Davis, are Chosen for that Purpose; and any Three of them at each end of the Town have Power to act.

John Curtis and John Brown, Jun'r, are chosen to make the Rates for this Year.

Item—it is voted, that Mr. Pierson's and the Town Rate shall be made in one this Year.

Item—it is voted, that Ephraim Burwell shall be Rate free this Year.

Committee chosen to end the Difference about the Neck.

TOWN MEETING, *December* 19th, 1681—It is agreed, there shall be a Committee of four Men from among ourselves chosen to join with the four Farmers, both joining together as a Committee, to end the long Difference between the Town and them concerning the Neck Money; which eight Men shall have Liberty finally to end that Difference if they can; and if they cannot agree them selves they have Liberty mutually to choose an Umpire to be the casting Voice; and both the Town and the Farmers are engaged together, to stand to what they shall do. The Umpire agreed upon both by the Town and the Farmers, is one of these three Men, (viz): Benj'n Price, Sen'r, Isaac Whitehead, Sen'r, or Benjamin Parkas; the Committee's work which is chosen, is to see whether the Town be indebted to the Farmers or not, and whose Right it is to pay it if any be due.

Item—Mr. Thomas Johnson, John Curtis, William Camp and John Brown, Jun'r, are chosen for the Committee.

TOWN MEETING, *January* the 1st or 2nd, 1681-2—Mr. Thomas Johnson and John Curtis are chosen Deputies for the Year ensuing.

Samuel Plum, Constable. John Brown, Jun'r, Clerk for the Town. Samuel Lyon and Samuel Harrison, Pounders.

Stephen Davis, John Catlin, William Camp, Joseph Walters, Samuel Harrison, Joseph Riggs, and John Brown, Jun'r, Town's Men.

Item—it is agreed by Vote, that the Difference between the Town and the Farmers shall be ended by the Committee already chosen.

Item—it is voted, that the Treasurer shall have no Salary.

TOWN MEETING, *January* 6, 1681-2—It is agreed, that what the Town's Men shall act and do according to the best of their Judgment for the Town's Good as they apprehend in making any act, provided it infringe not on any of the three things prohibited in the Town Book, shall be as binding as any Act made by the whole Town, for the Year ensuing.

Item—Edward Riggs is chosen Warner of Town Meetings for that end of the Town where he lives, for the Year ensuing.

TOWN MEETING, *January* 11th, 1681-2—Mr. Thomas Johnson is chosen Town Treasurer for the Year ensuing.

Item—Benjamin Baldwin is chosen to Warn Town Meetings, at that End of the Town where he lives, for the Year ensuing.

Item—Azariah Crane is chosen to look to the Young People, that they carry themselves civilly in the Meeting House in time of Divine Worship, for half this Year ensuing.

Joseph Riggs and Thomas Lyon are chosen Fence Viewers for the Year ensuing; and the Town doth allow them half the Fines, as they did before.

Item—there having been some uncomfortable Debate, about the Town's Men chosen the 1st or 2nd of January, 1681–2—The Town doth now again confirm their Choice.

Order to recon with the Treasurer.

TOWN MEETING, *February* the 24th, 1681–2—It is agreed, that all and every Person or Persons shall reckon with the Treasurer, and agree with him for the Payment of their Rates, within a Week's Time.

Item—it is agreed, that the foremost Seats in the Meeting House shall be filled with Men and Women, so far forth as Conveniency will permit.

Committee to seat the Meeting House.

Item—it is agreed that a new Committee shall be chosen, to appoint in which Seats Persons shall sit.

Item—it is agreed that the Town's Men shall be a Committee to seat the Meeting House, and they shall have Liberty to chuse two Men to join with them, which Town's Men together with those two shall have Power, from Time to Time to supply this Work.

Item—Samuel Plum and Thomas Ludington are made choice of, to join with the Town's Men in this Work.

For Killing Wolves and Bears.

Item—it is agreed that if any Person or Persons kill any Wolves or Bears, which they require pay for from the Town; they shall be only such Wolves and Bears that are killed within our Town Bounds, that they shall be allowed pay for.

TOWN MEETING, *April* 19th, 1682—There having been much Damage done by Reason of much defective Fences, and in special by a Piece of Fence against a Home Lott formerly given to Daniel Dod, upon account of his making and maintaining a Fence at the Front of his Lott, the Breadth of his Lott so given. And Altho' this Grant (to Daniel Dod) is not found upon the Record, Yet several Persons that was then Present do now declare, that they do fully remember that that Lott was given to Daniel Dod upon the afs'd Condition, as namely: Deacon Michael Tompkins, Deacon Richard Lawrence, Mr. Thomas Johnson, Stephen Davis, and William Camp, and also several others. Yet now Daniel Dod refuseth to make or maintain the same, only as his Proportion in Common with other, tho' made and maintained by him at first. Upon these Person's Testimony and the Complaint of Damage done by the Insufficiency of this Fence—The Town doth by Vote declare their Minds concerning the same, (viz): that Dan'l Dod is to make and maintain, from Time to Time, that Fence at the

Daniel Dod to make and maintain his Fence across his Lott.

front of his Lott, according to the Conditions he took the Lott by as is before exprest.

Fence Viewers to be paid. Item—the Town doth agree to stand by the Fence Viewers, and see that they shall be paid for the making or repairing any defective Fences which the owners refuse to make or repair, according as the former Country Order provides.

Carrying Mr. Pierson's wood for this Year. Item—Mr. Johnson, Joseph Walter, Mr. Ward, and Samuel Plum, are chosen to appoint the Time for the carrying Mr. Pierson's Wood, each Man in that Quarter where he liveth; and all Persons concerned in each Quarter is to attend the work upon one Day, when the Overseer doth Appoint it, he giving two or three Days Warning before Hand.

Item—Zachariah Burwell, Ephraim Burwell, and George Day, have the Grant to take so much Land at the Front of their Lotts toward the Two Mile Brook as William Camp, Thomas Ludington, and John Treat, who are appointed to lay it out shall lay to their Lotts; provided it prejudice not the Highway.

The way of rating in the Year 1682. TOWN MEETING, *September* the 24, 1682—It is agreed by Vote, that all Home Lotts and improved Lands shall pay a Penny p. Acre—that all Lands unimproved lying within Fence, and Meadow, a half Penny p. Acre. That the Second Division without the Common Fence and not Fenced in particular, shall be rated according to the Third Division without Fence, (viz): a farthing p. Acre. That all Heads, and Cattle, as they were the last Year.

Item—it is agreed, that two Men at each end of the Town shall go to each Inhabitant that is concerned to pay Rates, and demand a List of their Estate, within a Fortnight after this Day, and if any Person do refuse to give in a List of their Estate to them, then these Men now chosen shall give in a List, according to their best knowledge and best Information they can come at.

The Men now chosen for this purpose, are Samuel Harrison and Edward Ball for that End of the Town where they live. William Camp and Ephraim Burwell for that End where they live.

Item—it is agreed that the Minister's and the Town Rate shall be made in one this Year.

John Curtis and John Brown, Jun'r, are chosen to make the Rates this Year.

TOWN MEETING, *December* 4, 1682—Joseph Walters and David Ogden are chosen, to go to each Man that stands indebted to the Town in the Treasurer's Book, and make Demand thereof, or desire them to reckon with the Treasurer within a Week's Time; and if they have neither Meat, nor Corn, to pay, the Treasurer doth engage to putt them in a Way to pay their Debt with Timber; but if they will not pay nor reckon, then the Constable shall come with a Warrant and distrain for it.

TOWN MEETING, the 1st *January*, 1682-3—Mr. Thomas Johnson and John Curtis are chosen Deputies for the Year ensuing. Edward Ball, Constable. Thomas Huntington, Joseph Walters, Joseph Riggs, Samuel Harrison, Samuel Lyon, John Baldwin, Jun'r, and John Crane, Town's Men.

Mr. Johnson, Treasurer.

John Brown Jun'r, Clerk for the Town, also Warner of Town Meetings at that End of the Town where he lives.

Item—John Davis, Warner of Town Meetings at that end of the Town where he lives.

Jasper Crane and Samuel Potter, Fence Viewers.

Azariah Crane and Anthony Oliff, Pounders.

William Camp and John Brown, Jun'r, are chosen, to gather up a List as near as they can, of those that are behind in paying the Purchase for such Lands they have taken up and not paid for; also as near as they can, how many Acres such have taken up.

Item—John Baldwin, Sen'r, is chosen, to look that the Young People carry themselves orderly, in Times of Divine Worship.

TOWN MEETING, *February* 5th, 1682-3.—It is voted, that the Town's Men's Work for this year, shall be as it was in March the 19, 1673-4.

Item—it is agreed that there shall be a Committee chosen, to consider of some Things as they think may be for the Town's Good, in Order that our Deputies should promote the same at the General Assembly.

Committee to instruct the Deputies if they need.

Item—Mr. John Ward, Stephen Davis, Richard Harrison, Thomas Richards, William Camp, Joseph Walters, Ephraim Burwell, and John Brown, Jun'r, are chosen a Committee for this End.

A Committee to seek settlement.

TOWN MEETING, *March* 22, 1682-3—Mr. Ward, Mr. Johnson, Mr. Lyon, John Curtis, Edward Ball, and John Brown, Jun'r, are chosen Agents to endeavor in the Town's Behalf the obtaining a legal Settlement, with such Privileges from the Proprietors as they, the said Agents, shall think fit to be proposed for. As also, the obtaining a Charter for the whole Town Bounds, with as much Priviledge and Ease as they can. And any three of these have Power and may Act in the Town's behalf, and what they shall act and do, the Town shall and will own as their Act and Deed.

Town Meeting, *May* 11th, 1683—It is agreed by Vote, that for the two next Years one End of the Town from the cross Street shall find Mr. Pierson with wood one Year, and the other End of the Town the next Year. The North End of the Town is to begin.

Carrying Mr. Pierson's wood.

Item—Upon Mr. John Wilkins' Motion. The Town admitted him to be a Planter, he submitting to our Town Orders. The Town hath also given him Liberty to purchase an Accommodation in our Town, or take up a Tract of Land; provided it be no Ways prejudicial to Highways, or that other Men have not already surveyed, he paying the Purchase as others have done.

John Wilkins Admission to be a Planter.

Town Meeting, *May* 16, 1683—Whereas, there was a Covenant made with Mr. Robert Treat and Sarj't Richard Harrison, to make and maintain a sufficient Corn Mill, upon such Conditions as is in a Covenant exprest, made between them, the said Mr. Treat and Richard Harrison, and the Town, recorded in the Town Book, fol. 29. Be it known, that I, Richard Harrison, having bought Mr. Treat's Part of the Mill, and am obliged according to the Covenant and Conditions thereof afs'd, have formerly, and do now again make over, all my Right to the Mill unto my Sons Sam'l, Joseph, and George Harrison; they being become obliged unto the Town in all particulars mentioned in the said Covenant, to observe and keep the same, in all Respects as fully as I the said Richard Harrison was obliged to. And the said Samuel, Joseph, and George Harrison, have and do declare in the Town Meeting, their acceptance of the Mill, upon the same Conditions as is in the said Covenant exprest. Also the Town doth declare their Acceptance of the said Samuel, Joseph, and George Harrison, in their Father's stead—this was voted in the Meeting above said.

Item—Sarj't Richard Harrison hath Granted to him as his proper Right, half of the Mill Home Lott, on that side of the Lott next to Samuel Rose; by Exchange for a Parcel of Land laid out to himself and Mr. Treat, joining to the Mill Land, on the other side of the Mill River.

Item—the Millers do own, that the Six Acres of Meadow belonging to the Mill, lieth next to, and on that end of their Meadow next to Jasper Crane.

Town Meeting, 2nd *October*, 1683—It is agreed by vote, that all and every Person possessed of Lands in the Town of Newark, shall have their Names put into the List, to be called at Town Meetings from Time to Time.

Item—it is agreed by vote, that this second Day of October

shall be the Day for this Year, to bring in the List of their Estates, instead of the last Second Day of September.

Item—it is agreed by Vote, that the way of rating this Year shall be on Lands, Heads, and Cattle, as it was the last Year, viz: on Heads 14d. p. Head, Oxen 5d. p. Ox, Cows above 3 Years old 3d. p. Cow, Steers of 4 Years old 4d. each, Steers and Hieffers of 3 Years old 3d. each, Steers and Hieffers of 2 Years old 2d. each, Steers and Hieffers of one Year old 1d. each, Horses and Mares of three Years old and upwards 3d. each, Horses and Mares of 2 Years old 2d. each, Horses and Mares of one Year old 1d. each, all Swine of one Year old and upwards 1d. each, all Home Lotts and improved Lands shall pay 1d. p. Acre. All Lands unimproved lying within Fence, and Meadow, half penny p. Acre. The Second Division without the Common Fence and not Fenced in particular, shall be rated according to the Third Division without Fence, viz: a farthing p. Acre.

Item—John Curtis and John Brown, Jun'r, are chosen to make the Rates for this Year.

Item—it is agreed by vote, that those Persons as have not yet brought in a List of their Estates on this Second day of October, according to the Town Order, shall within seven days (from this 2nd of October above said) bring in a true List of their rateable Estate, to the Men chosen to make the Rates; and if any neglect so to do, William Camp and Ephraim Burwell are chosen for that end of the Town where they live, Edward Ball and Samuel Harrison are chosen for that end of the Town where they live, to go to the Houses of those as neglect and demand a List, and for their Pains shall have Six Pence a piece, for each List so fetched: which money is to be taken (by the Rate Makers) from their Rates as fetch any such List, and added to their Rates as are found Neglectors. And if any shall refuse to give in a List of their Estates, those as are thereunto appointed shall give in a List, according to the best of their Knowledge and others Information.

TOWN MEETING, *January* 1st, 1683—Mr. Thomas Johnson and John Curtis are chosen Deputies for the Year ensuing. William Camp, Constable. John Tichenor, Warner of Town Meetings at that End of the Town where he lives. John Ward, Turner, Warner of Town Meetings at that End of the Town where he lives.

Thomas Huntington, John Crane, John Baldwin, Jun'r, Samuel Lyon, Azariah Crane, Joseph Harrison, and Nathaniel Wheeler, Town's Men.

John Brown, Jun'r, Town Clerk.

John Curtis, Town Treasurer.

Stephen Davis, John Baldwin, Sen'r, Azariah Crane, John

Treat, Thomas Ludington, Jasper Crane, and Anthony Oliff, to lay out Highways.

WHEREAS, there is an Order made by Vote the 21 of March, 1675–6, for our Orderly attendance at Town Meetings, and for Want of due Execution many are remiss in their Attendance, by which means Town Business is much hindred, and some as do attend are much damnified by loosing their Time. We that are now present do assent, that all past offences upon this account be past by to this Day. And do now subscribe our names (provided that Three fourths of the Planters do subscribe) to submit to all and every Penalty in that Order before mentioned, upon our late Coming, total Absence, or irregular going away before the Meeting be dismissed. And Whereas, the said Order directs every Delinquent to give their Reasons to the Town. We do now agree and think it most fit, that Three Men in each End of the Town be Chosen, for each Person that is remiss to repair to within two or three Days at the most after the Meeting; and if their Reasons are satisfying to them, why they were absent, they shall be remitted their Fine; otherwise, within three Days after such Town Meeting their Names as are remiss shall be returned to the Constable, who is to gather up such Fines, and shall have half for his Pains.

Item—it is agreed, that the three Men at the South End of the Town are Joseph Walters, Stephen Bond, and Ephraim Burwell; and the Three at the North End of the Town are Deacon Lawrence, Stephen Davis, and Samuel Plum; for the Confirmation thereof, we have hereunto set our Hands this 9th of January, 1683. Note, that the other half of the Fines is to be delivered to the Treasurer for the Town's use.

John Ward,
Thomas Johnson,
Richard Lawrence,
William Camp,
Stephen Davis,
John Baldwin, Jun'r,
Samuel Plum,
John Ward, Jun'r,
Thomas Ludington,
John Baldwin, Sen'r,
Joseph Walters,
David Ogden,
Theophilus Pierson,
Anthony Oliff,
Samuel Lyon,
Ephraim Burwell,
Samuel Rose,
Thomas Pierson.
John Crane,
John Wilkins,
John Johnson,
Azariah Crane,
Joseph Johnson,
John Burwell,
Zachariah Burwell,
John Bruen,
Thomas Lyon,
John Curtis,
Edward Riggs,
Jonathan Tompkins,
Jabez Rogers,
Seth Tompkins,
Stephen Bond,
John Brown, Sen'r,
Henry Lyon,
Samuel Kitchell,
Robert Dalglesh,
Richard Fletcher,
John Brown, Jun'r,
Jonathan Sargant,
Samuel Potter,
Joseph Brown,
Edward Ball,
Thomas Brown,
Samuel Harrison,
Samuel Tichenor,
Joseph Riggs,
Joseph Harrison,
Thomas Richards,
Ebenezer Canfield,
John Tichenor,
Samuel Ward,
Nathaniel Ward,
John Ward, Turner,
John Treat,
Francis Lindly,
Daniel Abett.

Some propositions between the Town and John Gardner, towards an agreement for John Gardner to keep and provide for Richard Hore, (viz): that the said John Gardner doth agree with the Town, to take Richard Hore into his House (he coming well clothed with a good Leathern Suit) for Two Shillings and Six Pence a Week, in Money, or Pay equivalent; and doth further promise to keep him conveniently clean, and if he live not a Year, the said John Gardner shall have two Shillings and Six Pence a Week for so long as he doth live; and if he live above a Year, the said John Gardner doth engage to provide him with Cloaths and Victuals, that he suffer not, for the two Shillings and Six Pence a week afs'd, as long as the said Richard live and the Town see Cause to continue him there, and free the Town from further Trouble. In Confirmation hereof, John Gardner on his Part and Edward Ball in Behalf of the Town, have this 20th of Feb'y, 1690, set to their Hands.

JOHN GARDNER,
EDWARD BALL.

Town Meeting, *January* 9th, 1683—Anthony Oliff is appointed by the Constable to be the Constable's Deputy. Richard Fletcher and Anthony Oliff are chosen Fence Viewers for the Year ensuing. Thomas Lyon and Jabez Rogers, Pounders.

Seating the Meeting House.

Town Meeting, *Feb'y* 25th, 1683—It is agreed by Vote, that there shall be a Committee chosen to seat the Meeting House, and procure the mending the Seats that are broken.

Item—John Curtis, Mr. Johnson, Deacon Lawrence, Mr. Ward, John Brown, Jun'r, Stephen Davis, and William Camp, are chosen a Committee for this Purpose.

Item—It is voted that the Rule for them to proceed in to seat Persons by, is Office, Age, Estate, Infirmity, Decent or Parentage —all which are left to the Discretion of the Committee, to act in according to the best of their Judgments.

Item—John Conch is admitted a Planter in this Town.

Zopher Beach his Grant.

Item—Samuel Lyon hath Liberty to give Zopher Beach two Acres of Land, to build on.

Item—the Town's Men are chosen a Committee, to draw up some thing concerning the Act of Assembly about Horses and present to the Deputies, that we may not be hindred to take up our Horses out of the Woods.

Town Meeting, *March* 22, 1683-4—Azariah Crane, Joseph Riggs, Edward Ball, and Samuel Harrison, are chosen to lay out the Bounds between us and Hockquecanung, and to make no other Agreement with them of any other Bounds than what was formerly.

The Surveyors appointed by the Town to lay out Highways for convenient coming at Land and Meadow, upon the 13th of March, 1683-4, laid out from the great Highway that goes down to the lower End of the Great Neck, a Highway of two Rods Wide, upon that Point of Land between the Pond and Swamp and the Meadow, in the most convenient Place leading into the Meadow.

TOWN MEETING, *May* 30, 1684—It is voted, that there shall be a Committee Chosen to consider and draw up something as may be in Readiness, if Occasion be, to manifest our Right and Title to the Land we bought of the Heathen; and present the same to the Town, to have the Town's approbation if they like it.

Item—it is voted, that five Men shall be of this Committee, (viz): Mr. Johnson, Mr. Ward, John Curtis, Mr. Kitchell, Deacon Lawrence, and William Camp, which Committee have Liberty to call in the Help and Advice of any others, not of the Committee.

TOWN MEETING, *September* 29, 1684—It is voted, that all Land laid out for Home Lotts are to be rated for this Year, at two pence p. Acre; And all Land Second or Third Division which Men build House or Barn and dwell upon, shall to the Value of Six Acres pay two Pence p. Acre; and all other Land improved in the Neck or out of the Neck by Tillage, one Penny p. Acre; and all Lands improved for Pasture within or without the Neck, and Meadow, half penny p. Acre. All Heads, and Stock, as they use to be of late Years.

Item—John Curtis and John Brown, Jun'r, are chosen to make the Rates this Year.

Item—all Persons are appointed to carry a list of their rateable Estate to one of the Rate Makers, by the 6th of October next after this Date; and in Case any fail of so doing the Constable is appointed to fetch a List, and to have Six Pence of each Person he fetched a List from.

TOWN MEETING, *December* 22nd, 1684—It is voted that there shall be a Committee chosen to treat with the Governor.

Item—it is voted, that twelve Men shall be of this Committee. Item—Mr. Johnson, Mr. Ward, Mr. Kitchell, John Curtis, Deacon Lawrence, Thomas Huntington, John Brown, Jun'r, Joseph Walters, Thomas Ludington, Ephraim Burwell, Robert Dalglesh, and Joseph Johnson, are chosen for this Committee.

TOWN MEETING, *January* 1st, 1684-5—Thomas Huntington

and John Curtis, are chosen Deputies for the Year ensuing Benjamin Baldwin and Seth Tompkins, Warners of Town Meetings. Azariah Crane, Joseph Harrison, John Treat, Joseph Johnson, Thomas Pierson, Jabez Rogers and Edward Ball, Town's Men. Nathaniel Wheeler, Constable.

TOWN MEETING, *January* 7th, 1684-5—Jasper Crane, Joseph Riggs, and Jabez Rogers, are chosen Surveyors, to see the Highways mended, for the Year ensuing. John Curtis, Treasurer. John Brown, Jun'r, Town Clerk.

Thomas Richards, John Curtis, and John Brown, Jun'r, are chosen to make Inquiry into the old Treasurer's Accounts, and what they find amiss to rectify if they can.

Azariah Crane, Joseph Walters, and John Baldwin, Sen'r, are chosen to lay out Highways.

TOWN MEETING, *February* the 6th, 1684—Daniel Tichenor hath Liberty, according as Thomas Ludington, Samuel Lyon, and Nathaniel Wheeler shall appoint, to take up a piece of Land in the Common against the Rear of Samuel Lyon's Lott, he leaving a Rod or more in Breadth from the Corner of his own Lott, if these Three Men see cause for it.

Daniel Tichenor's Grant.

TOWN MEETING, *March* 9th, 1684-5—It is agreed to incourage those as will kill Wolves, that [they] shall have allowed them five shillings a Head of each grown Wolf killed within our Town bounds, besides what the Country allows.

Order to Kill Wolves.

Item—Mr. Johnson is chosen Surveyor, to join with Jasper Crane, Joseph Riggs, and Jabez Rogers, to see to mend the Highways for this Year.

Item—these four Surveyors have Power to agree among themselves and divide the Town Highways into four Parts if they see Cause. And also they have Power to call out Men as are concerned by their Agreement, to make and mend those Highways they are betrusted with.

Surveyors to make and mend Highways.

Item—it is agreed, that those Surveyors chosen to lay out Highways, if they take away land for Highways out of any Man's lotted Land, they have Power to repair them again with other Land. Also, those that were Surveyors formerly and have taken Land away from any Person or Persons for Highways, shall join with the now Surveyors to make their Land good to them again.

To make good the Land as is taken for Highways.

Item—it is agreed, that those Persons as want their Third Division of Land laid out, shall have it now laid out by the Town Surveyors, before any other Land be taken up, provided it be done between this Day and the first of April next ensuing.

Those as want third Division to take it up.

Item—John Curtis and William Camp are chosen for the Surveyors to perfect the Third Division.

Item—Joseph Brown and Thomas Brown have Liberty to take up Sixty Acres of land between them, when the Third Division is completed and they are willing to pay the Purchase—this Land is to be laid out by the aboves'd Surveyors, John Curtis and William Camp.

Item—Mr. Johnson, John Curtis, William Camp, Stephen Davis, and Edward Ball, are chosen as a Committee to treat with Elizabeth Town about the Bounds, and to issue it with them if they can.

Town Meeting, *June* 3, 1685—It is agreed that there shall be a Committee to treat with the Proprietors, about our Settlement—it is also agreed, that the Committee formerly chosen to that Purpose, shall still continue.

Town Meeting, *August* 13th, 1685—It is agreed, there shall be a Committee chosen to join with those sum'oned, to be assistant what they can in defending their and our just Rights and Titles to our Land.

Item—John Curtis, Edward Ball, Thomas Richards and John Brown, Jun'r, are chosen for that Purpose.

Town Meeting, *November* 7th, 1685—It is agreed, that the way of rating for this year, shall be as it was the last Year, 1684.

Item—John Curtis and John Brown, Jun'r, are chosen to make the Rates for this Year.

Item—Samuel Harrison, Edward Ball, Samuel Lyon, and John Treat, are chosen to go to each Man concerned in the Town Rates, and demand and take a List of their Estates; and if any Person refuse to give a List, then they are to take a List according to the best of their knowledge and others Information.

Item—William Camp and John Baldwin, Jun'r, are chosen, to go from House to House of those as have not subscribed to our fundamental Covenant, and return their answer to the Town.

Town Meeting, *January* 1, 1685-6—John Curtis and Thomas Richards are chosen Deputies for the Year ensuing. Joseph Harrison, Constable.

Item—it is agreed, that the Fence in the Common Line shall be made and maintained, sufficient from Time to Time to keep out Cattle and Swine—and also, that all Fences about Home Lotts shall be made and maintained, sufficient and good as above said.

Item—John Ward, Jun'r, and John Johnson, are chosen Fence Viewers. David Ogden and Jabez Rogers, Pounders.

TOWN MEETING, *January* 8, 1685-6—John Curtis and William Camp are chosen to lay out the Third Division of Land to those as Want it, they being called forth to do it between this and the first of April next—and if any as pretend to any Third Division and neglect calling them out as aboves'd, they shall loose their Claim to any Third Division.

Town's Men chosen for this Year are Stephen Davis, Mr. Samuel Kitchell, John Baldwin, Jun'r, and the four that were Town's Men last Year.

Item—Edward Ball is chosen to declare the Town's Business about the five Pounds that is in Difference between Mr. Johnson and the Town—note first, Mr. Johnson and the Town agreed to put it to Mr. Price, Mr. Whitehead, and Lieut. Rose to end.

Item—it is thought convenient that there shall be four Town Meetings in a Year, at a Time certain, (viz): the first upon the first day of January, the Second the first Second day of April, the Third the first second day of July, the fourth the first Second day of October, at which Meeting the Way of rating shall be agreed on; and that the Warning of these Meetings which shall be accounted legal, shall be by a Writing set up on the Meeting House Door, by the Clerk, 10 or 12 Days before the Day appointed by this Order—Also, it is further agreed, that if 10 or 12 Planters together with the Clerk, shall meet at about Ten of the Clock in the forenoon on the Day appointed, the Major Part of them so met, shall by this Order have Power to order and do any Thing or Things as shall be thought by them convenient to be done for the Town's Good; and the same to be binding to the whole for this Year, as if every Planter was present: and if the whole or a greater Part than the 10 or 12 as before said shall meet, the Major Part of them then met shall have the like Power to order and do as afores'd. And if there shall be any special Occasion for a Meeting at other Times, then to be warned with a Warrant from a Justice, in which Days the whole is to be present.

TOWN MEETING, *April* 5th, 1686—William Camp, Edward Riggs, Zachariah Burwell, Jasper Crane, Francis Lindly, John Baldwin, Sen'r, Stephen Davis, Samuel Harrison, and Samuel Plum, are chosen to lay out Highways for the Year ensuing—as also to lay out Passages to Men's Land as they shall call them out, they agreeing with them; they are also to make Amends in laying out Land, to repair those they take any Land from to make Highways with, and any Three of these have Power to act in ordinary Cases; but in difficult Cases any five: this is agreed to be done, between this and the first of June next after this Date.

Item—Mr. Johnson, Edward Ball, and William Camp, are chosen to treat and agree with Elizabeth Town Inhabitants about the Division line; and the Town leaves it with them, to take the best Way they can to accomplish it.

Item—Azariah Crane, Joseph Walters, Samuel Harrison, and Edward Ball, are chosen to go to each Person that is possessed of Land, and take an account of them how much each Man hath, and bring an Account to the Town the next Meeting.

TOWN MEETING, *April* 18th, 1686—It is agreed that there shall be a Committee chosen, to take an Account of the Third Division of Land and Meadow laid out by Deleplary, or our Town Surveyors; and every Man that hath taken up Land since the Third Division was agreed on to be taken up, shall bring in as true an Account as they can to the Committee, within Six Days after this Meeting; which Committee is according to Men's Estates to see how much each one hath exceeded what he should have taken up, or come short of what they might have taken up, and make Report thereof to the Town—And if any neglect to bring in an Account by the Time appointed, such shall pay the Charge for fetching it in their Rate.

Item—William Camp, Ephraim Burwell, and John Brown, Jun'r, are chosen for this Committee.

TOWN MEETING, *October* the 4th, 1686—It is agreed and voted, that the orders made the 4th of May, 1669, together with the order made the 10th of April, 1672, shall be now again renewed —it is also voted, that they shall stand in full Force in all Respects, only Sheep may have Liberty with Leave from the Town's Men or the Major Part of them, in such Seasons of the Year when they will in all likelihood do more Good than Hurt.

The way of rating 1686.

Item—it is agreed that the way of rating for this Year, shall be as it was the Two last Years.

Item—John Curtis and John Brown, Jun'r, are chosen to make Rates for this Year.

Item—it is agreed, that the Constable shall see that the Pounders shall take their Oaths before one of the Justices, some time within a week from this Day.

The Meeting being adjourned to the 18th of this Month—on which Day, Edward Ball and Joseph Harrison are chosen Town Attornies, to take Care that the Town Orders be put in Execution; and upon any Complaints made of the Breach thereof to prosecute the offender, and to have half what they can recover upon any Penalty for their Pains.

Item—Joseph and Thomas Brown have Liberty granted, to exchange their Father's Third Division of Land lying beyond

Elizabeth River, and to take up the Quantity thereof on this side Ruway River, below the Mouth of Stone House Brook.

TOWN MEETING, *January* 1st, 1686–7—John Curtis is chosen Deputy for the Year ensuing.

Item—George Harrison, Constable.

Item—Stephen Davis, Samuel Kitchel, John Baldwin, Jun'r, Seth Tompkins, Jasper Crane, Ephraim Burwel, and Thomas Richards, Town's Men

Item—the Town hath appointed any five of these Town's Men to meet with and agree together with the Justices, concerning what is to be done according to Acts of Assembly in Refference to Rates.

Item—Samuel Pierson is admitted a Planter, he submitting to all wholesome Town Orders.

Item—Jonathan and Thomas Davis have Liberty to possess what Land was laid out to them by William Camp, upon account of their Father's Purchase.

TOWN MEETING, *January* 24th, 1686–7—Joseph Walters and John Brown, Jun'r, are chosen, to Seal Measures and Weights.

Item—it is agreed, that Benjamin Baldwin's or Stephen Davis's half Bushel, shall be the Standard which shall be thought most suitable, and all Measures shall be sealed with an **N**, and all Weights shall be tried by brass Weights if they can be had, and if not, by Stephen Davis's Weights which have been Sealed at New York.

Item—John Curtis is chosen Treasurer for this Year.

Whereas—there is Liberty by Acts of Assembly, that each Town should chuse Seven Men to appoint whether Swine shall have their Liberty or be still restrained; as also to appoint what Fences shall be accounted sufficient: We do therefore chuse Stephen Davis, William Camp, Samuel Harrison, Thomas Richards, Edward Ball, Samuel Lyon, and John Brown, Jun'r, to act in this Matter.

Item—Jabez Rogers and Thomas Lyon are chosen Pounders for this Year.

Item—William Brant hath granted, to have three Rods of land by the Mill Brook as the Men appointed to view have agreed, with Priviledge of the . . . against it.

Item—it is agreed, that there shall be a Committee to treat with the Committee of the Proprietors, about our Settlement for the Town Bounds.

Item—John Curtis and Edward Ball are chosen to treat with and settle with the Proprietors if they can; receiving their Instructions from the Town.

Item—it is agreed that there shall be a Committee to give Instructions in the Town's Behalf (viz): Mr. Ward, Mr. Johnson, John Brown, Jun'r, Thomas Richards, and Daniel Dod.

Town Meeting, *January* 31st, 1686-7—Item—it is agreed that upon the fourteenth Day of February next, every one as hath Measures and Weights shall bring them to the Prison, that they may be tried, and sealed; and for cutting and Sealing every Measure, they are to have three Pence in Money, or four Pence in other Pay; and for Weights as they can agree.

Town Meeting, *February* 7th, 1686-7—It is voted that there shall be a Committee chosen, to take Notice of all Lands that Persons have appropriated to themselves, and regulate the same—The Committee chosen are Mr. Ward, Mr. Johnson, Stephen Davis, John Curtis, Samuel Harrison, Edward Ball, William Camp, Thomas Richards, Samuel Lyon, John Brown, Jun'r, Azariah Crane, Ephraim Burwell, and Joseph Harrison: this s'd Committee are to Order how a fourth Division of Land shall be laid out: it was agreed that there should be thirteen, that there might be a casting voice among them, if need should require.

Town Meeting, *January* 2nd, 1687-8—John Curtis is chosen Deputy for the Year ensuing.

Thomas Richards, Constable. Thomas Richards having agreed with George Harrison, the Town accepts George Harrison to be Constable in Thomas Richards's Stead, and the s'd George hath made Choice of Theophilus Pierson, to be his Deputy.

Item—the way of rating as formerly, which was after desisted from, and agreed upon to pay the Minister by Contributions for the Year 1687.

Item—Thomas Richards, Seth Tompkins, Jasper Crane, John Baldwin, Sen'r, Samuel Plum, Sen'r, Samuel Harrison and Anthony Oliff, are chosen Town's Men for This Year.

John Brown, Jun'r, Clerk. John Curtis, Treasurer.

Town Meeting, *March* 6th, 1687-8—Joseph Johnson and Daniel Tichenor, are chosen fence Viewers for this Year.

Town Meeting, *January* 9th, 1687-8—John Cockburn is admitted an Inhabitant among us.

Item—Stephen Davis, Azariah Crane, and Samuel Harrison, are Surveyors for Highways for this Year.

Item—Eleazer Tompkins hath granted, that he may take up a piece of Land upon his Father's account, upon Lighting hill.

January 9th, 1687-8—It is fully and unanimously consented to, and agreed upon by every Planter now present, all being called by Name; that they will from Time to Time pay or cause to be paid yearly, in their full Proportion equally, in a Rate that may be agreed on by the Major Part of the Town, to the Maintainence and Allowance now agreed upon for the upholding and preaching of the Word in our Town; and Eighty Pounds by the Year is agreed upon to be allowed to the present Minister, with his fire wood, and to be Rate free. Note, it is to be understood, that every man that doth now subscribe to this Agreement, he paying his Proportion in the Rate, shall not be liable to be prosecuted to make Payment for any that may be deficient in non-payment—In Confirmation hereof, we have hereunto set to our Names.

John Ward, Sen'r,
John Bruen,
Thomas Johnson,
Samuel Freeman,
John Curtis,
John Baldwin, Jun'r,
Seth Tompkins,
Micah Tompkins,
Samuel Ticenor,
Edward Ball,
Edward Riggs,
Samuel Kitchel,
John Cockburn,
Anthony Oliff,
Joseph Riggs,
Theophilus Pierson,
Azariah Crane,
Samuel Harrison,
Jasper Crane,
Joseph Harrison,
Thomas Pierson,
Samuel Dod,
George Harrison,
Sam'l Lyon,
Thomas Richards,
David Ogden,
Daniel Dod,
Stephen Davis,
Sam'l Plum, Sen'r,
John Crane,
Nathaniel Ward,
John Browne, Sen'r,
Zachariah Burwell,
Ephraim Burwell,
Thomas Browne,
John Tichenor,
Joseph Browne,
John Browne, Jun'r,
Joseph Walters,
Ebenezer Canfield,
Matthew Canfield,
Robert Dalglesh,
Francis Lindly,
Samuel Pierson,
Sam'l Rose,
Richard Lawrance,
Jonathan Sargent,
John Baldwin, Sen'r,
Hans Albers,
Jonathan Tompkins,
Joseph Johnson.

Town Meeting, *April* 30th, 1688—It is thought convenient, that there be a Committee chosen to endeavour a legall Settlement with the Proprietors, offering to give a legall Acknowledgment for our Lands within our Town Bounds as exprest in our Bill of Sale, and Priviledges suitable for us—The said Committee in their Offer, not exceeding the advice of such of their Neighbours as are most capable to give Advice in that Matter—Mr. Ward, Mr. Johnson, John Curtis, Joseph Harrison, Azariah Crane, Edward Ball, George Harrison, Thomas Richards, Jasper Crane, Thomas Ludington, John Treat and Joseph Johnson, are chosen a Committee for the Purpose afs'd.

TOWN MEETING, *November* 19th, 1688—It is voted that the Town's Men shall endeavor to get the Meeting House repaired, to keep out the Wett and Cold for the present; and also to repair the Seats, and provide Cedar Shingles to cover it when the Spring comes suitable, and be paid for it in a Town Rate.

Item—it is voted by the Major of those met, that the Way of rating for this Year shall be upon Heads, Stock, and Lands, as formerly; upon the same Prices as formerly.

Item—it is voted that John Curtis and John Brown, shall make the Rates for this Year: And all Persons are by this day Se'night to bring a List of their Estates to them.

TOWN MEETING, *February* 4th, 1688–9—Edward Ball is chosen Constable for this Year, or 'till a new one be sworn.

Item—it is voted to encourage killing wolves, that there shall be allowed for each grown Wolf, in a Town Rate 15s.

TOWN MEETING, *February* 11th, 1688–9—John Curtis is chosen Treasurer for this Year; it is also voted, that the Treasurer shall . . . thirty Shillings for this Year's Salary.

Item—it was voted, that there should be two men chosen to size ye Land as Deleplary laid out, and every one as imploys them shall pay them for it.

TOWN MEETING, *November* 25th, 1689—Daniel Tichenor is chosen fence Viewer, to join with Samuel Lyon till new ones are chosen.

Item—John Morris and Benjamin Harrison are chosen Pounders for this Year, or 'till new ones are chosen: notwithstanding, others may pound as they have Occasion.

John Johnson is chosen Pound Keeper.

TOWN MEETING, *January* 10th, 1689–90—The order made the 21st of March, 1675–6, was read, and there was none but approved it, and therefore it is now again confirmed to stand in Force.

Item—it is voted, that all Lands shall be rated as it was in the Year 1684. Item—Heads and Stocks are to be rated as formerly, (viz): Heads 14d. p. Head, Oxen above 4 Years old 5d. p. Head, 4 Year old Steers 4d. p. Head, Cows and 3 Years olds 3d. p. Head, Horses and Mares 3d. p. Head, all 2 Year olds, neat Cattle, and Horse kind 2d. p. Head, all Yearlings 1d. p. Head, Swine 1d. p. Head.

Item—John Curtis and John Browne is chosen to make the Rates for this Year.

Item—it is voted, that the Town's Men shall agree with . . . . . Shingles and Nails, and let him have Meadow.

Town Meeting, *March* 25th, 1689-90—It is voted, that there shall be a Committee chosen to order all affairs in as prudent a way as they can, for the Safety and Preservation of ourselves, Wives, Children and Estates, according to the Capacity we are in. Mr. Ward, Mr. Johnson, Azariah Crane, William Camp, Edward Ball, and John Browne, are chosen for a Committee, to join with those in military Capacity.

Town Meeting, *July* 18th, 1690—Jasper Crane is chosen Constable, for this Year or till another be sworn.

Item—Robert Young is chosen Pounder.

Town Meeting, 29th *September*, 1690—The Planters then met, voted that the Way of rating should be on Heads, Lands, and Stocks, as it hath been some Years before.

Town Meeting, 5th of *January*, 1690-1—It is voted, that the Soldiers Phillip Morris, Samuel Potter, and Benjamin Harrison, should be paid their Wages for the time they were out, according to our Agreement.

Item—Mr. Falconer is chosen to be Collector, to receive and make payment of this Money for the Soldiers.

Item—Joseph Johnson, Thomas Browne, John Treat, Azariah Crane, Daniel Dod, Zopher Beach, and Jonathan Sarjent, are chosen Town's Men for the Year.

Jabez Rogers, Constable for this Year, or till another be sworn.

Zachariah and Ephraim Burwell, fence Viewers.

Item—it is voted that John Curtis be joined with the Justices, to hear and determine all small Causes actionable, whether of Debts or Trespasses, not exceeding forty Shillings; according to the Acts of Assembly concerning small Courts.

Edward Ball and Daniel Tichenor, are chosen Pounders for this Year.

Town Meeting, *February* 20th, 1690-1—It is agreed, that Edward Ball should sign in the Town's Name, the agreement between John Gardner and the Town, for providing for Richard Hore.

Item—Edward Ball is chosen Town's Man, in the Room of Jonathan Sargent.

Town Meeting, *January* 29th, 1691-2—William Camp and Samuel Harrison, are chosen fence Viewers for the Year ensuing.

Theophilus Pierson is chosen Constable, for this Year or until another be chosen and Sworn.

Item—John Morris, Pounder.

TOWN MEETING, *February* 5th, 1691-2—It is voted, that the Comon line of Fence shall be righted up within a Week's Time; and by the first day of March next, the Gate belonging to John Ward and Matthew Canfield, removed to the upper end of the Lane, and all the Common fence made sufficient to keep out Cattle and Swine.

Item—Azariah Crane, Samuel Harrison, William Camp, and Edward Ball, are chosen to take the Care of the Poor and of Richard Hore, and to appoint what each Man shall pay for what is behind; and also, to appoint what each one shall pay for a quarter—they are also to see to remove him to Samuel Rose, or some other Place, and agree as reasonably as they can.

TOWN MEETING, *April* 2nd, 1692—It is voted, that Mr. Pierson shall be paid his Salary for that Time for which no Rates have been made, proportionable to the Rate made for two Years together (viz): '88 and '89.

John Curtis, is chosen Clerk.

TOWN MEETING, *August* 23rd, 1692—It was consulted, consented, and unanimously agreed, that Mr. John Pruden should be called to be their Minister; and in Case he should come and settle among them in that Work, they would freely and readily submit themselves to him and to his Dispensations and Administrations, from Time to Time in the Discharge of his ministerial Office and Works, as God shall assist and direct him therein by his Word and Spirit, for their Spiritual Good and Edification. It is also consulted, voted, consented to, and agreed by the said Inhabitants then convened, for Mr. John Pruden's Encouragement to come and settle among them, and that he may the better attend upon the Work of the Ministry as his Business, and for the more comfortable Sustainance of his Family in his Attendance therein; that he shall have £50 p. annum, and his Fire Wood free: to be paid yearly, according to several Contributions voluntarily subscribed by them, to Mr. Pruden or his Order, so long as he shall continue with them employed in the Ministry: this also voted.

It is moreover voted and agreed, that Mr. Pruden shall have and hold such a Propriatie, and other Conveniences for his Accommodations in the Town, as shall be agreed upon between him and the Committee appointed to treat with him (viz) Mr. Ward, Mr. Johnson, John Curtis, Azariah Crane, Jasper Crane, Thomas Ludington, and Stephen Bond, nominated and impowered by the Town for that Purpose.

August 23rd, 1692—The Result of a Treaty between Mr. John Pruden and a Committee chosen, constituted, and impowered by

14

the Inhabitants and Freeholders of Newark to act in their Behalf, is as followeth, (viz): It is concluded and agreed by the said Committee, that Mr. Pruden shall have and hold the accomo'dations purchased of Mrs. Falconer, for his own Propriatie, to him and his Heirs forever; he paying or causing to be paid the two last Payments indented for with Mrs. Falconer; excepting only five Pounds which the Town is to discharge besides what is already done, in prime Bill of Debt made to the s'd Mrs. Falconer —as Witness our Hands—subscribed, Mr. John Pruden. Committee for and in Behalf of themselves and their Neighbours—Mr. John Ward, Mr. Johnson, John Curtis, Azariah Crane, Jasper Crane, Thomas Ludington, Stephen Bond.

Town Meeting, 28th *October*, 1692—It was voted, whether the Charges for purchasing that Accom'odations that was Mrs. Falckner's, and the Charge of transporting Mr. John Pruden, should be equally levied on every person's Estate; and it was agreed with a unanimous Consent, that it should be so.

2ndly, It was also voted, that the Charge for the Payment and Transport should be Charged by a Rate, according to our Agreement formerly made, that is by Heads, Lands, and Stock. 3rdly, It was voted that Mr. Johnson and Jasper Crane should give Mr. Pruden Possession of the Accom'odations that was purchased of Mrs. Falkoner.

It was also voted, that Zachariah and Ephraim Burwell for the South end of our Town, and Samuel Harrison and Nathaniel Ward for the North end, for to see after the bringing the Wood for Mr. Pruden; and for to call out the People for that Purpose, when there is Need for his Supply therein.

Pounders chosen. John Gardner and Eleazer Lampson, are chosen Pounders.

It was voted, that the List of Estates for the Town Rate should be brought in, when the list of Estates to make the Country Rate was brought in, to the Constable.

Thomas Brown 500, Jasper Crane 200, of Shingles for the covering of the Meeting House.

Town Meeting, *Jan'y* 2, '92—Thos. Richards and Daniel Dod are chosen Deputies, for the Year ensuing.

John Baldwin, Sen'r, Constable.

Jasper Crane, Sam'l Harrison, Joseph Harrison, Nathaniel Ward, Seth Tompkins, Joseph Johnson and Zopher Beach, Town's Men.

Town Meeting, . . . 16—Thos. Richards, Azariah Crane, Edward Ball and John Gardner are chosen for to be a Committee for to treat with the Governor and Proprietors about our Settlements.

Benjamin Baldwin, Jabez Rogers, William Camp and Seth Tompkins are chosen, to collect the Money that is gathered by the Subscriptions in Newark, for the Maintainence of the Ministry in the year 1692.

TOWN MEETING, *January* 1st, 1693–4—John Treat and Azariah Crane, are chosen Deputies for the Year ensuing.

Item, Benjamin Baldwin is chosen Constable—and he hath chosen Jonathan Baldwin his Son, for his Deputy.

Item—it is voted that Robert Young may have Sixty Acres of land, where he can find it within our Town Bounds clear from any Claim of others—he paying the Purchase as others have done.

Samuel Harrison, Joseph Harrison, Nathaniel Ward, Jasper Crane, Thomas Davis, John Morris, and Theophilus Pierson are chosen Town's Men, for the Year ensuing. Jabez Rogers and Samuel Freeman, Pounders.

John Gardner and Eleazer Sampson, Fence Viewers.

Item—it is voted, that the Town's Men, John Treat, William Camp, and Ephraim Burwell, in the Town's Behalf on the one Part; and those that have their Home Lotts butting on the Neck on the other Part; to agree among themselves to settle the Common Fence against their Lotts: and if they cannot agree, they are impowered to choose some unconcerned to end it between them; and also to settle where the Common Line of Fence shall stand.

Item—Thomas Davis is chosen Collector to gather up the pay Rate, and if any Person or Persons do not pay their Proportion within a Fortnight's Time, then he is to make his Complaint to a Justice.

TOWN MEETING, *March* 5th, 1693–4—Joseph Wood is admitted Planter.

Item—Caleb Ward, Hendrick Henderson, Tunis Johnson, Hance Hendrickson, Bostyan Van Giese, Garret Laydicker, Eleazer Lampson, James Clizbe, Jonathan Tichenor, and William Brant, are admitted Planters.

Item—Zophar Beach is chosen by the Town, to be at the Court of Sessions, according to Act of General Assembly, in Case John Browne is wanting at that time.

Item—Whereas, there is much Prophanation of the Lord's Day in the Time of Worship, by the playing of Boys and Girls; therefore Daniel Tichenor and Thomas Lyon are chosen to look after them, and to correct them, or call them by Name, as they shall see Occasion, for this Year ensuing.

Item—it is voted that the Town Rate for this Year shall be made by the Estates given in for the Country Rate; only, Sheep shall be taken out and Heads put in, according to Town Agreement; and those that were assess'd in the Country Rate shall be assess'd in the Town Rate, if they do not bring in their Estates.

Deputies chosen. TOWN MEETING, *January* 1st, 1694-5—John Treat and Azariah Crane are chosen Deputies, for the Year ensuing.

Constable chosen. Thomas Davis, Constable for this Year, or untill another be chosen and sworn.

The way of rating 1694. TOWN MEETING, *January* 17, 1694—It is voted, that all Lands and Meadows shall be rated alike, for this Year.

Item—it is also agreed by Vote, that Lands and Meadows shall be rated at a farthing p. acre—Item, it is voted that Heads and Cattle shall be valued in this Rate, (viz): Heads £14, Oxen of 4 Years old and upwards £3, Steers of 3 Years old £2, Cows £2, Two Year old Steers and Hieffers £1 10s., 1 Year old 15s., grown Horses and Mares of 3 Years old and upwards £2 10s., Two Year olds £1 5s., One Year olds 15s. All Swine of one Year old and upwards, 10s.

Item—Zopher Beach and John Browne are chosen to make this Rate.

Item—the Constable is chosen to collect this Rate.

Town's Men chosen. Theophilus Pierson, John Morris, Daniel Dod, John Treat, and Azariah Crane, are chosen Town's Men for this Year. John Gardner, Pounder. John Baldwin and Samuel Freeman, Fence Viewers.

TOWN MEETING, *March* 4th, 1694-5—According to Acts of Assembly, each Town Hamlet have Power to chuse Men not exceeding Seven, to make orders for the prudential preventing Harm by Swine, and laying a Penalty on them. John Treat, Samuel Harrison, Theophilus Pierson, Nathaniel Ward, Joseph Harrison, Jasper Crane.

TOWN MEETING, *June* 19th, 1695—Thomas Davis hath Liberty to set up a Saw Mill, with Liberty to have use of Timber in any common Land; provided he shall let any of the Inhabitants have Boards, as cheap as others and before Strangers.

TOWN MEETING, *January* 1st, 1695-6—Mr. John Treat and John Browne are chosen Deputies, for this Year.

Item—it is voted, that the way to make the Rate for the Governor, Deputies, and other Town Charges, shall be by Heads, Stock, and Lands, as it was the last Year, and to be made in one Rate together.

Item—the Select Men chosen to make this Rate and receive the List of Men's Estates, are John Browne, Nathaniel Ward, Joseph Harrison, Joseph Johnson, and Theophilus Pierson, each Person is to give in a List of their Estates within a Week's Time after the Date hereof, or else are liable to be assessed by the Select Men.

Item—Thomas Browne is chosen Constable, for the Year ensuing. Eliphalet Johnson and James Clizbe, fence Viewers. John Baldwin, Sen'r, Paul Day, and Jabez Rogers, Pounders.

Item—the Select Men chosen to make the Rate, shall appoint the Time when the Cattle shall have Liberty to go into the Neck, and when they shall be prohibited, and also what Cattle shall go in.

TOWN MEETING, *August* 10th, 1696—Summoned by the Constable, with a Warrant from a Justice according to Act of Assembly. Item—it is voted that there shall be Seven Men chosen, to agree, and consider, and Order all prudential Affairs as shall be for the Securing the Neck, and Fruits in it, and concerning the Pound, and pounding Cattle, and where working Cattle shall be baited; and this Agreement to continue untill the Town, or major Part of them, agree otherwise.

Item—John Browne, Joseph Harrison, Samuel Harrison, Thos. Hays, Thomas Ludington, Eliphalet Johnson, and Jasper Crane, are chosen to be the Committee.

Item—it is voted, that Capt. John Curtis, Mr. John Treat, and Mr. Theophilus Pierson, shall endeavor the obtaining a well qualified Man for a School Master.

The Committee chosen August 10th, 1696, to order the prudential Affairs of the Neck, do this 10th of August, 1696, agree, that all Cows or any other Cattle that go into the Neck, (working Cattle and Sheep only excepted), shall be kept out of the Neck, by the last day of August or first of September next, under the Penalty of being pounded and paying Nine pence p. Head, to be paid by the owner of the s'd Cattle to the Party as pounds them, or else otherwise compound with them: working Cattle, and Horses that are worked with, have Liberty to go in untill the 12th or 13th Day of September; after which Time they shall be liable to be pounded, being found in Damage either in Corn or Grass, paying nine pence p. Head, to be paid as afs'd. And no Cattle, Cows, or Calves, shall have Liberty at all to go in before Harvest is in, under the Penalty of eighteen pence p. Head (every time so transgressing) Poundage, besides all Damage to be paid as afs'd; unless in the Spring, for such Time as shall be agreed on by us: but finding that most Damage is done in the Neck on Sabbath Days, We agree, that no Oxen or Horses shall be kept or baited in the Common field on Sabath Days, under the Penalty of nine pence p. Head, if it be proved afterwards that they have been so kept or baited, unless at such Seasons in the Spring, when Cattle are allowed to go in: Always provided; working Cattle have Liberty (unless Sabbath Days) to bait in the Neck with a sufficient keeper, when Men have occasion to work their Cattle, not Damnifying their Neighbours in their Corn or Mowing-Grass, at any Time of the Year—any Thing in this Agreement notwithstanding.

TOWN MEETING, *October* 23rd, 1696—Nathaniel Ward is chosen Clerk.

Officers chosen. TOWN MEETING, *January* 1st, 1696-7—Mr. John Treat, and Jasper Crane, are chosen Deputies for this Year.

Item—John Cooper is chosen Constable, for the Year ensuing or untill another be sworn.

Item—Joseph Harrison and Robert Young are chosen, to be concerned with the Justices in making the County Rate next March.

Item—it is voted, that the Way of rating this Year shall be by Heads, Stocks, and Lands, as it was in the Year '94; and the Men chosen to make the Town Rate, and to make Assessments upon those Persons that don't give in a List of their Estates are Joseph Harrison, Nathaniel Ward, Seth Tomkins, Zopher Beach, and Thomas Hayse: and each Person is to give in a List of their Estates to Zopher Beach or Nathaniel Ward, within eight Days after the Date hereof or they are liable to be assess'd, and the Constable is chosen to collect the Rate above said.

The Way of rating.

TOWN MEETING, *January* 6th, 1696-7—Joseph Harrison, Theophilus Pierson, Nathaniel Ward, Thomas Hays, and Jasper Crane are chosen, to be concerned in settling the Common Line of Fence for the Security of the Neck.

Item—Daniel Browne, John Dalglish, and Paul Day, are chosen Pounders for this Year. Hugh Robards and Samuel Camp, Fence Viewers.

Item—it is voted, that the Deputies shall have 5s. p. Day, for the last Year.

TOWN MEETING, *February* 15th, 1696-7—It is voted, that those Men that are chosen to settle the Common Line of fence against the Neck, shall have Power to call out the County Surveyors, to lay out such Highways as they shall see needfull for the Town's use.

Item—John Lindly is chosen Fence Viewer for the Year ensuing, in Samuel Camp's Stead.

TOWN MEETING, *July* 21st, 1697—Summoned by the Constable, with a Warrant from a Justice according to Act of Assembly.

Item—there is chosen by vote, Mr. John Curtis, Mr. John Treat, Thomas Richards, Mr. Theophilus Pierson, Eliphalet Johnson, Nathaniel Ward, to order the prudential affairs of the Neck.

TOWN MEETING, *January* 1st, 1697-8—Mr. John Treat, and Jasper Crane, are chosen Deputies for this Year.

Theophilus Pierson, Jasper Crane, and Thomas Richards are chosen, to agree with a School Master to keep School in this Town for this Year, according to Act of Assembly.

Matthew Canfield and Ebenezer Lindly, are chosen fence Viewers. Item—Daniel Tichenor, Obadiah Bruen, and Samuel Freeman, Pounders.

The Way of rating. TOWN MEETING, *April* 10th, 1698—It is voted and agreed upon, that the Way of rating to raise Money to discharge the Town Debts, shall be as it was the last Year.

Select Men chosen. Item—the Men chosen to make the Rate, are Nathaniel Ward, John Cooper, Thomas Richards, Joseph Harrison.

Item—it is voted, that Thomas Hayse, Joseph Harrison, Jasper Crane, and Matthew Canfield, shall view whether Azariah Crane may have Land for a Tan Yard, at the Front of John Plum's home Lott, out of the Common; and in case the Men above mentioned agree that Azariah Crane shall have the Land, he the said Azariah Crane shall enjoy it, so long as he doth follow the Trade of tanning.

TOWN MEETING, *September* 6th, 1698—It is agreed upon by vote, for Incouragement to those that will kill Woolves, that they shall have Twenty Shillings p. Head allowed them in a Town Rate, for this Year.

Men chosen to lay out Highways. TOWN MEETING, *December* 12th, 1698—Mr. Treat, Mr. Curtis, Jasper Crane, Samuel Harrison, are chosen by vote, to lay out Highways for the Town's use.

Item—Mr. Pierson, Joseph Harrison, are chosen by vote, to take Care of the Town's Poor.

Item—it is agreed upon by vote, that there shall be a School Master hired for this Town, the next Year.

TOWN MEETING, *January* 2nd, 1698-9—Mr. Treat, and Jasper Crane, are chosen Deputies, for the Year ensuing. Samuel Pierson, Constable.

Item—Capt. Curtis, Mr. Pierson, Thomas Richards, Joseph

Harrison, Nathaniel Ward, are chosen a Committee for to give Advice to the Deputies.

Item—Seth Tompkins and Eleazer Tompkins, are chosen fence Viewers, for the Year ensuing, John Gardner, Thomas Pierson, and Nathaniel Ward, Pounders.

Item—it is voted that those Men that are chosen to take Care of the Town's Poor, shall take Care to repair the Meeting House, and to keep it in Repair from Year to Year.

Item—Mr. Treat, Jasper Crane, Thomas Richards, Nath'l Ward, Mr. Pierson, John Morris, Eliphalet Johnson are chosen, to lay Penalties upon Swine.

Item—it is agreed upon by Vote, that the Town will raise £100 in a Way of Rate, for the upholding of the Worship of God amongst us for a Year.

Item—it is voted for to know, whether the Town would have Mr. Wakeman if he could be obtained, for to join with Mr. Pruden in helping him to carry on the Work of the Ministry, and if he cannot be obtained then some other.

Item—Mr. Pierson, Mr. Treat, Mr. Curtis, Jasper Crane are chosen, for to treat and agree with Mr. Wakeman and Mr. Pruden, for to see if they can be agreed with, and if Mr. Wakeman will not then some other, for a Year.

Town Meeting, *April* 5th, 1699—Summoned by the Constable, with a Warrant from a Justice according to Act of Assembly.

Item—Thomas Hays, Samuel Harrison, Zopher Beach, are chosen, to make up the Town's Accounts and assess Men in Order to making a Town Rate, and to make the Rate.

Item—it is agreed upon by Vote, the Way of rating for this Year shall be as it was formerly.

Item—that all Lands and Meadows shall be rated alike, and that Land and Meadow shall be rated at farthing p. Acre, Heads £14, Oxen of 4 Years and upwards £3, Steers of three Years old £2, Cows £2, two Year old Steers and Heiffers £1 10s., one Year old 15s., grown Horses and Mares of Three Year old and upwards £2 10s., two Year olds £1 5s., One Year old 15s., all swine of one Year old and upwards 10s.

Item—Mr. Curtis, Mr. Treat, Jasper Crane, George Harrison, Mr. Pierson, William Camp, Robert Young, are chosen a Committee, to treat and agree with Elizabeth Town if they can about our Bounds in Controversy, and to sue or defend if there be Occasion.

Town Meeting, *June* 9th, 1699—Item—it is agreed upon by vote, that We will send for the hon'rd and revered Counsel of Elders, and to favour us with the Sight of those Papers wherein the Issue of late Difficulties so far is contained.

Item—the Town did Vote their full Compliance with, and Acquiescence in that Issue.

Item—the Revered Mr. Pruden and Mr. John Brown are chosen by vote, to return our Thanks to the Revered Counsel for their faithfull and painfull Services for our Settlement; signifying we will take sufficient Care to defray the whole Charge of this their Journey and Trouble, till they return.

Item—Capt. Curtis, Mr. Treat, Mr. Pierson, and Thomas Richards are chosen by a full vote, to return our Thanks to the Revered Mr. Pruden for his hitherto Services amongst us; with a signification that We will speedily pay of our Arrears due to him by our particular Subscriptions: and by a full Vote we declare our Desire of his Continuance among us, and his Service at present in preaching the Word to us, till God shall favor us with some other Supply.

Item—it is agreed and voted, that we will allow him for his further Ministry according to what he formerly had, in Proportion to the Time We have occasion to use him as a Minister.

Item—it is voted, that all Persons, from 16 to 60 Years of Age, shall give to Mr. Pruden each of them one Load of Wood, for the Year ensuing; whether he serve the Town in the Ministry another Year, or no.

Item—it is voted, that Mr. Treat, Jasper Crane, Joseph Harrison are chosen a Committee, to join with such as the Church shall appoint, in speedily looking out for another Person to be on Trial, in order to Settlement in the pastoral Office in this Place.

Item—it is voted, that We will give to such Minister £50 p. Annum, for his Incouragement whilst on Trial; and that We will increase the Salary upon his Settlement, as he and We shall agree.

Item—Mr. Treat, Mr. Curtis, Mr. Pierson, and Thomas Richards, are chosen by Vote, to desire Mr. Pruden to carry on the Work of the Ministry with us, till God shall favour us with a Supply.

At a Town Meeting at *Newark* 11th of April, Anno 1699—The Town gave unto their Representatives their Thanks, for not consenting to the passing of an Act, entitled, an Act for redressing a force of our Neighbour Province; and because the said Act does Order the raising the sum of £675 Current Money of New York, and does not say for what End that Sum is raised, but leaves it to be disposed to such Uses as a few Men nominated in the said Act shall think fit; and to be remitted (by Bills of Exchange though obtained at extraordinary Rates) to such Persons, the Major Part whereof we have no reason to Trust nor give our Money unto, nor are we (or can be) any ways assured, that the said Persons will apply it to those uses the Commissioners will appoint, if they be any other than the paying the owner or owners of the Ship Hester, which we suspect to be the End of raising the Sum afs'd. The Town of Newark therefore do with one Voice, resolve, not to pay any Part of the Tax afs'd, nor to be aiding or assisting to the Constable or Sheriff, or any other Officer or Officers impowered or to be impowered to gather the said sum of £675, or any Part of it; but do resolve, as one Man to withstand all Force whatsover that shall be used for the gathering of it; because we know of no illegal force committed upon us by our neighbouring Province: and the said Town of Newark do order their Clerk to record this Resolve, in their Town Book. This also voted.

Item—it is voted, that Cattle shall have Liberty to go into the Neck without keeping, after Harvest.

Item—Samuel Harrison, Thomas Hays, John Morris are chosen by Vote, to give Notice when Cattle shall go into the Neck, and when they shall be taken out.

Item—Nathaniel Ward is chosen Collector, to gather the Town Rate.

At a TOWN MEETING, *August* 8th, 1699—The Committee formerly chosen, to look out for a Person upon Trial in the Work of the Ministry, desired the Advice of the Town as to the Person; the Votes being given in, they desired the Town to withdraw: the Committee having looked over the Votes, the Meeting was called in again, and it was agreed by Vote, that they would comply and acquiesce with the advice of the Major Part. Item —Mr. Wakeman was declared to be the Person made choice of.

At a TOWN MEETING in Newark, *October* 2nd, 1699—First—it was agreed by the generality of the Town, that they would endeavor to make a Purchase of a Tract of Land lying Westward of our Bounds, to the South Branch of Passaick River; and such of the Town as do contribute to the purchasing of the s'd Land, shall have their Proportion according to their Contribution—2ndly, That Mr. Pierson and Ensign Johnson are chosen, to go and treat with the Proprietors about the same, to obtain a Grant —3rdly, There was a Committee chosen (viz), Samuel Harrison, Thos. Davis, Robert Young, Daniel Dod, Nathaniel Ward, and John Cooper, to consider, agree, and put forward the Design abovesaid.

Item—it was agreed upon by Vote, that the Committee formerly chosen to confer and consult about such prudential Affairs as should offer, they shall be paid what is due to them, out of the Town Rate; they making up their Accounts with the Select Men chosen to make up the Town's Accounts.

TOWN MEETING being legally summoned, and assembled together this 16th of *November*, 1699—It was unanimously voted and agreed to, that Mr. Jabez Wakeman should be treated with, to be imployed in the Work of the Ministry.

Item—it is agreed upon by Vote, that we will give him for his Incouragement, for his Service in the Work of the Ministry, £60 for this Year.

At a TOWN MEETING, *February* 29th, 1699—it is voted, that Cattle shall be prohibitted from going into the Neck after Harvest, without keeping.

Item—Eliphalet Johnson, Paul Day, Samuel Freeman, Eleazer Bruen, are chosen Fence Viewers for the Year ensuing. Daniel Brown, and George Day, Pounders.

At at a TOWN MEETING at Newark, *April* 15th, 1700—Summoned by the Constable, by a Warrant according to Act of Assembly; It was particularly inquired of every Person, whether they desired Mr. Jabez Wakman to be called to the pastoral office in this Town, and they every one manifested their Willingness thereto, and also voted the same.

Item—John Lindsly is chosen Constable for this Year, or till another be chosen and sworn.

At a TOWN MEETING, *May* 9th, 1700—Mr. John Treat and Mr. Jasper Crane, are chosen Deputies.

Item—John Johnson or his Son, John Dalglesh, John Ogden, are chosen Pounders.

Item—Mr. Treat, Mr. Jasper Crane, Eliphalet Johnson, are chosen a Committee to join with the Church's Committee, to treat with Mr. Jabez Wakman about his taking the Office of a Pastor upon him in this Town.

At a TOWN MEETING, *August* 16th, 1700—Mr. Curtis, Mr. Treat, Mr. Pierson, Mr. Jasper Crane, Thomas Richards, Eliphalet Johnson, Seth Tompkins, are chosen a Committee, to procure a Settlement for Mr. Jabez Wakman in this Town.

Item—it was agreed upon by vote, that the Money to procure a Settlement for Mr. Jabez Wakman, shall be raised by way of Rate upon the Estates of the Subscribers.

TOWN MEETING, *September* 30th, 1700—It was unanimously voted by the Inhabitants then assembled, that Mr. Jabez Wake man should have £60 allowed him annually and every Year for his Salary, for his Labour in the Ministry amongst us.

Item—it was agreed upon by vote, that the aboves'd £60

should be raised by way of Rate, and the way of rating should be as the major Part of the Subscribers should agree upon.

At a TOWN MEETING, *January* 7th, 1700—Mr. John Treat, and Jasper Crane, are chosen Deputies for the Year ensuing. Samuel Freeman, Constable. Thomas Hays and Samuel Harrison, Overseers of the Poor.

Daniel Brown and John Dalglish, Fence Viewers—and to view from Camp's Gate by Daniel Tichenor's to the Bound Creek—John Morris and Joseph Ball, Fence Viewers—and to view from the River to Camp's Gate by Daniel Tichenor's.

At a TOWN MEETING, *February* 28th, 1700—Samuel Robards, John [Sam ?] Alling, John Medlos are chosen by vote, to go about to get the Subscription perfected to Mr. Wakeman's Deed of Gift.

Item, it is agreed upon by vote, that the Committee shall deliver the Deed of Gift to Mr. Wakeman, as the Town's Act and Deed.

At a TOWN MEETING, *November* 11th, 1701—It is agreed upon by Vote, that Mr. Wakeman's Salary of £60 for the Year past, shall be raised upon Estates as was agreed upon formerly, that is, all Lands and Meadow alike—and that Land and Meadow shall be rated at 5d. p. Acre, Heads £14, Oxen of four Years old and upwards £3, Steers of three Years old £2, two Year old Steers and Hieffers £1 10s., Yearlings 15s., Horses and Mares of three Year old and upwards £2 10s., Two Year Olds £1 5s., One Year old 15s., Cows £2, All Swine of one Year Old and upwards 10s.

The way of rating.

Item, Daniel Dod and Nathaniel Ward are chosen, to make the Rate of Mr. Wakeman's Salary.

Mr. Wakeman's Salary.

Item, it is agreed upon by Vote, that Mr. Wakeman shall have £80 allowed him Annually and every Year for his Salary, for his Labour in the Ministry amongst us.

Mr. Jabez Wakeman's Grant.

Item, it is agreed upon by Vote, that Mr. Jabez Wakeman shall have laid out to him, Sixty Acres of Upland and Ten Acres of Meadow in the Bounds of Newark if it can be found, if he settle among us to be our Minister; and Mr. John Curtis is chosen by Vote to lay out the Land above said.

At a TOWN MEETING, *January* 16th, 1701-2, Mr. John Treat, and Mr. Jasper Crane, are chosen Deputies for the Year ensuing. Samuel Dod, Constable. Joseph Ball, Samuel Huntington, and William Wilson, Pounders.

Item, Joseph Brown and Abraham Pierson, Fence Viewers.

Town Meeting, *November* 2nd, 1702—Summoned by the Constable, according to Act of Assembly.

Item, it is voted, that the Way of rating for Mr. Wakeman's Salary, shall be as it was the last Year.

Assessors chosen.

Item, Sarj't Samuel Harrison and John Morris, are chosen Assessors for the North End of the Town; and Sarj't Thos. Hays and Ensign Eliphalet Johnson, are chosen Assessors for the South End of the Town.

Item, it is voted that a List of the Estates shall be brought in to the Assessors, by this Sen'night.

Item, Capt. Curtis and Mr. Theophilus Pierson are chosen, to reckon with the Collectors and take an Account of the Town's Debts.

Item, it is voted, that there shall be a Gallery built at the North End of the Meeting House.

Item, it is voted that there shall be a Town Rate made, to discharge the Town's Debts.

Item, it is voted that the Town Rate shall be raised upon Estates, as Mr. Wakeman's Rate is.

Item, it is voted that those Persons that have killed Wolves since the last Town Rate, or shall kill any Wolves, shall be allowed Twelve Shillings p. Head.

Item, it is voted that those Creatures which People intend to kill for their Use, shall be Rate Free.

Item, Nathaniel Ward and John Cooper are chosen to make the Rates.

Town Meeting, *January* the first, 1703—James Nottman is chosen Constable, for the Year ensuing.

At a Town Meeting, *November* 2nd, 1703—Item, Jasper Crane and Samuel Pierson are chosen Overseers for the Poor. Thomas Williams, Azariah Crane, Jun'r, and Zachariah Burwell, Pounders.

Item, Samuel and Daniel Baldwin, Fence Viewers.

At a Town Meeting, *March* 10th 1704—It is voted that there should be a Shepherd hired for to keep the Sheep—Samuel Harrison, Robert Young, Eliphalet Johnson, and Thomas Hays, are chosen Sheep Masters.

Item, it is agreed upon by vote, that the Sheep Masters shall have Power to hire a Shepherd to keep the Sheep.

Item, Samuel Harrison and John Morris are chosen, to contrive and oversee the building a Gallery in the Meeting House.

Item, Mr. Treat, Mr. Curtis, Mr. Pierson, Joseph Harrison, George Harrison, and Eliphalet Johnson are chosen a Committee, for to draw up something in order to a regulation of Lands irregularly taken up.

At a TOWN MEETING, *October* 12th, 1704—It is agreed upon by Vote, that we will pay Mr. Wakeman's Salary for this Year as we paid the Last Year, or by the last Year's Rate.

Item, it is unanimously agreed upon by vote, that we will be in the speedy Use of Means, to see for a Man to supply the vacancy of the pastoral office in this Town among us.

Item, it is agreed upon by vote, that we will desire Mr. Pruden to preach the Word amongst us at present, or till We be otherways supplyed.

At a TOWN MEETING held at Newark, *April* 11th, 1705—It was voted, that the regulation of Fence in the Common Line shall be left or deferred, till some further Opportunity.

It was voted, that Samuel Lyon, Sen'r, and Nathaniel Wheeler, Jun'r, should be Fence Viewers, for that part of the Common Line from Mr. Treat's Lott to the Bound Creek; and Daniel Harrison and Joseph Ball, for the Remainder of the Common Line of Fence.

It was voted, that Samuel Harrison and William Camp should survey the Highway and vacant Land at the Landing, and that the Exchange with Thomas Richards and the Town is allowed, and ordered to be recorded accordingly.

Mr. Treat, Mr. Pierson, Mr. Samuel Robards, and Joseph Harrison are chosen to discourse Mr. John Barcly, Receiver General, about the Quit-Rents in behalf of the Town, and to give an Answer.

At a TOWN MEETING, *October* 1st, 1705—Mr. John Treat is chosen to be one of the Committee, to endeavor to get a Man upon Trial in the Work of the Ministry amongst us.

Item, the Town manifested their Desire by vote, that the Committee should make their application to Mr. Sam'l Sherman, to preach the Word amongst for Probation.

At a TOWN MEETING, *October* 30th, 1705—It was agreed upon by Vote, to petition my Lord Cornbury for Lisence, that we may have Leave to get and settle a Man in the Work of the Ministry of the Gospel, according to our own Presevasion.

Item, Mr. Pruden, Mr. Pierson and Sarj't John Morris are chosen by Vote, to draw a Petition—it is voted that the Clerk of the Town shall personate the Town in signing the Petition—Mr. Pierson is chosen to prefer it to my Lord Cornbury.

TOWN MEETING, *January* 22nd, 1705–6—Summoned by the Constable, it is voted that the Way of rating for defraying the Town's Debts shall be as followeth: Person of Sixteen Years old and upwards £14—all Land and Meadow at 5s. p. acre—all Cattle of One Year old and upwards at £2 p. Head—all Swine of One Year old and upwards at 10s. p. Head.

Item, John Cooper and Nathaniel Ward Sen'r, are chosen Rate makers.

Item, Nathaniel Ward Sen'r is chosen Collector, to collect the Town Rate.

Item, it is voted that the Price of Corn to pay the Town Rate shall be as followeth: Wheat 5s. p. Bushell, Rye 3s. p. Bus'l, Indian Corne 3s. p. Bus'l, Oats 1s. 9d. p. Bus'l, Flax 9d. p. pound.

Item, Joseph Harrison and Robert Young are chosen, to take account of what are the Town's Debts, in Order to make the Town Rate.

Item, it is agreed upon by Vote, that if any Person or Persons do leave open Gate or Barrs belonging to the Neck, they shall be fined according to Town Order.

Item, Nath'l Ward and John Cooper are chosen Assessors, for the Town Rate.

Item, it was granted to John Johnson, that he should have that Piece of Land betwixt his own Land at Canfield's Meadow and the Highway, for what the Town owed him, or for that Debt for which he sued Thomas Richards and had Judgment against him.

John Johnson's Grant this was voted Aug't 29th tho' omitted recording till now.

At a Town Meeting, *February* 19th, 1705–6—The Question was asked the Town, whether they was satisfied with the Information that the Church had from Mr. Sherman's own Mouth, concerning his Circumstances from the Place from whence he came—It was consented to by Vote they was.

Item, it was also voted by the Town, that they would have no farther Treaty with Mr. Sherman upon the account of a Settlement amongst us.

Item, Eliphalet Johnson, Mr. Jasper Crane, Mr. Pierson, Deacon Azariah Crane were chosen by Vote, to return the Town's answer to Mr. Sherman abovesaid.

Item, it was voted to try the Town's Mind, whether they would seek for a Supply in the pastoral Charge amongst us, in inviting a Man amongst us upon Trial; which was manifested by Vote.

Item, Mr. Pierson was chosen by Vote to be the Town's Messenger to send, to endeavor to get a Man upon Trial in the work of the Ministry amongst us.

Item, Mr. Pruden, Mr. Jasper Crane, Deacon Crane, Robert Young, and Joseph Harrison were chosen by Vote, to give Mr. Pierson Power, Direction, and Instruction in that matter, in the Town's Behalf.

Item, it is voted, that if any Person or Persons do set Fire within the Common Line, or Neck, or Meadow, before Notice be given by the Beat of the Drum, he or they shall forfeit 20s— which shall be for the Town's use.

At a TOWN MEETING, *February* 25th, 1705-6—It is granted to John Gardner by Vote, that he should have half the Breadth of that Gusset of Land next Jasper Crane's Line so running from the Brook up to his Land, and John Baldwin should have the Rest.

John Cooper is chosen Town Clerk, for the Year ensuing.

Item, Joseph Harrison, John Morris, and Nathaniel Ward, are Chosen for to settle a Table of Fees for the Town Clerk.

At a TOWN MEETING, *May* 17th, 1706—It was voted and agreed upon, to improve Mr. Samuel Whitlesse in the work of the Ministry among us, for the Space of One Year.

Item, it was also voted that Mr. Whittlesse should have £60 in Money or equivolent, for his first Year's Salary.

Item, it was also voted, that the £60 should be raised by Way of Rate, and the Way of rating as was agreed upon for our last Town Rate.

Item, Thomas Davis and John Morris, are chosen Overseers of the Poor for this Year. Hugh Robards and Henry Lyon, Fence Viewers for the South End of the Town, and William Wilson and John Rogers for the North End.

Item, It was also voted, that Mr. Theophilus Pierson, Capt. Eliphalet Johnson, Deacon Crane, and Joseph Harrison, should carry the Town's Message to Mr. Whittlese.

At a TOWN MEETING, *August* 26th, 1706—It was voted that Mr. Whittlesey should be treated with, about his settlement in the Work of the Ministry among us—Deacon Azariah Crane, Capt. Eliphalet Johnson, Mr. Theophilus Pierson, and Thomas Richards are chosen, to deliver the Town's Message and to treat with him about the Settlement.

TOWN MEETING, *March* 31st, 1707—It was voted that the Major Part should Rule the Minor, in affixing Mr. Whittlesey's Salary.

It was also voted, that John Cooper should have a piece of the Parsonage Land for his Improvement, for the space of Seven Years, about Six or Seven Acres adjoining to Sarj't. Ward.

It was also Voted, that Mr. Whittlesey should have Sixty-five Pounds Annually, for his Labour in the Ministry among us.

Item, it was also Voted, that they would and were willing to be helpfull to Mr. Whittlesey, in procuring a Settlement for him in Convenient Season.

Item, it was also voted, that Deacon Crane, Mr. Pierson, and Sarj't Joseph Harrison, should carry the Town's Proceedings to Mr. Whittlesey.

TOWN MEETING, *October* 27th, 1707—It was voted, that the Way of rating for the Poor shall be as the last Town Rate was made, and Sarj't Ward and John Cooper are chosen to make said Rate.

Item, it was also voted, that a Rate for Mr. Whittlesey's Salary should be made, in the same Way as it was last Year; and Serj't Nathaniel Ward and John Cooper are chosen to make the Rate.

Item, Sarj't Joseph Harrison and Robert Young are chosen by vote, to collect, demand, and recover Mr. Whittlesey's Rate for the Year 1707, and also to demand and recover Mr. Whittlesey's Rate for the Year 1706—that is to say the Arrears.

TOWN MEETING, *March* 21st, 1708—Mr. Pierson was chosen by vote, to go to New England to endeavor to procure a Minister, and the Committee that was before chosen, (viz): Mr. Pierson, Deacon Azariah Crane, Mr. Jasper Crane, Sarj't Joseph Harrison, Robert Young, and Lieut. Samuel Alling were appointed to give him his Instructions in the Management of that Affair.

TOWN MEETING, *June* 3d, 1709—Upon Mr. Pierson's Return, he made a Report to the Town of the Progress he had made in that Matter, and that with good Advice from the Elders he made his application to Mr. Nathaniel Bowers, where he received this Encouragement, that if the Town would signify their Desire therein he would give us a Visit; which was put to Vote, and very unanimously voted that there should be a Messenger sent to Hudson's River on the 16th Inst. June, to wait upon him to Newark.

TOWN MEETING, *June* 22nd, 1709—The Town was then asked whether they desired any farther Improvement of Mr. Bowers upon Trial or not, which was very unanimously voted to the Affirmative and not one to the Contrary, it was also agreed that he should be treated with for his Continuing among us for one Year.

It was also voted the Committee before chosen should treat with him, for the Time of Trial among us.

It was also voted, that the offer to Mr. Bowers for the first Year should be £70, with the Use of the Parsonage House and Land, and his Transportation; and so proportionably to the Time they should agree with him for.

It was also Voted, that the afs'd Sum of £70—with the said Charges should be paid by Way of Rate, according to our former Way of Rating.

At a Town Meeting, *October* 21st, 1709—It was agreed upon, that Mr. Bowers's Rate for his Salary, should be raised according to usual Way of Rating for the Minister—Also, Sarj't Nath'l Ward and John Cooper, Assessors and Rate Makers for said Rate—Also, Caleb Ward and Nathaniel Wheeler, Jun'r, Overseers of the Poor, and Assessors for this Year—Also, Lieut. Sam'l Alling and James Nottman, are chosen Collectors of Mr. Bowers's Salary.

Mr. John Treat, Mr. Theophilus Pierson, Mr. Jasper Crane, Sarj't Joseph Harrison, and Zopher Beach are chosen, to draw up some wholesome Orders about the Neck, and also to provide a Man to be with the Surveyor General in drawing the line between Newark and the intended Hurley [Survey?].

At a Town Meeting, *March* 20th, 1709-10—The Inhabitants of Newark were called one by one, and examined, whether they were so far satisfied with Mr. Bowers the present Minister, as to Give him a Call in Order to his Settlement, and to make Provision for the same—and all agreed and consented so to do excepting two Men.

Item, it was voted that Mr. Bowers should have £80 p. annum for his Salary and the Use of the Parsonage, he keeping of it in Repair.

June 29th, 1710, upon a Lecture Day, Mr. John Treat and Sarj't Joseph Harrison were appointed and made choice of by vote, to deliver the Subscription to Mr. Bowers which was drawn up and signed by the greatest Part of the Town for the Payment of his Yearly Salary.

At a Town Meeting, *August* 28th, 1710—The Town were desired to signify by vote, whether they were willing that Mr. Bowers should be called to Office in this Town, and there was not one appeared to the negative—Also, Mr. Theophilus Pierson, Mr. John Treat, Capt. Eliphalet Johnson, Deacon Crane, and Sarj't Joseph Harrison were made Choice of, for the Management thereof in Order to his Ordination.

Town Meeting, *November* 6th, 1710—Sarj't Nathaniel Ward and John Cooper were chosen, to assess and make Mr. Bowers's Rate for his Salary for the Year ensuing, and Mr. Samuel Alling and James Nottman Collectors; and that a List of the Estates of the Subscribers should be given in to the said Ratemakers, on or before the first Day of December next ensuing.

Town Meeting, *November* 5th, 1711—Sarj't Nathaniel Ward and John Cooper were chosen, to assess and make a Rate for Mr. Bowers's Salary for the Year ensuing, and Mr. James Notman and Mr. Sam'l Alling are chosen Collectors; and that a List of the Estates of the Subscribers should be given in to Sarj't Ward, on or before the 1st of December next.

Town Meeting, *March* 3rd, 1711-12—John Dalglish and Joseph Baldwin, are chosen Overseers of the Poor for the Year ensuing. John Richards and Samuel Cooper are chosen Assessors, for making of a Rate for the Poor, and other necessary Charges allowed by an Act of Assembly—and Joseph Bruen is chosen, for the making of a Pound—John Dalglish, Pound Keeper—John Baldwin, Miner [Jun'r], and Judah Penington, Fence Viewers—Mr. Joseph Harrison and John Cooper, were chosen to meet for the County.

Town Meeting, *February* 21st, 1711—The Inhabitants of Newark were asked, whether they were willing to come to an Agreement with the Inhabitants of Elizabeth Town about settling the Bounds between them and us, which was unanimously consented unto: And in Order thereunto by Vote chose a Committee to endeavor for an Agreement, (viz): Mr. John Treat, Mr. Jasper Crane, Capt. Johnson, Mr. Theophilus Pierson, Mr. Joseph Harrison, Sarj't John Morris and John Cooper—did likewise put into their Hands the full Power of agreement, and did verbally by Words engage to rest satisfied with what the said Committee should do in that Affair.

Item, it was also voted, that the said Committee should take all care, and use all regular means for the procurement of a Town Pattent.

Town Meeting, *May* 25th, 1713—It was agreed upon by vote, that the Charges for procuring of a Town Pattent should be raised as Mr. Bower's Salary (that is to say) all Lands and Meadows at £25 p. Hundred Acres, all Cattle and Horses one Year old and upwards at £2 p. head, all Male White Persons at Sixteen Years old and upwards at £14 p. head.

Item, Ensign Samuel Cooper and James Brown, were chosen Rate makers and Assessors—Item, David Ogden, Collector.

Town Meeting, *November* 2nd, 1713—Samuel Cooper and David Ogden, were chosen Assessors and Rate makers for Mr. Bowers's Rate, the ensuing Year.

Item, Joseph Bruen and James Brown, are chosen Collectors for the said Rate.

Newarke,
County of Essex.

A Town Meeting, held *Apreill* ye 12th 1714, by Vertue of A warrant Given under ye hands of ye Trustees for ye Said Town for ye Time being, the Inhabitants being mett, ye Town Pattent was Published.

John Cooper was Chosen Town Clerke by Vote of ye Inhabitants. Also Persons Chosen by Vote to Regulate ye Common Line of fence, and to order other Prudentiall affaires in ye Neck, (viz): Capt. Eliphelet Johnson, Leiu^tt Sam^ll Aling, Leiu^tt Jonathan Crane, Leiu^tt John Moris, & Serg^t John Dalglish.

James Broun is Chosen Overseer of ye poor for ye Ensuing Year. Mr James Notman & Nathaniel Wheeler are Chosen Sheep Masters for ye Year Ensueing.

A Town meeting held at Newark *Sep'tr* ye 28th 1714. John Cooper was then again Chosen Town Clerk and Sworn Truly to perform that Trust, & Sam^ll Cooper was Chosen and Sworn to officiate in ye Clerks absence, in Taking ye Minites and to Transmit them to ye Clerk to be Recorded.

The Persons Chose apreill ye 12th to Regulate ye affaires in ye Neck, are again Confirmed for that Service.

Joseph Peck is Chosen by Vote, to be a Trustee for ye Town of Newark, to Suply ye place of Mr. John Treat Deceased, to fill up ye Number of Ten.

Leiu^tt Sam^ll Aling & Ensign Sam^ll Cooper are Chosen by Vote, to Take Care that ye Subscription for Mr. Bowers his Sallery be filled up at ye North End of ye Town, & Capt. Eliphelet Johnson & Ensign Nat^ll Wheller for ye Same at ye South End.

James Broun is Chosen Overseer of ye poor, for ye Year Ensueing.

It was also ordered by Vote, y^t ye old floor in ye Meeting house Should be made use of for ye Making a floor in ye Schoolhouse in the Midle of ye Town.

John Ogden is Chosen Constable by Vote, to Execute Such Matters and things as ye Trustees of ye Said Town Shall find Nessesary to be Done by Vertue of ye Town Pattent.

Town Meeting, *November* ye 1st, 1714—Assessors & Collectors Chosen for Mr. Bowers his Rate, (viz): Sam^ll Cooper & David Ogden are Chosen Assessors & Rate Makers: & Joseph Bruin & James Broun, Collectors.

Town Meeting, *January* ye 20th, 1714–15, it was then agreed by Vote, y^t John fford Should have Liberty to Sett a Mill below ye old Mill, and that he Should have a quarter of an Acre of Land.

David Ogden & Joseph Burwell was also Chosen by vote, to agree with those persons who Laid out ye Common Line fence, what they Should have for their work.

TOWN MEETING, *March* ye 8th, 1714–15—Sam^{ll} Aling & David Ogden were Chosen, to Meet ye Justices in order to agree about ye County Tax.

Town Meeting Aprell ye 28th, 1714.

The Severall Persons hereafter Named were Chosen by Vote, (viz): Capt. Eliphelet Johnson, Mr. Sam^{ll} Aling, Mr. Jonathan Crane, Leiu^{tt} John Morris, & Serg^{tt} John Dalglish, To Regulate Common Line ffence Relateing ye Neck, & to order other Prudentiall affaires In ye s'd Neck, the which orders & Regulation being Made is as followeth, (viz): That all ye Common Line fence Shall be Deemed & Esteemed Sufficient, when it is made and Maintained According to ye Act of Generall Assemblely, & not otherwise, Excepting from ye Bound Creek to ye Bridge by ye Two mile brook Landing, and John Bradburys by ye Main River: which Shall be made So as to Secure ye Neck & Then it Shall be accounted Sufficient, & not otherwise.

The Severall Persons hereafter Named whose Land Joines upon ye Common Line, (viz): Hugh Robarts, Daniel Broun, Thomas Broun, James Broun, Thomas Peirson, The Lot formerly belonging To Mr. John Treat Deceased, The front Thereof to be made and Maintained for ye Proportion of fence belonging to that Estate, Judah Penington, Eleazer Tompkins, John Tompkins, Seth Tompkins, John Baldwin, Joseph Baldwin, Daniel Baldwin, Samuel Baldwin, Timothy Baldwin, Elnathan Baldwin, Epherim Price, And Samuel freeman: all ye above Mentioned Persons whose Land Bounds upon ye Common ffeild, Each of them & their Successors Shall Secure ye Common ffeild against his or their own Lotts: all apparent Damages Happening in ye Sd feild Through any of ye abouesd Lotts to be born & paid by ye person or persons through whose ffence it Shall appear to be done: all ye Rest of ye Sd ffence to be under Veiw by ffence Veiwers Chosen to Veiw ye Same, which they Shall be oblidged to Do once Every Three Months, & oftener if need Require. Itt is also ordered that Each Person Do mark his her or their ffence with ye Two first Letters of their name at Each End, and for Neglect therof Each Person to forfeit one Shiling, to be paid to the aforesd fence Veiwers.

All apparent Damages Happening Through any Defective ffence, ye owner of ye Said ffence through which it Shall be made appear to be Done Shall pay ye Damages accruing thereby:

The ffence Veiwers finding Defective fence Shall Give Seasonable Notis to ye owner thereof to make it up: & if Neglected by ye owner the fence Veiwers to Do it themselves, or cause it to be Done, and to be paid Duble Wages by the owner thereof for ye Same.

All unruly Cattel & horsees being found trespassing in the Common feild, ye owner of such unruly Creature Shall pay to the Pounder or pounders when pounded, one Shiling and Sixpence pr. head. for all Cattell or horses put or Left in ye Neck without a keeper Shall pay one Shiling and Sixpence Per head when Pounded. ffor all Such Cattle and horses as Shall break out of pastures in ye Common feild, & all others that Shall be found in ye Neck, when Pounded ye owner or owners thereof Shall pay Nine pence pr. head.

There Shall be no baiting Cattle horses or sheep in ye Sd Neck, Except it be by persons upon their own Land.

all Sheep being found Trespasing in ye Sd Neck shall be pounded, and ye owner of them Shall pay Two pence pr. head.

The Pounders Pounding any Creatures out of ye Said Neck, they shall fourthwith Give Notice thereof to ye owner if to be found, if not to be Proceeded with according to ye Act of Assembly.

for Rescuing any Cattle or other Creature above mentioned from the Pounder or Pounders, by any person or persons, Such person or persons Rescuing ye Same Shall Pay the Sum of forty Shilings for Each time: if ye Rescue be made by any under Covert, In that Case ye Same Penaltie of forty Shilings Shall be paid by ye Parent Master or Mistriss of Such Son or Servant, by whom it Shall be Commited.

For any Gates or bars that Shall be Left open in ye Common Line, by any person or persons, they Shall forfeit five Shilings, to be paid to the Complainer & also pay all Damages hapening therby: if ye person Leaveing it open be under Covert, then & in that Case to be paid by ye parent Master or Mistriss of Such Son or Servant, by which ye Same Shall appear to be Left open.

The Names of ye Persons Concerned in ye Sd Common Line, with their Proportion of fence annexed to their Names Successively, begining at ye bound Creek and Thence Runing Northwardly to ye Main River—

	Chains.	Links.	½ Links.
John Canfield		25	
John Dalglish	1	50	
Two Widow Cundits		30	
James Wheeler	1	60	
Deacon Azariah Crane for ye first Gate	2	50	
Hezekiah Johnson in ye Same Gate		30	
Mr. James Notman from ye Creek to ye Gate and from ye Gate to Ebenezer Tompkins			
Ebenezer Tompkins		22	½
Mr. Joseph Harrison	1	15	
Ebenezer Lindsley		07	½
Joseph Baldwin of Milford		07	½
Johanus Vreelandt		80	
Capt. Eliphelet Johnson	5	66	
Josiah Ogden		95	
Widow Sarah Huntington	2	05	
Joseph Crane		59	
Thomas Johnson		59	
George Day from Thomas Johnson to ye North Side of ye Two Two mile brook for his Joining on ye Neck being	8	50	
Aling Wilkison		10	
Robert Camell		10	
Mr. Benjamin Lyon		25	
John Richards	2	—	
Samuel Harison	1	20	
Daniel Crane		80	
Abraham Vreelandt		55	
Joseph Ball	1	15	
Daniel Harrison one Length of fence		15	
Henry Lyon the Second Gate			
Daniel Harison	1	60	
Nathan ffoster		30	
Samuel Tompkins		32	½
Doctr James Pronost		25	½
Nathaniel Crane		15	

	Chains.	Links.	½ Links.
Samuel Camp	2	10	
Abraham Kitchell	2	—	
Lawrants Arentsen Deceast		30	
Jacob Vralman		25	
Daniel Dod		50	
Robert Hayes	2	60	
Widow Martha Beech		27	½
Joseph Riggs		10	
John Goden		17	½
Benjamin Harison		12	½
David Ogden	1	—	
Robert Young		40	
John Cooper		27	½
Widow Martha Dod		50	
Jonathan Peirson	3	80	
Benjamin Baldwin	1	05	
Samuel Peirson		75	
John Ward		60	
John Rogers	2	10	
Joseph Wood		50	
Daniel Dod		70	
Martin Tichenor		75	
Harmanus Garetson		40	
Daniel Clark		50	
John Lindsley		25	
Thomas Ball		40	
Mr. John Prudden and ye Widow Margeret Pruden	1	65	
Joseph Jones		15	
Jonathan Lindsley		07	½
Thomas Gardner		20	
John Johnson		70	
Edward Riggs		25	
Nathaniel Wheeler	1	50	
Jonathan Serjant	1	55	
Joseph Lindsley		25	
Mathew Williams		70	
Jasper Crane		72	½
Samuel Ward Junr		20	
Samuel Day		20	
Joseph Wheeler		15	
Jonathan Sayer		70	

Town Meeting, *August* 10th, 1716—Sarj't John Linsly and Joseph Bruen, were chosen Overseers of the Poor for the Year ensuing.

Town Meeting, *August* 30th, 1716—It was voted by the Town, to chuse a Committee to se out some Way to procure a Minister for the Town, to supply the Place of Mr. Nathaniel Bowers, dec'd. The Committee chosen for that affair was Deacon Azariah Crane, Capt. Eliphalet Johnson, Mr. Sam'l Alling, Mr. Josiah Ogden, Mr. Jonathan Crane, Mr. Thomas Davis and John Cooper.

There was also chosen two Men, to seat the Three Men that were chosen to seat the Meeting House, (viz): James Nuttman and Lieut. John Morris.

Town Meeting at Newark, *March* 12th, 1716–17—By virtue

of an Act of Assembly, on the Second Tuesday of s'd Month Mr. Sam'l Alling and Mr. David Ogden were chosen Freeholders, to meet the Justices for the present Year.

Item, David Ogden was chosen Assessor for the provincial Tax, and Samuel Alling, Collector.

Item, Lieut. John Morris, Mr. Jonathan Crane, Samuel Harrison, Jun'r, and Mr. Benjamin Lyon, are chosen Surveyors of the Highways.

Item, it was also voted that the Parsonage Land should be run out according to the Pattent, and that they would defray the Charge of doing it.

Item, Joseph Baldwin, Jun'r, and Abraham Kitchel, were chosen Sheep Masters for the ensuing Year.

TOWN MEETING, *March* 11th, 1718-19—Mr. Thomas Davis and Lieut. Nathaniel Wheeler are chosen, together with Sarj't Samuel Ward and Samuel Camp, Surveyors of Highways for the ensuing Year. John Ogden and John Cooper are chosen Freeholders, and the s'd John Cooper is chosen Assessor, and David Ogden, Collector for the provincial Tax. Abraham Pierson and Joseph Rogers, Overseers of the Poor. Joseph Bruin and Robert Hays, Sheep Masters, and Capt. Morris and James Brown are chosen, to make up acco'ts with the Sheep Masters. Robert Crane and Thomas Longworth, Pounders.

They have also agreed to renew the Line between Newark and Ackquackonong, the first Monday in April next.

April 6th, 1719—The Line was then Renewed, and there was present from Newark Deacon Azariah Crane, Mr. James Nottman, Joseph Peck, Joseph Ball, Joseph Baldwin, Moses Ball, Doct'r Jacob Arent, John Cooper, Thomas Stagg—from Acquackonong Mr. Michael Vreelandt, Thomas Uriansen, Garret Harmanusen.

TOWN MEETING, *December* 16th, 1718—After an Orderly beginning, a Letter of Recom'endation from Mr. Andrew, of Mr. Webb, was read well accepted. It was agreed upon by vote, to agree with Mr. Webb for Three quarters of a Year upon trial—It was also agreed upon, to give him for the Time at the Rate of £70 a Year. It was also agreed upon, to raise the Money by Way of Rate.

TOWN MEETING, *November* 2nd, 1719—There was then chosen David Ogden, and Samuel Cooper, Assessors, and Joseph Ball and John Crane, Jun'r, Collectors, to assess and collect Mr. Webb's Rate for the Year ensuing; and it was agreed upon, that the Estates in order to make the same should be given in to the s'd Assessors, at or before the 25th of December next.

TOWN MEETING, *November* 20th, 1719—It was then agreed upon, to make a Town Rate for the Support of the Poor in the Town of Newark—John Cooper was chosen to assess the said Rate, for which it was agreed upon he should have Twenty Shillings—Mr. Joseph Harrison, Mr. James Nottman, Capt. John Morris and Lieut. Jonathan Crane were chosen, to inspect the acco'ts of the Debts what should be allowed, and to give an acc't to the Assessor how big the Rate should be made, and of the Species and Prices the same should be paid in; and the same to be paid by the first Day of February next ensuing—also, Samuel Baldwin and Judah Penington are chosen Fence Viewers, for the Year ensuing.

TOWN MEETING, *March* 8th, 1719-20—John Cooper and Jonathan Crane, were chosen Freeholders for the ensuing Year. Joseph Crane, Caleb Ward, Henry Lyon and Samuel Harrison, Jun'r, Surveyors of Highways. Joseph Peck and Nathan'l Baldwin, Overseers of the Poor—David Ogden, Assessor, and Samuel Cooper, Collector of the provincial Tax.

March 14th, 1721—At a TOWN MEETING by Virtue of an Act of Assembly, were chosen for Overseers of the Poor for the Year ensuing, Thomas Longworth and Thomas Richards—Surveyors of the Highways, Thomas Davis, Sam'l Alling, Jonathan Sayer and Sam'l Cooper—Assessor, John Baldwin, Jun'r—Collector, Capt. John Morris—Freeholders, Joseph Crane and David Ogden —Capt. Ogden and Sam'l Cooper were chosen Freeholders, and John Baldwin, Assessor. Mr. Jonathan Crane, Collector—Daniel Dod, Samuel Pierson, Joseph Harrison and Joseph Riggs, Surveyors—Joseph Ball and Israel Candfield, Overseers of the Poor.

At the same Meeting it was agreed by vote, that the Trustees or the major Part of them should have Power with Capt. Samuel Harrison and Lieut. Sam'l Dod, to let out the Common Land or any Part thereof to dig for Mines, to such Person and on such Terms as they shall agree upon. Isaac Lyon, Pounder—the old Fence Viewers stand—Joseph Bond, Clerk for keeping the Book for Strays.

TOWN MEETING, *March* 8th, 1725—Was chosen, John Cooper, Assessor, and Jonathan Crane, Collector for the provincial tax—John Crane and Elihu Crane, Overseers of the Poor—Mr. Sam'l Farrand, Joseph Pruden, Stephen Brown, and Joseph Tutle, Surveyors of Highways, and John Crane, Sheep Master.

TOWN MEETING, *November* 7th, 1726—John Baldwin, Jun'r, and John Crane, Jun'r, were chosen Assessors and Rate makers for Mr. Webb's Salary for that Year ensuing—and Joseph Pruden and Epenetus Beach, Collectors.

TOWN MEETING, *March* 11th, 1728-29—John Crane, Jun'r, was chosen Assessor, and Elihu Crane, Collector—Capt. David Ogden and Lieut. Sam'l Cooper, Freeholders—Jonathan Pierson, Joseph Johnson, Jun'r, Joseph Rogers, and Thomas Richards, Surveyors of the Highways—Joseph Tutle, Clerk for entering of Strays—Eliphalet Johnson and Jonathan Ward, Overseers of the Poor.

TOWN MEETING, *March* 10th, 1729-30—Capt. David Ogden was chosen Assessor, and Sam'l Alling, Collector. Capt. David Ogden and Lieut. Sam'l Cooper, Freeholders. Jonathan Pierson, Thomas Richards, John Crane, Jun'r, and Thomas Curry, Surveyors of the Highways. Eliphalet Johnson, Jun'r, and Jonathan Ward, Overseers of the Poor. Joseph Bond, Clerk of Strays. Capt. Ogden, Sam'l Cooper, Nathaniel Johnson, Israel Canfield, Jonathan Pierson and Edward Riggs, Fence Viewers. John Keney [Kinney], Pounder.

TOWN MEETING, *November* 3rd, 1730—John Baldwin and John Crane were chosen Assessors, and Thomas Serjeant and Nath'l Camp, Collectors of Mr. Webb's Rate for the ensuing Year.

TOWN MEETING, *March* 9th, 1730-1—By virtue of an Act of Assembly, the several Officers were chosen, (viz): John Baldwin, Assessor, and James Wheeler, Collector. Eliphalet Johnson, Jun'r, John Crane, Joseph Harrison and Joseph Riggs, Surveyors of Highways. Joseph Bruen and Joseph Tutle, Overseers of the Poor. Capt. David Ogden and Lieut. Sam'l Cooper, Freeholders. Joseph Bond, Clerk of Strays. Isaac Lyon, Pounder. Capt. Ogden, Lieut. Cooper, Jonathan Pierson, Nath'l Camp, Hugh Roberts and Joseph Tutle, Fence Viewers.

TOWN MEETING, *November* 1st, 1731—John Baldwin and John Crane were chosen Assessors, and Thomas Sargeant and Israel Canfield, Collectors of Mr. Webb's Rate for the ensuing Year.

TOWN MEETING, *March* 14th, 1731-2—The Persons hereafter named were chosen by vote, Capt. David Ogden and Lieut. Sam'l Cooper, Freeholders. John Baldwin, Assessor for the provincial tax. Mr. Jonathan Crane, Collector. Daniel Dod, Sam'l Pierson, Joseph Harrison, and Joseph Riggs, Surveyors. Joseph

Ball and Israel Canfield, Overseers of the Poor. Isaac Lyon, Pounder—the old Fence viewers stand—Joseph Bond, Clerk of Strays.

The same Day was a Meeting Ordered by the Trustees by Virtue of the Town Pattent; at the said Meeting it was agreed on by a vote, that the Trustees or the major part of them shall have full Power with Capt Samuel Harrison and Lieut. Daniel Dod, to let out the Common or Town's Land or any Part thereof to dig for Mines, to such Person and on such Terms as they shall agree upon.

TOWN MEETING, *November* 6th, 1732—John Baldwin and John Crane were chosen Assessors for Mr. Webb's Rate, and Benjamin Co and Joseph Riggs, Collectors, for the ensuing Year.

TOWN MEETING, *March* 13th, 1732–3—At which were chosen the several Officers following—Timothy Tutle, Assessor, and Mr. Jonathan Crane, Collector, Capt. David Ogden and Lieut. Sam'l Cooper, Freeholders. Joseph Harrison, Joseph Riggs, John Ogden, Jun'r, and Benjamin Co, Surveyors of the Highways. Joseph Bond, Bookeeper for the Strays. Nath'l Johnson and Thomas Serjeant, Overseers of the Poor. Capt. Ogden, Sam'l Cooper, Joseph Tuttle, Israel Canfield, Capt. Wheeler and John Johnson, Fence Viewers for the common Line fence in the Neck —and Isaac Lyon, Pounder.

TOWN MEETING, *November* 5th, 1733—John Crane and Joseph Canfield were chosen Assessors, and Stephen Baldwin and Obadiah Bruen were chosen Collectors, of Mr. Webb's Rate for the ensuing Year.

TOWN MEETING, *November* 4th, 1734—John Crane and Benjamin Canfield, were chosen Assessors for Mr. Webb's Rate for the ensuing Year, and John Ogden, Jun'r, and John Ward, Collectors.

TOWN MEETING, *March* 11th, 1734–5—Pursuant to the Act of Assembly, the several Officers hereafter named were chosen by vote, (viz): John Crane, Assessor, Mr. Jonathan Crane, Collector. Eliphalet Johnson, Jun'r, and John Ogden, Jun'r, Freeholders. John Ogden, Jun'r, Benjamin Co, John Johnson and David Pierson, Surveyors of Highways. John Cooper, Clerk for Strays. Silas Halsey and Daniel Tichenor, Overseers of the Poor. Israel Canfield, Nath'l Camp, Robert Crane and Moses Ball, Fence viewers for the Com'on Line. Nathaniel Ward and Nathaniel Andress, Pounders. John Crane, Daniel Harrison, Nathaniel

Andress and Joseph Riggs chosen, to take Care for the ringing the Bell, sweeping the Meeting House, and to take Care of the Disorders among Persons on the Lords Day, and to use all lawfull Endeavors to suppress the same.

TOWN MEETING, *December* 18th, 1735—The Town being assembled together, there was a vote put, whether the Inhabitants were willing that the Common Land should be leased out to any Person, for to search and dig for Mines, which was carryed in the affirmative and not one Person opposing it.

2ndly, There was also another vote put, who they would chuse to act in that Affair and to lease Out the Town's Land—which with one Voice they made Choice of the Trustees of the said Town and the Pattentees of the Commonage, or the major Part of them.

TOWN MEETING, *March* 9th, 1735-6—Pursuant to an Act of Assembly, the several Persons were chosen, (viz): Benjamin Canfield, Assessor, and Mr. Jonathan Crane, Collector. Eliphalet Johnson, Jun'r, and John Ogden, Jun'r, Freeholders. Daniel Tichenor and Obadiah Bruen, Overseers of the Poor. George Harrison, Christopher Wood, Robert Crane and Sam'l Ward, Jun'r, Surveyors. John Cooper, Book Keeper for Strays. Nathaniel Andress, Thomas Sargeant and Thomas Winter, Pounders. Mr. Webb to have the use of Burying place for Pasture this present Year—and it was then offered to the Persons disatisfied with the Persons chosen before to regulate the Common Line Fence, to leave the Matter to Persons wholly unconcerned.

TOWN MEETING, *November*, 1736—John Crane and Benjamin Canfield are chosen Assessors, and Stephen Baldwin and Obadiah Bruen, Collectors for Mr. Webb's Rate for the ensuing Year. The Committee Chosen to agree with Mr. Burr was Mr. Jonathan Crane, Mr. Samuel Farrand, Mr. James Nutman, Mr. Jonathan Pierson, Mr. John Crane and John Cooper.

TOWN MEETING, *December* 21st, 1736—It was then put to vote, whether the Town desired Mr. Aaron Burr should have a Call, for further Improvement in the Work of the Ministry among us, as a Candidate for further Trial; which was carried in the affirmative, nemine contradicente.

It was also voted, whether Mr. Webb should be improved with Mr. Burr, untill the End of the Year now begun should be ended, which was carried in the affirmative; and it was left to the Committee above named to agree what Sum should be raised for Mr. Webb, for the Remainder of the Time to the expiration of the said Year on the 4th Day of January: the Committee agreed that there should be the sum of £80 raised for Mr. Webb's Salary, for the Year now running, on Condition that if any Person or Persons should find Fault and not consenting to pay the same, then Mr. Webb to deduct one Sixth Part of this Rate and allow the same out of it.

On the 30th Day of December, 1736—The Committee treated with Mr. Aaron Burr, for farther Improvement among us in the work of the Ministry as a Candidate, and agreed with him for One Year to commence from the 10th Day of January next, for which service he is to have the sum of £60.

TOWN MEETING, *March* 8th, 1736-7—Pursuant to an Act of Assembly, the several Persons was chosen, (viz): Benjamin Canfield, Assessor. Mr. Jonathan Crane, Collector. Eliphalet Johnson, Jun'r, and John Ogden, Jun'r, Freeholders. Nath'l Johnson, Robert Crane, Samuel Plum and Samuel Ward, Jun'r, Surveyors of Highways. Moses Ball and Joseph Riggs, Overseers of the Poor. John Crane to record Strays.

At the same time the feed [of] the burying Place was sold to James Banks, for the insuing Year for 40s. to be paid to the support of the Poor, except so much as is necessary to repair the Fence of s'd burying Place.

TOWN MEETING, *March* 6th, 1737-8—John Crane and Benjamin Canfield was chosen Assessors, and Benj'n Co. and Daniel Harrison, Jun'r, Collectors of Mr. Aaron Burr's Rate for the ensuing Year.

TOWN MEETING, *March* 14th, 1737-8—Pursuant to an Act of Assembly, the several Persons were chosen, (viz): Joseph Riggs, Assessor, Jonathan Crane, Collector of the Cuntry Rate. Eliphalet Johnson, Jun'r, and John Ogden, Jun'r, Freeholders. John Johnson, Sam'l Ward Jun'r, Amos Williams Jun'r, and John Dod, Surveyors of Highways. Daniel Harrison and Daniel Pierson, Overseers of the Poor. John Crane, to record Strays. Timothy Crane and Caleb Wheeler, Pounders for the Great Neck, and John Lyon for the Little Neck. Nathaniel Anderson, Pound Keeper.

At the same Meeting, Samuel Alling and John Crane was appointed to order the ringing of the Bell and Sweeping the Meeting House, also to take Care of the burying Yard fence—it was also voted that Hanah Shingelton should sweep the Meeting House, provided she sweeps it clean and for the same Wages as it was done for last Year. The feed of the burying Place was sold to Isaac Lyon for the ensuing Year, for the sum of £2 11s. 8d., to be put to the same Use as it was last Year.

At the same Time Mr. Jonathan Crane, Nathaniel Johnson, John Johnson, Isaac Lyon, Zopher Lyon, Joseph Lyon, and Joseph Robards, petitioned for Liberty to build a Hovel near the Meeting House, to shelter Horses, and Liberty was granted by Vote. It was also Voted, the Regulators of the Common Line Fence elected for the last Year, be continued Regulators thereof for the ensuing Year. Voted also, that Joseph Bonnel, Thomas Price, Matthias Metfield, Esq'r., shall determine and ascertain to the above Regulators, what Part and how much shall be by them deemed and regulated as Common Line fence; and that their Regulation so made, shall be binding and obligatory to all Persons concerned in Interest in Lands contained within the Neck or Necks of Land included within the Common Line, untill it shall be otherwise determined by another Vote of sd. Town of New Ark.

Town Meeting, *March* 12th, 1738-9—Thomas Longworth and John Crane were chosen Assessors, and Jonathan Sergeant and Sam'l Parkhurst, Collectors of Mr. Burr's Rate for the ensuing Year.

Town Meeting, *March* 13th, 1738-9—Pursuant to an Act of Assembly, the several Persons were chosen, (viz): John Crane, Assessor, and Samuel Alling, Collector. John Low and Nathaniel Johnson, Freeholders. Joseph Day, David Williams, Daniel Harrison and Daniel Pierson, Surveyors of Highways. Nathaniel Anderson, Josiah Gilbert, Samuel Freeman and John Dod, Overseers of the Poor. Thomas Longworth, Clerk for recording of Strays. The same Time, the feed of the burying Place was sold to Nathaniel Anderson, for the ensuing Year for 28s.

At a Town Meeting *October* 24th, 1739—Jonathan Crane Esq'r., Col'l Josiah Ogden, and Samuel Farrand Esq'r., were chosen a Committee, to treat with the People of Elizabeth Town about settling a Line between the two Towns.

Town Meeting, *March* 3d, 1739-40—Jonathan Crane and John Crane were chosen Assessors, and Daniel Tichenor and Stephen Baldwin, Collectors of Mr. Burr's rate for the Ensuing Year.

Town Meeting, *March* 11th, 1739-40—Pursuant to an Act of Assembly, the several Persons were chosen, (Viz): Samuel Dod, Assessor. Samuel Farrand, Esq'r., Collector. George Harrison and Nathaniel Camp, Freeholders. Nathaniel Baldwin, David Williams, Daniel Harrison, and Zopher Lyon, Surveyors of Highways. Josiah Gilbert and Nathaniel Anderson, Overseers of the Poor—and Samuel Alling, Clerk to record Strays.

At the same Meeting, Nathaniel Wheeler, Robert Crane, John Johnson, and David Bruen, were chosen to be viewers of the Common Line fence—and Timothy Crane and Jonas Crane, Pounders. Also, the feed of the burying yard was sold to Nathaniel Anderson, for £2 1s. 2d.

TOWN MEETING, *March* 10th, 1740-1—Pursuant to an Act of Assembly, Doct'r William Turner was chosen Assessor, and Samuel Farrand Esq'r., Collector for the ensuing Year. John Johnson Jun'r, David Bruen, Josiah Beech and Samuel Parkust, Surveyors of Highways. Nathaniel Anderson and Isaac Lyon, Overseers of the Poor. John Crane Clerk for recording estrays. Nathaniel Wheeler and Samuel Alling, Sheep Masters. At the same Time, the feed of the burying Place was Sold to Nath'l Anderson for £2 2s. 2d.

TOWN MEETING, *March* 3d, 1740-1—Jonathan Crane and John Crane were chosen Assessors, and James Wheeler and Samuel Alling, Collectors of Mr. Burr's Rate for the ensuing Year.

TOWN MEETING, *March* 24th, 1740-1—William Turner was chosen Assessor, in Order to make a Rate for the Poor in Newark for the Ensuing Year.

TOWN MEETING, *March* 9th, 1741-2—pursuant to an Act of Assembly, Amos Williams Jun'r was chosen Assessor, and Sam'l Alling, Collector, for the ensuing Year. Uzal Ogden and Thomas Longworth, Freeholders. Joseph Pierson, Ryneer Van Geese, Emanuel Cocker, and John Johnson Jun'r, Surveyors of the Highways. John Crane, recorder of Strays—and Isaac Lyon and David Ogden Jun'r, Overseers of the Poor. At the same Time, the burying Yard was sold to Doct'r William Turner for the Year ensuing, for £1 18s. 6d.

TOWN MEETING, *March* 8th, 1742-3—Pursuant to an Act of Assembly, Joseph Robards was chosen Assessor, and Joseph Riggs, Jun'r, Collector for the ensuing Year. George Harrison and Nathaniel Camp, were chosen Freeholders. Joseph Pierson, Ryncer Vangessee, Silas Halsey and Joseph Camp, Surveyors of Highways. Jonathan Peirson and Jonathan Sargeant, Overseers of the Poor—and Joseph Robards, Assessor of the Poor's Rate. and John Crane, Clerk to record Strays. At the same Time it was voted, that any Person should be fined 20s. one half to the Complainer and the other half for the Use of the Poor—that cuts any Tree or Trees, Spires or Hoop-Poles upon any Part of the Parsonage, except so much as is necessary for diging or carrying of any Stones any Person may want for building or other Uses. Nathaniel Wheeler, Nathaniel Johnson and Nathaniel Camp, were chosen to run out the Parsonage Meadow, and to prosecute Trespassers on the same in the Trustees Name. The feed of the burying yard was sold to Isaac Lyon, for 22s.

TOWN MEETING, *March* 7th, 1742-3—Jonathan Crane and Samuel Farrand were chosen Assessors, and David Crane and Nathaniel Chandler, Collectors of Mr. Burr's Rate.

TOWN MEETING, *March* 11th, 1743-4—Pursuant to an Act of Assembly, Joseph Robards was chosen Assessor of all Rates, and Joseph Riggs, Collector for the ensuing Year. George Harrison and Nathaniel Camp, Freeholders. Nathaniel Harrison, John Cundit, Epenetus Beach and Thomas Eagles, Surveyors of Highways. Jonathan Pierson and Jonathan Sergeant, Overseers of the Poor. Also Nathaniel Crane and Gideon Van Winkle—and John Crane, Clerk to record Strays—at the same time it was agreed, that the Inhabitants of Second River and the Body of the Town of Newark should act in all affairs relating to the Poor, separately and severally by themselves, and that all Fines and Assessments shall be collected for the Use of each Division where they are collected: and to prevent Disputes about which shall be esteemed Inhabitants of Second River, and which of the Body of Newark, the Division was agreed to be as followeth, (viz): Beginning at Passaick River, at the Gulley near the House of Doct'r Pigot, thence North West to Second River, thence up the same to the Saw Mill belonging to George Harrison, thence a direct Line to the North East Corner of the Plantation of Stephen Morris, thence to the Notch in the Mountain leaving William Crane's House to the Southward, thence on a direct line to Stephen Van siles, thence Westwardly to Passaick River leaving said Van siles Bars and Abraham Francisco's to the Northward of s'd Line: and it was agreed, that all on the Northward of s'd Lines should be esteemed Inhabitants of Second River, and all on the Southward of the Body of Newark, excepting Levi Vincent, Johanes Kiper and his Son Thomas Cadmus. John Low desired, that himself and his Father might be reconed or esteemed Inhabitants of Second River, since they belong to that Society.

TOWN MEETING, *March* 5th, 1743-4—John Crane and Jonas Crane, were chosen Assessors of Mr. Burr's Rate—and Silas Halsey and Thomas Boes, Collectors.

TOWN MEETING, *March* 12th, 1744-5—Pursuant to an Act of Assembly, Elijah Crane was chosen Assessor of the County and Poor Rates. Joseph Riggs, Collector. Nathaniel Camp and Isaac Lyon, Freeholders. Samuel Huntington and Capt. John Johnson, Overseers of the Poor. Samuel Plum, Daniel Harrison, John Cundit and Nathaniel Harrison, Surveyors of Highways. John Crane, Clerk for Strays. Amos Robards, John Crane, John Johnson, John Cundit and Jonathan Sergeant, a Committee to treat with Elizabeth Town about the Difference between Newark and s'd Elizabeth Town. Same Time, the feed of the burying yard was sold to Joseph Riggs for 24s. 9d.

TOWN MEETING, *March* 11th, 1745-6—pursuant to an Act of Assembly, Jonathan Day was chosen Assessor for County, Poor, and Taverns Rates. Stephen Baldwin, Collector. Nathaniel Camp and John Cundit, Freeholders. David Harrison, Jonathan Sergeant, Ebenezer Hedden and Timothy Ball, Surveyors of Highways. Samuel Huntington, John Johnson Jun'r and Gideon Van Winkle, Overseers of the Poor. John Crane, Clerk for Strays. Samuel Alling, Sheep Master. Feed of the burying Yard sold to Eliphalet Johnson Esq'r for 26s. John Crane and Samuel Alling to repair the fence of the burying Yard. At the same Meeting it was voted, that any Person or Persons cutting Wood or Timber on the Parsonage, within the space of Seven Years from this Time, shall forfeit 10s. for each offence—and David Crane, Emanuel Cocker and Samuel Plum to prosecute such offenders.

TOWN MEETING, *March* 3d, 1745-6—Deacon Samuel Alling and Jonathan Sergeant were chosen Assessors, and Elijah Baldwin and Nehemiah Baldwin, Collectors of Mr. Burr's Rate for the Year 1746.

TOWN MEETING, *March* 2nd, 1746-7—John Crane and Samuel Alling were chosen Assessors, and Caleb Sayr and Zopher Beach, Collectors of Mr. Burr's Rate.

At a TOWN MEETING, *March* 10th, 1746-7—Pursuant to an Act of Assembly, Ebenezer Lamson was chosen Assessor, and Samuel Alling, Collector for the Town, also for the Poor's Rate. Nathaniel Camp and John Cundit, Freeholders. Benjamin Co and Emanuel Cocker, Overseers of the Poor. James Nicholson, Joseph Hedden, Jonathan Tichenor and Samuel Beach, Surveyors of Highways. John Crane, Book-keeper for Stray Creatures. Abraham Cadmus, Overseer of the Poor for Second River. It was also unanimously voted, that whoever shall cut any Wood or Timber on any of the Land called the Parsonage Land, shall forfeit for every Cart-load 10s.—and so in Proportion for a greater or lesser Quantity—for the Use of the Poor—also to forfeit the Wood and Timber, to be fetched away by any Person for the Use of the Poor—the Person carting the Wood or Timber to be paid by the Overseer of the Poor. It was also voted the said Lands should remain unmanured, and let the wood stand, untill it is otherwise altered by a Town Vote. Joseph Peck, Josiah Linsley, Emanuel Cocker, David Crane, Samuel Plum and David Bruen were chosen, to take Care of the Parsonage Lands and prosecute Offenders. It was voted that there should be a Pound made on the West side of the School house, joining to the Land of Abiel Canfield dec'd. The feed of the burying Yard was hired to Capt. Cocker, for 26s.

At a TOWN MEETING, *March* 8th, 1747-8—Pursuant to an Act of Assembly, Daniel Lamson was chosen Assessor, both for the Town and Poor's Rate. Samuel Alling, Collector. Joseph Day and George Harrison, Freeholders. Joseph Hedden, James Nicholson, Daniel Harrison, and John Roberts, Surveyors of Highways. Isaac Lyon and James Nicolson. Overseers of the Poor—also Abraham Cadmus, Overseer of the Poor for Second River. John Crane, Clerk for Strays. Emanuel Cocker, Caleb Sayre, Timothy Pierson, and William Wheaton, Pounders. Jonathan Sergeant, Regulator of the Common Line fence, in the Place and Stead of Samuel Plum. The feed of the burying Yard was to Joseph Riggs, for 20s.

March 6th, 1748-9—John Crane and Samuel Alling were chosen Assessors of Mr. Burr's Rate, and John Young and Thomas Canfield, Collectors of the same.

TOWN MEETING, *March* 14th, 1748-9—Pursuant to an Act of Assembly, Nathaniel Farrand was chosen Assessor of the County and Poor's Rates. David Ogden, Collector. George Harrison and Joseph Day, Freeholders. Isaac Lyon and Nathaniel Camp, Overseers of the Poor—also Garrabrant Garrabrants for Second River. John Cundet, David Williams, Hugh Roberts and Ephraim Wheeler, Surveyors of Highways. John Crane, Clerk for Strays. The same Time Samuel Plum, John Plum, Samuel Ball and Thomas Canfield were chosen Pounders, for the ensuing Year. It was voted, that Samuel Alling should have Liberty to feed the burying Yard with Sheep and Calves the Year ensuing, he taking Care of the Repair of the Fence.

TOWN MEETING, *March* 5th, 1740—Nathaniel Chandler and Elijah Baldwin, Assessors, and Nathaniel Baldwin and Obadiah Bruen, Collectors of Mr. Burr's Rate.

TOWN MEETING, pursuant to an Act of Assembly, *March*

13th, 1749–50—Nathaniel Farrand was chosen Assessor of the County and Poor's Rates. David Ogden, Jun'r, Collector. George Harrison and Joseph Day, Freeholders. Eleazer Bruen, Abner Ward, Ebenezer Farrand and Israel Baldwin, Surveyors of Highways. David Ogden, Esq'r, and Isaac Lyon and Garrabrant Garrabrants, Overseers of the Poor. John Crane, Clerk for Strays for the ensuing Year. The same Time, Nathaniel Johnson, David Ogden, Jun'r, Nathaniel Camp, Daniel Tichenor, John Crane and Capt. Nathaniel Wheeler, a Committee, to manage the affair with Hugh Robarts relating to the Bounds of the Parsonage Meadow. The vote was renewed for preserving the Wood on the Parsonage Land, which was passed March 10th, 1746–7, and Josiah Ward, Samuel Plum, Josiah Linsly, Joseph Peck, John Crane, James Banks and William Turner, to take Care of said wood and prosecute Offenders.

Whereas, great Strifes and Contentions have been had, moved and stirred up between Hugh Robarts and John Robarts of Newark in the County of Essex and Province of New Jersey, and the Inhabitants of Newark afs'd concerning the Bounds of the Meadow of the said Hugh and John Robarts, and the Meadow called the Parsonage Meadow near the Mouth of Bound Creek. And Whereas, by a Vote at a Town Meeting in Newark the 13th day of March last past Capt. Nath'l Wheeler, Nathaniel Camp and Daniel Tichenor were chosen a Committee, to manage the affair relating to said Difference—And We, John Stites, Esqr. and John Halsted, Esqr.—and John Chandler, being indifferently chosen by the said Parties in Difference as Arbitrators, to settle, determine, and final End to make of said Difference concerning the Premises afs'd. We the said Arbitrators, having heard and duly considered the several Proofs and Allegations relating to the s'd Differences do order and determine, that the Bounds between the Meadow of the said Hugh and John Robarts and the Meadow called the Parsonage shall be as followeth, (viz): Beginning at a Stake standing at the Head of a small Branch of Tide Pond Creek so called, Nine Chains and five Links on a North Twenty two Degrees and fifteen minutes West course from the Westward side of the Mouth of said Creek at Bound Creek—And from the Stake running North Sixty five Degrees and Thirty Minutes Twelve Chains and fifty Seven Links, to a Stake standing by a Branch of Oyster Creek—And from thence along the several Courses of said Branch to said Oyster Creek—As Witness our Hands this Twenty Seventh Day of September Anno Dom. One Thousand Seven Hundred and fifty.

JOHN STITES,
JOHN HALSTEAD,
JOHN CHANDLER.

A True Copy taken by me,
JON'N SERGEANT, Clerk.

TOWN MEETING, Pursuant to Act of Assembly, *March* 12th, 1750-1—Nathaniel Farrand was chosen Assessor, of the County and Poor's Rates—Uzal Ogden, Collector. Nathaniel Camp and Nathaniel Harrison, Freeholders. Isreal Baldwin, John Sydenham, Isaac Pierson and Thomas Brown, Surveyors of Highways. Obadiah Bruen, John Alling, George Harrison and Ary King, Overseers of the Poor—and John Crane, Clerk for Strays for the ensuing Year. The feed of the burying Yard was sold to Doct'r Turner, for £1 0s. 6d.

March 4th, 1750-1—Elijah Baldwin and Eleazer Baldwin were chosen Assessors, and John Alling and Thomas Brown Collectors of Mr. Burr's Rate.

TOWN MEETING, Pursuant to an Act of Assembly, *March* 10th, 1752—Nathaniel Farrand was chosen Assessor for the County and Poor's Rate. Uzal Ogden, Collector. Nathaniel Camp and Nathaniel Harrison, Freeholders. Elijah Baldwin, Thomas Brown, Ezekiel Ball and Nehemiah Hedden, Surveyors of Highways. Joseph Camp, John Cundet, and Ary King, Overseers of the Poor—and John Crane, Clerk for Strays for the ensuing Year. The feed of the burying Yard was sold to Nathaniel Anderson, for Twelve Shillings. It was voted that Dogs might be killed, if found from Home out of Sight of the Person who has the Care of such Dog or Dogs.

TOWN MEETING, *March* 13th, 1753—Pursuant to an Act of Assembly, Nathaniel Farrand was chosen Assessor for County and Poor's Rate. Uzal Ogden, Collector. Nathaniel Camp and Nathaniel Harrison, Freeholders. Ezekiel Ball, Nehemiah Hedden, Daniel Tichenor and David Crane, Jun'r, Surveyors of Highways. Josiah Beech, Elijah Crane, Timothy Ball, William Crane and Ary King, Overseers of the Poor—and John Crane, Clerk for Strays for the ensuing Year. At the same Meeting, Joseph Johnson, Joseph Riggs, and Nath'l Camp were chosen to take Care about the burying Yard fence, and to endeavor to get Money subscribed for building a Pail Fence. The Day before this Meeting, Nathaniel Farrand and Elijah Crane were chosen Assessors, and Samuel Alling and Nathaniel Johnson, Collectors of Mr. Burr's Rate.

March * * * 1754—Joseph Riggs and Nehemiah Baldwin were chosen Assessors and * * * * * * and Samuel Huntington Collectors of Mr. Burr's Rate.

March 12th, 1754—At a TOWN MEETING pursuant to an Act of Assembly, John Dod the 3rd was chosen Assessor of both

County and Poor's Rates, and John Crane, Collector. David Rogers, Timothy Crane, Ezekiel Crane and Jonathan Tompkins, Surveyors of the Highways. Elijah Crane, Josiah Beach, Timothy Ball, William Crane and Ary King, Overseers of the Poor. John Crane, Clerk for Strays. Jonathan Sergeant, Town Clerk —and for Overseers of the Highways Caleb Wheeler, David Bruen, Joseph Camp, Isaac Pierson, William Gray, Jonas Ball, Joseph Riggs, Jun'r, Joseph Farrand, Noah Crane, Thomas Lyon, Sen'r, Samuel Jones, Samuel Pierson, Jun'r, Daniel Cundict—And Nathaniel Camp, Joseph Day, John Cundict and Nathaniel Harrison a Committee, to agree with Elizabeth Town about Settling a Line between the two Towns. It was voted, that it shall be the same Forfeiture of Twenty Shillings for every Tree that is cut on the Parsonage, half to the Complainer as the Act of the Assembly is in other Cases, the other half of the Money to the Poor. Also, the Parsonage Meadow was rented to Jonathan Crawford, for 46s, to be paid to John Ogden, Esqr.

March 3rd, 1755—Elijah Baldwin and Samuel Crane were chosen Assessors, and Samuel Parkhurst and Samuel Morris, Collectors of Mr. Burr's Rate for the Year ensuing.

March 11th, 1755—At a TOWN MEETING, pursuant to Act of Assembly, the following Officers were chosen, (viz): John Dod the 3rd, Assessor of all Rates, and John Crane, Collector. Nath'l Camp and Nathaniel Harrison, Freeholders. John Gildersleve, John Vincent, Isaac Pierson and Samuel Ball, Surveyors of Highways. Josiah Beech, Elijah Crane, Timothy Ball, William Crane and Ary King, Overseers of the Poor. John Crane, Clerk for Stray Creatures. Daniel Tichenor, Hendrick Coeyman, Jacobus Kidney, Simeon Riggs, John King, John Tichenor, Joseph Hedden, Nathaniel Ball, John Van Winkle, Jun'r, Zebulon Ward, Daniel Lamson, David Crane, Jun'r, Nath'l Ward, David Ward, Jun'r, Peter Pruden, William Williamson, Levi Vincent, Matt. Phillips and Joseph Mun, Overseers of the Highways. Feed of the burying Place sold to Joseph Riggs, for 15s. 3d.

March 9th, 1756—At a TOWN MEETING pursuant to Act of Assembly, the following Officers were chosen, (viz): John Dod 3rd, Assessor of all Rates. John Crane, Collector. Nath'l Camp and Nathaniel Harrison, Freeholders. David Johnson, Isaac Pierson, Samuel Ball and Peter Pruden, Surveyors of Highways. Timothy Ball, William Crane, Elijah Crane, Josiah Beech, Ary King and Peter Degarmo, Overseers of the Poor. John Crane, Clerk for Strays. Peter Jacobus, Sanders Cockefair, Jun'r, Cobus Vandike, Johanes Queeman, Jun'r, Jonathan Shores, Isaac Ball,

Abel Ward, Elihu Crane, Jedidiah Crane, Ebenezer Canfield, John Lyon, Samuel Crowell, John Young, Jonas Hinman, Helmegh Yourolman, Robert Ward, Daniel Dod, Jun'r, Caleb Brown, Nathaniel Williams, Jun'r, Zopher Bedford and Thomas Gold, Overseers of Highways. Isaac Lyon, Samuel Plum, Jonathan Sergeant, James Nuttman, David Williams, and Nathaniel Wheeler a Committee, to inspect Encroachment on the Parsonage. The above Time the Feed of the burying Place sold to Eliphalet Johnson, Esqr., for 15s. 6. The Parsonage Meadow was sold for the Year ensuing to Nathaniel Camp, for £2 7s., to be divided between the 3 Ministers, (viz): 2 in the Town, and one at the Mountain.

March 8th, 1757—At a Town Meeting pursuant to an Act of Assembly, John Dod 3rd, was chosen Assessor, both for County and Poor's Rates. Elijah Crane, Collector, and also Clerk for Strays. John Crane and Joseph Camp, Freeholders. David Johnson, Samuel Ball, Isaac Pierson and Peter Pruden, Surveyors of Highways. Samuel Plum, Samuel Huntington, Joseph Riggs, Jun'r, Nathaniel Ogden, Jacobus Kidney, and John Vincent, Overseers of the Poor. Amos Robards, Samuel Jones, Peter Bestedy, Daniel Deen, Ezekiel Johnson, Ebenezer Hedden, Jacob Spier, Peter Garrebrant, Nathaniel Wheeler, Jun'r, Jabez Harrison, Samuel Medlis, Caleb Harrison, Joseph Crane, Jun'r, Jedediah Crane, Abraham Urianson Vanriper, Casparus Van Winkle, Helmegh Youralman, Joshua Burwell, and Abraham Riker, Jun'r, Overseers of Highways. At the same Time the Parsonage Meadow was hired for the ensuing Year to * * * * * * for * * *.

Also the feed of the burying Yard to Josiah Crane, for 21s.

At a Town Meeting, *March* 14th, 1758—John Dod 3rd, was chosen Assessor of all Rates, both for County and Poor. Elijah Crane Collector, and also Clerk for Strays. John Crane and Joseph Camp, Freeholders. Garrebrant Garrebrantson, Helmegh Jerolman, Stephen Harrison, Jun'r, and David Peck, Surveyors of Highways. Samuel Plum, Elijah Baldwin, Alexander Cockefare, Jun'r, Jacobus Kidney, Joseph Harrison and John Gildersleeve, Overseers of the Poor. Samuel Jones, John Robinson, Samuel Morris, Stephen Crane, Joseph Crane, John Spier, Cornelius Cadmus, Abraham Vangeson 3rd, David Beech, Hendrick Spier, Benjamin Baldwin, Peter Garrabrants, Jonathan Harrison, Elijah Bruen, Ezekiel Tichenor and Eliakim Crane, Overseers of Highways. At the same time Capt. Joseph Johnson, and John Crane were chosen, to enquire after and Collect the Monies which the burying Yard and the Parsonage Meadow were hired for before, and for the Year ensuing. The feed of the burying Yard was sold, for 16s. 5d. for the Year ensuing to Elijah Baldwin.

Also, the Parsonage Meadow was hired to Caleb Wheeler, for £2 5s.

1759—*March* 13th—A Town Meeting was held at the Court house in Newark, the following Officers was then chosen for the ensuing Year—John Ogden Esq'r., Moderator. Elijah Crane, Town Clerk, and also Clerk for the Strays. John Crane and Joseph Camp, Freeholders. John Treat Crane, Benjamin Johnson, Ezekiel Johnson and Jedediah Crane, Surveyors of the Highways. Samuel Plum, Elijah Baldwin, David Williams, and Bethuel Pierson, Overseers of the Poor. Abraham Van Riper and Sanders Cockefair Jun'r., Assistants at Second River. John Dod, 3rd Assessor. Elijah Crane, Collector. Joseph Johnson Esq. and John Crane, Collectors for the Parsonage and the burying Yard. Capt. Joseph Riggs, Nathaniel Harrison, Lieut't Nathaniel Camp, John Crane and Deacon Peck a Committee, to settle a Line in the Parsonage Land with John Ogden Esq'r. by his Land. Overseers of the Highway Samuel Plum, David Brown, Matthew Winne, Isaac Poulesson, Hendrick Van Gieson, Samuel Whittimore, Jedidiah Hedden, John Hedden, Jun'r, Nathan Baldwin, James Nesbit, Jonathan Squire, Aaron Baldwin, Samuel Nuttman, Caleb Davis, Joseph Mun, Levi Vincent, John Muchmore, John Cockefair, Jeremiah Martin, John Corter, Solomon Crane and Samuel Harrison Jun'r. The Parsonage Meadow was let for One Year to Elijah Bruen, for £3. Also, the burying Yard was let to John Vander Pool, for 20s. 6d. drawn out and given to S'd Collectors.

March 12th, 1760—At a Town Meeting held at the Court house in Newark, the following Officers were chosen for the ensuing Year, (Viz): Joseph Camp, Esq'r, Moderator. Samuel Hayes, Town Clerk. Nathaniel Farrand, Assessor. Solomon Davis, Collector, and Book-keeper for Strays. John Crane and Joseph Camp, Freeholders. Ebenezer Lindsly, David Harrison, Isaac Ball and Joseph Baldwin Jun'r, Surveyors of the Highway. Samuel Plum, Elijah Baldwin, Abraham Van Ryper and David Williams, Overseers of the Poor. Overseers of the Highway, Samuel Plum, Isaac Myer, Solomon Davis, Daniel Tichenor Jun'r, Phillip Courtland, John Kingsland, Ezekiel Ball, Eleazer Hedden, Samuel Freeman Jun'r, Caleb Harrison, Peter Garrabrant, Enoch Powlson, Samuel Jones, Jonathan Squire, Zebulon Ward, Ebenezer Ward, William Crane and Isaac Ryker Jun'r.

Item, it was voted to take a Girl of Theophilus Burwells, now with Samuel Pierson, into the Care and Charge of the Overseers of the Poor of the Town, for the present Year.

Item, Whereas David Young of Hanover in Morris County is

thought by some, to be Heir at Law of our Parsonage Patents, as he is Heir of Robert Young the oldest Patentee, it is thought by some proper that this Vote be put—Whether the Trustees of the first Presbiterian Church at Newark shall apply to s'd David Young for a Deed of Conveyance to them in Trust, that so the said Trustees may be the better enabled to be Guardians for the same. This Vote was accordingly put, and therefore it was accordingly unanimously voted, that the Trustees of the first Presbiterian Church in Newark should procure a Deed from the s'd David Young, for the said Parsonage Lands in Trust, in Order that they may be the better enabled to take Care of the same for the said Church. The Parsonage Meadow was let the ensuing Year to Joseph Riggs, for 59s. 6d. The feed of the Burying Yard to William Grant, to take Care of the Fence.

At a TOWN MEETING, *March* 10th, 1761—The following Officers were chosen, (viz): Joseph Riggs Esq'r, Moderator. John Dod, 3d Assessor. Elijah Crane, Collector, and Clerk for Strays. John Cundit and Samuel Pennington, Freeholders. Isaac Ball and Joseph Baldwin Jun'r, Surveyors of Highways. Samuel Plum and Elijah Baldwin, Abraham Van Riper and David Williams, Overseers of the Poor. Joseph Hedden, Jonathan Tompkins, Samuel Crowel, John Van Winkle Jun'r, Aaron King, Henry Earl Jun'r, John Peck, Jonas Ball, Samuel Cundit Jun'r, Capt. Ely, Samuel Ogden, Joseph Taylor, William Crane, Aaron Jacobus, Abraham Ryker, Joseph Wright, Abraham Garrabrant, Ichabod Sayre, Nathaniel Ogden, Elias Crane, Samuel Gouverneur, James Banks Jun'r, Joseph Robarts, Eliphalet Johnson, Joseph Riggs, Abraham Van Ryper Jun'r and Thomas Freeman, to be Overseers of the Highways. Joseph Ball, Elias Crane and David Rogers, were chosen Pounders for the Neck.

It was voted that the Overseers of the Poor should build or hire a House, and keep the Poor of the Parish to Labor, agreeable to an Act of Assembly in that Case made and provided.

It was voted that William Grant should have the feed of the burying Ground, and to keep the Fence in Repair.

It appearing to the Heirs and Descendants of the first Settlers of Newark, Inhabitants of s'd Town, That the Proprietors of the Eastern Division of the Province of New Jersey, by their Governor and Council by Letters Patent dated the 10th Day of December, Anno Dom. 1696 did grant to John Curtis, Robert Young and others, sundry Tracts of Land Lying in Newark for the Uses and Purposes therein mentioned; among which several Lotts and Parcells of Land and one Lott of Meadow were granted, for the Use of a Parsonage—And that since the granting the s'd Letters patent, the Heirs and Descendants of the first Settlers of s'd Town of Newark have divided into three several Societies within s'd Town for public Worship of God, distinguished by the Names of The Church of England, The first Presbiterian Society, and the Mountain Society—and that many Disputes have frequently arose among the Heirs and Descendants of the first Settlers of New-Ark, relating to the property of said last mentioned Lands and Meadow, whereby the real Benefit and Advantage which might otherwise be made of the same is greatly obstructed and hindered—and that at a Town Meeting held at Newark afs'd, In March last, during the Time of the Small Pox being in Town, and when but very few of the Inhabitants were present, and without any previous Notice being given to the Inhabitants of said Town of any Intent of their passing a Vote relating to said Lands called the Parsonage Lands—it was then and there voted by the majority of the few then present, that Application should be made to One David Young, Heir to the Surviving Trustee mentioned in said Letters Patent, to obtain a Deed for the same Lands last mentioned to the Committee or Trustees to the first Presbiterian Society or Congregation, and that a Deed was accordingly obtained for the Use of One Society Only, which has given great dissatisfaction to the Inhabitants of said Town in general. Wherefore, to End s'd disputes, and that the same may be amicably adjusted and the Use intended by said Letters Patent be carried into Execution—it is voted and agreed at a very full and public Town Meeting as follows—

1st, That said Deed, so obtained as afs'd from David Young Heir of the Surviving Trustee mentioned in s'd Letters patent, is contrary to the real Intent and Desire of the majority of the Heirs and Descendants of the first Settlers of Newark, and to the Spirit and Design of said Letters Patent, and against the Use intended to be thereby granted.

2ndly, That as the Heirs and Descendants of the first Settlers of Newark have three Societys or Congregations for the publick Worship of God—each having a distinct or separate Minister to support—It is voted and agreed, that the said Lands granted by said Letters patent to lye for a Parsonage be equally divided in Quantity and Quality exclusive of the Improvements made thereon, among said Three Societies or Congregations.

3rdly, It is further voted and agreed, that John Cundit, Bethuel Pierson, Daniel Pierson Esq'r, James Nutman, John Crane and Elijah Baldwin, or any four of them be Agents to divide and allot said Lands to said Societies or Congregations in manner afs'd, and when so divided and allotted to apply to the Governor, Council and General Assembly, to confirm the same by a Law to be made for that Purpose to each Society, agreeable to s'd Division for the Use in s'd Letters Patent mentioned.

TOWN MEETING, *March* 9th, 1762—The following Officers were chosen: Nehemiah Baldwin, Moderator. Samuel Hayes, Town Clerk. John Dod the Third, Assessor. Elijah Crane, Collector and Clerk for Strays. John Cundit and Sam'l Pennington, Freeholders. James Nutman, William Camp, Samuel Harrison Jun'r, and Abraham Vanriper, Overseers of the Poor. Ezekial Ball and Obadiah Hedden, Surveyors of Highways. Thomas Brown, David Crane, Timothy Crane, Isaac Plum, William Dow, Tunis Jeroleman, Daniel Williams, Ebenezer Canfield, William Crane, Jedediah Hedden, Silas Dod, Israel Crane, Caleb Harrison, Nathan Ward, Josiah Lindsly, Arthur Perry, Samuel Billiard, Caleb Camp, Thomas Seagler, Hendrick Vanderhoof, Robert Baldwin, Robert Ward and Timothy Freeman, were chosen Overseers of Highways. Joseph Ball, Elias Crane and David Rogers, were chosen Pounders for the year ensuing, to take Care of the Neck.

The hon'ble David Ogden Esq'r having signified to the People, that at the Desire of some or all of the four Persons herein after mentioned whom he called Agents for the Town—the other two being those chosen out of the first Presbyterian Church in Newark refusing to be concerned in it—he had drawn a Draught of an Entry proposed to be made at a Town Meeting held at Newark on the Ninth Day of March 1762—which he read as follows—

John Cundit, Bethuel Pierson, Daniel Pierson and James Nutman, four of the Persons appointed by a vote of the Inhabitants of this Town of Newark, at their last annual Meeting on the Second Tuesday in March Last, for the dividing of the Parsonage Lands and Meadow Belonging To s'd Town, Made their Report this day of their Haveing so far Executed the Trust in them Reposed as to make a Division of s'd Parsonage Lands and Meadow, which report was read at the Publick Town Meeting held this Day for said Town, and approved of and Confirmed by a majority of the Inhabitants of s'd Town at their s'd. Meeting, subject Nevertheless to such Alterations as is herein After Mentioned: which Report is in the Words following, viz: the Question being Put, whether the s'd Agents for the Town, or any four of them might receive and Consider the division by them made as afs'd, and Hear such Objections thereto Against the Equality thereof as any Person or Persons shall think Proper to offer—and Make all Reasonable Alterations—it was Carried by a Vote of the Majority of s'd Town, that the s'd Agents for the Town or any four of them Shall and May have 4 Months from this Time to Hear the Objections of any person, or persons within s'd Town, who shall Think themselves Grieved Against the Equality of s'd division, and make such alterations therein as shall Be Just and Equal; and that After the Expiration of s'd four Months, the s'd division now Made or such other division as shall within that Time Be Agreed on as afs'd, the s'd agents or any four of them are requested by the Inhabitants of s'd Town to Take all Proper Measures to make Effectual and Binding on all Parties.

A Number of the Principal Members of the first Presbiterian Church in New Ark Objected Against it, and Insisted upon it that the Men was Not Legally Chosen—that the Vote pass'd Last Annual Town Meeting was not fairly obtained —a Majority being at that Time on the Negative, and that there was at Least Two Hundred Persons present at the Town Meeting in March 1760, when the Vote about the Parsonage was so Unanimously Obtained, &c. However, upon Mr. Ogden's and some others strongly urging and repeatedly insisting upon it, the Moderator put the Vote and it was carried in the negative by a majority of those present, it being a very full Town Meeting, (viz): that the Division should not be confirmed even with the Limitations above mentioned.

Town Meeting, *March* 8th, 1763—The following Officers were chosen—John Ogden, Esqr, Moderator. Joseph Robards, Assessor. Elijah Crane, Collector and Clerk for Strays. Samuel Huntington and Bethuel Pierson, Freeholders. Caleb Wheeler and William Camp, Surveyors of Highways. William Camp, James Nuttman, Nath'l Ogden, John Gildersleeve, Abraham Van Riper at Second River, Overseers of the Poor. Thomas Browne, David Crane, Timothy Crane, Isaac Plum, William Dow, Theunis Jerolman, Daniel Williams, Joseph Crane, David Peck, William Crane, Silas Dod, Israel Crane, Caleb Harrison, Aaron Baldwin, Arthus Perry, Samuel Billard, Caleb Camp, Thomas Seagler, Jeremiah Martin, Robert Baldwin, Andrew Teed, and Timothy Freeman, Overseers of Highways—David Taylor appointed in the Room of Andrew Teed, dec'd.

Town Meeting, *October* 3rd, 1763—Warned by the Constable, held at the Court House at Newark—it was voted that Two Hundred Pounds proclamation, shall be raised for the use of the Poor in Newark afs'd.

At a Town Meeting held *March* 13th, 1764—Joseph Riggs Esq'r, Chosen Moderator. John Dod Jun'r, Assessor. Elijah Crane, Town Clerk, Collector, and Book Keeper for Stray Creatures. Nath'l Camp and Stephen Morris, Freeholders. Caleb Harrison and Abraham Van Ryper, Surveyors of the Highway. Samuel Plum, Nathaniel Ogden, and Abraham Van Ryper, Overseers of the Poor. Voted, that £150 proclamation be raised for the Poor. That the Overseers shall hire a House for the Reception of the Poor. Overseers of the Highways—William Crane, Zopher Beech, Samuel Billard, Daniel Riggs, Matthew Harrison, Uzal Ward, Sam'l Pierson, Justice Dow, John Kingsland, Hendrick Van Winkle, John Van Winkle, Peter Garrabrant, Helmegh Jeroleman, John Morris, Josiah Ward at Canoe Brook, Nathan Baldwin, Isaac Cundit, Tim. Williams, David

Cundit and Alexander Vance. Voted, that the Parsonage Meadow be hired for the ensuing Year—said Meadow rented for £2 12s. to Josiah Quinby, Joseph Mun and Ichabod Harrison. Nehemiah Baldwin, James Nutman, and Amos Harrison Esq'rs, to receive the Money, equally to be paid to the Priests of said Town.

At a TOWN MEETING, held 12th of *March*, 1765—Doctor Burnet, chosen, Moderator. Elijah Crane, Town Clerk. John Dod Jun'r, Assessor. Elijah Crane, Collector. Isaac Longworth and Caleb Camp, Freeholders. Joseph Hedden, Jun'r and Josiah Pierson, Surveyors of the Highways. Samuel Plum, Nathaniel Ogden and Abraham Van Ryper, Overseers of the Poor. Samuel Plum, chosen Pounder.

It was voted, to Farm let all the Poor out for one whole Year from the Date hereof by way of Vendue, and whoever is the last Bidder shall take the charge of them immediately. It was also further agreed, that whoever takes them should have the Benefit of all the Fines belonging to the Poor, within said Year. Also, the Benefit of all the Money that may arise from Stray Creatures. They was Vendued of to Daniel Cundit being the lowest Bidder, for the sum of £159—proc'n Money—which said Sum was agreed to be raised by way of Rate within said Year. The following Men chosen Overseers of the Highways—Samuel Hayes, William Camp, Elihu Crane, Jedediah Freeman, Jonathan Lyon, Jedediah Hedden, John Earle, William Dow, Esq'r, Theunis Jerolman, Noah Crane, John Cockefair, Enoch Powlesson, John King, Jonathan Cundit, Abraham Van Geison, Peter Garmo, Rheuben Harrison, David Bedford, Joseph Williams, Obadiah Force, Thomas Denman, Ralph Tucker and David Williams.

A TOWN MEETING, held at the Court house in Newark the 11th of *March*, 1766—Joseph Riggs Esq'r, chosen Moderator. Elijah Crane, Town Clerk. John Dod Jun'r, Assessor. Elijah Crane, Collector. Isaac Longworth and Caleb Camp, Freeholders. Joseph Hedden Jun'r and Josiah Pierson, Surveyors of the Highways. Samuel Huntington and Isaac Cundit, Overseers of the Poor—Dr. Abraham Van Ryper for Second River. Elijah Crane, Clerk for Strays. Samuel Huntington, Pound Keeper. Matthias Crane and Joseph Ball, Pounders. Paul Beech, Capt. Joseph Riggs, Sam'l Gouverneur, Thomas Brown, Joseph Crowell, Alexander Vance, Ezekiel Ball, Hendrick Francisco, John Garrabrant, Peter D. Garmo, Wm. King, Samuel Williams, Hendrick King, Benj'n Williams Jun'r. Joseph Harrison, Joshua Baldwin, Ralph Tucker, Capt. Wm. Ely, Hendrick Van Winkle, Levi Vincent, John Peck, John Gordon, Daniel Cundit, Joseph Williams Jun'r and Thomas Lyon, Overseers of Highways.

It was voted that £180, proc'n Money, be raised for the Poor for the ensuing Year.

Voted that the Inhabitants might take Care of their Hay in the Meadows, the 24th of this Inst't March.

March 10th, 1767—At the TOWN MEETING, at the Court house was chosen the following Officers, for the Year ensuing—John Ogden Esq'r, Moderator. Elijah Crane, Town Clerk. John Dod Jun'r, Assessor for all Rates. Elijah Crane, Collector, and Clerk for Strays. Nath'l Camp and William Crane, Freeholders. John Peck and Ichabod Harrison, Surveyors of the Highways.

By a Vôte passed it was agreed, that all the Poor that then was or should be brought on the Town, within One Year from the Date hereof, should be farmed out for the ensuing Year, and that they should be set up at Vendue—agreeable whereto they were set up and Struck off to Caleb Camp, he being the last Bidder; and he agreed to Keep the same said Poor the ensuing Year or to the 10th Day of March 1768, for the sum of £147 15s. Light money, and he being the lowest Bidder they were struck of to him accordingly for £147 15s. Light money. Samuel Huntington, Capt. Camp and Ezekiel Ball, Overseers of the Poor—Capt. Garrabrant, Do. for Second River. Overseers of the Highways—Sam'l Gouverneur, Uzal Ward, Paul Beech, Dan'l Tichenor Jun'r, Alexander Vance, Ezekiel Ball, Obadiah Hedden, Cornelius Jones, George Parsonett, Daniel Taylor, John Range, John Ogden over the Mountain, Aaron Dod, Sam'l Pierson Sen'r, Dan'l Cundit, Daniel Dean, John Waters, Obadiah Force, Sam'l Pierson Jun'r, Elijah Squire, John Dod, Carpenter, Benjamin Baldwin, Job Brown, Claus Garrabrant, Helmegh Jerolman, David Griffith, John Kingsland, Jeremiah Martin, Tho's Pierson, Tho's Denman, John Pierson.

August 4th, 1767—We the Surveyors of the Highways for the Town of Newark, do nominate and appoint Jabez Harrison to be an Overseer of the Highways in the Room of Uzal Ward—and Joseph Baldwin 3rd, in the Room of John Range.

JOHN PECK,
ICHABOD HARRISON.

March 8th, 1768—A TOWN [MEETING] held at the Court House for the Town of Newark—the following Officers were then chosen for the ensuing Year—John Ogden Esq'r, Moderator. Elijah Crane, Town Clerk. John Dod Jun'r, Assessor. John Camp, Collector. Elijah Crane, Clerk for the Stray Book. William Camp and Eleazer Lamson, Freeholders. Moses Ogden and Alexander Vance, Surveyors of the Highways. The Poor of this Town was farmed out for the ensuing Year to the Town

Meeting in March next, Caleb Wheeler being the lowest Bidder, accordingly he is to take and Keep said Poor for the Sum of £143 10s.—Light Money. Samuel Huntington, Caleb Wheeler, Ezekiel Ball, Nathaniel Ogden and Capt. Garrabrants, Overseers of the Poor. Voted, that the People may secure their Hay in the Meadow Tomorrow, at Ten of the Clock in the Morning. Joseph Hedden Jun'r, Obadiah Hedden, Caleb Camp, James Banks, Garret H. Spier, Joseph Hedden, Josiah Crane at the Farms, Lawrence Ward, Nath'l Ogden, Sam'l Freeman Jun'r, Joseph Baldwin 3rd, John Riker, David Harrison, David Cundit, Ephraim Camp, John Muchmore, Enoch Powlson, Tho's Gould, Bethuel Pierson, Solomon Crane, Silas Baldwin, Isaac Reeves, Tho's Cadmus, Abraham Van Ryper, Weaver, Matthew Winne, Benj'n Mun, Eliphalet Johnson, Samuel Johnson, James Force, Tho's Seagler, Overseers of the Highways.

Voted by a great majority, That the Parsonage Lands belonging to the Town of Newark be divided between the Three Congregations of the first Settlers of Newark, (to wit): The first Presbyterian Church in Newark, the Church of England, and the Mountain Society. But the Trustees of the first Presbyterian Church in Newark being present, advised the People then met to let the Parsonage alone, declaring the Title to be Invested in them, and forbid them passing the former or any other Vote relating to the Parsonage—publickly protested against it and desired their [protest?] might be entered upon the Town Book—which was granted.

Voted by a great majority, that Sam'l Penington and Ebenezer Baldwin on the part of the first Presbyterian Church of Newark, Thomas Longworth and Capt. James Nutman on the part of the Church of England—and Bethuel Pierson and Capt. Abraham Ogden on the part of the Mountain Society—should be the Men to divide the Parsonage belonging to the Town of Newark between said Congregations, agreeable to the foregoing Vote—But Sam'l Pennington and Ebenezer Baldwin declared they would not act.

At a Town Meeting held for and in the Town of Newark at the Court House the 14th *March*, 1769—the following Officers were chosen and appointed to act the ensuing Year as follows—John Ogden Esq'r, Moderator. John Ogden Jun'r, Town Clerk. Abraham Ogden and Isaac Longworth, Freeholders. John Camp, Collector, and Clerk for Strays. John Dod Jun'r, Assessor. David Cundit and Benj'n Williams Jun'r, Surveyors of the Highways. Samuel Huntington Sen'r, Ezekiel Ball, Caleb Camp, Nathaniel Ogden and Garrabrant Garrabrants, Overseers of the Poor. And Overseers of the Highways were as follows—Joseph Hedden Jun'r, Sam'l Hayes, Alexander Vance, Ezekiel Ball,

Thomas Pearsal, Jonathan Squire Jun'r, Obadiah Hedden, John Freeman, Benj'n Baldwin, George Parsonet, Manning Force, Jonathan Dickenson, Sam'l Williams, John Jones son of Sam'l Jones, Daniel Taylor, Reuben Harrison, Thomas Gould, Silas Baldwin, David Williams, Joseph Pierson, Levi Vincent, Amos Dod, Timothy Davis, Benj'n Williams Sen'r, Phillip V. Cortlandt, Ab'm Van Ryper Sen'r, Ab'm Vangeson 3rd, John Waters. William Camp and Bethuel Pierson, Freeholders last chosen. Caleb Camp bid off the Poor at £100—Light money, and is to keep them in sufficient Victuals and Cloathing, give Schooling to such Children as require it, which s'd Schooling &c. is left at the Direction and Discretion of Samuel Huntington one of the Overseers; and the s'd Camp is to take all that shall legally be brought on the Town, and farm the whole from March 14th 1769 to the second Tuesday in March 1770.

Memorandum—William Camp and Eleazer Lamson were proposed to be elected Freeholders, as were also the before mentioned Isaac Longworth and Abraham Ogden; the mode of election was the same as used on the Election of all the other officers at this Meeting, (viz): by holding up of the Hands and the majority appearing clear and indisputable in favor of said Mess'rs Longworth and Ogden, the Moderator directed their being elected Freeholders to be entered by the Clerk on the Minutes—which was accordingly done. Soon after, Nathaniel Camp the Father of said William Camp, seconded by others, objected to the above Election and proposed William Camp and Bethuel Pierson Candidates for a new Election; and that the same should be determined by poling or going down in the Street, and seperating and counting the Votes for the different Candidates—which was waved by the Moderator as the former Election appeared perfectly clear and conclusive, but on the matter's being insisted upon ordered that the remaining Business of the Meeting should be first gone through, and that then any reasonable Objections against the above of the Freeholders should be heard—which being done, the above Proposal of going down into the Street was again moved for—but the afs'd majority who had voted for the s'd Mess'rs Longworth and Ogden, conceiving any Election set aside the first (so clearly determined) would introduce the greatest Confusion in Town Meetings, as there would be no end to electing so long as any one Person remained dissatisfied and had any other Candidate to propose, and therefore, they conceiving the Business of the Meeting to be finished departed. However, great part of the remaining Inhabitants went into the Street, and the Majority of the said remaining Inhabitants voted that s'd William Camp and Bethuel Pierson should be Freeholders.

N. B. The first Court of Quarter Sessions determined that s'd

Longworth and Ogden should serve as Freeholders for the ensuing Year.

At a TOWN MEETING, held *August* 30th, 1769—According to Order of the Justices, on account of the Death of John Camp the late Town Collector—The Town met and chose James Banks Esq'r, Moderator. Elijah Crane, Town Collector, to act for the remainder of this Year.

At a publick TOWN MEETING, held the 13th Day of *March*, 1770—the following Persons were chosen Officers for the ensuing Year—Joseph Riggs, Sen'r, Moderator. Caleb Camp, Town Clerk. John Dod, Assessor. Elijah Crane, Collector, and Clerk for the Strays. Jonathan Sayre and Joseph Alling, Surveyors of the Highways. Nathaniel Camp and Abraham Ogden, Freeholders. Samuel Huntington, Caleb Camp, Ezekiel Ball, Ichabod Harrison and Theunis Jerolman, Overseers of the Poor. Overseers of the Highways are as follows—Sam'l Huntington, Sen'r, Joseph Hedden, Sen'r, Recompense Crowell, Peter Garrabrant, Jacob Spier, Ichabod Harrison, Jabez Baldwin, Daniel Dean, David Morehouse, Capt. Garrabrant Garrabrants, Joseph Bruen, Moses Roberts, Solomon Davis Andrew McMyers, Manning Force, William Ely, Sen'r, Thomas Williams, Jun'r, Nath'l Beech, Joseph Williams, Dan'l Riggs, Zebina Ward, Daniel Miller, Simeon Van Winkle, Samuel Cundit, Abel Freeman, Helmegh Jerolman, and Jedediah Lindsly.

Put to Vote, whether the Fines and the Strays should be given to the Farmer of the Poor or not—it was carried in the negative. The Poor was set up to be farmed out for the ensuing Year, and they was bid of to be kept by Caleb Camp, at £157, Light Money. Money to be raised for the Poor, £160.

At a TOWN MEETING, held the 12th Day of *March*, 1771, the following Officers were chosen for the ensuing Year—William Camp, Moderator. Caleb Camp, Town Clerk. John Dod, Assessor. Obadiah Bruen, Collector, and Clerk of the Strays. David Cundit and Caleb Camp, Freeholders. Stephen Harrison, Thomas Williams, Surveyors of the Highways. Samuel Huntington, Caleb Camp, Ezekiel Ball, Ichabod Harrison and Theunis Jerolman, Overseers of the Poor. Overseers of the Highway as follows—William Camp, Uzal Ward, Matthias Lyon, Ezekiel Ball, David Brown, Jedediah Crane, Obadiah Hedden, Silas Baldwin, Dan'l Williams, Joseph Harrison, Sen'r, John Kingsland, Abraham Winer, Ephraim Camp, Henry Earle, Abr'm Riker, John Edwards, George Parsonet, Daniel Taylor, Matthew Cundit, Moses Osborn, David Baldwin, Sam'l Dod, Jun'r, George Wells, James Segler, Dan'l Cundit, Sen'r, Samuel Pierson. John Cockefair, Epaphras Cook, Joseph Hedden, Sen'r.

Proposed whether the Poor be farmed out as in former Years —it was carried in the affirmative, and was accordingly farm'd out to Bethuel Pierson, he being the lowest Bidder at £148 10s. —Light Money—and is to provide and do for them and for the Town, agreeable to the Direction of the Year 1769.

It was further agreed and voted, that as there is a Dispute between the Township of Newark and the Township of Elizabeth, about the Residence of Thomas King and Wife, and Patience Jennings and her children, that none of s'd Persons shall be chargeable this Year 1771 to said Bethuel Pierson.

Voted, that upon a Letter from Edward Thomas, Overseer of the Poor for the Township of Elizabeth, proposing for the Township of Newaık to keep Thomas King and his wife and pay their own Costs hitherto accrued, and the Township of Elizabeth should keep Patience Jennings and her three Children and pay their own Costs hitherto accrued, being read—that the Overseers of the Poor, this Day chosen, be a Committee for the further Management of this Cause, and that they answer Mr. Thomas's Letter and proceed in the Matter as they shall think most for the advantage of the Township of Newark—and that they also approve the Steps taken by the Overseers the last Year, in their Proceeding in their Causes.

Voted, that there be £200 Light Money raised for the Use of the Poor for the Year 1771—Fines and Strays and Tavern Rates included.

Voted, that any Cattle that shall be found trespassing in the Salt Meadows shall be pounded by the Person who shall find them trespassing, and that the Poundage shall be one Shilling p. Head—and the Person who shall pound them shall receive it of the owner of s'd Cattle—and that John Crane be Pound keeper at 3d. p. Head. Put to vote, whether every Man may have a Court Yard before his House of Ten feet wide—it carried in the negative.

At a publick Meeting, held at the Court House in and for the Town of Newark on the 10th Day of *March*, 1772—the following Officers were chosen for the Year ensuing—The hon'ble David Ogden, Esq., Moderator. Isaac Longworth, Town Clerk. John Dod, Assessor. Obadiah Bruen, Collector, and Clerk for Strays. David Cundit and Isaac Ogden, Esqr., Freeholders. Joseph Hedden, Jun'r, and James Banks, Surveyors of the Highways. Samuel Huntington, Caleb Camp, Ezekiel Ball, Ichabod Harrison and William King, Overseers of the Poor. William Camp, Isaac Longworth, Nathaniel Johnson, Isaac Crane, Joseph Baldwin, Samuel Hayes, Henry Squire, Samuel Billard, George Parsonet, David Crane, Josiah Quinby, Jonathan Wade, John Jones, Zachariah Burwell, Nath'l Ogden, Daniel Cundit, Thos. Gould,

James Raymond, Caleb Harrison, John Range, Samuel Cundit, Jun'r, Daniel Dod, Derick Mowrson, Joseph Meeker, Peter Jacobusen, John Kingsland, William Dow, Esqr., Obadiah Hedden, Overseers of the Highways. By virtue of an Order from David Ogden, Esq., Dated Ap'l 22nd, 1772, and sent p. Ezekiel Ball—this Day I make the entry of the underwritten—Charles Gillam, Overseer of the Highway.

The Poor was taken by Bethuel Pierson for the ensuing Year, for £157, Light Money. It was voted to raise £180 Proclamation, for the support of the Poor. It was voted, that any Cattle that shall be trespassing on the Salt or fresh Meadows (not belonging to the owner of the Cattle) shall be subject to be pounded—and any Person that shall pound any Cattle (trespassing as above) shall be entitled to one Shilling a Head for each.

At a publick TOWN MEETING held at the Court house in Newark on the 9th Day of *March*, 1773—the following Officers were chosen for the ensuing Year, (viz): The Hon'ble David Ogden, Esqr., Moderator. Isaac Longworth, Town Clerk. John Dod, Assessor. Obadiah Bruen, Collector, and Clerk of Strays. Isaac Ogden, Esqr., and David Cundit, Freeholders. Samuel Pierson, Jun'r, and Benjamin Williams, Jun'r, Surveyors of Highways. Daniel Cundit, Caleb Camp, Samuel Penington, Ezekiel Ball and William King, Overseers of the Poor. Isaac Ogden and Sylvanus Baldwin, Constables.

Voted unanimously, that a Committee should be chosen to take Care of the Priviledges of the Town, and agreeable thereto, Isaac Ogden, Esqr., William Camp, John Peck and Moses Baldwin, were chosen to take Care of the Priviledges of the Town, especially the Watering Place near Capt. Joseph Riggs's, and to make Report thereof at the next Town Meeting. William Camp, Joseph Alling, Caleb Camp, Nathan Baldwin, Matthias Winants, Manning Force, Williams Cook, Daniel Van Seluf, Alexander Vance, Josiah Quimby, Ichabod Harrison, John Range, Amos Dod, Thomas Gould, Reuben Harrison, Benjamin Baldwin, William Dow, Esqr, John Kingsland, Timothy Freeman, John Crane, Jun'r, Obadiah Hedden, Jonathan Williams, Helmegh Jerolman, Jonathan Cundit, Thomas Seagler, and Zenas Pierson, Overseers of the Highways. Voted to farm out the Poor. Also voted, that the Money arising from Fines and Strays in the Year 1773 shall be paid to the Person that takes the Poor the above Year. The Poor was taken by Caleb Wheeler for the Year 1773, at £107, Light Money. Voted to raise £110 proclamation, for the Poor for the Year 1773. The vote concerning pounding, past in the Year 1772, is again voted for the Year 1773. Thomas Saffen is chosen Pounder for the ensuing Year, and to have 4d. a Head for his Service.

At a Publick Town Meeting, held at the Court House in Newark on the 8th Day of *March*, 1774—the following Officers were chosen for the Year ensuing, (viz): Isaac Ogden, Esqr., Moderator. Isaac Longworth, Town Clerk. Voted, that the Town Clerk shall be exempted from working on the Highways for the ensuing Year. John Dod, Assessor. Obadiah Bruen, Collector, and Clerk of Strays. Isaac Longworth and David Cundit, Freeholders. Joseph Hedden, Jun'r, and Jonathan Sayre, Surveyors of Highways. Samuel Huntington, Caleb Camp, Daniel Cundit and William King, Overseers of the Poor. Isaac Cundit and Isaac Ogden, Constables. Isaac Ogden, Esqr., William Camp, John Peck, and Moses Baldwin, to take Care of the Priviledges of the Town. Capt. Anthony Rutgers, John Alling, Paul Beech, Capt. Eliphalet Johnson, Job Camp, Amos Dod, John Range, John Kingsland, Sam'l Ogden, Aaron Ward, John Francisco, Thomas Gould, Ezekiel Ball, Jotham Harrison, Thos. Williams, Jun'r, Joseph Tompkins, Jun'r, Enos Baldwin, John Pierson, Daniel Dean, David Morris, Samuel Pierson, Henry Wade, Garret Spier, Richard Harrison, Jun'r, Obadiah Hedden, John Devesne, John Browne, Joseph Browne, William Dow, Esqr., Gershom Kilburn, and Isaac Cundit, Overseers of the Highways.

Voted to farm out the Poor, and that on the following Conditions—1st, That John Ogden and Amos Harrison, Esqrs., with Samuel Huntington and Caleb Camp, or any three of them, be a Committee to inspect the Poor on the first Monday in every Month, and to see that they are well provided with Cloaths and Provisions and otherways well taken Care of—and that the Poor shall be now inspected and shall be well cloathed, and so delivered to the Person that shall hire them, and at the Expiration of the Year the s'd Person shall deliver them up as well cloathed as he receives them—and if he should refuse or neglect to do it, then the Inspectors shall cloath them and deduct the Expence thereof out of the Monies that are to be paid Him for the Support of the Poor. 2ndly, That the Poor Children shall be constantly sent to School at the expence of the Person that takes them. 3rdly, That if the Poor shall chuse to go to a Place of publick Worship, the Person that farms the Poor shall procure Carriages for them to go there—if they live at a Distance from a Place of publick Worship.

The Poor was taken by Joseph Riggs, Esqr., for the Year 1774, for Ninety Nine Pounds and five Shillings Light Money—and he is to have the Benefit of the Fines and Strays. Voted, to raise £120 proc'n for the Poor for the Year 1774.

Voted, that a School house may be built on any of the Comon Land in Newark—and the particular Place shall be where a major Part of the Subscribers in Value shall appoint. Thomas Saffen is chosen Pounder.

At a Publick Town Meeting, (agreeable to warning given as directed by an Act of Assembly) held at the Court House in Newark the 6th Day of *June*, 1774—in Order to chuse a Collector for the Town of Newark, in the Stead of Obadiah Bruen, dec'd. Isaac Ogden, Esqr., was chosen Moderator. John Ogden, Esqr., was chosen Collector.

Voted, that a Pound may be built on the Watering Place near Capt. Joseph Riggs's, and that untill the Dispute concerning the Watering Place is decided between the Town and Capt. Riggs, a Pound may be built adjoining the East Corner of Elihu Crane's Lott, near his House. Samuel Huntington, Robert Nichols, and Joseph Mun, were chosen to treat with Capt. Riggs concerning the disputed Lands at the Watering Place, and nominate Men to settle the Dispute between the Town and Mr. Riggs.

At a Publick Town Meeting held at the Court House in Newark on the 14th Day of *March*, 1775—the following Officers were chosen, (viz): Isaac Ogden Esq'r, Moderator. Isaac Longworth, Town Clerk—and to be exempt from Work on the Highway for his Services. John Dod, Assessor. John Ogden Esq'r, Collector, and Clerk of Strays. David Cundit and William Camp, Freeholders. Samuel Huntington, Solomon Davis, John Peck, William King and Enos Baldwin, Overseers of the Poor. Isaac Cundit and Isaac Ogden, Constables. Timothy Cundit and Joseph Tompkins Jun'r, Surveyors of the Highways. William Camp, Jonathan Sayre, Benj'n Coe, Jun'r, Sam'l Curry, John Ogden Jun'r, Jerod Harrison, Josiah Quinby, Dan'l Taylor, Elijah Squire, John Pierson, Stephen Williams, Lewis Miller, Abraham Garrabrant, Isaac Dod, Caleb Harrison, Aaron Dod, John Range, Thomas Gould, Timothy Bruen, Jun'r, Walling Egberts, Hendrick Brown, Joseph Kingsland, Helmegh Jerolman, John Kingsland, Casparus Van Winkle, Caleb Camp, Eliphalet Johnson, Ezekiel Ball, Maning Force, David Morehouse, David Little, Joseph Meeker, Recompense Crowell, James Smith, Jun'r, Bethuel Pierson, Jonathan Cundit, Reuben Harrison, Daniel Cundit, and Ephraim Morris, Overseers of the Highways.

Voted to farm out the Poor. Voted, that Joel Osborn's oldest Son be put out by the Overseers of the Poor. Also, that one of Joel Osborn's Daughters shall be put to Capt. Eliphalet Johnson, at the Discretion of the Overseers of the Poor.

Voted, that Joseph Hedden Jun'r may build a boat on the Town Wharf. Voted, the Farmer of the Poor shall not be at any Charge with Elizabeth Godden's Child. Voted, the Monies arising for Fines and Strays, shall be Paid to the Farmer of the Poor this Year. Henry Squier took the Poor for One Year, for which he is to have £93 17s.—Light Money.

Voted unanimously, that One Acre and an half of Land in the

Town Commons at the North End of the Town, may be taken up for the Use of the new Academy lately erected on s'd Land. Voted, that Lewis Ogden Esq'r, William Camp, Isaac Ogden Esq., Capt. Anthony Rutgers, Joseph Hedden Jun'r, Samuel Hayes, and Joseph Alling, or any four of them be a Committee to lay out one Acre and an half of Land, for the Use of the Academy in such Manner as they shall think proper.

Voted, to burn the Meadows on the 28th Day of March.

Caleb Wheeler, Paul Beech, and Benj'n Coe Jun'r, were chosen Sheep Masters.

Voted, to raise Ten Pounds proclamation, to be paid to Joseph Hedden Jun'r for which he agrees to purchase a Bound Book in folio not less than 5 Quire, and to "transcribe the Old Town Book into the new one" in a legible fair hand.

Voted, the Town will indemnify Samuel Curry, in the Possession of his Tan Yard, and that William Camp, Eliphalet Johnson and Thomas Candfield be a Committee to give Sam'l Curry a Lease. Thomas Saffen is chosen Pound keeper, and to have 4d. proclamation p. Head, Poundage.

At a Publick Town Meeting held at the Court House in Newark on the 12th Day of *March*, 1776—the following Officers were Chose—Isaac Ogden Esq'r, Moderator. Isaac Longworth, Town Clerk.

Voted, that the Town Clerk draw an Order on the Town Collector, To pay Joseph Hedden Jun'r Ten pound proclamation, for Coppying the Old Town Book.

John Dod, Assessor. John Ogden Esq'r, Collector, and Clerk of Strays. David Cundit, and Jonathan Sayrs, Freeholders. Paul Beech and Jonathan Crane, Surveyors. Samuel Huntington, Solomon Davis, John Peck, William King and Enos Baldwin, Overseers of the Poor. Isaac Ogden and Isaac Cundit, Constables. Hendrick I. Browne, Christopher Stymats, John Range, Lewis Crane, Thomas Gould, Stephen Williams, Matthias Ross, Dan'l Cundit, Michael D. Vreland, Lewis Baldwin, Thomas Griffith, Peter Beach, Ephraim Camp, Zenas Pierson, John Edwards, Effingham Townly, Matthew Cundit, Samuel Pierson, Jeptha Baldwin, Uzal Ball, Jediah Freeman, Benjamin Baldwin, Joseph Brewin, Moses Baldwin, David Browne, Caleb Harrison, Daniel Dod, Mathias Lyon, David Little, Isaac Denman, Joseph Baldwin, Nath'l Andruss, Ebenezer Ward, Caleb Sayrs, John King, Gerrit Spier, And Abram Garrabrant, Overseers of ye High Ways.

Voted to burn ye Medow Next Saturday.

Sam'l Currey, pound keeper, to have One Shilling p. head for Horses and Cattle and 2d. per head for Sheep.

Voted to Farm out the Poor, Also to put out ye Widow Heddens Oldest boy.

Voted the Fines and Strays Shall go to the Farmer of the poor. Amos Freeman Took the poor at £101 10s. 0d. Light Money.

Voted to raise £110 0s. 0d. prock. for the use of the poor. Jonathan Lyon, Thomas Canfield, Samuel Hays, Sam'l Penington, Josiah Hornblower, Isaac Ogden Esq'r, Daniel Cundit, Lewis Ogden Esq'r, Benjamin Williams, Joseph Munn, Joseph Tompkins Jr., Nath'l Camp, John Range, Israel Crane, Capt. Leslie, Jos. Hedden Ju'r, Matthias Ward, Elijah Squire, Manning Force and David Cundit and Jonathan Sayrs be A Committee. Voted 11 makes A Quorum.

Mr. Joseph Riggs having Applied to the Town Meeting, to Leave the Dispute Subsisting Between this Town and Himself to Arbitration, The Town Agreed to the Same on this Condition, to Witt: that in Case the said Dispute Should be Determined in Mr. Rigg's Favor, that then he Will Convey the Land Agreed to be Convey'd by A former Contract made with Mr. Currey, Agreeable to the Said Contract, And for the Sum therin Specified, and that the Costs of S'd Arbitration Shall go with the Event of the Suit, Unless the S'd Arbitrators Should find part of the Land in Said Currey's Possession to Belong to Mr. Riggs. And Other Part to the Town; in which Case the S'd Arbitrators are to Order the Costs to be paid by Which Party they think proper: to which Conditions the S'd Mr. Riggs Agreed. The Town then Appointed the Following persons, to Witt: William Camp, Eliphelet Johnson, and Caleb Camp as a Committee to Enter into Arbitration Bonds with Mr. Riggs, and to Chuse the Arbitrators.

At a Town Meeting, held at the Court house in Newark the 10th *March*, 1778, the following Officers were Chosen, Joseph Riggs, Esqr., Moderator. Aaron Ogden, Clerk. Ebenezer Baldwin, Bethuel Pierson, Freeholders. John . . . Assessor. Nath'l Farrand, Collector, and Clerk of Strays. Enos Baldwin, Samuel Huntington, Sen'r, Josiah Quimby, John Garrabrant, Over-Seers of the Poor. Joseph Alling, David Crane, Surveyors. Caleb Camp, Josiah Hornblower, Joseph Riggs, Commissioners of Appeals. Sylvenus Baldwin, John Tichenor, Nathaniel Andross, Joseph Crane, Joseph Meeker, Manning Force, William Baldwin, John Morris, William King, Constables. Voted, That the poor be Taken Care of by the Overseers of the poor. No poor money to be raised this Year. · Voted, That all Cattle, Horses, Hogs, Sheep, or Geese, found Running at Large are subject to be pounded, unless they have a Keeper—poundage 3s. p. head.

At an annual Town Meeting, held at Newark the Ninth day *March*, 1779, the following Officers were Chosen, Joseph Riggs, Esq., Moderator. Aaron Ogden, Clerk. John Dod, Assessor.

Nathaniel Farrand, Collector, and Clerk of Strays. Ebenezar Baldwin, Bethuel Pierson, Freeholders. Caleb Wheeler, Sen'r, Josiah Quimby, Enos Baldwin, Garrabrant Garrabrant, Overseers of the Poor. Abraham Ogden, Stephen Harrison, Jun'r, Surveyors. Caleb Wheeler, Sen'r, Joseph Riggs, and Josiah Hornblower, Commissioners of Appeals. Edward Fleming, John Ward, Nathaniel Camp, Jun'r, Timothy Andross, Jeremiah Martin, John Dovosne, Benjamin Williams, Jonathan Hedden, Constables. David Crane, pound Master. Voted, that the poor be Taken Care of by the Overseers of the poor. Voted, That Eight Hundred pounds be Raised for the Poor.

Voted, That the Meadows shall not be burn'd untill the 1st April. Voted, that Justice Cundit Take The Town Charter into his Charge, untill Called for By Proper Authority. Voted, that all Horses and Cattle, found on the Salt Meadows not the property of the Owners of the Cattle, shall pay a fine of 10s. and be subject to poundage.

Voted, that the Reverend Alex'r McWhorter, Mr. Chapman, Josiah Hornblower, Joseph Riggs, and Lewis Ogden, be a Committee, to give such instructions to our Legislatures in this County from time to time as Occasion may require.

The Proceedings of Town Meeting for 1780 is Lost.

At a Town Meeting, held at Newark the 13th *March*, 1781, The following Officers were chosen—Joseph Riggs, Esqr., Moderator. Aaron Ogden, Town Clerk. John Dod, Assessor. Nathaniel Farrand, Collector, and Clerk of Strays. Caleb Wheeler, William Dow, Esqr., Joseph Baldwin, Elijah Squire, Assistants to the Assessor. Joseph Alling, Thomas Williams, Freeholders. Daniel Cundit, Isaac Dod, Benjamin Coe, Jun'r, Commissioners of Appeals. Joseph Thomkins and Zebulun Jones, Surveyors. Joseph Baldwin, Garribrant Garrabrant, Josiah Quimby and Joseph Harrison, Overseers of the poor. Sylvenus Baldwin, Josiah Quimby, Joseph Canfield, Nathaniel Taylor, Jacob Ward, Sam'l Cocker, John Devosne and Josiah Taylor, Constables. Robert Johnson, Joseph Lyon, Joseph Riggs, Isaac Reves, and William Dow, were Chosen to give such Instructions to Our Legislature from time to time as Occasion may require.

Voted, that Two hundred and fifty pounds be Raised for the poor.

At an Annual Town Meeting, held at the Court house in Newark the 12th *March*, 1782, the following Officers were Chosen, Doc'r William Burnet, Moderator. Aaron Ogden, Town Clerk. John Dod, Assessor. Nathaniel Farrand, Collector, and Clerk of Strays. Caleb Wheelar, Jun'r, William Dow, Elijah Squire and Lewis Baldwin, Assistants to the Assessor. Matthias

Ward and Stephen Harrison, Freeholders. Josiah Pierson, Joseph Baldwin, and Joseph Riggs, Commissioners of Appeals. Benjamin Coe, Jun'r, Joseph Harrison, Joseph Riggs, and Garribrant Garribrant, Overseers of the poor. Sylvenus Baldwin, Martin Hill, Josiah Quimby, Obed Denham, James Farrand, Jabez Williams, Samuel Ratan and Thomas pool, Constables. Robert Johnson and Benjamin . . . . . Jun'r, Surveyors.

Voted, that a Lawsuit be Commenced against the Widow Davis on acc't of Wessells.

Voted, that the said Wessells Remain in the hands of the Overseers of the poor, untill the suit is Determined.

Voted, that the poor be farmed out and that the Farmer be allowed all the fines on Strays, and one hundred pounds proc. p. Year.

Voted, that Two Hundred be Raised for the poor this Year. Natha'l Andross, Pound Master.

At an annual Town Meeting, Held at the Court house in Newark the 11th *March*, 1783, The following Officers were Chosen. Caleb Camp, Moderator. Aaron Ogden, Town Clerk. John Dodd, Assessor. Nathaniel Farrand, Collector, and Cl k of Strays. Caleb Wheeler, Jun'r, Joseph Baldwin, William Dow and Elijah Squire, be Assistants to the Assessor. Stephen Jarrison and Matthias Ward, Freeholders. Josiah Pierson, John Ogden, Jun'r, Thomas Williams, Commissioners of Appeals. Zebulon Jones and Joseph Tomkins, Surveyors. Benjamin Coe, Jun'r, Rynear Brown, Josiah Quimby, and Joseph Harrison, Overseers of the Poor. Sylvenus Baldwin, Obadiah Bruen, John Tichenor, Jacob Brookfield, Josiah Quimby, Stephen Fordham, Benjamin Lyon, Henry Ratan and William King, Constables.

Voted, that three hundred and fifty pounds be Raised for the use of the poor the ensuing Year. David Banks, Esqr., Pound Master.

At an Annual Town Meeting, held at Newark the 9th *March*, 1784, the following Officers were Chosen for the ensuing Year—Caleb Camp, Moderator. Aaron Ogden, Town Clerk. John Dod, Assessor. Abial Canfield, Collector, and Clerk of Strays. Doct'r Wm. Burnit, Jun'r, Isaac Munn, William Dow, Elijah Squire, Assistants to the Assessor. Caleb Camp, Doc'r John Cundit, and Israel Hedden, Commissioners of Appeals.

Joseph Banks and Luther Baldwin, Surveyors. Benjamin Coe, Jun'r, Stephen Harrison, Rynear Brown and Joseph Harrison, Overseers of the Poor.

Sylvenus Baldwin, Alexander Eagles, John Tichenor, Jabez Baldwin, Stephen Fordom, Thomas Tison, Timothy Ward, and Benjamin Lyon, Constables.

Robert Nichols and Stephen Harrison, Freeholders.

Voted, that the poor be farmed out.

Voted, that to Prevent Disputes, if any Person or Persons of the poor shall be adjudged by the Justices To be Removed for Non Residence, that the Expence shall fall on the Town and not on the farmer.

Voted, That Two hundred and fifty pounds be Raised the ensuing Year, for the Support of the poor.

Benjamin Coe, Farmer of the Poor at One hundred and Ninety Six pounds proc.

Moses Combs, Pound master.

At an Annual Town Meeting, Held at Newark the Eighth day *March*, 1785, the following Officers were Chosen for the ensuing Year—Caleb Camp, Moderator. Aaron Ogden, Town Clerk. Samuel Curry, Collector and Clerk of Strays. John Dod, Assessor. Caleb Camp, Doc'r Cundit, Israel Hedden, Commissioners of Appeals. Abial Canfield and John Lindley, Freeholders. Daniel Williams and Amos Harrison, Surveyors. William King, Isaac Alling, Josiah Quimby, Enos Baldwin and Rubin Harrison, Overseers of the poor. Sylvenus Baldwin, John Gifford, John Tichenor, Josiah Quimby, Stephen Fordom, Gerrit Hogwert, Isaac Force and Daniel Harrison, Constables.

Voted, that to Prevent Disputes if any Person or Persons of the Poor shall be Adjudged by the Justices to be Remov'd for Non Residence, that the expence shall fall on the Town and not on the Farmer of the poor.

Voted, that the poor be Farmed out.

Voted, That Two hundred pounds be Raised the ensuing year, for the support of the Poor. Amos Freeman, Farmer of the Poor at One Hundred and thirty nine pounds Ten Shillings.

Voted, that Moses Combs be pound Master.

Voted, that John Brown be pound Master at Second River.

At an annual Town Meeting held at the Court house in Newark the 14th day of *March*, 1786, The following Officers were Chosen for the ensuing Year—Caleb Camp, Esqr., Moderator. John Burnet, Town Clerk, and Clerk of Strays. John Dod, Assessor. Silvanus Baldwin, Collector. Samuel Hayes, Amos Harrison and Wm. Dow, Commissioners of Appeal. Abiel Canfield and John Lindsley, Freeholders. George Ogilvee and Joseph Banks, Surveyors of the High Way. Isaac Alling, Josiah Quimby, Enos Baldwin, Reubin Harrison and William King, Overseers of the Poor. Silvanus Baldwin, Alex'r Eagles, Josiah Quimby, Daniel Harrison, Ebenezer Dod and Aaron Tompkins, Constables. David Sayrs, Israel Hedden, Benj'n Coe, Jun'r, Isaac Alling, John Crane, Caleb Wheeler, Caleb Parkhurst, Eleazer Hedden, Josiah Tichenor, Capt. Amos Dod, John Tucker,

William Ely, Jacob Deen, George Harrison, Nathaniel Taylor, Eleazer Ogden, Thomas Baldwin, Asher Brown, Thomas Corey, Benj'n Meeker, Samuel Muchmore, James Jacobus, Isaac Tichenor, John Duren [Durand], Joseph Pierson, Matth's Lyon, Jacob H. Vreelandt, James Speer, Hendrick B. Brown, John Van Winckle, Elias Speer, Jacob Brookfield, Wm. Gould, John Mun, John Meeker, William Stockman, Obadiah Hedden, Samuel Pierson, Daniel Taylor, Doct'r John Condict, Samuel Perry, Thomas Williams, William Corbit, John Vreelandt, Stephen Crane, Joshua Ward, and Samuel Miller, Overseers of the High Way. And then the following Votes were taken—

1st. That the Pound be removed to the place where it formerly was, adjoining the School House in the middle of the Town.

2d. That Wm. Grant be keeper of the Pound, and John Brown for Second River.

3d. That 1s. p. Head be paid for all Cattle that shall be Pounded, 8d. to the Person who shall drive them to the Pound, and 4d. to the Keeper of the Pound.

4th. That if any Cattle shall be privately taken out of the Pound, the owners of them shall notwithstanding pay the Poundage.

5th. That the Poor be farmed out for the ensuing Year.

6th. That Obadiah Tompkins be farmed out, seperately from the rest of the Poor.

7th. That the Poor be farmed out untill the first Monday in May 1787.

Joseph Lyon agreed to keep Obadiah Thompkins for 5s. proc. p. Week, and it was agreed to give him 5s. proc. p. week for keeping him, from the first day of April 1786 to the first Monday in May 1787.

William Stockman agreed to keep all the Poor of the Township of Newark, besides the s'd Obadiah Thompkins, from the first Day of April 1786 to the first Monday in May 1787, which it was agreed to give him One Hundred and Seventy Nine Pounds, Proc.

8. That Two Hundred Pounds be raised for the use of the Poor the ensuing Year.

9. That there shall be a large Swinging Gate on the Road that leads to the Salt Meadow, below and near the Hand that points to the Ferry, and that all Cattle which shall be found without a Keeper below the Gate shall be liable to be Pounded.

10. That any Gentlemen have leave to build an House for a Public Market, in the Broad Street.

The following was read and unanimously agreed to—

It is taken for granted, that the Issuing of Paper Money upon Loan would be of great advantage to this State, Especially to the eastern Division of it and a Bill for this Purpose has passed the

House of Assembly, which is now before the Council for their Concurrence: but it is said, that it is not like to pass in its present Form.

We shall therefore be deprived of the Advantage of a Paper Currency, unless a Compromise should take place.

And a Compromise has been proposed in the Council or between the Council and Assembly, which is this—

That the Holders of Certificates should be entitled to borrow the Money upon their Public Securities, in the same manner as Land-Holders will be Entitled to borrow Money upon their Lands, or that a certain Proportion of the Money should be appropriated to the payment of the Interest of Certificates, and thus all the Inhabitants of the State will have an Equal Chance of being benefited by the Money.

It is well known that the Part of the State where the Army lay, hold more Certificates than the Western Division do, and therefore it is supposed, that if a Measure of this Kind Should be adopted, it would be of peculiar advantage to the Inhabitants of this and the adjacent Counties, who performed more services and afforded more supplies for the Army of the United States, than all State besides, and therefore it is probable that they have more Certificates. Some of our Representatives request that their Constituents would instruct them upon this Head, that they may know how to conduct themselves in this Business, as they look upon it a matter of great Importance in which the County is deeply interested. It is therefore proposed and requested, that the following Vote be put—

Whether in the present situation of Affairs, this Town Meeting approves of our Representatives in Council and Assembly consenting, that a Law should pass Entitling the Original Holders of Public Securities to borrow the Money to be Emitted upon Loan, they giving their Certificates for Securities in the same manner as Land Holders shall be Entitled to borrow money by mortgaging their Lands.

At the Annual Town Meeting held at the Court House in Newark the 23d Day of *April* 1787, The following Officers were Chosen for the ensuing Year—

Caleb Camp Esq'r, Moderator. John Burnet, Town Clerk and Clerk of Strays. John Dod Jun'r, Assessor. Silvanus Baldwin, Collector. Israel Hedden, William Dow and Amos Harrison, Commissioners of Appeals. Abial Camfield and John Lindsly, Freeholders. Aaron Harrison and John Crane, Surveyors of the Highways. Nath'l Beach, Josiah Quimby, William King, Enos Baldwin, and Robert Gould, Overseers of the Poor. Silvanus Baldwin, Alexander Eagles, Josiah Quimby, Nath'l Condict, Eleazer Dod, John Ogden of Swines field, Nath'l Taylor and

David D. Crane, Constables. Daniel Johnson, Nathan Baldwin, Benj'n Williams, Nathaniel Taylor, John Durand, William Corby, Richard Harrison, Zenas Pierson, John Tichenor Jun'r, Jotham Harrison, Joseph Pierson Jun'r, Joseph Davis, Simeon Baldwin, John Vreeland, Thomas Force, Jun'r, Daniel Williams, Col. J. Cummings, Samuel Curry, Israel Hedden, Elijah Hedden, Caleb Wheeler, Jun'r, Simon Hedden, Samuel Hays, Jesse Robards, Abial Hays, Eleazer Dod, David Earl, Eleazer Hedden, Sam'l Farrand, Stephen Crane, Adonijah Dod, Henry Speer, Joel Condict, Daniel Woodruff, Daniel Zeluff, Corey Meeker, Samuel Muchmore, Stephen Lyon, Thomas Gould, Jacob Brookfield, Joshua Ward, William Kingsland, William Burnet, Jun'r, Isaac Rowleson, Thomas Seglar, Francis Speer, Daniel Tuers, John Jordon, and Moses Baldwin, Overseers of the High way.

And then the following Votes were taken—

1st. That the Pound be removed near Mr. Samuel Curry's Barkhouse.

2nd. That David D. Crane be keeper of s'd Pound, and John Brown for Second River.

3rd. That 1s. p. Head be paid for all Cattle that shall be Pounded, 8d. to the Person who shall drive them, and 4d. to the Keeper of the Pound.

4th. That if any Cattle shall be taken Privately out of the Pound, the owners of them shall notwithstanding pay the Poundage.

5th. That the Poor be farmed out the ensuing Year.

6th. That the Overseers send the Poor Children to School, at the expence of the Town.

7th. That the fines and Strays go to the Town the ensuing Year.

Zenas Pierson agreed to keep all the Poor of the Township of Newark, from the first Monday in May, 1787, till the first Monday in 1788, for which it was agreed to give him Two Hundred Pounds, proc.

8th. That Silvanus Baldwin be Town Constable, for the ensuing year.

9th. That Two hundred & Twenty-five Pounds be raised for the use of the Poor, the ensuing year.

10th. That all Cattle found in the road below the Gates in the Neck, without a keeper, shall be liable to Poundage.

At an annual TOWN MEETING, held at the Court house in Newark the 28th Day of *April*, 1788, The following Officers were Chosen for the ensuing year—Caleb Camp, Moderator. John Burnet, Town Clerk, and Clerk of Strays. John Dod, Jun'r, Assessor. Silvanus Baldwin, Collector. Israel Hedden, Wm. Dow and Amos Harrison, Commissioners of Appeals.

Abiel Canfield and John Lindsley, Freeholders. John N. Cumming and Abra'm Spear, Surveyors of the Highway. Wm. King, Alex'r Eagles, Josiah Quimby, Robert Gould, and David Little, Overseers of the Poor. David D. Crane, Silvanus Baldwin, Alex'r Eagles, Nath'l Condit, Josiah Quimby, Isaac Force, and Ebenezer Dod, Constables. David D. Crane, Town Constable.

Dan'l Johnson, Sam'l Huntington, Moses Tichenor, Stephen Crane, Jun'r, John N. Cumming, Ebenezer Ward, Jeremiah Bruen, James Thompson, Joseph Woodruff, John Sandford, Joseph Gould, Helmeck Sipp, Sam'l Pierson, Zadock Baldwin, Nath'l Lindsley, Dan'l Taylor, Amos Condict, Nath'l Squire, Jedidiah Lindsley, John Wright, Wm. Burnet, Jun'r, Sam'l J. Ward, Jonathan Hedden, Branard Dickerson, Wm. Bond, Elijah Lyon, Isaac Gillom, Thomas Baldwin, Obadiah Crane, Norris Baker, John Davis, Benj'n Reave, John Peck, Henry Kent, Isaac Van Geson, Jacob Vreelandt, Abr'm Mowerson, Timothy Bruen, Wm. Stockman, Joseph Crane, Joseph Ball, Caleb Johnson, Henry Rutan, Elias Osburn and Anthony King. Total (45).

And then the following Votes were taken—

1st. That David D. Crane be Keeper of the Pound, and John Brown for Second River.

2nd. That 1s. p. head be paid for all Cattle that shall be pounded, 8d. to the Person who shall drive them to the Pound and 4d. to the Keeper of the Pound.

3rd. That if any Cattle shall be taken privately out of the Pound, the Owners of them shall notwithstanding pay the Poundage.

4th. That the Poor be farmed out for the ensuing Year.

5th. That the Farmers send the Poor Children to school the ensuing Year.

6th. That the Fines and Strays go to the Town for the ensuing Year.

7th. That three hundred Pounds be raised for the use of the Poor, the ensuing Year.

Caleb Camp agreed to keep all the Poor of the Township of Newark, from the first Monday in May, 1788, to the first Monday in May, 1789, which it was Agreed to give him Two hundred and forty five Pounds.

8th. John Peck, David Banks, and John Condit, Esqr., were chosen and appointed a Committee, to settle with the Freeholders of the Township for the ensuing Year.

9th. That the Money raised by the Dog tax, shall be appropriated to the encouragement of raising Sheep and Wool in this Township.

The increase of Sheep and the consequent production and increase of Wool being of the highest importance to the interest and prosperity of this Country, and the inhabitants of this Township being disposed to encourage and promote so laudable a design do agree to give the following premiums upon the Conditions following, viz:

To the Person who shall shear off of his own Sheep in the Spring of 1789, the greatest quantity of good clean Wool, the sum of ten pounds.

To the Person who shall shear the next greatest quantity as above s'd, the sum of eight Pounds.

To the Person who shall Shear the third greatest quantity, the sum of six pounds.

To the Person who shall shear the fourth greatest quantity, the sum of five pounds.

To the Person who shall Shear the fifth greatest quantity, the sum of three pounds.

To the Person who shall Shear the sixth greatest quantity, the sum of two pounds.

No person shall be entitled to either of the above s'd premiums, unless he shall reside within this Township, and unless he shall appear before David Banks, Esqr., on or before the tenth Day of June, 1789, and shall make oath to the quantity of Wool he shall have Sheared as above s'd. And the s'd David Banks is hereby authorised to give Orders upon the Collector of the Township, in favor of the persons who shall appear to be entitled to the above s'd premiums—and the s'd Collector is hereby directed to pay such Orders, which shall be sufficient vouchers in the settlement of his accounts. And if it should so happen, that two or more persons shall produce the same quantities of Wool, then such premiums as they are entitled to shall be equally divided between them.

10th. That the Executors of Sam'l Curry, Dec'd, shall be released from the Payment of £5, being five years rent of the Tanyard which he hired of the Town.

11th. That the Town Committee or Trustees be authorized to draw on the Town, for any expences arising from any suit that may be commenced by them.

12th. That the Town Clerk meet with the Justices, and bring forward the acc't of the Overseers of the Poor the ensuing Year.

13th. That John Peck, Esqr., David Banks, Esqr., Caleb Camp, John Crane, Sam'l Hays, Ebenezer Ward, Elias Baldwin, Elijah Squire and Doc'r J. Condict, be Town Trustees to take care of the priviledges of the Town, agreeable to the Town Charter.

J. BURNET, Town Clerk.

At an annual Town Meeting, held at the Court House in New-Ark the 27th Day of *April*, 1789—The following Officers were chosen for the ensuing Year—Caleb Camp, Esqr., Moderator. John Burnet, Town Clerk, and Clerk of Strays. John Dod,

Jun'r, Ass'r. Silvanus Baldwin, Collector. Israel Hedden, Wm. Dow, and Amos Harrison, Commiss'rs of Appeal. Abiel Camfield and Abraham Spier, Freeholders. John C. Crane and Zenas Pierson, Surveyors of the Highway. Alex'r Eagles, Josiah Quimby, Elijah Squire, Robert Gould and John Brown, Overseers of the Poor. David D. Crane, Town Constable. David D. Crane, John Gifford, Silvanus Baldwin, John Drew, Nath'l Condict, Josiah Quimby, Girshom Kilburn, James McGinnis, and Isaac Force, Constables. Isaac Plum, Viner V. Zandt, Luther Baldwin, Samuel Hays, Aaron Ogden, Caleb Pierson, Joseph Robards, Elias Osborn, Elijah Durand, Aaron Quimby, Samuel Mun, Jun'r, John Smith, Jun'r, Amos Mun, Abraham Rheock, Ezra Baldwin, Samuel Baley, Nath'l Taylor (Short Hill), Joseph Pierson, Daniel Taylor, Elijah Squire, John Perry, Abraham Spier, Aaron Harrison, David Day, Henry Kingsland, Joseph Tompkins, Jonathan Hutchings, Henry Wade, Abel Dod, John Berry, John Jordan, Abner Ball, Thomas Sigler, Josiah Baldwin, Abraham V. Riper, Robert Gould, Caleb Martin, Stephen Parkhurst, Henry Rutan, Israel Crane, Nath'l Andress, Amos Dod, Thomas Sidmun, Abraham Harrison, Wm. Burnet, Jun'r, Samuel M. Ward, and Jacob Denman, Overseers of the Highway. James Jacobus, Overseer of the Road by order of Two Magistrates. J. B.

And then the following Votes were taken—

1st. That Stephen Hays be Keeper of the Pound, and John Brown for Second River.

2d. That 1s. p'r Head be paid for all Cattle that shall be Pounded; 8d. to the Person who shall drive them to the Pound, and 4d. to the Keeper of the Pound.

3d. That if any Cattle shall be taken privately out of the Pound, the Owner shall notwithstanding pay Poundage.

4th. That the Poor shall be farmed out the ensuing year.

5th. That the Farmer shall send the Poor Children to School, the ensuing year.

6th. That the fines and Strays go to the Town for the ensuing year.

7th. That all horses and horn'd Cattle found in the Road in the Neck, without a Keeper, is liable to Poundage.

8th. That Two hundred and fifty pounds be Raised for the use of the Poor, the ensuing year.

Henry Squire agreed to keep all the Poor of the Township of New-Ark, from the first Monday in May, 1789, to the first Monday in May, 1790, for which it was agreed to give him two hundred and fifteen Pounds.

9th. That the Dog tax for the year 1788, be appropriated for the use of the Poor.

10th. That the Town Committee call a Town Meeting to settle some business (they have to settle) of Importance.

JOHN BURNET, Town Clerk.

At an annual TOWN MEETING, held at the Court House in New-Ark, *April* 26th, 1790, the following Officers were chosen for the ensuing year—

Caleb Camp, Esqr., Moderator. John Burnet, Town Clerk, and Cl'k of Strays. John Dod, Jun., Assessor. Silvanus Baldwin, Collector. John N. Cumming, Abraham Spier and Amos Harrison, Commissioners of Appeals.

Abiel Camfield and Amos Harrison, Freeholders.

Nathaniel Beach and Samuel Hays, Surveyors of the Highway.

Alex'r Eagles, Stephen Harrison, Esqr., Robert Gould, Henry W. Wade, and Abraham Joralman, Over's of the Poor.

Zebulon Jones, Esqr., and Caleb Wheeler, Jun'r, Town Committee in the room of John Ogden, Esqr., resigned, and Nathaniel Camp, dece'd. Stephen Hays, Town Constable. Silvanus Baldwin, John Gifford, Nath'l Canfield, Stephen Hays, Gershom Kilburn, Nath'l Condict, Josiah Quimby, Ezra Baldwin, James McGinnis, Constables.

Caleb Camp, Esqr., Samuel Hays, Isaac Alling, Moses Baldwin, John Wiley, Caleb Wheeler, Jun'r, Joseph Camp (Farms), Daniel Harrison, Thos. Baldwin, Ezekiel Ball, Abijah Harrison, John H. Brown, Peter H. Garrison, Nath'l Crane, Benjamin Crane, Uzal Dod, Aaron Edwards, William Corby, Christian Bone, Zenas Pierson, Simeon Harrison, Abijah Harrison, Joseph Tompkins, Israel Blundige, Peter Halleck, John Edwards, Abraham Rheack. Branard Dickerson, Thomas Force, Aaron Ball, Ab'm Stegar, Helmech Joralmon, Moses Baldwin (Farms), Ichabod Baldwin, Pell Sid, William Ely, Garrabrants A. Garrabrants, Paiminus [Parmenus] Riggs, John Ogden (O. Mountain), Joseph Gould, John Berry, Eleazer Hedden, Daniel Condict, Henry Rutan, Daniel Brown, Thos. Gardner, Jun'r, Elihu Pierson, Wm. Sandford, John Jordan, George Harrison, Joseph Baldwin (Crane Town), Joseph Ward, James Spier, Anthony Waters, Jos. Woodruff, and Samuel Huntington, Overseers of the Highway.

And then the following Votes were taken, (viz:

1st. That Stephen Hays be Keeper of the Pound, and John Brown for Second River.

2nd. That One Shilling p'r head be paid for all Cattle that shall be pounded, 8d. to the person who shall drive them to the Pound, and 4d. to the keeper of the Pound.

3rd. That if any Cattle shall be taken privately out of the Pound, the owners of them shall notwithstanding pay the poundage, or if taken from the person driving them to the Pound.

4th. That the Poor be farmed out for the ensuing year.

6th. That the Fines and Strays go to the Town for the ensuing year.

7th. That two hundred pounds be raised for the use of the Poor, the ensuing year.

8th. That the Dog Tax for the year 1789, be appropriated for the use of the Poor. John Robards agreed to keep all the Poor of the Township of New-Ark, from the first Monday in May, 1790, to the first Monday in May, 1791, for which it was agreed to give him Two Hundred and fifteen Pounds.

J. BURNET, Town Clerk.

At an annual TOWN MEETING, held at the Court House in Newark, on Monday, *April* 11th, 1791, the following Officers were chosen for the ensuing year—

Zebulon Jones, Esqr., Moderator. John Burnet, Town Clerk, and Clerk of Strays. John Dod, Jun'r, Assessor. Silvanus Baldwin, Collector. John N. Cumming, Abraham Spier and Amos Harrison, Commissioners of Appeals. Abiel Camfield and Amos Harrison, Freeholders. Henry Squier and Joseph Thompkins, Surveyors of the Highway. Alexander Eagles, Stephen Harrison, Esqr., Elijah Squire, Robert Gould and Ab'm Joralmon, Overseers of the Poor. Stephen Hays and Nathaniel Canfield, Town Constables. Nath'l Canfield, Stephen Hays, Silvanus Baldwin, John Gifford, James McGinnis, Nathaniel Condict, Gershom Kilburn, James Conklin, Wm. King and Josiah Quimby, Constables. Samuel Hays, Benjamin Coe, Isaac Plume, Jon'th. Sayrs, David D. Crane, Caleb Wheeler, Jun'r, Abner Ward, Nich's A. Garrabrant, Benjamin Williams, John Ogden, (Swine Field), Amos Robards, Job Brown, Eleazer Hedden, Nath'l Foster, Daniel Williams, Jun'r, Jephia Condict, John H. Brown, Nathan Tichenor, David Day, Nath'l Crane, John Crane, Nathaniel Taylor, John W. Smith, Jonathan M. Baldwin, Samuel Mun, David Morris, Isaac Freeman, James Spier, Anthony Waters, Josiah Brown, John Lyon, Recompence Crowell, Elijah Case, John Vreelandt, Caleb Ward, Richard Harrison, John Meeker, Isaac Winants, Ezekiel Ball, William Bond, Thaddeus Russell, Garret P. Jacobus, Abraham Spier, Lewis Miller, Linus Baldwin, Nathaniel Edwards, Chris'n Bone, Joseph Davis, Daniel Harrison, Eleazer Dod, John Winner, Enos Farrand, Zenas Pierson, William Hornblower, John Drew, Abraham Garrabrants, Abram V. Riper, Abraham Rheoc, Thomas Marr, Thomas Deane and Cornelius V. Gieson, Overseers of the Road.

And then the following Votes were taken, viz:

1. That Stephen Hays be Keeper of the Pound, and John Brown for Second River.

2. That one Shilling per Head be paid for all Cattle and Hogs that shall be pounded, 8d. to the Person who shall drive them to the Pound, and 4d. to the Keeper of the pound, and 6d. be paid for Sheep.

3. That if any Cattle, Hogs or Sheep, shall be taken privately out of the Pound, the owners of them shall pay the Poundage, or if taken from the Person driving them to the Pound.

4. That the Poor be farmed out this year.

5. That the Farmers shall send the Poor Children to school this Year.

6. That the Fines and Strays go to the Town this Year.

7. That Two hundred pounds be raised for the use of the Poor this Year.

8. That John Peck and John Lindsly, Esq'rs, be a Committee to settle with the Overseers of the Poor, and report to the next Annual Town Meeting.

9. That the Dog tax for the Year 1790 be appropriated to the use of the Poor.

Sayrs Robards agreed to keep all the Poor of the Township of Newark, from the first Monday in May, 1791, to the first Monday in May, 1792, for which it was agreed to give him One hundred and Ninety Seven Pounds, Ten Shillings—£197 10s.

ZEBULON JONES, Moderator.

J. BURNET, Cl'k.

At an Annual TOWN MEETING, held at the Court House in Newark, *April* 9th, 1792, The following Officers were chosen for the ensuing Year—

Caleb Camp, Esqr., Moderator. John Burnet, Town Clerk, and Cl'k of Strays. John Dod, Jun'r, Assessor. Silvanus Baldwin, Collector. Ephraim Morris, Joseph Harrison and Thos. Williams, Commiss's of Appeals. Abiel Canfield and Amos Harrison, Freeholders. Samuel Hayes and Moses Baldwin, Surveyors of the Highway. Stephen Harrison, Alex'r Eagles, Abraham Joralman, Ezra Baldwin and William Ely, Jun'r, Overseers of the Poor. Silvanus Baldwin, John Gifford, James Conklin, Nath'l Canfield, Gershom Kilburn, David Taylor, Nath'l Condict, Josiah Quimby, and William King, Constables. Caleb Sayres, Ephraim Morris, George Harrison, James Jacobus, Aaron Harrison, Jotham Harrison, Simeon Harrison, Egbert Egbert, Francis Speer, Isaac Van Gieson, Gershom Kilburn, Isaac Cadmus, John Sandford, Amos Freeman, Joel Condict, John Squire, Eleazer Dod, Israel Crane, Joseph Pierson, Jun'r, Joseph Gould, John J. Brown, Joseph Thompkins, Jun'r, Jacob Dean, Francis Outwater, Zebina Ward, Christopher S. Stegar, John Pierson, John Corby, Elias E. Baldwin, Stephen Fordham, William Mutchmore, Isaac Longworth, Jacob Denman, William Camp, Nathan Tichenor, Jonathan Day, Nicholas Joralman, Caleb M. Baldwin, John Peah, Caleb Camp, Moses Gardner, Daniel Taylor, Jun'r, Isaac Condict, William Burnet, Jacobus Joralman, William Hand, Abiel Hayes, Zenas Freeman, Erastus Pierson, Nath'l Taylor, Abner Ball, Overseers of the Highway.

And then the following Votes were taken, viz:

1st. That Rev'd Moses Combs be Keeper of the Pound, and John Brown for Second River.

2d. That one Shilling per head be paid for all Cattle and Hogs that shall be Pounded, 8d. to the Person who shall drive them to the Pound, and 4d. to the Keeper of the Pound, and that 6d. be paid for Sheep.

3d. That if any Cattle, Hogs or Sheep shall be taken privately out of the Pound, the owner of them shall notwithstanding pay the Poundage; or, if forcibly taken from the Person driving them to the Pound.

4th. That the Poor be farmed out in four Classes this Year.

5th. That the Farmers shall send the Poor Children to School this Year.

6th. That the Dog tax for the Year 1791, be appropriated to the use of the poor.

Joseph Lindsly agreed to keep the first Class of the Poor for fifty pounds—William Stockman, the fourth and Second Class, for one hundred and two pounds.

Zenas Pierson, the third Class for forty six pounds, from the first Monday in May, 1792, to the first Monday in May, 1793.

CALEB CAMP, Moderator.

J. Burnet, Cl'k.

At an Annual Town Meeting, held at the Court House in Newark, *April* 8th, 1793, The following Officers were chosen for the ensuing year—

John Lindsly, Esqr., Moderator. John Burnet, Town Cl'k and Cl'k of Strays. John Dod, Jun'r, Assess'r. Silvanus Baldwin, Collector. Ephraim Morris, Joseph Harrison and Thomas Williams, Commissioners of Appeal. Abiel Canfield and Amos Harrison, Freeh's. Aaron Harrison and Simeon Harrison, Surveyors of Highways. Alex'r Eagles, Stephen Harrison, Abraham Joralman, Wm. Ely, Jun'r, and Ezra Baldwin, Overseers of the Poor. Silvanus Baldwin, John Gifford, Nath'l Canfield, Josiah Quimby, David Taylor, Nath'l Condict, and Wm. King, Constables.

Samuel Huntington, Isaac Alling, Samuel Hay, Nath'l Camp, Enos Baldwin, David Morehouse, Calvin Ely, Joseph Harrison, Joseph Rogers, Pell Tidd, John Michael Vreelandt, Timothy Ball, Nathan Squire, Isaac Kingsland, Stephen Smith, Ethan Baldwin, Timothy Brewin, Benj'n Coe, Abraham Sigler, Aury King, Thomas Cadmus, Joseph Camp, Cyrus Freeman, Silas Baldwin, Elikam Crane, Jun'r, Matthew Dod, Jedidiah Lindsly, Elijah Lyon, Henry Earl, Silas Cook, Sam'l Mun, Jacob Vreelandt, Capt. Henry Joralman, Wm. Wheton, Sam'l Perry, Thaddeus

Russell, Enos Condict, Jonathan Wade, Joseph Keen, Stephen Beach, Moses Edwards, Josiah Quimby, Abraham Harrison, David Meeker, Nicholas O. Garrabrants, Amos Mun, Aaron Ward, John Jordan, Hendrick Franisko, James Townley, Joseph Pierson, Thomas Parsell, Ebenezer Canfield, Enos Pierson, Aaron Beach, Joseph Pierson, Caleb M. Baldwin and Isaac Plum, Overseers of the Highway.

And then the following Votes were taken, viz:

1st. That one Shilling p. head be paid for all Cattle and Hogs, that shall be pounded, 8d. to the person who shall drive them to the Pound, and 4d. to the Keeper of the Pound, and that 6d. be paid for Sheep.

3d. That if any Cattle, Hogs or Sheep, shall be taken privately out of the Pound, the owners of them shall notwithstanding pay the Poundage; or, if forcibly taken from the person driving them to the Pound.

4th. That Moses Combs be Keeper of the Pound, and John Brown for Second River.

5th. That the Poor be farmed out in four Classes this Year.

6th. That two hundred pounds be raised for the use of the Poor this Year.

7th. That the Justices and Overseers shall bind out all the Poor Children this Year.

8th. That the Salt Meadow shall not be burned this Year.

9th. That the Dog Tax for the Year 1792 be appropriated to the use of the Poor.

Nath'l Taylor agreed to keep the first Class of the Poor for the sum of Twenty Eight Pounds Ten Shillings.

Thomas Sidman the second Class, for Thirty Seven Pounds.

Josiah Tichenor the third Class, for the sum of Forty nine Pounds ten Shillings, and Joseph Camp the fourth Class for the sum of Twenty nine Pounds fifteen shillings, from the first Monday in May 1793 to the first Monday in May 1794.

JOHN LINDSLY, Moderator.

J. Burnet, Cl'k.

At an Annual Town Meeting, held in the Court House in Newark *April* 14th, 1794, the following Officers for the ensuing year were Chosen—

Zebulon Jones, Moderator. John Burnet, Town Clerk and Clerk of Strays. John Dodd, Jun'r, Assessor. Silvanus Baldwin, Collector. Caleb Wheeler, Amos Harrison, and Ephraim Morris, Commissioners of Appeal. Abiel Canfield, and Amos Harrison, Freeholders. Stephen Hays and Amos Condict, Surveyors of the Highway. Abiel Canfield, Joseph Davis, Stephen Harrison, Joseph Harrison, Abram Jerolaman and David E·

Tichenor, Overseers of the Poor. Silvanus Baldwin, John Gifford, Nath'l Canfield, James Clark, William King, Amos Freeman, Josiah Quimby, Samuel Jones and David Taylor, Constables.

David Ross, Caleb Sayrs, Nath'l Camp, Isaac Plum, James McGinnis, Joseph Keen, Moses Robarts, Jared Harrison, Henry Jarolaman, Halamer Jarolaman, Isaac Luker, Anthony Waters, Nehemiah Hedden, Moses Osborne, John Lindsley, Francis Lawrence, Peter H. Garrison, David Banks, Zenas Pierson, Eathan Baldwin, Dan'l Teirs, John Lamb, Isaac Kingsland, Dan'l Harrison, Joel Williams, W. S. [Watsesson], William Stockman, Linus Dodd, Dan'l Dodd, George Harrison, Cyrus Pierson, John Pierson, Abial Hays, Abram Hyar, Aaron Tompkins, Sam'l M. Ward, John Jordan, Abram Queman, Pell Teed, Joseph Green, Jonathan Crane, Stephen Moorhouse, John Vreelandt, Garret V. Waggoner, Moses Baldwin (Newark), Joseph Jones, Nathan Tichenor, Jotham Johnson, Egbert Egberts, Mathias Chitterlin, Abram Sigler, Joel Condict, and William Holmes, Overseers of the Highway.

And then the following Votes were taken, viz:

First. That one Shilling p'r head be paid for all Cattle and Hogs that shall be pounded, 8d. to the person who shall drive them to the pound, and 4d. to the Keeper of the pound, and that 6d. be paid for Sheep.

Second. That if any Cattle, Hogs, or Sheep shall be taken privately out of the Pound, the owners of them shall notwithstanding pay the Poundage; or, if forcibly taken from the person driving them to the Pound.

Third. That Moses Tichenor be Keeper of the Pound, and John Brown for Second River.

Fourth. That the pound be removed above the House of Jonathan Keen.

Fifth. That the Poor be left in the hands of the Overseers, to be taken care of at their Discretion.

Sixth. That the Dog Tax for the year 1793 be appropriated for the use of the Poor.

Seventh. That the sum of Two Hundred Pounds be raised for the use of the Poor this Year.

ZEBULON JONES, Moderator.

J. Burnet, Cl'k.

At an Annual Town Meeting, held in the Court House in Newark *April* 13th, 1795, the following Officers for the Ensuing Year were Chosen—

William Burnet, Moderator. John Burnet, Town Clerk, and Clerk of Estrays. Isaac Mun, Assessor. Silvanus Baldwin, Collector. Amos Harrison, Nath'l Camp and Jasper Ten Brook, Commissioners of Appeal. Abiel Canfield and Amos Harrison, Freeholders. Joseph Rogers and Aaron Harrison, Surveyors of the Highway. Abial Canfield, David E. Tichenor, Stephen Harrison, Jonathan Wade, Joseph Davis and Abraham Joralaman, Overseers of the Poor. John Gifford, Nath'l Canfield, James Clark, Joseph Robarts, Ezekiel Ball, Josiah Quimby, David Taylor, William King and David Ayres, Constables. Nath'l Bruen, James McGinnis, Isaac Davis, Stephen Hays, Sam'l Hays, Josiah Baldwin, Abraham Cadmus, James Dod, Enos Pierson, Simeon Williams, Joseph Campbell, Moses Combs, Pell Ted, Nath'l Camp, Jonathan Sayres, David Earl, Jonathan Hedden, Thomas Baldwin, Zenas Pierson, Henry Mandeville, James Dod, William Ely Jun'r, John Kidney, Noah Matthews, Henry I. Speer, Christopher Interest, Sam'l Huntington, Jacob Foster, John Harriot, Nath'l Crane, David Rogers, Joseph Tompkin's Jun'r, Isaac V. Geeson, Egbert Egberts, Francis Beatty, Justus Baldwin, Timothy Brewin, John Dod Jun'r, Joseph Rogers, Abial Hays, Ziba Tompkin, Ryner Brown, Job Brown, Aaron Ball, Joseph Harrison and John Van Winkle, Overseers of the Highway.

And then the Following Votes were taken, Viz—

1. That two Shillings p'r head be paid for all Cattle and Hogs that shall be pounded—1s. 6d. to the person who shall drive them to the pound, and 6d. to the Keeper of the pound, and that 1s. be paid for Sheep, 9d· to the driver and 3d. to the Keeper of the pound.

2. That if any Cattle, Hogs or Sheep shall be taken privately out of the pound; The Owners of them shall notwithstanding pay the poundage, Or if forcibly taken from the person driving them to the pound.

3. That Benjamin Lyon be Keeper of the pound, and John Brown for Second River.

4. That the Overseers of the Poor, after settling their acco'ts shall render them Annually at this Meeting.

5. That the Poor be left in the Hands of the Overseers, to be taken care of at their discretion.

6. That the Dog Tax for the year 1794 be appropriated for the use of the Poor.

7. That the sum of three Hundred Pounds be raised for the use of the Poor this Year.

WM. BURNET, Moderator.

J. BURNET, Clerk.

At a TOWN MEETING in the Court House in Newark, *April* 11th, 1796, the following Officers for the insuing Year were duly Chosen—

Amos Harrison, Moderator. Jabez Parkhurst, Town Clerk,

and Clerk of Estrays. John Dod Jun'r Assessor. Silvanus Baldwin, Collector. Caleb Camp Esq'r Judge of next Election. Ephraim Morris, Amos Harrison, Nathaniel Camp, Commissioners of Appeal. Abiel Canfield and Amos Harrison, Chosen Freeholders. Abraham Speer and Amos Condit, Surveyors of the Highways. Abiel Canfield, David Tichenor, Stephen Harrison, Joseph Davis, Jonathan Wade, and Abraham Cadmus for Second River, Overseers of the poor. Joseph Robords, David Ayres, John Gifford, Josiah Quimby, William King, Nathaniel Canfield, David Taylor, James Bruen, Aaron Dod Jun'r, Nathaniel Andress and John Brown, Constables.

It was agreed by the Town Meeting, that the poundage of Cattle &c. should remain as the law directs.

Henry Jaralman, Abraham Cadmus, John King Sen'r, Nehemiah Baldwin, George Harrison, Thomas Cadmus, Matthias Ward, Phillip Kearney, John P. Crane, Zenas Williams, Jacob Foster, Aaron Tompkins, John Johnson, Caleb Brown, Isaac Munn, Samuel Lindley, Samuel Hays, Thomas Ball, Joseph Condict, Zadock Baldwin, Christian Bone, Robert Gould, John Berry, Josiah Smith, Josiah Baldwin, Isaac Van Geeson, Stephen Morehouse Jun'r, Nathaniel Dod Jun'r, Cornelius Speer, John A. Van Geeson, Jonathan Kent, Linus Pierson, John Speer Jun'r, William Kingsland, Nathaniel Crane, Jonathan Baldwin, Zenas Freeman, Parmenus Riggs, Samuel Billington, Linus Dod, David Ross, Zebediah Ward, Johnson Nichols, Peter H. Garritse.

Daniel Tues, John Parrot, Thadeus Russell, Eathen Baldwin, Jasper Ten Brook, Paul Hurton, Peter Cook, Uriah Smith, Eliakim Crane, Nathaniel Harrison, Josiah Tichenor, Stephen Hays, Cornelius Vincent, Elias Osborn, John Morris, Overseers of the Highway.

And then the following Votes were passed, Viz:

1. That the poor be left in the hands of the Overseers, to be taken Care of at their discretion.

2. That the dog Tax be appropriated for the use of the poor.

3. That the sum of Five Hundred pounds be raized for the use of the Poor this Year.

4. That the Overseers of the poor render an account of the whole expence of the poor, at the next Town Meeting.

5. That the Town give all the liberty they possess to the propriators of the School House at the North End of the Town, for them to remove said School House on the Upper Common.

AMOS HARRISON, Moderator.

J. Parkhurst, Cl'k.

At an annual Town Meeting, held at the Court house in Newark *April* 10th, 1797, The following Officers for the ensuing year were duly chosen—

Caleb Camp Esq'r, Moderator. Jabez Parkhurst, Town Clerk, and Clerk of Estrays. John Dodd Jun'r, Assessor. Sylvanus Baldwin, Collector. Amos Harrison Esq'r, Judge of next Election. Amos Harrison Esq'r, Major Nathaniel Beach, and Ephraim Morris, Commissioners of Appeal. Abiel Camfield and Amos Harrison Esq'r, Chosen Freeholders. Caleb Camp Esq'r and Jotham Harrison, Surveyors of the Highways.

John Brown, Joseph Davis, Aaron Munn, Capt. Jonathan Wade, Capt. David Tichenor and Abiel Camfield, Overseers of the Poor. James McGinniss, Josiah Quimby, Moses Williams, Amos Freeman, Joseph Robords, Elias A. Baldwin, John Gifford, Nathaniel Canfield and Moses Ward, Constables.

Israel Curry, Pound Master for Newark. John Brown Sen'r, Pound Master for Second River.

Doct'r William Burnet, Major Nathaniel Beach, Thomas Speer, Abraham Berger, Henry Cadmus, Jacob Ward, Joseph Crane, Henry Rattan, Peter Garritse, Enos Williams, James Siglar, John Speer, Abraham Siglar, William Ely Ju'r, Frederick Vincent, Amos Freeman, David Munn, Cyrus Freeman, David Pierson, Amos Tyrrill, Capt. Thomas Baldwin, Abiel Hays, Samuel Camp, John Johnson, Stephen Peck, Caleb Parkhurst, Sylvanus Baldwin Jun'r, Jabez Camfield, Egbert Egberts, Richard Harrison, Elias Baldwin, Moses Quinby, Thomas Ball, Peter H. Garritse, Oliver Crane, Aaron Williams, Elias A. Baldwin, Capt. Isaac Gillam, John Van Winkle, Sayres Coe, John Morris, John P. Crane, Col. Matthias Ward, Simon Hedden, John Jordan, Samuel Stivers, Joseph Clizbe, Samuel Rattan, Stephen Plum, Aaron Tompkins, Caleb Ward, Samuel Tompkins, Thaddeus Russell, Robert Gould, Joseph Kingsland, Daniel Dodd, Capt. Zenas Pierson and Jonathan Wlliams, Overseers of the Highway.

And then the following Votes were passed—

1. That the Poor be left in the hands of the Overseers (as the year past).

2. That the Dog Tax be applied to the use of the Poor.

3. That the sum of Five Hundred pounds Proclamation money, be raised for the use of the Poor the ensuing year.

4. Resolved (on motion of Mr. William Hornblower) That the Poor of Second River (which have been supported by the Parish of Second River separately) be in future included in the Poor of the Township of Newark, and that they be supported together with the said Township's Poor at large, from the first Monday in May next, and that all the accounts respecting the said Poor previous to that day be paid by the two parties seperately.

CALEB CAMP, Moderator.

J. Parkhurst, Cl'k.

At an Annual Town Meeting, held at the Court House in Newark on the 9th day of *April*, 1798—The following Officers for the ensuing year were duly chosen—

Col. John Condit, Moderator. Jabez Parkhurst, Town Clerk, and Clerk of Estrays.

John Dodd, Assessor. Sylvanus Baldwin, Collector.

Major Amos Harrison, Judge of next Election. Nathan Squire, Nathaniel Beach and Abraham Speer, Commissioners of Appeal. Abiel Camfield and Major Amos Harrison, Chosen Freeholders.

Caleb Wheeler and Nathan Squire, Surveyors of Highway.

Abiel Camfield, John Brown, Aaron Munn, and Capt. David E. Tichenor, Overseers of the Poor.

William S. Pennington, Abraham Speer, Nathaniel Crane, Jotham Harrison and Caleb Camp, Town Committee.

Elias A. Baldwin, Joseph Robords, Nathaniel Canfield, William King, James McGinniss, Joseph Dodd, Moses Williams Junior, Josiah Quinby and Uzal Baldwin, Constables.

John Brown, Samuel Curry, Samuel Munn and Thomas Baldwin, Pound Masters.

Nehemiah Baldwin, Anthony Van Cisco, Jarid Rutgers, Stephen Fordham, John Parrot, Enos Farrand, David Sayre, Elias Crane, Moses Robords, John Vincent 2nd, Aaron Johnson, Abiathar Dodd, Aaron Roffe, Ethan Baldwin, Abiel Hayes, David Earle, Joseph Kingsland, Thomas Williams, Aaron Crowell, Abner Crowell, Nathaniel Condit, Jabez Pierson, Matthias Ward, Stephen Hayes, Jonas Smith, Matthias Dodd, Samuel Farrand, Enos Lyon, Joel Condit, Ebenezer Striker, John E. Baldwin, Aaron Baldwin Jun'r, Thomas Sydenham, Moses Dodd, Simon Condit, Moses Crowell, Daniel Dodd, Amos Munn, John Spear, Henry Kingsland, John Pake, Henry Striker, Doct'r William Burnet, Caleb Parkhurst, David D. Crane, Joseph Miller, John Winne, Moses Baldwin, Joseph Siglar, Abraham Spear, Isaac Van Gesen, David Munn, Joseph Condit, Daniel Lindly, John H. Brown and Abraham Jaralman, Overseers of the Highway.

The following Votes were passed—

First. That the next Annual Election for the State Legislature be opened at the House of Samuel Munn at Orange, and held there during the first day of the same, and that on the Second day it be opened and closed at the Court House in Newark.

Second. That the next Town Meeting be held at the Court House.

Third. That the Clerk of Estrays have Liberty to publish an account of the Estrays, when he may think proper.

Fourth. That the Roads be repaired by labour and not by hire.

Fifth. That permission be granted for the Erection of two more public Pounds, Viz—One on the Common between Samuel Munn's and Moses Williams's at Orange, and another near the House of Capt. Thomas Baldwin.

Sixth. That the Town Committee be authorised to build the Pounds, and Keep them in repair.

Seventh. That the sum of Twenty Pounds be raised this Year, for the expence of the Pounds.

Eighth. That the Poor be left in the Care of the Overseers, as the last Year.

Ninth. That the Sum of Two Hundred pounds be raised for the use of the Poor this Year.

Tenth. That the Dog tax be applied to the use of the Poor this Year.

Eleventh. That the Town Committee be requested to meet at the House of Johnson Tuttle, at nine o'clock on the morning of the 12th instant, in order to divide the Highways into districts, to Erase the names of all supernumerary Overseers, and transact such other business as the Law authorizes them to perform.

Twelfth. That all Horned Cattle, Horses, Hogs and Sheep which may be pounded, shall be driven to the Pound which is nearest the place of trespass; and if any person shall drive said Cattle &c. to any pound situated more than One Mile farther than the pound which is nearest to said place of trespass, such driving shall be deemed unlawful, and the offender shall forfeit and pay to the owner of said Cattle, horses, hogs or Sheep the amount of double their lawful poundage.

Thirteenth. That the lawful poundage shall be as follows Viz: horned cattle and horses one shilling per head, Hogs two shillings per head and and Sheep six pence per head, New York Currency. One third part of the amount of the poundage shall be retained by the pound Master, and the other two thirds he shall pay to the person driving such cattle to the pound.

Fourteenth. That all cattle found in the road without a keeper, below the first Great Swamp bridge shall be liable to poundage.

Fifteenth. That a certain paper which has been handed to the Town Clerk, to lay before the Town Meeting, be read, it being an address to both Houses of Congress praying that they would "take some Effectual measures to restrain the arming of our "merchant Ships, and that they will not involve the Country in "an immense increase of debt by instituting or augmenting a "national maratime force; but avoid both as the best means to "prevent being led into war."

The said address being read and some debate ensuing, a motion was made and seconded that the Town Meeting adjourn till Monday next, in order to be more fully informed concerning the dispatches to Government from our Envoys in France. A Vote being taken on this motion it was negatived. A vote then passed almost Unanimously, that

The said Petition be adopted as the sentiments of this Town Meeting, and that two Copies of the same be forwarded to Congress, the One directed to the Vice President of the Senate, and the other to the Speaker of the House of Representatives, with a request that they lay the same before their respective Houses.

JOHN CUNDIT, Moderator.

J. Parkhurst, Clerk.

At an Annual Town Meeting, held at the Court House in Newark on the eighth day of *April*, 1799, The following officers for the ensuing year were duly chosen—

Major Amos Harrison, Moderator.

Jabez Parkhurst, Town Clerk, and Clerk of Strays.

Major John Dodd, Assessor.

Voted, that the person who may be chosen Collector of the Township shall give sufficient security for the faithful performance of his duty, and also that the Town Committee have power to demand and receive such security.

Isaac Ward was chosen Collector of the Township.

Major Amos Harrison was chosen Judge of next election.

Nathaniel Beach, Nathan Squier and Abraham Speer, Commissioners of Appeal.

Samuel Pennington and Nathan Squier, Chosen Freeholders.

Stephen Hayes and Samuel Condit, Surveyors of the Highway.

Abiel Camfield, John Brown, Ephraim Morris, Aaron Munn and David E. Tichenor, Overseers of the Poor.

Caleb Bruen, Abraham Speer, Nathaniel Crane, Jotham Harrison and Thomas Baldwin, Town Committee.

Joseph Robords, Elias A. Baldwin, Nathaniel Canfield, Abijah Dodd, Joseph Dodd, Josiah Quimby, Uzal Baldwin, Moses Williams and William King, Constables.

Samuel Curry, Samuel Munn, Thomas Baldwin and John Brown, Pound Masters.

Nathaniel Camp, Caleb Wheeler, Moses N. Combs, Simon Hedden, John Sandford, Aaron Johnson, Abraham Ward, Nehemiah Hedden, Overseers of Highway, Newark.

Jonathan Davis, Uzal Baldwin, Samuel Munn, Joseph Williams, Samuel Brown, William Stockman, Caleb Baldwin, Elihu Crowell, Ebenezer Canfield, Orange.

John J. Brown, Abraham King, Samuel Rattan, John Speer, Joseph Kingsland, Peter Van Winkle, William Holmes, Belleville.

Thomas Bennet, Joseph Keen, John King, Daniel Dodd, Jesse Baldwin, Israel Crane, John Baldwin, Nathaniel Dodd, Jun'r, Ephraim Van Gieson, Peter Garritse, Isaac Van Gieson, John Van Winkle, Peter Winne, George Harrison, Bloomfield.

John E. Baldwin, Ethan Baldwin, Timothy Ball, Obadiah

Crane, and Ebenezer Havens, Overseers of the Highways, Camp-Town and North Farms.

☞ The following Votes were passed—

1st. That the Annual Election for Members of Assembly, &c., shall be opened, held and closed as it was last Year.

2nd. That all the Constables give security for the faithful discharge of their duty.

3d. That all Cattle found trespassing on the Salt Meadows shall be liable to double the lawful poundage, viz: two shillings per head, and any person who may find them trespassing whether on his or their Meadow or not, shall have liberty to pound them.

4th. That the Common lawful poundage be the same as last year.

5th. That the Township Committee be authorised to keep the pounds in repair.

6th. That the Dog tax be applied to the use of the Poor this Year.

7th. That the Poor be left in the care of the Overseers of the Poor as they were last year.

8th. That Two Hundred Pounds be raised for the use of the Poor this Year.

9th. That the Clerk of Estrays have liberty to publish an account of the Estrays, at such times as he may think proper.

10th. That the twelfth vote of last Town Meeting, respecting driving Cattle, &c., to the nearest Pound be continued in force.

AMOS HARRISON, Moderator.

J. PARKHURST.

At an annual TOWN MEETING, held at the Court House in the Township of Newark, on Monday, the 14th day of *April*, 1800, the following Officers for the ensuing year were duly chosen—

Amos Harrison, Moderator.

Jabez Parkhurst, Town Clerk, and Clerk of Estrays.

John Dodd, Assessor.

Amos Harrison, Judge of next Election.

Isaac Ward, Township Collector.

Samuel Condit, Stephen Fordham, and Robert B. Campfield, Commissioners of Appeal.

Nathan Squier and Samuel Pennington, Chosen Freeholders.

Stephen Hayes and Samuel Condit, Surveyors of the Highways.

Abiel Campfield, John Brown, Nehemiah Baldwin, Aaron Munn and Caleb Camp, Overseers of the Poor.

Jabez Parkhurst, Nathaniel Crane, John Dodd, Jotham Harrison, and Thomas Baldwin, Town Committee.

Isaac Ward, Elias A. Baldwin, Moses Roff, Nathaniel Canfield, Uzal Baldwin, Abijah Dodd, Josiah Quimby, Moses Williams and William King, Constables.

Stephen Hayes, John Brown, Thomas Baldwin and Samuel Munn, Pound Masters.

Overseers of the Highways—

For the Town of Newark, &c.—Nathaniel Camp, Joseph T. Baldwin, Joseph Brown, Jun'r, Edward Earle, Jacob Foster, Hiram Freeman, Simon Hedden, Elijah Andress.

For Orange, &c.—Amos Freeman, Abijah Harrison, Stephen Day, Matthias Dodd, Ezra Gildersleeve, Samuel Munn, Isaac Condit, Isaac Munn, Jabez Pierson, Henry Townley, Nathaniel B. Gardner, Aaron Ball, Davis Kilbron, Joel Condit.

For Camptown, &c.—Edward Badgly, David Day, Jabez B. Baldwin and Abiel Hayes.

For Bloomfield, &c.—Samuel C. Ward, William Sandford, Matthias Baker, Enos Farrand, Thomas Hayes, Simeon Crane, Peter H. Garritse, Abraham Garrabrants, Cornelius Speer, Peter Egbert, Job Dodd, John Van Dyck, Henry Cadmus, Joseph Kingsland, Nathaniel Dodd, Daniel Tues.

For Belleville, &c.—John H. Brown, Thomas Speer, Abraham Cadmus, Jared Rutgers and John Speer, Jun'r.

The following votes were passed—

1st. That the Town Committee shall demand security of the Township Collector and Constables, in the sum of One Thousand Dollars Each, for the true and faithful performance of their respective official duties.

2nd. That the Poor of the Township be left under the Care and Management of the Overseers of the Poor as usual.

3d. That the sum of Twelve Hundred Dollars be raised for the use of the Poor this Year.

4th. That the Dog Tax be appropriated to the use of the Poor this year.

5th. That the next Annual Election for Members of the State Legislature, &c., be opened at the House of Bethuel Pierson at Orange, and continued there during the first day of the same, and that the said Election on the Second Day be opened, held and Closed at the Court House in Newark.

6th. That all Cattle found Trespassing on the Salt Meadows shall be liable to a poundage of four Shillings per head, and any person finding them so trespassing may pound them.

7th. That the Pound in the Town of Newark be removed, and placed as near the Centre of the Street in front of the Place where it now stands as may be found convenient.

8. That John Dodd, Caleb Parkhurst and Doct'r Isaac Pierson be a Committee, to act in behalf of this Township in concert

with such other Committees as may be appointed in the other Townships for the like purpose, Viz: for the purpose of recommending to the people, suitable persons to be supported as Candidates for Members of our next State Legislature and Congress.

AMOS HARRISON, Moderator.

J. PARKHURST, Town Clerk.

At an Annual TOWN MEETING held at the Court House in Newark on Monday *April* 13, 1801, The following Township Officers for the Ensuing Year were duly chosen—

Amos Harrison, Moderator.

Jabez Parkhurst, Town Clerk, and Clerk of Estrays.

John Dodd, Assessor.

Isaac Ward, Collector.

Amos Harrison, Judge of next Election.

Samuel Condit, Stephen Fordam, and Robert B. Campfield, Commissioners of Appeals.

Jabez Pierson and Jabez Campfield, Surveyors of the Highways.

Samuel Pennington and Aaron Munn, Chosen Freeholders.

Abiel Campfield, John Brown, Nehemiah Baldwin, Aaron Munn and Caleb Camp, Overseers of the Poor.

Jabez Parkhurst, Abraham Speer, John Dodd, Jonathan Condit and Thomas Baldwin, Township Committee.

Elias A. Baldwin, Elihu Crane, Nathaniel Campfield, William King, Abijah Dodd, Josiah Quimby, Moses Williams and Moses Croell, Constables.

Abiel Campfield, John Brown, Samuel Munn, and Thomas Baldwin, Pound Masters.

Caleb Parkhurst, David D. Crane, Johnson Nichols, Isaac Andruss, Jacob Simpson, Stephen Plum; and for Camptown &c. Moses Robards, Joseph Wilbur, Joseph Camp, Ethan Baldwin, David Ball, Samuel Pierson, John E. Baldwin and Obadiah Crane, Overseers of the Highways.

Bethuel Pierson, Linus Pierson, Cyrus Pierson, Amos Freeman, Josiah Baldwin, Samuel Condit, David Pierson, Daniel Williams and Moses Harrison, Overseers of the Highways for Orange.

And Overseers of the Highways for Bloomfield &c.: Joseph Keen, Isaac Baldwin, Squier Baldwin, James McInnis, James Wharry, Isaac Van Gieson, John Parrot, Benjamin Crane, Nathaniel Crane, Abraham Speer, Joseph Kingsland, Isaac I. Kingsland, John H. Van Winkle, Peter Helme, Henry J. Van Winkle, Stephen King, Henry H. Brown, James T. Jaralmen, Charles Hedenburg and Francis Speer.

The following Votes were passed:

1st. That the Township Committee shall demand security of the Township Collector in the sum of Two Thousand Dollars—and of the Constables in the sum of One Thousand Dollars each, for the true and faithful performance of their respective Official duties.

2. That the poor of the Township be left under the Care and management of the Overseers of the poor as usual.

3. That the sum of Thirteen Hundred Dollars be raised for the use of the Poor this Year.

4. That the Dog Tax be appropriated to the use of the poor this year.

5. That the next annual Election for Members of the State Legislature &c. be opened at the house of Samuel Munn at Orange, and continue there during the first day of the same, and that the said Election on the Second day be opened, held and closed at the Court house in Newark.

Adjourned.

AMOS HARRISON, Moderator.

J. PARKHURST, Town Clerk.

At an annual TOWN MEETING, held at the Court house in Newark On Monday *April* 12, 1802,

The following Township Officers for the ensuing year were duly chosen.

Amos Harrison, Moderator.

Jabez Parkhurst, Town Clerk and Clerk of Estrays

John Dodd, Assessor.

Isaac Ward, Collector of the Township.

Amos Harrison, Judge of Election.

Jabez Pierson, Jabez Camfield, Surveyors of Highways.

Samuel Pennington and Samuel Condit, Chosen Freeholders.

Abiel Campfield, John Brown, Nehemiah S. Baldwin, Aaron Munn and Caleb Camp, Overseers of the Poor.

Samuel Hayes, Abraham Speer, John Dodd, Caleb Tichenor and Thomas Baldwin, Township Committee.

Stephen Fordham, William S. Pennington, Doctor Isaac Pierson, Caleb Camp and Samuel Hays, Committee to Enquire into and ascertain the priviliges of the Town under the antient Charter—and to call a Town Meeting if they think it necessary, to fill up the board of Trustees under said Charter to the number of ten.

Elias A. Baldwin, Nathaniel Canfield, Jediah Crane, William King, Abijah Dodd, John Quimby and Moses Williams, Constables.

Abiel Camfield, John Brown, Samuel Munn and Thomas Baldwin, Pound Masters.

Jonathan Lyon, Joseph Camp, Timothy Osborne, David Day

Abraham Harrison, Timothy Ball, Joseph B. Ball, Job Brown, William Stockman, David Munn, Noah Matthews, Enos Pierson, Samuel Crane Ward, Josiah Williams, William Perry, Israel Curry, Jacob Simpson, John Sandford, Charles Hedenburg, Abraham Cadmus, Joseph Kingsland, Hendrick Van Winkle, John Morris, William Kingsland, John Van Winkle, Peter Winner, John Van Dyk, Joseph Siglar, John E. Baldwin, Joseph Pierson, Elias Van Arsdale, Caleb Parkhurst, Aaron Baldwin, Benjamin Coe, Nathaniel Dodd, James Siglar, Rynear A. Van Geson, Cornelius Speer, Samuel Sandford and James Van Winkle—of Bloomfield—Joseph Munn, Joseph Woodruff, Abraham Cadmus Junior, Daniel Ball, Samuel Farrand. [Overseers of Highways.]

The following Resolves were passed:

1st. That the Business relative to supporting and disposing of the Poor be hereafter taken up, and finished by the Town Meeting previous to the Election of any other township Officers, than the Moderator and Clerk.

2nd. That the Township Committee shall demand security of the Township Collector in the sum of Two Thousand dollars, and of the Constables in the sum of One Thousand dollars Each, for the faithful performance of their respective Official Duties, and that the mode heretofore practised of accepting one Constable as security for another be discontinued.

3d. That the Poor of the Township be left under the care and management of the Overseers of the poor, as usual.

4th. That the sum of Fifteen Hundred dollars be raised for the use of the Poor this Year.

5th. That the Dog Tax be appropriated to the use of the poor.

6th. That the next annual election be opened at Orange at the house of Bethuel Pierson—and continue there the first day, and adjourned to the Court House in Newark the second day, as usual.

7th. That the Town Committee do meet hereafter on the first Monday in April Annually, for the purpose of Examining and settling the accounts of the Overseers of the poor &c.

N. B.—Samuel Condit, Robert B. Camfield and Stephen Fordam were appointed (at the aforesaid meeting) Commissioners of Appeal.

Adjourned.

AMOS HARRISON, Moderator.

J. Parkhurst, Town Clerk.

At a Special Town Meeting duly called by advertizements according to law, for the purpose of "Enquiring into the encroachments made on the Public Lands and Highways within the

Township of Newark, and to consider of, and determine on the propriety of prosecuting the persons who have made encroachments on the said Public Lands and Highways within the Township of Newark, and for making provission for defraying the Expences of such prosecutions."

Amos Harrison Esquire was chosen Moderator, and Jabez Parkhurst, Clerk.

The Committee appointed by the last annual Town Meeting to make Enquiry relative to the Encroachments made on the public lands and Highways &c. made report in the following words, Viz:

"The Committee appointed by the last annual Town Meeting in April, to make Enquiry relative to the Public Lands and Roads in the Town of Newark, and the Encroachments made thereon, Report—

That the first Inhabitants of the Town purchased all the lands of the Indian Natives, and held and possessed the same for a considerable time without any other title. During this possession they divided off to each Individual Inhabitant such part as reasonably fell to his Lott according to agreements made with the whole, which divisions were usually confirmed by a Vote of the Town Meeting, and Entered in the Town Book now in the possession of the Town Clerk.

That besides the Grants to Individuals the Inhabitants of the Town—Reserved to themselves for certain public purposses—In the first place, Large Extensive Roads without any precise dimensions to the same, varying according to local circumstances in many cases arising from the broken situation of the ground, and often exceeding Eight Rods in width. In the Second Place—Large pieces of ground for sundry public purposses such as a "Parsonage"—"Burying Ground"—"Training place"—"a Market Place"—and "a Watering place" and in fact all the lands not particularly and specifically given to some Individual were reserved to the use of the Town. After this occupation and possession of the Lands for a considerable time by the Inhabitants of the Town, the Eastern Proprietors set up a right to the Lands, and demanded of the Inhabitants a quit Rent for the same.

This demand was however resisted with great Spirit by the Inhabitants, who refused to pay the quit rent and they were finally abandoned by the Proprietors. But notwithstanding this many of the Inhabitants thought proper to obtain from the Proprietors Grants or Patents for their Lands; And, the Inhabitants of the Town in the Year 1695 or '96 took of the Proprietors a Patent for their Reservations including Roads of uncertain dimensions in the name of Certain Trustees.

The Committee cannot learn that the Proprietors Ever granted any Lands adverse to the original Divission made by the Inhabitants, nor adverse to their Reservations, nor in any way to disturb the Inhabitants in the disposal of their Lands according to their Original plan under the Indian purchases; but only granted Patents for the confirmation of the original lots as previously sett off and allotted to each Individual.

That on the beforementioned Public Lands and Roads so as aforesaid reserved by the Inhabitants and confirmed by the Patent from the Proprietors, Individuals have been constantly making Encroachments.

The Lands thus Encroached upon being Enclosed with the Antient Lotts, it is in many cases difficult to ascertain the ancient boundaries, the Land Marks in many Cases being destroyed or removed.

But many Encroachments are so recent as to be Easily ascertained, and the Land Marks precisely traced, described and ascertained—Especially where Encroachments have been made on Public Lands and in many cases on Public Roads.

The Committee think that the encroachments on and about the Antient Watering Place are wanton and without a shadow of Right, that some of the Trespassers Emboldened by the remissness of the Inhabitants openly avow their intentions to maintain and defend not only their former Encroachments; but threaten to fence in the whole of the Public Lands and set the Town at defiance.

It is with pain the Committee observe that the manly and En lightened policy of our Ancestors in providing Lands for Public uses and Capacious Streets, at once calculated to preserve the Health of the People, and to adorn, beautify, and render commodious the Town, has been greatly circumscribed by the narrow and selfish dispositions of some of their Descendants and the shameless avarice of more modern Settlers.

(Signed) CALEB CAMP,
SAM'L HAYES,
WILLIAM S. PENNINGTON,
STEPHEN FORDHAM.

Which Report having been read—The Meeting Resolved unanimously,

1st. That the Township Committee of the Township of Newark are hereby authorised to prosecute in behalf of the said Township, any person or persons who have made encroachments on the Public Lands and Highways and, also all those Persons who may hereafter encroach on the same.

2nd. That the said Committee be authorized in such cases as they think proper and beneficial to the Town, to consent on the part of the Town to settle Controversies relative to the Public Lands and Roads, by Arbitration or Reference.

3d. Resolved by a very large majority—That the sum of Two Hundred pounds be raised and assessed on the Inhabitants of the Township of Newark the ensuing year, to be appropriated to the purpose of prosecuting for the privileges of the Town, viz: for the recovery of such Common Lands and Highways as are encroached on, as far as the appropriation of the same shall be found necessary.

The Town Meeting adjourned to meet again according to Law.

AMOS HARRISON, Moderator.

J. PARKHURST, Town Clerk.

At an Annual TOWN MEETING held at the Court House in Newark, on Monday, *April* 11th, 1803, the following Township Officers for the ensuing year were duly chosen—

Amos Harrison, Moderator.

Elias A. Baldwin, Town Clerk.

Aaron Coe, Clerk of Estrays.

John Dodd, Assessor.

Isaac Ward, Township Collector.

Amos Harrison, Judge of Election.

Jabez Pierson, Jabez Canfield, Surveyors of the Highways.

Samuel Pennington, Samuel Condit, Chosen Freeholders.

Abial Canfield, John Brown, Nehemiah S. Baldwin, David D. Crane, Aaron Munn, Caleb Camp, Overseers of the Poor.

John Dodd, Abraham Speer, Samuel Hays, Thomas Baldwin, Caleb Tichenor, Town Committee.

Elias A. Baldwin, Nathaniel Canfield, John Hedden, Jun'r, Japhiah Harrison, John Quimby, Moses Williams, Abijah Dodd and William King, Constables.

Abial Canfield, John Brown, Samuel Munn, Thomas Baldwin, Pound Masters.

Robert B. Canfield, Nathan Squire, Stephen Fordham, Commissioners of Appeals.

Nehemiah Hedden, Henry Lyon, Sayre Roberts, Thomas W. Baldwin, Daniel Brown, Isaac Gilliam, Ebenezer Baldwin, Amos Freeman, Jonas Smith, Abraham Winans, John Dean, Richard Harrison, Benjamin Crane, Elijah Williams, Israel Brundridge, Jotham Clark, Moses Fatout, Minard Quoman, James Joralmon, Joseph Kingsland, John Rikeman, Henry H. Joralmon, John H. Brown, Peter Van Winkle, John Winne, George Harrison, Ephraim Morris, Isaac J. Tichenor, Joseph Pierson, Jun'r, John Crawford, Caleb Bruen, Uzal Baldwin, Ezra Baldwin, Samuel Dodd, Isaac Van Gieson, Nicholas Garrabrant, Garrett G. Speer, John Siglar, John Parrott, Parmenas Dodd, Doct'r John Ward, Samuel L. Ward, Nehemiah Baldwin, Joseph L. Keen, John P. Crane, Caleb Baldwin, John Tichenor, Overseers of the Highways.

The following Resolutions were passed—

1st. That the business relative to supporting and disposing of the poor, be hereafter taken up and finished by the Town Meeting previous to the election of any other Township Officers than the Moderator and Clerk.

2d. That the Township Committee are hereby instructed to demand Security of the Township Collector in the sum of Two thousand dollars, and of the several Constables in the sum of One thousand dollars each, for the faithful performance of their respective official duties, and it is hereby enjoined on the said Committee, that they will not except of one Constable as security for another.

3d. That the sum of fifteen hundred dollars be raised for the use of the poor this year.

4th. That the poor of the Township be left under the care and management of the Overseers of the poor as usual.

5th. That the Dog Tax be appropriated to the use of the poor as usual.

6th. That the next Annual Election be opened at Orange at the House of Samuel Munn and continued there during the first day of the same, and adjourned to the Court House in Newark, as usual.

7th. That the Township Committee do meet annually on the first Monday in April, for the purpose of examining and settling the accounts of the Overseers of the poor.

Adjourned.

AMOS HARRISON, Moderator.

Elias A. Baldwin, Town Clerk.

At an Annual Town Meeting held at the Court house in Newark, on Monday, the ninth day of *April*, 1804, The following Resolutions were passed, and the Township officers for the ensuing year duly Elected, viz:

Caleb Camp, Moderator.

Elias A. Baldwin, Town Clerk, &c.

John Dodd, Assessor.

Isaac Ward, Township Collector.

Caleb Camp, Judge of Election.

Jabez Canfield and Caleb Tichenor, Surveyors of the Highways.

Amos Harrison and Sam'l Pennington, Chosen Freeholders.

Abial Canfield, James Tichenor, David Munn, John Brown and Nehemiah S. Baldwin, Overseers of the Poor.

John Dodd, Abraham Speer, Samuel Hays, Thomas Baldwin and Caleb Tichenor, Township Committee.

Robert B. Canfield, Nathan Squire and Stephen Fordham, Commissioners of Appeals.

Abial Canfield, John Brown, Samuel Munn, Thos. Baldwin and Ephraim Morris, Pound Masters.

Elias A. Baldwin, Japhiah Harrison, Aaron B. Miller, Nathaniel Canfield, William King, Abijah Dodd, Nathaniel Dodd, Moses Williams, John Quimby, and John Hedden, Jun'r, Constables.

Caleb Bruen, David Johnson, Caleb Camp, Ethan Baldwin, Abraham Harrison, Timothy Ball, Aaron Crowell, Jabez Pierson, Jotham Quimby, Samuel Munn, Alexander Dean, Henery Baldwin, Aaron Harrison, Ebenzer Canfield, Eleazer Hedden, Samuel Perry, Zenas Pierson, Dan'l Williams, Joseph Campbell, Moses Fatout, Jotham Clark, John Crawford, Jonathan Keen, Samuel Huntington, Jabez B. Baldwin, Abraham Sanford, Joseph Kingsland, Gerard Rutcus, Anthony Francisco, John H. Brown, Herman Lynkford, Aaron King, George Harrison, Nehemiah S. Baldwin, Samuel Dodd, Ephraim Morris, Joseph L. Keen, Henery Van Winkle, Linas Baldwin, Sam'l W. Baldwin, Francis Speer, Daniel Siglar, John Vreelandt, Garrabrant A. Garrabrant, Robert Van Gieson and James Van Winkle, Overseers of Highways.

The following Resolves were passed—

1st. That all the Children now on the Town, under the age of fourteen Years, are to be under the care and direction of the Overseers of the Poor. And all other persons now on the Town and all that may or shall hereafter become a Town Charge (including Children) are to be farmed out, and the farmer to indemnify the Town from the first Monday in May next to the first Monday of May following.

2d. That the sum of two thousand dollars be raised for the use of the poor this year.

3d. That the Dog Tax be appropriated for the use of the Poor, as usual.

4th. That the bisiness relative to supporting and disposing of the Poor be hereafter taken up and finished by the Town Meeting, previous to the Election of any other Township Officers than the Moderator and Clerk.

5th. That the Township Committee be authorized and instructed, to give the Trustees of Market Street School house a Title for a lot of land.

6th. That the Township Committee do meet annually on the first Monday in April, for the purpose of examining and settling the accounts of the Overseers of the Poor, &c.

7th. That the next annual Election be opened at the house of Bethuel Pierson at Orange and continued there during the first day of the same; and adjourned to the Court house in Newark, as usual,

The Poor sold this year for Eight hundred and fifty dollars, Benjamin Coe the purchaser.

Adjourned.

CALEB CAMP, Moderator.

ELIAS A. BALDWIN, Town Clerk.

At an Annual TOWN MEETING, held at the Court house in Newark, on Monday, *April* 8th, 1805, The following Resolves were passed, and the Township Officers for the ensuing year duly chosen, Viz:

Amos Harrison, Moderator.

Elias A. Baldwin, Town Clerk, and Clerk of Astrays.

John Dodd, Assessor.

Isaac Ward, Township Collector.

Caleb Camp, Judge of Election.

Stephen Hays, Caleb Tichenor, Surveyors of the Highways.

Amos Harrison, Sam'l Pennington, Abraham Speer, Chosen Freeholders.

Abial Canfield, James Tichenor, Caleb Camp, David Munn, Isaac Dodd, Jun'r, John Brown, Overseers of the Poor.

John Dodd, Abraham Speer, Samuel Hays, Thomas Baldwin, Caleb Tichenor, Township Committee.

Nathaniel Beach, John Harrison, Stephen Fordhom, Commissioners of Appeals.

Aaron B. Miller, Japhia Harrison, Nath'l Canfield, Jonathan Keen, William King, Isaac Dod, John Quimby, William Williams, John Hedden, Jun'r, and Alex'r Laurence, Constables.

Abial Canfield, John Brown, Thos. Baldwin, Pound Masters.

Caleb Bruen, Elias Van Arsdale, John C. Burnet, Joseph Wilber, Ezra Baldwin, Elihu Crane, John Johnson, Caleb Camp, Ethan Baldwin, Abial Hays, David Hand, Aaron Crowel, John Linsley, Esqr., Caleb Quimby, Timothy Williams, John Harrison, Aaron Williams, Abijah Harrison, Ebenezer Canfield, Israel Brundrage, Henry Townley, Jonathan Williams, Japhia Condit, John Harthorn, Amos Terril, Abraham Stivers, Joseph Kingsland, Peter Cadmus, John Brown, Jun'r, Henery Kingsland, Abraham King, George Harrison, Job S. Dodd, Daniel Kilburn, Sam'l Pitt, Thos. Sidman, Henery Van Winkle, Thos. Crane, John Baldwin, Francis Speer, Abraham Siglar, James Siglar, Moses Siglar, Ephraim Van Gieson, James Van Winkle, Overseers of the Highways.

Resolves passed—

1st. That the poor be left in the hands of the Overseers of the Poor.

2d. That a poor house be built.

3d. That the dog Tax be appropriated for the use of the Poor, as usual.

4th. That the sum of fifteen hundred dollars be raised for the use and support of the Poor this year.

5th. That John Y. Baldwin supply the place of Jesse Baldwin as Trustee of the new Town dock.

6th. That the Township Committee do meet on the first Monday in April, for the purpose of examining and settleing the accounts of the Overseers of the Poor.

7th. That the next Annual Election be opened at the house of Sam'l Munn, at Orange, and continue there during the first day of the same; and adjourned to the Court House in Newark as usual. Adjourned.

AMOS HARRISON, Moderator.

ELIAS A. BALDWIN, Town Clerk.

N. B.—As in the Original Charter of the Town priviliges there is a piece of land granted to the Town for a Watering place—the same Lands are claimed by sundry persons. The dispute has not been finally disicded in Law.

Propositions have been made by the claimants afs'd to settle the dispute in an amicable manner.

Therefore Resolved, provided the claimants afs'd adhere to their propositions—The Town Committee are hereby authorized and instructed to relinquish the claim of the Town to said lands, and to grant such acquittances or Releases as may be proper on the occasion, and should Legislative aid be found necessary to confirm the title in the af'd Claimants at any future period, it is agreed that the Town Committee sign a petition to the Legislature when presented by the claimants af'd to that effect.

At an Annual TOWN MEETING, held at the Court house in Newark on Monday the 14th day of *April* 1806. The following Resolves were passed and the Township Officers for the insuing Year duly chosen, Viz:

Aaron Munn, Esq., Moderator.

Elias A. Baldwin, Town Clerk.

John Dodd, Nathan Squire, Elias A. Baldwin, Assessors.

Henry Stryker, Isaac Dodd, Jun'r, Annanias Baldwin, Township Collectors.

Robert B. Canfield, John Harrison, Surveyors of the Highways.

Aaron Munn, Judge of Election.

Amos Harrison, Sam'l Pennington, Chosen Freeholders.

Isaac Nichols, Joseph T. Baldwin, Caleb Camp, Caleb Tichenor, Isaac Dodd Jun'r, John Brown, Overseers of the Poor.

Resolved—That all Cattle hereafter impounded notice shall be given to the owner or owners thereof within one week after impounding the same.

David D. Crane, Stephen Hays, Israel Crane, Stephen D. Day, Tho's Baldwin, Township Committee.

Abraham Winans, Stephen Fordham, Stephen Hays, Commissioners of Appeals.

John Brown, Tho's Baldwin, Jabez Canfield, Pound Masters.

James Whitlock, Jonathan Keen, Isaac A. Ward, John Quimby, Noah Matthews, Alexander Laurence, Isaac Dodd and John A. King, Constables.

John Alling, Caleb Sayre, Uzal Sayre, Stephen Hays, Sylvanus Baldwin, Moses Crowell, Jacob Plum, Joseph Sayre, John Harrison, Joseph Matthews, James Williams, Benjamin B. Williams, Josiah Baldwin, Moses Roberts, Moses Taylor, Jonas Smith, John Corby Jun'r, Caleb Camp Esq'r, Ethan Baldwin, Obadiah Crane, David Beach, Aaron A. Gardner, Timothy Bigalow, Joseph Crane Jun'r, Ezekiel Ball, John H. King, Edward Earl, Abraham Bergen, Henery J. Van Winkle, Tho's Cadmus Jun'r, Oliver Crane, Yellis Mandeville, Henery Osborn, Smith Ward, David Doremus, Sylvanus Baldwin, Japhia Condit, David Taylor, Henery Speer, Joseph Jones, Tho's Crane, Rhyneer Van Gieson, David Riker, James Ward, Abraham Van Cisco, Simon Condit, Joseph Kingsland, Simeon Stivers, Jotham Condit, Abr. Mercelle Jun'r, Peter Helms, Abr. Rutan, Overseers of the Highway.

Resolves passed—

1st. That the Township Committee be authorized to make good all damages done to the Court house at the time of holding Town Meetings therein, and to cause the same to be swept and cleaned after each Meeting.

2d. That the Resolves of the Town Meeting passed at the last Town Meeting held April 1805, respecting the Town lands, be resinded.

3d. That the Note or Notes, Obligation or Obligations or any other security entered into by any person or persons respecting the Town lands commonly called the watering place, be rendered and given up by the Township Committee to the persons who entered into or gave the same.

4th. That all persons are hereby forbid to enter upon, and take possession, for private use, the public lands adjoining the Tanyards of Nathaniel Beach and others, known by the name of the Watering place, and that these Resolves be published in the Centinel of Freedom for three weeks successively.

5th. That the Township Committee, together with the Assessors, be authorized to divide the Township into three destricts, for the purpose of Assessment and Collection, and that each person be taxed in the Destrict where he resides for all his Taxable property in the Township.

6th. That the dog Tax be appropriated for the use of the poor, as usual—And that the sum of Twenty five hundred dollars be raised for the support of the poor the ensuing year.

7th. That the Township Committee be instructed to pay unto Samuel Pennington or to the director of the board of Chosen Freeholders the sum of forty five dollars and sixty two cents.

8th. That the next Annual Election open at the house of John Ming in Orange, and continued there during the first day, and adjourned to the Court house in Newark, as usual.

Adjourned to meet again according to Law.

April 14th, 1806.

AARON MUNN, Moderator.

ELIAS A. BALDWIN, Town Clerk.

Agreeable to the fifth Resolve passed at the last annual Town meeting, a meeting of the Township Committee and Assessors, was held at the house of Samuel Munn in Orange on the ninth day of May, 1806—when it was agreed, that the following should be the division lines. Beginning at the Green Island in Pasaik River; and runing from thence to the Boiling Spring on lands of Phinehas Baldwin, Dec'd; and from thence to the Bridge at the Slough between the houses of Jonathan Baldwin and Elihu Pierson; and from thence to the Bridge near Silas Dodd's; and from thence to the Bridge near Martin Richards; and from thence to Turkey Eagle Rock on the top of the first Mountain, which we agree shall be the line between the Bloomfield Ward and the Wards of Newark and Orange. And also, that the line between Newark Ward and Orange Ward shall begin at the af'd Boiling Spring; and from thence runing to Peck's Bridge on Great Meadow Brook; and from thence to the Bridge called Coleman's Bridge; and from thence following the River called Elizabeth or Elizabeth River to the line of the Township of Elizabeth.

Witness our hands this ninth day of May, 1806.

D. D. Crane, Thos. Baldwin, Stephen Hays, Stephen D. Day, Township Committee.

Elias A. Baldwin, John Dodd, Nathan Squire, Assessors.

At an annual TOWN MEETING held at Newark on Monday, the 13th day of *April*, 1807, The following resolves were passed, and the Township Officers for the ensuing year duly chosen, viz:

John N. Cumming, Moderator.

Elias A. Baldwin, Town Clerk.

John Dodd, Assessor.

Ananias Baldwin, Town Collector.

John N. Cumming, Judge of Election.

Nehemiah S. Baldwin, Nathaniel Crane, Surveyors of the Highways.

Israel Crane, William Halsey, Chosen Freeholders.

Benjamin Coe, Isaac Nicholes, John Brown, Caleb Camp, Overseers of the Poor.

John Dodd, David D. Crane, Thomas Ward, Stephen Hays, Joseph Sandford, Township Committee.

Jonathan Keen, Edward Jones, Japhia Harrison, Isaac Dodd, Jun'r, Alex'r Lawrence, John Brown, Jun'r, Constables.

Sam'l Pennington, Abraham Speer, Joseph Wilber, Commissioners of Appeals.

Joseph Canfield, John Brown, Pound Masters.

Joseph Wilber, Uzal Johnson, Ebenezer Havens, Caleb Bruen, Ezra Baldwin, Jotham Clark, Uzal Sayre, James Vanderpool, Archibald Mercer, Joseph L. Keen, Job S. Dodd, David Ward, Nathaniel Dodd, John Osborn, Jacob Vreelandt, Stephen King, John P. Sanford, Joseph Siglar, John Williams, James J. Jaroleman, John Garrabrant, Samuel H. Rutan, Araham Speer, Eleazer Crane, David Riker, Peter Egberts, and John Van Winkle, Overseers of the Highways.

Resolves passed—

1st. That the sum of fifteen hundred dollars be raised this year for the use of the poor—And that the poor be left in the hands of the Overseers of the poor, as usual.

2d. That the dog tax be appropriated for the use of the poor, as usual.

At an Annual Town Meeting held in the Township of Newark, on Monday, the 11th day of *April*, 1808, The following resolves were passed, and the Township Officers for the ensuing year were duly chosen:

Col. Thomas Ward, Moderator.

Elias A. Baldwin, Town Clerk, &c.

John Dod, Assessor.

Ananias Baldwin, Collector.

Robert B. Canfield, Judge of Election.

Thos. Ward and Israel Crane, Chosen Freeholders.

Nathaniel Crane, Nehemiah S. Baldwin, Surveyors of Highways.

Sam'l Pennington, Abraham Speer, Joseph Wilber, Commissioners of Appeals.

Abraham Speer, David D. Crane, Stephen Hays, John Dodd, Joseph T. Baldwin, Township Committee.

Benjamin Coe, Caleb Camp, John Brown, Isaac Nichols, John Osborn, Overseers of the poor.

Jabez Canfield, Seth Woodruff, John Brown, Pound Masters.

Ananias Baldwin, Edward Jones, Jonathan Keen, Japhia Harrison, Isaac Dodd, Alexander Lawrence and John P. Cadmus, Constables.

Jonathan Andruss, Jonathan Lyon, David Johnson, Caleb Parkhurst, Joseph Bruen, Sayre Coe, David Rogers, John Crawford, Matthias Plum, Joseph T. Baldwin, John Hawthorn, Moses Crane, Joseph Davis, David Ward, Sam'l Dodd, Isaac Ball, Aury King, George Harrison, John Stimus, Moses Siglar, Abraham

Cadmus, Harmonus Speer, Yellis Manderfield, Henery Jaroleman, Jun'r, John H. Van Winkle, Nehemiah Crane, Caleb Baldwin (Bloomfield), Moses Harrison, John Parrot, John H. Brown, John A. Van Riper, Overseers of the Highways.

Resolves passed—

1st. That Seth Woodruff, William Halsey and Robert B. Canfield, be a Committee to settle all matters in dispute (if any there may be) respecting the poor of the Township of Newark and the Township of Orange.

2d. That the Township Committee, at the next annual Town Meeting have leave to apply for a rehereing respecting the unsettled accounts of Isaac Ward late Collector of the Township of Newark.

3d. That the sum of fifteen hundred dollars be raised for the use and support of the poor, and that they shall be disposed of as usual.

4th. That all hogs or swine found running at large in the public streets or highways, shall and may be taken up and pounded at the expence of the owner or owners thereof at the rate of fifty cents per hed—twenty five cents to the use of the poor—twelve and a half cents to the driver and twelve and a half cents to the pound Master. This resolve extends no farther than from Col. Sam'l Ogden's down to Joseph Beach's—and from high Street to the East Back Street.

5th. That the next annual Election be opened at the house of Jacob Ward in Bloomfield and continued there during the first day, and adjourned to the Court house in Newark as usual.

6th. That the Township Committee meet on the first Monday in April annually, for the purpose of examining and settling the accounts with the Overseers of the Poor.

Adjourned.

THOS. WARD, Moderator.

ELIAS A. BALDWIN, Town Clerk.

An Act for the preservation of Sheep in the Township of Newark.

Whereas the Legislature of this State by a Law passed on the thirteenth day of March Eighteen hundred and Six, did authorize the Inhabitants of the several Townships at their Annual Town Meetings to order to be levied, Assessed and Collected, such tax on Dogs, in addition to the Tax already imposed by Law—and to make such other by laws as a Majority of each Town Meeting may deem expedient for the protection of their Sheep.

Therefore 1st be it enacted by the Inhabitants of the Township of Newark in the County of Essex, that the Assessors of this Township shall at the Time of Assessing the other taxes for the use of the Township, County, or State, assess every Master or Mistress of any family in which a Dog or Dogs of six months old and upwards are kept whether by themselves or any Child, Servant or other person whomsoever, the following sums of money, viz: If only one Dog is kept by one family, One Dollar. If two Dogs are so kept, five dollars and for every Dog so kept above two, the further sum of twenty dollars, which Tax shall be construed to include the Tax heretofore authorized by law, and shall be collected at the same time and in the same manner in every respect, with the other Taxes raised in the Township, except that the Assessor and Collector shall be each intitled to six cents for every Dog returned in the Duplicate agreeably to this Act.

2d. And be it enacted that if any person shall deny that he or she have any property in any Dog so assessed in his or her name, or shall refuse to give a fair account of the number or age of the Dog or Dogs to remain about his or her house, he or she shall be deemed to be the owner of such Dog or Dogs and be liable to the payment of the Tax aforesaid, and moreover shall be liable to a fine of ten dollars for every Dog so harboured and not returned to the Assessor when by him required, to be recovered before any Justice of the peace in this Township by the Collector of the same, and to be applyed as is herein after directed.

3d. And be it enacted, that the amount of the said Tax after deducting the charges of Assessing and Collecting the same and all fines which shall be recovered by virtue of this Act, shall be appropriated, exclusively to making good any losses sustained by the Inhabitants of this Township by the destruction of their Sheep by Dogs where no legal remedy can otherwise be had for the same: and for this purpose, the ballance of this fund which may remain unappropriated in the hands of the Collector at the expiration of his office, shall be paid to his successor, or shall be placed at interest to form a permanent fund to be applyed exclusively to the object contemplated by this Act, at the discretion of the Township Committee.

4th. And be it enacted, that where any Inhabitant of this Township shall sustain damages by his or her Sheep being killed by Dogs, it shall be Lawful to call on two respectable freeholders of the Township who shall view the Sheep so killed, and if it shall appear to their satisfaction that the said Sheep were killed by a Dog or Dogs, and that the owner of such Dog or Dogs cannot be discovered, the said viewers shall make return in writing to a Justice of the peace of this Township of such their belief, together with the damages appraised by them on oath or affirmation, which said Justice shall under his hand direct the Collector of the Township to pay the amount out of the monies specially appropriated for this purpose, if he should have a sufficient sum in his hands to pay the same—together with one dollar for the services of each of the said appraisers, and fifty cents for the services of the said Justice:—Provided that the person so claiming damages shall previously subscribe on oath or affirmation on the back of said, to be certified by the said Justice, that he or she doth not know by whose Dog or Dogs the damages was occasioned, and that whenever it shall come to his or her knowledge, he or she will give information thereof to the Collector of the Township whose duty it shall be to prosecute forthwith for the amount, and when recovered to apply the same as herein before directed.

5th. And be it enacted, that it shall be lawful for any Inhabitant of this Township who shall see any Dog chase, worry or wound his Sheep or Lambs, to kill such Dog; and if such person does not kill such Dog, and shall give notice thereof to the owner or possessor of such Dog, If such owner or possessor shall not kill, or cause the Dog to be killed within forty eight hours after such notice, he or she shall forfeit the sum of thirty dollars; to be recovered before any Justice in the Township by the owner of said Sheep or Lambs, to his or her use, with cost of suit.

6th. And be it enacted, that the Dog or Dogs meant to be subject to the Taxes and penaltys above named, shall extend to Dogs of all sizes and sexes.

At an Annual Town Meeting held at the Court house in Newark on Monday, the 10th day of *April*, 1809, The Officers for the ensuing year were duly chosen and Resolves passed as follows—

Samuel Pennington, Moderator.

Daniel Brown, Town Clerk.

John Dodd, Assessor.

Ananias Baldwin, Collector.

Aaron Mun, Judge of Election.

Thomas Ward and Israel Crane, Chosen Freeholders.

Abraham Speer, Caleb Camp and Samuel Pennington, Commissioners of Appeals.

Abraham Speer, Aaron Johnson, Stephen Hays, John Dodd, and James Vanderpool, Township Committee.

John Brown, Benjamin Coe, David Nichols, Isaac Dodd, Overseers of the Poor.

Samuel B. Brown, Jabez Campfield, Peter Wilt, Pound masters.

Robert B. Campfield, William Halsey and Seth Woodruff, Street Commissioners.

Edward Jones, David Thorp, Japhiah Harrison and Thomas Crane, Isaac Dodd, and Alexander Lawrence, Constables.

Nathaniel Crane and Nehemiah S. Baldwin, Surveyors of Highways.

Cooper Crane, Caleb Parkhurst, Henry Tichenor, Sayres Coe, James Black, William Burges, Jabez Campfield, Edward Blackford, Abner Ward, Joseph T. Baldwin, David James, Jun'r, Eleazer Crane, Lewis Baldwin, Samuel Dodd, Abraham Sigler, Peter Egbert, Thomas Speer, John P. Sanford, John Stimats, James Hornbloer, Jared Rutgers, John A. Van Riper, Henry Van Winkle, Jacob Cooman, Tunis Garrabrant, James Sigler, Isaac Kingsland, George Harrison, Isaac Baldwin, Stephen Morris, Ephraim Cockafeir, John Winneer, Joseph L. Keen, Garret I. Speer, John Tuis, Overseers of the Highways.

Resolved—

1st. That a paper containing the division of the Poor between the Townships of Newark and Orange be recorded, and filed by the Clerk.

2. That sixteen hundred Dollars be raised this year, for the use and support of the Poor.

3. That the Poor be disposed of by the Overseers, &c., as usual.

4. That the Street Commissioners, viz: Robert B. Campfield, William Halsey and Seth Woodruff, be instructed to proceed to execute the law respecting streets, &c., and that the Faith of the Town be pledged to defray the expences of the same.

5. That the aforesaid street commissioners be appointed a committee to confer with the inhabitants residing in the neighborhood of certain vacant lands known by the name of the watering ground, respecting the width of the street, &c. And the said Committee be authorized to receive fifteen hundred Dollars, in payment for part of said lands. It shall also be the duty of the said Committee to apply to the Legislature for a Law to authorise the said Committee to sell the said vacant lands.

6th. That two public Pounds be provided in addition to the common Pound, for the impounding of Hogs, viz. one at the South, and the other at the North end of the Town, and that each hog, after remaining in the Pound more than 24 hours, have three cents worth of feed per day, which shall be given him by the pound master, and to be paid for by the owners of the hogs. And that every hog after remaining in the Pound more than seven days, shall be sold at public Vendues, which shall be held on Saturdays between 5 and 7 o'clock P. M.

Hogs subject to be impounded—All of two months old and upwards found in the public streets, or out of the enclosures of their owners. Rate of Poundage, and Bounds, the same as last year.

7. That the Dog tax be continued the same as last year.

8. That all Cattle found on the Salt Meadow, not on the land of their owners, shall be liable to be impounded.

9. That liberty be granted to the Inhabitants of this Town to

build a Fish Market on the common between Mr. Aaron Harrison's and Mr. J. Ashton's.

10. That the annual Election be opened at Bloomfield on the first day, (at the time appointed by law) and close at the Court house in Newark on the second day.

Division of the Poor between the Township of Newark and Orange.

Agreeable to notice, The Township's Committees of the Townships of Newark and Orange met at the house of Moses Condit, Inn-keeper at Orange on the 3rd day of June, 1808; for the purpose of dividing the Poor of the said Townships not heretofore agreed upon; and the said Committees amicably agree to the following division.

The Township of Orange by the Committee agreed, and it was accepted by the Committee of Newark, that they take as quota the following persons, and the remnant to be provided for by the Township of Newark. Samuel Parrett, Hannah Ball, Joel Osborne, Abner Osborne, Child, Joannah Williams, Widow of Moses Owens, and two children, John Congar, James Humes, Susannah Humes, Robert Davis, Widow Hannah Price, and Children, and James Ryon.

The Committees directed their Chairmen to make out two Certificates, one for each Town, and sign the same.

In conformity to the said order of the Committees, we the Subscribers do certify that the foregoing division of the Poor is just and true, as agreed upon by the Committees respectively, as witness our hands this seventeenth day of August, 1808.

D. D. CRANE, Chairman of the Newark Committee.

STEPHEN D. DAY, Chairman of the Orange Committee.

SAM'L PENNINGTON, Moderator.

DAN'L BROWN, Town Clerk.

At an Annual TOWN MEETING, held at the Court house in Newark, on Monday, the 9th day of *April*, 1810, The Officers for the ensuing year were duly chosen and resolves passed as follows, viz:

Aaron Munn, Esqr., Moderator.

Isaac Headley, Town Clerk.

John Dodd, Assessor.

Ananias Baldwin, Collector.

Aaron Munn, Judge of Election.

Robert B. Campfield, Israel Crane, Chosen Freeholders.

Abraham Speer, Caleb Camp, Samuel Pennington, Commissioners of Appeal.

Robert B. Campfield, Seth Woodruff, Joseph T. Baldwin, Street Commissioners.

Abraham Speer, John Dod, Stephen Hays, Nehemiah S. Baldwin, James Vanderpool, Town Committee.

John Brown, Benjamin Coe, John H. Osborn, David Nichols, Overseers of the Poor.

Edward Jones, Joseph Sayrs, Japhiah Harrison, David Thorp, Alexander Lawrence, Isaac Dodd, Constable.

Joseph Sayrs, Jun'r, Nathaniel Crane, Surveyors of the highways.

Jabez Canfield, Pound Master.

Resolved—

1st. There shall be but one Pound in the Town.

2nd. That two thousand Dollars be raised for the support of the poor for the present year.

3rd. The Overseers shall not sell the poor at Auction.

4th. That a Committee be appointed to dijest; and at a future meeting, exhibit some place [plan?] relative to errecting a poor house in the Town. The Committee to consist of the following persons, viz: Samuel Pennington, John Dodd, John Dow, Isaac Andruss, Seth Woodruff, Epaphras Hinsdale, Caleb Camp, James Vanderpool, Joseph T. Baldwin.

5th. That the dog tax shall be as it has heretofore been.

6th. That the Annual Election shall be opened at the house of Jacob Ward at Bloomfield, and closed at the Court house in Newark.

7th. That a tax of $500 be raised to defray the expences of Surveying the Town Plot.

8th. That the Street Commissioners be paid for their services the last year.

9th. That the Inhabitants of this Town will not abandon their right in the old burying ground.

10th. That a Committee of five be appointed to enquire into the Town's right respecting the burying ground.

11th. That the Committee consist of the following persons—William S. Pennington, Isaac Andruss, James Vanderpool, Silas Condict, Seth Woodruff.

12th. That the said Committee be instructed to make due enquiry respecting the right of the burying ground, and if they find it invested in the Inhabitants of the Town they shall demand it of the Trustees, and if they refuse to give it up they shall propose leaving to a refference; but if those pacific measures prove ineffectual the Committee are authorized to call a special Town Meeting.

13th. That the purchasers of that lot of land commonly called the watering place, shall pay one third of the money on the receipt of the deeds, and the other two thirds on the first of May, 1811.

14th. That the hog law be and remain as it was the last year, except that the hogs shall be subject to be pounded at any Season of the year.

15th. That Goats shall be subject to be pounded any season of the year, their poundage to be two shillings.

AARON MUNN, Moderator.

ISAAC HEADLEY, Town Clerk.

At an Annual TOWN MEETING, held in the Court room at Moses Roff's tavern, *April* 8th, 1811, The following Officers were chosen for the year ensuing, viz:

Aaron Munn, Esqr., Moderator.

Isaac Andruss, Town Cl'k and Cl'k of Estrays

John Dodd, Assessor.

Ananias Baldwin, Collector.

Aaron Munn, Judge of Election.

Robert B. Campfield, Israel Crane, Chosen Freeholders.

Ab'm Speer, Caleb Camp, Sam'l Pennington, Com. of Appeals.

John Alling, Joseph Sayrs, Jun'r, Seth Woodruff, Street Commissioners.

Abr'm Speer, John Dodd, Stephen Hays, Nehemiah S. Baldwin, Joseph T. Baldwin, Town Committee.

John Brown, John H. Osborn, David Nichols, Benjamin Coe, Overseers of the Poor.

Jonathan Keen, Joseph Sayrs, Japhia Harrison, Isaac Dodd, Squire Baldwin, Harmonus King, Constables.

Job S. Dodd, Joseph Sayrs, Jun'r, Surveyors of Highway.

Jabez Campfield, John Brown, Pound Masters.

The following resolutions were then adopted, viz:

1st. That the Poor be left in the hands of the Overseers, as in the last year.

2d. That the sum of twenty five hundred dollars be raised for the use of the Poor the ensuing Year.

3d. That the chosen freeholders of this Township, be instructed to concur in the proposition for building a County Poor house.

4th. That the next Election for County Officers be opened at Isaac Ward's at Bloomfield, and closed at Moses Roffs in Newark.

5th. That the next Annual Town Meeting be held at Moses Roffs tavern in Newark.

6th. That the same *Law* respecting the impounding of Hogs and Goats shall be in force this year, as was in the last.

7th. That the Town Clerk be allowed five dollars for his services, in addition to the fees allowed him by law.

The following persons were then elected Overseers of the highways, viz: Sam'l Foster, Ogden Johnson, Joseph Bruin, Sam'l

Pennington, Jediah J. Nichols, John Alling, Uriah Burdge, Elihu Crane, Seth Woodruff, Joseph T. Baldwin, John Sandford, Minard Queman, Cornelius Jacobus, Ezekael Wade, Joseph Kingsland, Adrion Post, Thomas Speer, Ab'm Pake, Rich'd Craig, Alex. Williams, David Taylor, John Garrabrant, Ab'm Speer, Stephen Fordham, Caleb Baldwin, Joseph Morris, Isaac J. Ward, Thomas Keen, Nehemiah Ward, Moses Dodd, Henry Kingsland, John G. Garrabrant. No further business appearing the Town meeting was adjourned.

AARON MUNN, Moderator.

ISAAC ANDRUSS, Town Clerk.

At a special TOWN MEETING, held at the Court room at Moses Roff's tavern, pursuant to public notice, *June* the 24th, 1811, Aaron Munn, Moderator, and Isaac Andruss, Clerk.

The object of this Special Town Meeting was to take into consideration the propriety of purchasing, with a part of the money arising from the sale of the *Watering place*, a lot of land in the Town platt of Newark whereon to build a *Town House.*

After the object of the meeting had been fully explained, and much conversation and debate had taken place, upon a motion being made and seconded, it was Resolved,

1st. That one thousand five hundred and seventy five Dollars and fifty cents, of the monies arising from the sale of the watering place be and is hereby appropriated, to purchase a lot of land lying South of Stephen Roff's tavern in the Broad Street, being a part of the old Court house ground, containing sixty four feet in front, and running back to the burying ground, for the purpose of building a *Town house* thereon, and that the Township Committee be directed to take a deed for the same, in the name of the Inhabitants of the Township.

2d. That a committee of seven persons be appointed, with full powers, to contract for, or build a *Town house* on said lot of land, in such a way, or manner as they may think best calculated to serve the interests of the Town, and that the following persons be the Committee, Viz: William S. Pennington, Smith Burnet, Robert B. Campfield, Stephen Hays, Isaac Andruss, James Vanderpool, and Aaron Munn.

A letter was received and read in the Town Meeting, from the Selectmen of *Newberry port,* addressed to the Town Officers of Newark, giving an account, of very great distress and damage experienced in that Town from a late fire, which had consumed more than two hundred houses—And praying for the benevolent aid of their fellow citizens, it was resolved that the address be handed back to the Town Committee and that they be instructed to cause the same to be published in the Newspaper published in this Town, and that the Town Committee be directed to open a subscription and circulate the same througout the Township, for the benefit of the sufferers. And that after the subscription has had a general circulation the money raised be forwarded by the Town Committee in the name of the Township, to the Selectmen of *Newberry port*, for the benefit of the sufferers.

ISAAC ANDRUSS, Town Clerk.

At an annual TOWN MEETING, held in the Court Room at Moses Roff's Tavern, *April* 13th, 1812, the following Officers where chosen for the year ensuing, viz:

Aaron Munn, Esqr., Moderator.

Silas Hayes, Town Clerk, and Clerk of Estrays.

James Hedden, Assessor.

Joseph L. Wheeler, Collector.

Aaron Munn, Esqr., Judge of Elections.

Robert B. Campfield, Esq., Joseph T. Baldwin, Chosen Freeholders.

Samuel Pennington, Esq., Caleb Camp, Esq., James Vanderpool, Commissioners of Appeals.

Seth Woodruff, John Alling, Jabez Camfield, Street Commissioners.

David D. Crane, Esqr., Stephen Hayes, Nehemiah S. Baldwin, Joseph T. Baldwin, Silas Condit, Town Committee.

David Nichols, Obadiah Woodruff, Overseers of the Poor.

David Roff, Joseph Sayrs, Jotham Baldwin, Japhia Harrison, Constables.

Joseph W. Camp, David Doremus, Surveyors of Highway.

Jabez Camfield, Pound Master.

The following reasolutions where then adopted, viz:

1st. Resolved, That the same law respecting the pounding of Hogs and Goats shal be in force this year as was in the last.

2nd. That the sum of *Two Thousand* Dollars be raised for the use and support of the poor the ensuing year.

3rd. That a Committee of three persons be appointed to call upon the trustees of the first Presbyterian Church in Newark, for a surrender of the possession of all the town lands, now in their possession, which where, by a late act of Assembly vested in the town, wether held by them, or persons holding under them, and, that in case the said Corporation refuse to surrender any lands which the Committee are of opinion belong to the Town, that the said Committee have authority to call a special town meeting.

4th. That Joseph C. Hornblower, Seth Woodruff and William Halsey, be a Committee to call on the trustees of said church.

5th. That the poor be left in the hands of the overseers of the poor as in the last year.

6th. That the accounts of the Street Commissioners be examined by the Town Committee, and that a sum not to excede One hundred Dollars be raised for said Commissioners, provided however that said Committee shall deem it expedient.

The following persons where then elected as Overseers of the high ways, Viz:

Joseph Wilbur, Stephen Johnson, Caleb Camp, Esq., Samuel Pennington, David Nichols, John Alling, Moses Fatout, Jabez Camfield, Samuel Williams, Joseph T. Baldwin, David Sayrs, Jun'r.

It was then agreed that the next election for County Officers be held at Stephen Roff's Tavern in Newark.

No further business appearing Town Meeting adjourned.

AARON MUNN, Moderator.

S. HAYES, Clerk.

At an annual TOWN MEETING, held at Moses Roff's Court room, *April* 12th, 1813, when the following officers where chosen for the ensuing year, viz:

Aaron Munn, Esq., Moderator and Judge of Election.

Silas Hayes, Town Clerk and Clerk of Estrays.

James Hedden, Esqr., Assessor.

Joseph L. Wheeler, Collector.

Robert B. Campfield Esq'r, Samuel Pennington Esq'r, Chosen Freeholders.

Caleb Wheeler, Nehemiah S. Baldwin, Stephen Hayes, Commissioners of Appeals.

John Alling, Jabez Camfield, Silas Condit Esq'r, Stephen Hayes, Nehemiah S. Baldwin, Town Committee.

Obadiah Woodruff, David Nichols, Overseers of the Poor.

David Roff, Jotham Baldwin, Joseph Sayrs, Japhia Harrison, Constables.

Seth Woodruff, Nehemiah S. Baldwin, Surveyors of High way.

Jabez Camfield, Pound Master.

John Alling, Seth Woodruff, Jabez Camfield, Street Commissioners.

The following Reasolutions where then adopted, Viz:

Resolved 1st. That Hogs be subject to poundage that run at large and that their poundage be fifty Cents, that all Hogs that remain in pound for four days, shall be then advertised by the Pound Master for Sale for three days, advertisements to be posted at three different places, viz. at Moses Roff's, at the pump opposite Capt. Gifford's in Broad Way and at Jacob Plum's store in north part of the town, and that the pound master be allowed twenty five cents for advertising, to be paid by the owner or owners of such Hogs so advertised—that this law extend to all the township except that part which lies South and South West of David Hayes'.

2nd. That Twenty two hundred Dollars be raised for the support of the poor of this township the ensuing year.

3rd. That Five hundred Dollars be raised for the Schooling of poor children, to be placed in the hands of the Town Committee for said purpos.

4th. That the poor remain in the hands of the Overseers of the poor the ensuing year.

5th. That the elections be held at Stephen Roff's.

6th. That John N. Cumming, Anthony Dey, Caleb S. Riggs, William Halsey and Joseph C. Hornblowers, Esquires, be permitted to erect at their own expence or by voluntary contribution, under the direction of the Township Committee, a pale fence, with proper gates, railings and walks round the two Commons in the North part of the town, to wit, the Common in front of Gen'l Cumming's, and the military common on which the Episcopal church now stands, provided that the said commons are to be and remain for the original public use in the town patent designated, under the direction of the township Committee, and be subject to the futur order and controul of the Town Meeting. And the erections round the Military common to have gates sufficiently large to admit Collums of Military Troops to pass and repass.

The following persons were then appointed overseers of the high ways, viz:

Zophar Lyon, Stephen Johnson, Josiah Brewin, Sam'l Pennington, Johnson Nichols, Richard Sweazy, Isaac Sayrs, Caleb Sayrs, Jabez Camfield, Seth Woodruff, Joseph T. Baldwin, and David C. Brown.

No further business appearing Town Meeting Adjourned.

SILAS HAYES, Clerk.

At an annual TOWN MEETING, held at Moses Roff's Court Room, *April* 11th, 1814, when the following Officers where chosen for the ensuing Year, viz:

Aaron Munn, Esqr., Moderator.

Silas Hayes, Town Clerk and Clerk of Estrays.

James Hedden, Esqr., Assessor.

Joseph L. Wheeler, Collector.

Aaron Munn, Esqr., Judge of Election.

Robert B. Campfield, Esqr., Seth Woodruff, Chosen Freeholders.

Caleb Wheeler, Nehemiah S. Baldwin, Stephen Hays, Commissioners of Appeals.

John Alling, Jabez Camfield, Stephen Hays, Nehemiah S. Baldwin, James Vanderpool, Town Committee.

Jabez Camfield, Henry L. Parkhurst, Surveyors of Highways.
Obadiah Woodruff, Moses Roberts, Overseers of the Poor.

David Roff, Joseph Sayrs, Japhia Harrison, Jotham Baldwin, Constables.

Moses Smith, Seth Woodruff, John Alling, Street Commissioners.

Jabez Camfield, Jonathan Miller, Samuel B. Brown, Pound Masters.

Jos. C. Hornblower, Silas Condit, Edward Jones, James Vanderpool, David Hayes, William Tuttle, Aaron Munn, Committee to examine the Poor Schools.

Overseears of the High Ways—Israel C. Crane, Samuel Baldwin, Samuel Whitaker, Edward Jones, Ezra Baldwin, Stephen Sayrs, William Burdge, James Serring, Abner Ward, Jr., Jonathan Miller, and John I. Plume.

The following Reasolutions where then adopted, Viz:

1st. That the roads be worked by tax.

2nd. That Four Thousand Dollars be raised for the working the roads.

3rd. That Twenty Seven Hundred Dollars be raised for the support of the Poor and that Five Hundred Dollars be appropriated for the schooling of Poor Children.

4th. That Poor Children who have a residence be schooled.

5th. That the Poor remain in the hands of the overseears as the year past.

6th. That the Town Committee have authority to raise a sum on loan, not exceeding Two Thousand Dollars in anticipation of the road Tax.

7th. That the Hog Law and poundage be as it was last year.

8th. That this meeting do instruct their Freeholders to use their influence to join with the County to build a County Poor House, and If they refuse to endeavour to get the property sold that is now purchased and the money divided in proportion to the money advanced.

9th. That the election open at Stephen Roff's and close at Moses Roff's.

No further business appearing—Adjourned.

SILAS HAYES, T. Clerk.

At a Special Town Meeting, held at the Court Room of Moses Roff's, on Saturday, the 30th of *April*, 1814, Call'd at the request of sundry Inhabitants of the Township, to reconsider the several reasolution of working the High ways by tax for raising by tax Four Thousand Dollars for road Tax and the empowring the Town Committee to borrow on Loan a sum not exceeding Two Thousand Dollars in anticipation of the road tax.

The meeting proceeded to business, when Aaron Munn, Esqr., was chosen Chairman, and Silas Hayes, Clerk.

The following reasolutions where then adopted:

1st. That the first reasolution of the last Annual Town Meeting declaring the Highways to be worked by tax for the ensuing year that the same be repealed.

2nd. That the Second reasolution passed at the last annual Town meeting, authorizing the raising by tax the sum of Four Thousand Dollars for road tax that the same be repealed.

3rd. That the sixth reasolution passed at the last annual Town Meeting, authorising the Town Committee to borrow on Loan a sum not exceeding Two Thousand Dollars in anticipation of the road tax that the same be repealed.

The business of the meeting having gone through agreeable to the advertisements, it adjourned.

SILAS HAYES, Town Clerk.

At an extra Town Meeting, held at Moses Roff's Court Room, for the purpos of appointing an Assessor to supply the vacancy occasioned by the resignation of Col. James Hedden and to hear the report of the Committee appointed in respect to the poor and poor House.

Aaron Munn, Esqr., Chairman.
Silas Hayes, Sect'y.
John Thompson, Assessor.

The following Reasolution was then adopted:

That a Committee of six persons, Viz—Lewis Thibou, Caleb Camp, Esq., Silas Condit, Robert B. Campfield and Samuel Pennington be and are hereby appointed to fix on a sight for building or hireing a situation for the Poor.

No further Business the meeting adjourned.

SILAS HAYES, Clerk.

A Special Town Meeting, held at the House of Moses Roff's, on Tuesday, the 18th *October*, 1814, agreeable to public notice, on the subject of the Poor House.

The Committee appointed to procure a situation for the Poor, reported and recommended the Purchase of a certain House and lot situated in Mulberry street, formerly the property of Jotham Baldwin. The report being considered, was adjourned to the next meeting, when it was

Resolved, that the subject of this meeting be adjourned untill Tuesday, the 25th inst., at 6 o'clock in the evening at this place, at which time the Town will be call'd upon to adopt the report of the Committee in purchasing the above mentioned situation.

Meeting adjourned.

SILAS HAYES, Clerk.

A Special TOWN MEETING, held at the House of Moses Roff, agreeable to public Notice, on Tuesday, the 25th *October*, 1814, on the subject of the Poor House.

The report noted in the Minutes of the last meeting on this subject, was again made by the Committee appointed at a previous Town Meeting, and after deliberation it was resolved that the subject be postponed untill Wednesday evening, the 2nd of November next, at 6 o'clock, and in order that general Information may be given, the following reasolution was adopted, viz:

Resolved, That this meeting do instruct the Town Clerk to cause Hand bills to be distributed on the day preceding the meeting, setting forth the object and time of the meeting, and that he engage the Bell man to give notice through the streets on the afternoon preceding the meeting, and do direct the Town Committee to pay for the same.

No further business appearing, adjourned.

SILAS HAYES, Town Clerk.

A Special TOWN MEETING, held at Moses Roff's Court Room, *Nov.* 2nd, 1814, on the subject of the Poor House.

The Committee appointed to procure a situation for the Poor again reported their proceedings on the subject, Recommending the purchase of the House and Lott late the property of Jotham Baldwin situated in Mulbery Street. When after considerable debate and investigation, the following reasolution was taken on the subject, Viz:

1st. That this meeting deem it expedient at this time to hire a situation for the convenience of the poor.

2d. That the Town Committee do hire a House and Lands sufficient for the convenience of the Poor within the Town Plot for three Years.

3d. That the Town Committee are hereby instructed to present a petition to Legislature of this State praying for a Law to exemp the Town of Newark from being subject to a tax for the purpos of a County Poor House.

No further Business appearing, adjourned.

SILAS HAYES, Town Clerk.

A Special TOWN MEETING, held agreeable to public Notice, on Tuesday, the 6th *December*, 1814, at the Court room of Moses Roff's, on the subject of the Poor House, call'd at the request of the Town Committee.

Aaron Munn, Esq., was chosen Chairman.

Mr. Vanderpool in behalf of the Town Committee explained the object of the meeting, viz: that the reasolution of last Town Meeting requiring the Town Committee to hire a situation for the Poor within the Town Platt could not be put into effect, embraceing the interest of the Town and the accommodation of the Poor. The Town Committee suggested the propriety of purchasing instead of hireing a situation for the poor. After deliberation the meeting was adjourned untill Tuesday, the 13th inst., for a more general attendance, to be held at this place at 6 o'clock in the evening, to take into consideration the report of the Town Committee on the subject of the Poor House. Also to take into consideration the propriety of Issuing Tickets as a circulating medium for the convenience of the Town.

Ordered that the Town Clerk be required to give public notice of the adjourned Town Meeting in the Newark Centinel, setting forth the time and object of said meeting.

Adjourned.

SILAS HAYES, Town Clerk.

Special Town Meeting *December* 13, 1814—The Town Committee again reported to the meeting the impropriety and impossibility of hireing a Situation within the Town Platt for the Poor.

The following reasolution was adopted, Viz: That Whereas the Town Committee having found it impractable to procure a situation for the poor within the Town Platt therefore resolve that the Town Committee are hereby authorised to hire or purchase a situation for the poor within the Township of Newark.

The subject of Issuing Tickets as a circulating medium for the Benefit of the Town was discuss'd and adjourned indefinitely.

SILAS HAYES, T. Clerk.

At an *annual* Town Meeting of the Inhabitants of the Township of Newark held at Moses Roff's this Tenth day of *April* A. D. 1815—

Aaron Munn, Moderator and Judge of Election. James W. Burnett, Clerk and Clerk of Estrays.

On motion being made and seconded this meeting was adjourned for one hour, to meet again at this same place, which being duly done and the 7th Sec. of the Act of the Legislature, being read, as required by Law, proceeded to Buisness, when was duly Elected

For Assessor, Seth Woodruff.

Collector, Joseph L. Wheeler.

Chosen Freeholders, Seth Woodruff, James Van Derpool.

Commissioners of Appeal, Nehemiah S. Baldwin, Jabez Canfield, Col. Stephen Hayes.

Surveyors of Highway, Henry L. Parkhurst, Ezra Baldwin.

On Motion &c. The Report of Township Committee was read and accepted in part, to wit, relative to monies received and Expended.

Report of Overseers of the Poor being called for, was read by Oba. Woodruff, Overseer.

Report of Town Committee relative to the purchase of a Poor House, for the accommodation of the Poor of this Township, together with a Preamble and Resolutions accompanying the same were severally Read, and on motion &c. the said Resolutions were adopted and sanctioned by unanimous Vote of this meeting.

It was submitted for the consideration of this meeting, the propriety of selling the Poor House and Farm recently purchased by the Town Committee for the purpose of procuring a more Eligible situation and one more adjacent the Houses of *Public Worship*, and after considerable debate this Meeting Resolved to dispense with the Sale.

On Motion &c. the Sum to be raised the ensuing Year for the Benifit and Support of the Poor shall be Three Thousand Two Hundred Dollars, of which sum Five Hundred Dollars shall be appropriated for the use of the Poor School of this Township, and that the sum of One Thousand Dollars, be loaned if necessary, till such time as the same shall be duly collected.

Resolved that the Overseers of the Poor, consist of two persons to wit

Overseers of Poor, David Hayes, Lewis Thibou.

Town Committee, John Alling, Jabez Canfield, Stephen Hayes, Nehemiah S. Baldwin, James Van Derpool.

Constables, Japhia Harrison, Ashbel Green, Isaac Crawford, Uzal McGinnis, Joseph Sayres.

Street Commissioners, Col. Isaac Andruss, Edward Jones, Joseph T. Baldwin.

Pound Masters, Jabez Canfield, Nehemiah J. Crane, Samuel B. Brown.

Overseers Highway, Abner Kilburn, Capt. Joseph Bruen, Hugh K. Toler, Henry Parkhurst, Ezra Baldwin, Edward Jones, Jedediah Crane, David Cook, Matthias Plum, John C. Burnet, John P. Decatur.

Committee appointed to superintend the Poor School Established for the Benefit of the Poor Children of this Township Reported and submitted an Address to this meeting, which was read.

Whereupon the following persons were chosen as a Committee for the same purpose the Ensuing Year to wit:

Joseph C. Hornblower, Silas Condit, Edward Jones, David Hayes, William Tuttle, Isaac Andruss, William Ward, Committee to Superintend Poor Schools.

Resolved that the Roads shall be worked by Labour the Ensuing Year.

Resolved, that Hogs found trespassing shall not be liable to be pounded.

A motion was made seconded and carried that the Town Committee be instructed to Enclose the Old Burying Ground, and see that it be Kept in good fence, and that the same be not Leased or Hired for the purpose of pasturing Horses, Oxen or Cows.

It was submitted that a Town House be Erected and Built in this Township and a motion taken accordingly and Resolved that a Committee be appointed to consider of the propriety and Expediency of such proceeding, and to report in Writing at the next annual Town meeting, and the following persons were duly appointed as such Committee to wit:

Seth Woodruff, Isaac Andruss, Silas Condit, Isaac Nichols, Rob't B. Canfield.

Resolved—That the Ensuing Election open at Stephen Roffs and Close at Moses Roffs.

No further Business appearing before this Meeting, the Same was closed Sine die.

JAMES W. BURNETT, Town Clerk.

The following is a Copy of the Preamble and Resolutions submitted to the Town Meeting by Township Committee, (vide Minutes):

The Township Committee hav'g reported that they had applied to the Legislature of this State and obtained an Act Entitled "An Act to authorise the Inhabitants of the Township of Newark in the County of Essex to Build or Purchase a Poor House."

And also that they had entered into certain Articles of Agreement in writing on behalf of this Township with Captain Aa. Johnson, for the purchase of the dwelling House and farm whereon he lately lived situate in the Township of Newark, as lately surveyed by Stephen Hayes Junior, for the sum of Four Thousand Five Hundred Dollars.

Whereupon Resolved that this Township do accept the Priveledges of the said Act of the Legislature, and do appoint the said dwelling House and Farm, so as aforesaid agreed by the said Township Committee to be purchased from the said Aaron Johnson, to be the place in the said Township of Newark to be purchased for a Poor House according to the terms of the said Act.

Resolved, That the said Township Committee be and they are hereby empowered to take possession of the said Dwelling House and farm for the use of the Poor of the Township, and to receive from the said Aaron Johnson a Deed for the same—and thereupon the Inhabitants of the Township of Newark in the County of Essex and their Successors shall become bound to pay to the said Aaron Johnson his Executors, Administrators and Assigns the sum of Four Thousand five hundred Dollars, the consideration money, in manner following to wit—$500 on the first day of January next with Interest on the whole sum or Purchase money from the first day of April Instant, and One thousand Dollars Yearly and Every year thereafter untill the whole Purchase money be Paid, with Interest to be paid Annually on the whole sum remaining unpaid according to the Terms of the said Agreement so made with the said Aaron Johnson, And that this Township is pledged and bound to provide the necessary funds to make good the said Payments.

At a Special TOWN MEETING, holden this ninth day of *September*, A. D. 1815, for the purpose of appointing a Township Collector, (vice Joseph L. Wheeler, resigned) agreeable to previous notice, Col. Isaac Andruss was duly appointed Moderator.

The object of this meeting being explained, the 7th Section of the "Act incorporating the Inhabitants of Townships, designating their meetings" being read, and the said meeting qualified agreeable to Law, proceeded to Buisness, when after due consideration James W. Burnett was by a majority of votes appointed *Township Collector* for the Year. No further Business coming up, this Town Meeting was adjourned *sine die.*

JAMES W. BURNETT, Town Clerk.

At an Annual TOWN MEETING of the Inhabitants of the Township of Newark, convened on the 8th day of *April*, 1816, at the house of Moses Roff, and from there adjourned to the Session house of the 1st Presbyterian Church, the following Officers were elected for the ensuing year, and the proceedings as follow adopted:

Gen. John N. Cumming was chosen Moderator.

William Ward, Town Clerk and Clerk of Estrays.

Seth Woodruff, Assessor.

James W. Burnett, Collector.

Samuel Pennington, Robert B. Camfield, Chosen Freeholders.

Nehemiah S. Baldwin, Jabez Camfield, Col. Stephen Hayes, Commissioners of Appeal.

Henry L. Parkhurst, Ezra Baldwin, Surveyors of Highway.

Isaac Nichols, Lewis Thibou, Overseers of the Poor.

Ashbel Green, Joseph Sayres, Japhia Harrison, David Ball, Jacob Peshine, Constables.

John I. Plume, Seth Woodruff, William S. Pennington, Street Commissioners.

Jabez Camfield, Nehemiah J. Crane, Samuel B. Brown, Pound Masters.

Elias Wood, Joseph W. Camp, Caleb Earle, Samuel Pennington, James Black, David Nicholls, Jedediah Crane, David Cook, Matthias Plum, Thomas Eagles, Joseph T. Baldwin, Overseers of Highway.

John Alling, Jabez Camfield, Stephen Hayes, Nehemiah S. Baldwin, James Vanderpool, Town Committee.

Aaron Munn, Judge of Election.

Joseph C. Hornblower, Silas Condit, Edward Jones, David Hayes, William Tuttle, Isaac Andruss, William Ward, Committee for the Poor School.

On motion, Minutes of the last annual meeting relating to Hogs were corrected—in place of the word "*trespassing*," the sentence, "*hogs found running at large in the streets*," was substituted.

Mr. Vanderpool, in behalf of the Town Committee, produced and read a detailed report concerning the state of the poor, and other subjects, which report was accepted:—Whereupon it was resolved, that said Annual report be entered on the town books, and that the clerk be instructed to transcribe the same, and that a reasonable compensation be allowed him for such service.

Resolved, that 2,800 dollars be appropriated for the maintenance of the poor for the ensuing year.

That the Street Commissioners be compensated for their services, at the rate of One Dollar p'r day, and that they exhibit their accounts for such allowance at the Annual Meeting.

That they be authorised at the public expence to procure a copy of a map of the town now in the office of the County Clerk.

That One Hundred Dollars be raised by a tax, to be levied exclusively upon the inhabitants of the Town Plot, for the use of the Commissioners toward regulating the Streets; and that in every case of difficulty or opposition which, in the faithful performance of their duty may occur;—such as running and ascertaining lines, or prosecuting or defending the common rights of the township; the town will support them, and indemnify them in any loss or damage so sustained.

That after this date all hogs found running at large within the town plot may be impounded—the name of the person who brings or sends them to be left with the pound Master. The rate of poundage for each hog shall be Fifty cents: twelve and a half to the pound master, twelve and a half to the person impounding, and twenty five cents to the town.

Report of the Committee on the proposition to build a town house was read. Whereupon on Motion, Resolved, that the subject be referred back to the same Committee for further consideration, and that the Committee be instructed to apply to the Legislature for a Law to authorize the selling of such portions of the town property as may be deemed necessary to accomplish the proposed object.

Resolved, that the poll of the next election be opened and closed at the house of Stephen Roff.

Resolved, that the management of the Charity School devolve exclusively upon the Superintendants of that establishment, and that they be authorised generally to conduct and regulate its concerns in such way as they may deem most conducive to the promotion of its welfare, and the accomplishment of the designs of the institution.

Resolved, that the roads be worked as the last year, by labour.

Resolved, that the town Committee take charge of the burying ground.

Meeting adjourned.

WM. WARD, Cl'k,

(Copy.)

Report by the Township Committee of the receipts and expenditures for the township of Newark in the support of the Poor, and for other purposes, from April, 1815, to April, 1816.

The ballance reported to be on hand the last annual report..		$396 49½
Out of which was paid to David Nicholls late overseer of the poor the sum of..........	$42 37	
To Obadiah Woodruff do..........	14 30	
To Moses Roberts do..........	37 90	
To James Connor for school teaching..........	13 33	
		107 90
Which left an unexpended ballance of..........		$288 59½

Applicable to the support of the poor, the education of poor children and damage done to Sheep.

The amount of the duplicate Tax list for 1815 and '16 is..........	$4,150 00	
The amount of the Dog tax..........	71 00	
Making the total sum raised of..........		$4,221 00

From which deduct—

Paid Joseph Pierson, State tax..........	$423 89	
" Township Collector's fees..........	114 00	
" Assessor's fees..........	114 00	
" Commissioners of Appeal..........	14 84	
" Taxes returned bad..........	136 21	
" Direct and township taxes..........	15 76	
Error, tax assessed to Baldwin & McGinnis..........	5 00	
Which makes a total sum to be deducted of..........		823 68
And leaves for the use of the Township..........		$3,397 32
To which add unexpended funds last year..........		288 59½
		$3,685 91½

And which is applicable to the following objects—

Due to the account for damage done to sheep........................... $74 60
Nett am't of Dog tax the last assessment 58 04

Making a sum applicable to dam'ge done to sheep.. 132 64

Due to the acc't for education of poor children........................ 187 58¼
Appropriation by vote of last annual town meeting.................... 500 00

Making a sum applicable to the education of poor children....................... 687 58¼
The sum applicable to the support of the Poor... 2,865 69
3,685 91¼

State of the funds applicable to the support of the Poor, for the payment due on the Poor House farm, for building, repairs, and furnishing the same.

Receipts on hand from last year.............. .. $26 41
The am't arising from taxes as before stated is..... 2,865 69

To which add rec'd for fines.

From Caleb Sayres..........................	$ 1 00
" David D. Crane, Esqr.....................	5 00
" Joseph T. Baldwin, Esq..................	12 00
" Smith Burnet, Esqr.................... ...	15 00
" Stephen Hayes, Jun'r, Esq................	2 00
" Aaron Munn, Esq.........................	2 00
" Japhia Harrison.........................	10 00
Rec'd for two Pedlar's licences..............	1 20

Making a total sum of.............................. $2,940 30

The expenditures which have been made on acc't of the Debt, for the purchase of the Poor House farm, the building, repairs, and furnishing the same, is as follows—

There has been paid to Captain Aaron Johnson the payment due to him by Contract on the 1st of January last, on acc't of principal.............. $500 00
There has been expended in build'g and repairs............................... $648 84
Deduct the sale of a Cistern and barrack.. 45 50
Leaves.................................. 603 34
There has been paid for household furniture and stock on the farm.......................... 193 49
Making a total sum of expenditure, the property of the township of.. 1,296 83

The expenditures which have been made for the support of the poor are as follows:

Interest paid Capt. Aaron Johnson		225 00	
Paid Ebenezer Haven's salary		350 00	
Expences paid for cloathing and provisions furnished the poor house	592 39		
Deduct am't of produce sold from the Poor house farm	252 26		
Leaves the sum of		700 13	
Lewis Thibou, Overseer of the Poor, has paid for the support of paupers that could not be removed to the poor house, conveying paupers to their place of residence and his own services—amounting to		175 79¼	
David Hayes, Overseer of the Poor		25 05	
Paid Physician's bills, amounting to		55 21	
" Magistrates' bills		16 00	
" Jacob Peshine, Constable		15 00	
" Advertising by the Collector		1 50	
" Funeral charges		17 75	
" J. C. Hornblower, Esq., Council Fee		10 00	
" Newark Mutual Fire Insurance Company for policy of Insurance on the Poor house for 5 Years		19 80	
" Interest on $1100 borrowed for the use of the Township by vote of last annual Town Meeting		36 37	
" Moses Roff, Township Committee's bill of expences		21 71	
" Township Committee's Bill		75 00	
Which makes the current expences for the support of the Poor amount to the sum of			1,744 31¼
To which add the permanent expenditure			1,296 83
Makes a total expenditure from the funds applicable to the support of the Poor of			$3,041 14¼
And leaves a deficiency of		100 84¼	

State of the fund which has been specifically appropriated by vote of Town Meeting for the education of Poor Children.

There was a ballance due to this account from the last year amounting to	187 58¼	
Appropriation by vote of last annual town meeting	500 00	
Makes a total of		687 58¼

From this fund has been made the following expenditures—

To David Rogers, Teacher, the sum of	292 18	
" Augustus M. Hay	20 31	
" Albion Pool	2 00	
Paid for fuel	21 13	
		336 62
Which leaves a balance for educating poor children of		$350 96¼

State of the funds arising from the Dog tax applicable to the payment of damage done to sheep.

There was a ballance due to this account from the last year of....................................	$74 60	
The nett am't of Dog tax from last assessment.....	58 04	
Making a total sum of..............................		132 64

From which has been made the following expenditures—

To Joshua Baldwin for sheep damage......................	8 53
Leaves an unexpended fund for damage done to sheep of..	$124 11

From this statement the funds of the Township will appear to be as follows:

An unexpended ballance for the education of Poor children is....................................	$350 96½	
An unexpended ballance for damage done to sheep of	224 11	
Which makes together the sum of......... :.........		475 07½
From this sum deduct the deficiency of funds for the support of the Poor..		100 84½
Leaves the amount of funds unexpended.................		374 23
To which add the use of the burying ground let for pasturing of Sheep, after deducting repairs of fence............		21 00
Makes a total of unexpended funds belonging to the Township..		$395 23

All which is respectfully submitted.

By order of the Township Committee.

(Signed) JAMES VANDERPOOL, Cl'k.

Newark, April 8th, 1816.

At a Special TOWN MEETING, convened agreeably to public notice at the house of Moses Roff, *Aug.* 13, 1816.

William S. Pennington, Esq., Moderator.

Mr. Vanderpool, in behalf of the Township Committee, submitted the following resolution, which was adopted unanimously:

Resolved, That the Township Committee be, and they are hereby authorized to purchase in the behalf of the township, for the use the Poor house, a piece of Meadow offered for sale by Capt. Aaron Johnson, containing between six and seven acres, and to pay for the same at the rate of Fifty five Dollars p'r Acre, and to enter into engagements on the part of the Township to pay at such time as the Committee may agree upon with Capt. Johnson, and the funds of the town are hereby pledged for the fulfilment of the Contract.

Meeting adjourned.

WM. WARD, Cl'k.

At an Annual TOWN MEETING, convened at the house of Moses Roff, on the 14 day of *April*, 1817—

Silas Condit, Esq., was chosen Moderator, and William Ward, Clerk.

After which proceedings it was resolved to adjourn to 2 o'clock in the afternoon, at the Session house of the 1st Presbyterian Church.

Session house, 2 o'clock P. M.

Section 7 of the law relating to town meetings having been read as prescribed, Meeting proceeded to business.

William S. Pennington, Esq., moved the following resolution, which was adopted:

Resolved, That it be a rule of this Town Meeting, that on all Annual Town Meeting days every question to be submitted to the consideration of the meeting respecting the working of the high ways, maintenance of the poor, raising of money, or any other matter, involving the pecuniary interest of the town, shall be proposed and offered for consideration, and disposed of before the meeting proceed to the choice of Officers—the Moderator and Clerk excepted—and not afterwards on that day. And that this rule shall not be annulled or altered unless on public notice thereof given in the newspaper of the town at least ten days before an annual town meeting, and then to be proposed and decided on before the meeting proceed to the choice of Officers—the Moderator and Clerk excepted.

The Town Committee submitted a Report, which was read by Mr. Vanderpool, and the same ordered to be accepted and filed.

Report of the Free School Committee was read, together with a letter addressed to the trustees by the teacher of the school, which were accepted—Whereupon resolved, that the Town Committee be authorized to discharge the difficiency of the School fund represented in said report, amounting to $16 97-100ths.

Resolved, that *Three thousand two hundred dollars*, be appropriated for the support of the poor the ensuing year.

That *Four hundred dollars* of the appropriation be applied for the support of the Free School.

Officers chosen for the ensuing year:

William Ward, Town Clerk, and Cl'k of Estrays.

Isaac Nicholls, Assessor.

James W. Burnett, Collector.

Samuel Pennington, Robert B. Campfield, Chosen Freeholders.

Col. Stephen Hayes, Nehemiah S. Baldwin, Jabez Camfield, Commissioners of Appeal.

Henry L. Parkhurst, Ezra Baldwin, Surveyors of Highways.

Lewis Thibou, Isaac Nicholls, Overseers of Poor.

William S. Pennington, Lewis Thibou, Silas Condit, Street Commissioners.

Samuel B. Brown, Jonathan Andruss, Jonathan Miller, Ebenezer Havens, Pound Masters.

Uzal Hedden, Isaac Youngs, Elias Roberts, Samuel Pennington, Richard Sweezy, Sears Coe, Jedediah Crane, Uzal Sayres, Obadiah Woodruff, Moses Hedden, Robert Baldwin, Henry Baker, Overseers of Highway.

John Alling, Jabez Camfield, Stephen Hayes, Nehemiah S. Baldwin, James Vanderpool, Town Committee.

Ashbel Green, David Ball, Joseph Sayres, Jonathan Keen, Japhiah Harrison, Constables.

Col. Stephen Hayes, Judge of Election.

Joseph C. Hornblower, Silas Cond't, Edward Jones, David Hayes, William Tuttle, Isaac Andruss, William Ward, Free School Committee.

Committee for building Town house reported having done nothing in the business.

Street Commissioners reported having done nothing.

Resolved, that the Street Commissioners be instructed to take all legal and proper measures to remove any encroachments on the road, or obstructions in the highway.

Resolved, that the roads the ensuing year be worked by labour, by districts.

Resolved, that the hog law of last year be revived, with this alteration—that the driver shall be entitled to 25, and the pound master to 12½ cents a head.

Resolved, That the poll of the next annual election be opened and closed at the house of Stephen Roff, Innkeeper, Newark.

Resolved, that the next annual town meeting be opened at the house of Moses Roff, at 1 o'clock P. M.

Meeting adjourned.

WM. WARD, Cl'k.

At an Annual Town Meeting, commenced at the house of Moses Roff, on the [13] day of *April*, 1818, and from there adjourned to the Session House of the 1st Presbyterian Church, in the town of Newark—the following Officers were chosen for the ensuing year, and the following proceedings adopted:

Gen. John N. Cumming, Moderator.

William Ward, Town Clerk, and Clerk of Estrays.

Isaac Nicholls, Assessor.

James W. Burnett, Collector.

Samuel Pennington, Robert B. Camfield, Chosen Freeholders.

Col. Stephen Hayes, Nehemiah S. Baldwin, Jabez Camfield, Commissioners of Appeal.

Moses Roberts, Ezra Baldwin, Surveyors of Highway.

Isaac Nicholls, Aaron Ward, Overseers of the Poor.

William S. Pennington, Lewis Thibou, Silas Condit, Street Commissioners.

Samuel B. Brown, Ebenezer Havens, Capt. DeKay, Col. Isaac Andruss, Pound Masters.

Joseph Camp, Isaac Young, Thomas Camfield, Sylvanus Baldwin, Samuel Pennington, Edward Jones, Jedediah Crane, David Cook, Moses Fatout, Joseph T. Baldwin, D. Baker, John Ransley, Overseers of Highway.

Jabez Camfield, Col. Stephen Hayes, Nehemiah S. Baldwin, James Vanderpool, Lewis Thibou, Town Committee.

Jonathan Keen, Joseph Sayres, Ashbel Green, Silas C. Baldwin, Japhia Harrison, Constables.

Silas Condit, Judge of Election.

Joseph C. Hornblower, Silas Condit, Edward Jones, David Hayes, William Tuttle, Isaac Andruss, William Ward, Trustees of Free School.

Resolutions adopted—

The Annual report of the Township Committee having been read,

Resolved, that the same be accepted, and that the Report be entered in the town book.

The Annual report of the Free School was read, and on motion accepted.

Resolved, that Two thousand nine hundred dollars be appropriated toward the maintenance of the poor the ensuing year.

Resolved, That Two hundred dollars be appropriated for the support of the Free School the ensuing year.

Resolved, that the Town Committee be required to inspect the old burying ground, and that they be empowered and instructed to remove all nuisances, and prevent trespassing on the same, to mend the fences, to raise and otherwise regulate the head stones which they may find out of order.

Resolved, That the Town Committee be authorized to take measures to procure a new burying ground, and report at a special, or at the next Annual Town Meeting.

Resolved, That the Town Committee be authorized to open a passage from the Main street into the old burying ground, and that they cause the lower grounds therein to be raised, that the passage across them may be rendered more convenient.

Resolved, that this meeting deem it expedient to adopt measures to erect a town house upon the town lot in the main street.

Resolved, that William S. Pennington, James Vanderpool, Silas Condit, Isaac Nicholls, Lewis Thibou, be chosen a Committee to carry the above resolution into effect, and to report a plan at some future town meeting.

Resolved, that the above Committee be instructed, in case they shall deem it expedient, to report at a special town meeting to be called at their request, any time between this date and the first Monday in June next.

Resolved, that the roads be worked as the last year by labour, by districts.

Resolved, that the Town Committee be authorized to purchase a lot of land late the property of Abraham Lyon, without the buildings, should they deem the measure expedient.

Resolved, that the hog law be continued the same as last year, and that it be in force throughout the whole year.

Resolved, that the next annual town meeting be held in the session room of the 1st Presbyterian church, to commence at 1 o'clock in the afternoon.

Resolved, that the poll of the next annual election be opened and closed at the house of Stephen Roff, Newark.

Resolved, that the Town Clerk be allowed Five dollars for his Services, in addition to the fees allowed him by law.

WM. WARD, Town Clerk.

At a Special TOWN MEETING, convened agreeably to law, on Monday, *Mar.* 1, 1819, at the house of Moses Roff, Inn-keeper, Newark,

William S. Pennington, Esq., was chosen Moderator, when the following resolution was adopted:

Resolved, that the Town Committee be authorized and instructed to lease out the Town Lot in the Main street, opposite to the 1st Presbyterian Church, in such proportions as they may deem most advisable, for a term not exceeding five years.

Meeting adjourned.

WM. WARD, Town Clerk.

At An Anual TOWN MEETING of the Inhabitants of the Township of Newark, held at the Session room of the 1st Presbyterean Church in the Town of Newark on the 12th day of *April*, A. D. 1819—

Silas Condit, Esq., was chosen Moderator, and Nathan F. Wood, Town Clerk.

When the following Resolutions were adopted:

Resolved, that the Town Committee be instructed to Investigate the situation of the Lot of Land belonging to the town on which the Market now stands, and call on the subscribers who built the Market, and if they relinquish their claims to take possession and apply it to the use of the Town.

The report of the Town Committee was then Read, and on motion, &c., was ordered to be accepted and filed.

Resolved, that the Town Committee be instructed to Lease out the Town Lot in Front of the 1st Presbyterian Church untill wanted for a publick purpose.

Resolved, that the Town Committee be instructed not to Lease out any part of said Town Lot for to be built upon.

The report of the School Committee was read, and on motion made and Carr'd, was Accepted and filed.

Resolved, that the sum of Four hundred Dollars of the sum to be raised for the maintainance of the poor be appropriated for the educating of poor children.

Resolved, that the sum of Twenty six hundred Dollars be raised the ensuing year to be appropriated for the maintainance of the Poor.

The Following officers were then chosen:

Assessor—Isaac Nichols.

Collector—James W. Burnet.

Chosen Freeholders—David Beach, Lewis Thibou.

Commissioners of Appeal—Col. Stephen Hayes, Nehemiah S. Baldwin, Jabez Camfield.

Surveyors of Highways—Moses Roberts, Ezra Baldwin.

Overseers of the Poor—Isaac Nichols, Lewis Thibou.

Street Commissioners—Wm. S. Pennington, Esq., Lewis Thibou, Silas Condit.

Pound Masters—John P. Crane, James Searring, Henry L. Parkhurst, Ebenezer Havens, Samuel Baldwin.

Town Committee—Jabez Camfield, Col. Stephen Hayes, Nehemiah S. Baldwin, James Vanderpool, Lewis Thibou.

Constables—David Ball, Japhia Harrison, Joseph Sayres, Samuel Searring, Ashbel Green, Jonathan Keen.

Silas Condit, Esq., Judge of Elections.

Trustees of Free School—Joseph Wilbur, John C. Burnet, James Tichenor, David Hayes, Wm. Tuttle, Isaac Andruss, Esq., Silas Condit, Esq.

Overseers of Highways—Joseph T. Baldwin, Gen. John N. Cumming, George Holden, Caleb Sayres, Abner Ward, Jedediah Crane, David Nichols, William Burge, Caleb Campbell, Moses Roberts, James Camfield, Josiah Meeker, Joseph W. Camp.

Resolved, That the Town Committee be instructed to fit up and prepare a room in the upper part of the Market for the use of the Free School at the Town expence.

Resolved, that hogs Running at large be subject to Poundage the present year, and that the Poundage be three shillings, i. e. two shillings to the driver and one shilling to the Pound Master.

No further Business Meeting adjourned to Meet Again on the 2nd Monday in April, 1820, at one o'clock P. M. in this place.

SILAS CONDIT, Moderator.

Attest—NATHAN F. WOOD, Cl'k.

At an Annual TOWN MEETING of the Inhabitants of the Township of Newark Held in the Session House of the 1st Presbyterean Church in the Town of Newark on Monday the 10th Day of *April* 1820,

Silas Condit Esq'r was Chosen Moderator.

Nathan F. Wood, Clerk.

The 7th Section of the Law relating to Town Meetings having Been read as prescribed, Meeting proceeded to Business. When the following resolutions were adopted:

The Annual report of the Township Committee having been read, Resolved that the report be accepted and filed.

The Articles of Agreement Between Town Committee and Aaron Munn respecting the rent of the Burying Ground was read. The amount of the rent was $40—and Reported by said Town Committee as due from Aaron Munn to the Town, it was

Resolved that the sum of $10 be abated from the above Claim against Aaron Munn.

Resolved that the Town Committee be authorised to Borrow any sum not Exceeding One Thousand dollars for the use of the Town, to be repaid when the taxes for the present year are paid.

Resolved that the sum of Twenty Eight hundred dollars be raised the Ensuing year to be appropriated toward the maintainance of the poor.

The report of the School Committee was read and ordered to be accepted and filed.

Resolved that the Sum of Four hundred dollars of the sum to be raised for the maintainance of the poor Be appropriated for the Education of poor Children.

Resolved that the Town Committee be Instructed to select a suitable place for a Burying Ground and to call a Special Town Meeting when they think proper and make report of such place or places, that The Town may act upon it.

The Following Officers were then Chosen:

Isaac Nichols, Assessor.

James W. Burnett, Collector.

Samuel Pennington, James Vanderpool, Chosen Freeholders.

Stephen Hayes, Jabez Camfield, Joseph W. Camp, Commissioners of Appeal.

Henry L. Parkhurst, Moses Roberts, Surveyors of Highways.

Isaac Nichols, Lewis Thibou, Overseers of the Poor.

Silas Condit, Wm. S. Pennington, Caleb S. Riggs, Street Commissioners.

Zadock Baldwin, Jonathan Andruss, Zadock Meeker, Pound Masters.

Stephen Hayes, Jabez Camfield, Moses Smith, Silas Condit, John Taylor, Town Committee.

Samuel Searring, Japhia Harrison, David Ball, Stephen Howel, Jonathan Keen, Joseph Sayres, Constables.

Joseph Wilbur, John C. Burnett, James Bruen, John Taylor, James Tichenor, David Hayes, William Tuttle, Silas Condit, Trustees of Free School.

James Keen, Moses Fatout, Caleb S. Riggs, Abner Ward, Geo. Neilson, Sayres Coe, William Burge, Silvanus Baldwin, Moses Roberts, Caleb Earl, Stephen Foster, Jos. W. Camp, Overseers of the Highway.

Stephen Hayes, Judge of Election.

Resolved That Hogs running at Large be subject to Poundage the present year and that the poundage be three Shillings i e 2s. to the driver and 1s. to the Pound Master.

Resolved That the Poll of the next Annual Election be open'd and closed at the House of Mr. Stephen Roff Inkeeper Newark.

Resolved That the Next annual Town Meeting Be held in the session room of the first Presbyterean Church in this Town to Commence at 1 O'Clock P. M.

Meeting adjourned.

SILAS CONDIT, Moderator.

NATHAN F. WOOD, Clerk.

At a Special TOWN MEETING Convened agreeable to Law on Tuesday *May* 30th, 1820, at the House of Moses Roff Innkeeper, Newark.

Aaron Munn Esq'r was chosen Moderator.

When the following resolution was adopted.

Resolved that the further Consideration of the purchasing a Town Burying Ground, (for which purpose this Meeting was Called) Be postponed Indefinately.

Meeting adjourned accordingly.

N. F. WOOD, Clerk.

At an Annual TOWN MEETING of the inhabitants of the Township of Newark held in the Session house of the 1st presbyterian Church in the Town of Newark on Monday the 9th day of *April* 1821,

Joseph C. Hornblower Esq'r was chosen Moderator,
Philo Sanford " Clerk.

The laws respecting town meetings having been read and the act to prevent routs, riots &c., as prescribed by law, the meeting proceeded to business, when the following resolutions were adopted and Officers chosen, the report of the Town Committee was read, resolved that the same be accepted, resolved that the report of the fire wardens be read, resolved that the Town Committee be authorised to raise the sum of One thousand eight hundred dollars for the expences of the town for the Ensuing year, resolved that a special Committee be appointed to inquire into the situation of the Town Docks, and to report at an annual or special meeting for that purpose, and to settle with the trustees of the said Docks and receive the money if any for the use of the Town. This Committee to consist of Three; The following Gentlemen were chosen Viz: Caleb S. Riggs, David D. Crane,

Sam'l Pennington; resolved that the surplus fund arising from the dog tax be appropriated to the support of the poor.

A letter from the Clerk of the Board of Directors of the Newark and Mount pleasant turnpike Co. addressed to the Moderator of this Meeting, being read, on motion Ordered that the same be laid on the Table: It being stated to the meeting that Ebenezer Havens while keeper of the poor house had sold certain articles of produce as agent for the town Committee amounting to about forty dollars (40) and which had been lost by the failure of the person to whom the sale was made and that he had been charged with the amount in settlement with the Town Committee, on motion resolved that the sum of forty (40) dollars be refunded to him: Resolved that the tax on dogs be raised to the sum of three dollars the Ensuing year, resolved that the sum of four hundred dollars raised by the Town for the use of the poor be appropriated to the support of the free school. resolved that it is Expedient to procure a place for a public burying Ground, resolved that a Committee of three be appointed to purchase the land, the following Gentlemen were Chosen, Viz David D. Crane, Caleb S. Riggs, Samuel Pennington; resolved that the Committee have power to purchase a lot containing not less than Two acres nor more than four acres for the burying ground, and that the sum of Two hundred and fifty dollars be appropriated towards the payment of said lot, resolved that the town Committee be authorized to borrow the residue of the money that may be wanted to complete the purchase of said lot.

resolved that all the Town lands that are now in the possession of or belonging to the town or that may hereafter be owned by the town be placed under the care and Superintendance of the town Committee; resolved that it is Expedient to build a town house the present year, resolved that a Committee of Seven be appointed to Carry into Effect the build of the town house, the following gentlemen were chosen Viz: Lewis Thibou, John Pionier, Isaac Nichols, Caleb S. Riggs, Smith Burnett, Ephraim Bolles, William Halsey.

Resolved that five hundred dollars be raised towards the building of the Town house and that the Committee have power to borrow any sum not Exceeding five Thousand dollars to carry into Effect the building of the town house; resolved that the vacancies occasioned by the death of two of the trustees of the town docks, be filled by the following Gentlemen Viz David D. Crane, James Vanderpool.

The following officers were then Chosen:

Isaac Nichols, Assessor.

James W. Burnett, Collector.

Samuel Pennington, James Vanderpool, Chosen Freeholders.

Stephen Hayes, Jabez Campfield, Joseph W. Camp, Commissioners of Appeals.

Henry L. Parkhurst, Moses Roberts, Surveyors of Highways.

Isaac Nichols, Lewis Thibou, Overseers of the poor.

Silas Condit, William S. Pennington, Caleb S. Riggs, Street Commissioners.

Zadoc Baldwin, Jonathan Andruss, John Maginnis, Ebenezer Havens, Pound Masters.

Stephen Hayes, Jabez Campfield, Moses Smith, Silas Condit Joseph W. Camp, Town Committee.

Stephen Hayes, Judge of Elections.

David Ball, Jacob Osborn, Joseph Sayres, Japhia Harrison, Benjamin Jarves, Constables.

Joseph Wilbur, John C. Burnett, James Bruen, David Hayes, William Tuttle, Silas Condit, John Taylor, James Tichenor, Trustees of the Free Schools.

John P. Sanford, Moses Faitoute, Henry Holden, John Alling, James Searing, Johnson Nichols, William Burdge, Enoch Bolles, Caleb Earle, Joseph Lyon, Overseers of the Highways.

Resolved that the poll of the next Annual Election be opened and closed at the house of Mr. Stephen Roff Innkeeper Newark.

Resolved that hogs running at large be subject to poundage the present year and that the poundage be four Shillings i. e. two Shillings for the driver and two Shillings for the pound Master.

Resolved that the roads be worked by labor the present year.

Resolved that the next annual town Meeting be held in the Session room of the 1st presbyterian Church in this Town to commence at 1 O'Clock P. M.

Meeting Adjourned.

JOS. C. HORNBLOWER, Moderator.

PHILO SANFORD, Clerk.

At a Special TOWN MEETING of the inhabitants of the Township of Newark, held in the Session house of the first presbyterian Church, on Monday, the 11th *June*, 1821, made choice of James Vanderpool, Esq., Moderator for the meeting.

The law respecting routs, riots, &c., having been read the following resolutions were adopted—Resolved, that the vote taken at the last Annual Town Meeting respecting Dogs be reconsidered. Resolved, that the vote of the last Annual Town Meeting laying a tax of three dollars on dogs, be and the same is hereby rescinded.

Resolved, that it is inexpedient to apply to the legislature at their next session for a law to raise money by tax to purchase a public burying ground or to build a Town house.

Meeting Adjourned.

PHILO SANFORD, Clerk.

Proceedings of the Annual TOWN MEETING of the Township

of Newark, held in the Session house of the first Presbyterian Church in Newark on the Second Monday in *April*, 1822,

Joseph C. Hornblower, Esq., was chosen Moderator, and Philo Sanford, Clerk.

The meeting being organized, and that part of the Act of Assembly read which by law is required to be read at the opening of every Annual Town Meeting. The reports of Committees were called for.

The Annual report of the Township Committee being read, on motion,

1st. Resolved, That the same be accepted and filed.

A Member of the Township Committee having stated to the meeting that Mrs. Savage had Presented to the Committee a bill of Fifty Dollars for services rendered to Robert Montgomery who had been badly injured by a scald, but that the Committee did not feel authorized to Pay the same, not knowing whether the Town was legally chargeable with the case and maintainance of the said Montgomery.

2nd. On motion, it was Resolved, That this meeting do recommend to the Township Committee to Pay to the said Mrs. Savage a sum not exceeding Twenty five Dollars on the said Bill.

The Committee to whom was referred at the last annual Town Meeting the subject of the Town Docks, made a report, which being read, on motion

3d. Resolved, That the report be accepted and filed, and the Committee discharged.

4th. Resolved, That so much of the report of the Committee on the Town Docks as relates to the lower or new Town Dock be referred to the Town Committee; and so much of the said report as relates to the upper or old Town Dock be referred to a select Committee of three persons, with authority to adopt such legal measures as they may deem expedient to ascertain and establish the Town rights in regard to the said Dock or landing place, and to recover the Possession thereof if necessary.

5th. Resolved, that Caleb S. Riggs, William S. Pennington and Samuel Pennington be that Committee.

6th. Resolved, That the sum of One hundred Dollars be raised and appropriated to the use of the last named Committee for the Purpose aforesaid.

The Trustees or Directors of the Free School under the care of the Town, made their annual report, which being read,

7th. Resolved, That the same be accepted and filed.

8th. Resolved, That the surplus fund of the Dog tax, which by a vote of the last Annual Town Meeting was transferred to the general fund, be transferred to the credit of the fund arising from the Dog tax, to be applied to the purposes to which that tax is by law appropriated, and That the Township Committee be directed to apply the same to the satisfaction of such balances as may be due to individuals for damages done by Dogs to Sheep during the past Year.

9th. Resolved, That the Township Committee be instructed to pursue legal measures to prevent trespasses upon the Upper and the Military Commons, and to protect the same from encroachments and injuries by carriages passing over the same.

10th. Resolved, That the Highways be maintained by hire.

11th. Resolved, That the sum of Two thousand Dollars be raised for the maintainance of the highways this year.

12th. Resolved, That the Township Committee apportion the sum above voted to be raised to each overseer of the highways that may be appointed in the several districts as now laid out; the amount of taxes that may be raised in said districts which said several sums so apportioned shall be exclusively for the maintainance of the highways in the said several districts where raised; Provided that the tax shall be applied to the districts in which the person taxed may reside.

13th. Resolved, That the sum of Twelve hundred Dollars be raised this year for the support of the Poor.

14th. Resolved, That the sum of Four hundred Dollars be raised this year for the support of the Free School under the care of the Township.

It being stated to the meeting that three vacancies existed in the Board of Trustees of the Town Docks by the resignation of David D. Crane and . . . . . and the removal of John Y. Baldwin.

Mr. John Alling, Nehemiah Tunis, and Lewis Thibou, were elected to supply the vacancies.

15th. On motion, Resolved, That the meeting proceed to the election of Township Officers for the ensuing year.

The following were Chosen:

Isaac Nichols, Assessor.

James W. Burnet, Collector.

James Vanderpool, Samuel Pennington, Chosen Freeholders.

Stephen Hayes, Jabez Camfield, Joseph W. Camp, Commissioners of Appeal.

Ezra Baldwin, Moses Faitoute, Surveyors of Highways.

Isaac Nichols, Lewis Thibou, Overseers of the Poor.

Silas Condit, William S. Pennington, Caleb S. Riggs, Street Commissioners.

Zadoc Baldwin, Robert Hayes, John Maginnis, Pound Masters.

William Tuttle, Ephraim Bolles, Joseph W. Camp, Jabez Campfield, Samuel Pennington, Town Committee.

Stephen Hayes, Judge of Election.

David Ball, Jacob Osborne, Joseph Sayres, Constables.

Joseph Willbur, John C. Burnet, James Bruen, David Hayes,

William Tuttle, Silas Condit, John Taylor, James Tichenor, Trustees of the Free School.

Israel C. Crane, Caleb Earle, John Baldwin, Ezra Baldwin, Johnson Nichols, James Searing, Matthias Plum, Lewis Thibou, Moses Faitoute, John I. Plume, Samuel Baldwin, James Tichenor, Overseers of the Highways.

16th. Resolved, That the poll of the next annual election be opened and Closed at the House of Mr. Stephen Roff, Inn-keeper, Newark.

17th. Resolved, That hogs running at large be subject to poundage the present year, and that the Poundage be four Shillings, I. E. Two Shillings for the driver and two Shillings for the Pound Master.

18th. Resolved, that the next annual Town Meeting be held in the Session house of the first Presbyterian Church in this Town to commence at half past one o'clock P. M.

Meeting Adjourned.

JOS. C. HORNBLOWER, Moderator.

PHILO SANDFORD, Clerk.

SPECIAL TOWN MEETING, Newark, *Nov* 11th, A. D. 1822.

At a special Town Meeting of the inhabitants of the Township of Newark, convened in the Session room of the first Presbyterian Church by Order of the Town Committee for the purpose of supplying the vacancy in the Town Committee occasioned by the death of Mr. Jabez Campfield; also a vacancy in the Commissioners of Appeal occasioned by the death of the same Gentleman—Also to take into consideration the propriety of applying to the Legislature for a modification, &c., of certain Laws.

Jos. C. Hornblower, Esq., Chosen Moderator.

1st. Resolved, That James Vanderpool, Esq., be chosen to supply the vacancy in Town Committee.

2d. Resolved, That James Vanderpool, Esq., is chosen to fill the vacancy in the Commissioners of Appeal.

3d. Resolved, That it is expedient to apply to the Legislature for a modification of the existing Laws, so as to exempt all regular members of the fire Engine Companies of this Town from personal labour not exceeding three days on the Highways whenever the same shall be worked by labour, and from tax when the same shall be worked by taxes, not exceeding three Dollars; provided that in case such quantity of labour or tax of any member shall exceed those amounts, such excess shall be worked or paid by such member.

4th. Resolved, That a copy of the foregoing resolution, signed by Moderator and Clerk of this meeting, be forwarded to the representatives in the Legislature from this County.

Meeting Adjourned. Nov. 11th, 1822.

PHILO SANFORD, Cl'k.

Annual Town Meeting A. D. Eighteen hundred and twenty three.

Proceedings of the Annual Town Meeting of the Township of Newark held in the Session house of the first Presbyterian Church in Newark on the Second Monday in April One thousand Eight hundred and twenty three.

Isaac Andruss Esq'r was chosen Moderator, and Philo Sanford Clerk.

The Meeting being organized and that part of the act of assembly read which by Law is required to be read at the opening of Every Annual Town Meeting the reports of Committees were called for.

The Annual report of the Township Committee being read, on motion,

1st. Resolved that the same be accepted and filed.

2ond. Resolved that Caleb S. Riggs, Elias Van Arsdale, and Theo. Frelinghuysen be a Committee to Examine into settle and determine a dispute now Existing between the Township Committee and the Assessor and the representation of the late Collector James W. Burnet dec. respecting the fees of said Officers respectively arising out of the Assessment and Collection of the tax of the last year.

And that the same Committee Enquire and determine whether the allowances made by the Township Committee to the Magistrates in pauper cases and others which Enter into the Accounts of the said Committee are correct or not.

3d. Resolved that William S. Pennington, Silas Condit, Thomas Ward, E. E. Boudinot and Samuel Pennington be a Committee on the subject of the upper Town Dock and that they have power and authority to accept the offer of Aaron Ward Except that part which requires the Town to repair the Dock, and that in case he shall not agree thereto that the said Committee have power to take such measures to recover possession of said dock as they may Judge necessary and proper and that the sum of One Hundred dollars be appropriated in addition to the former appropriation for the aforementioned purposes.

4th. Resolved, That the manure which shall remain in the public Streets within the Town plot of Newark after the 21st day of the present month and all that shall hereafter accumulate shall be considered as belonging to the Town. And it shall be the duty of the Superintendant of the Poor House Establishment to gather it from time to time for the use of the Township Farm in his charge.

Whereas there are several small pieces of land within the Town plot of Newark which are described on the map filed in the County Clerk's office made by the Commissioners appointed by law to survey and locate the Streets in the Town Plot and are in the said Map and Survey denominated Vacant ground and there is also a piece of ground whereon the Market stands adjoining Market street and the dock or landing place called the old Town dock all which are public or community property but the legal title to which does not appear to be vested in the Township as a Corporation or to be owned by any individual, but which with the other Vacant ground if any within the Town, ought to be vested in the Township as owner that it may be protected and improved as circumstances shall require: Therefore

Resolved that a suitable act for that purpose be prepared and application made to the Legislature to Enact the same into a Law with such provisions therein as may be deemed reasonable and for the public good.

Resolved That Caleb S. Riggs, Silas Condit and Wm. S. Pennington be a Committee to carry this resolution into Effect.

Resolved That the sum of Two thousand dollars be raised for the maintainance of the highways this Year.

Resolved That there be not more than three Overseers of the roads and highways within the Town Plot of Newark comprehending the roads leading into and out of the Town Plot as far as they are worked by the people of the Village and as comprehended in the present district: That it be recommended to the Township Committee to keep the whole of the said roads and highways in one district to the end that the said three Overseers may act in . . . . And that it also be recommended to the said Overseers to devise a judicious plan with respect to the said and highways and work the same accordingly. And it is further resolved that all the funds raised or to be raised for working the roads and highways be applied and Expended by the said three Overseers of a majority of them in the pursuit of such plan as far as may be done consistently with the public welfare.

Resolved That the sum of Eighteen hundred dollars be raised this year for the support of the poor.

Resolved That the sum of Four hundred dollars be raised this year for the support of the Male Free School under the care of the Township.

Resolved That the sum of three hundred dollars be raised this year for the support of the female Free School in the Union School house.

Resolved That the Meeting proceed to the Election of Township Officers for the Ensuing Year.

The following were chosen:

Assessor, Isaac Nichols.

Collector, Abm. Ward Jr.

Chosen Freeholders, James Vanderpool, Samuel Pennington.

Commissioners of Appeal, Stephen Hayes, James Vanderpool, Joseph W. Camp.

Surveyors of Highways, Moses Faitoute, Ezra Baldwin.

Overseers of the Poor, Lewis Thibou, Isaac Nichols.

Street Commissioners, Silas Condit, Wm. S. Pennington, Caleb S. Riggs.

Pound Masters, Zadoc Baldwin, Robert Hayes, John Baldwin, Jonathan Andruss, Caleb Campbell, George Holden.

Town Committeee, William Tuttle, James Vanderpool, Stephen Dodd, Joseph W. Camp, Sam'l Pennington.

Judge of Elections, Stephen Hayes.

Constables, David Ball, Jacob Osborn, John Searing, Benj. S. Jarvis, Joseph Sayres.

Trustees of the Male Free School, Joseph Wilbur, John C. Burnet, James Bruen, David Hayes, William Tuttle, Silas Condit, James Tichenor, John Taylor.

Overseers of Highways in the Town Plot, Caleb S. Riggs, Lewis Thibou, Samuel Pennington.

Overseers of Highways at Camptown and Lyons Farms, Israel C. Crane, James Canfield, Joseph W. Camp.

To supply the Vacancy in the Trustees of the lower Town Dock occasioned by the resignation of Caleb Wheeler, Ephraim Bolles.

Resolved That Hogs running at large be subject to poundage the present Year and that the poundage be Four Shillings I. E. three shillings for the driver and one Shilling for the pound Master.

Resolved That the Poll of the next annual Election be opened and closed at the house of Mr. Stephen Roff Innkeeper Newark.

Resolved That the next annual Town Meeting of the Township of Newark be held in the Session house of the first Presbyterian Church in the Town to commence at One O'Clock P. M.

ISAAC ANDRUSS, Moderator.

PHILO SANFORD, Clerk.

Special TOWN MEETING of the inhabitants of the Township of Newark Conven'd in the Session house of the first Presbyterian Church on Saturday 31st day of May A.D. 1823 for the purpose of taking into consideration the Expediency of enlarging the Poor house and if thought Expedient to authorise the raising of funds for carrying it into effect.

Aaron Munn Esq. was chosen Moderator for the Meeting.

Resolved That the Town Committee be authorised to make such additions to the Poorhouse as in their opinion is necessary.

Resolved That the Town Committee be authorised to borrow any sum not Exceeding Seven hundred dollars for the above mentioned purpose.

Meeting adjourned.

AARON MUNN, Moderator.

PHILO SANFORD, Clerk.

Newark Annual Town Meeting, In Eighteen Hundred and Twenty Four.

Agreeable to previous Notice, the Annual Town Meeting for the Township of Newark was held in the Session House (Attached to the 1st Presbyterian Church) on the Second Monday the 12th of April, 1824—

When Joseph C. Hornblower, Esq., was chosen Moderator, and Archibald Woodruff, Clerk.

The House being called to order the Clerk was instructed to read the 7th Section of the Act which relates to Town Meeting and also the Riot Act.

Caleb S. Riggs, Esq., on the Committee respecting vacant parcels or Lots of Land in the Town Plat of Newark, Reported that a Law was passed at the last sitting of the Legislature (which was read) and which said law vested said Lots or Parcels of Land, Including the old Town Dock, In the Inhabitants of the Township of Newark.

Resolved, That said Lands and Dock be placed under the direction and care of the Township Committee.

The Annual Report of the Township Committee was called for, Read, Accepted and ordered to be filed.

The Report of the Committee respecting the Charge made by Justices of the Peace in certain cases and of Collector's Fees was made and the Committee discharged.

The Committee appointed to adjust the difference with Aaron Ward respecting his encroachments on the old Town Dock, made no special Report thereon. But it was Resolved to reject Mr. Ward's former proposal, and continue the same Committee, and they are hereby instructed to take such Legal measures as they may deem expedient for the recovery of said Dock and the Town rights therein.

Resolved, That the Roads be districted and Worked upon the same plan and in the same way as the last Year.

Resolved, That Two Thousand Dollars be raised for the working the Roads or Public Highways this year.

Resolved, That the sum of Four Hundred Dollars be raised for the support of the Male Free School.

Resolved, that the sum of Four Hundred Dollars be raised for the support of the Female Free School held in the Union School House.

Resolved, that the sum of Two Thousand Dollars be raised for the support of the Poor—each of the above several sums are for the ensuing year.

Resolved, that the sum of Eight Hundred Dollars be raised for the purpose of Paying the Ballance due for Building an addition to the Poor house.

Resolved, That the Township Committee be instructed to pay

the respective ballances due the Overseers of the Highway, as Reported by the said Township Committee in their Annual Report for the last Year.

Resolved, That this meeting now proceed to the election of Township Officers for the ensuing year, Commencing with the Choice of Constables.

Five Constables were chosen, viz:—Benjamin S. Jarvis, Jacob Osborn, John Searing, David Ball and Joseph Sayres.

List of Officers Elected as Follows:

Assessor—Isaac Nichols.

Collector—Abraham K. Ward.

Chosen Freeholders—James Vanderpool and Moses Smith.

Commissioners of Appeal—Joseph W. Camp, Robert B. Campfield and James Vanderpool.

Surveyors of the Highways—Moses Faitoute and Ezra Baldwin.

Overseers of the Poor—Moses Smith and Caleb Carter.

Street Commissioners—William S. Pennington, Caleb S. Riggs and Silas Condit.

Town Committee—William Tuttle, Samuel Pennington, Wm. S. Pennington, Moses Smith and Ephraim Bolles.

Judge of Election—Robert B. Campfield.

Trustees of the Male Free School—James Tichenor, John C. Burnet, Joseph Wilbur, Silas Condit, Wm. Tuttle, James Bruen, John Taylor and David Hayes.

Overseers of the Highways—Caleb S. Riggs, Samuel Pennington and Nehemiah Tunis.

Overseers at Camptown and Lyon's Farms—James Canfield, Israel C. Crane and Joseph W. Camp.

Pound Masters—William Stevens, Elihu Pierson and Robert Hayes.

Resolved, That Hogs running at large are liable to be drove to the Pound, and Charged for each Hog Fifty Cents, that is to say—Twenty Five Cents to be paid to the Driver and Twenty Five Cents to be allowed the Pound Keeper.

Resolved, That a Committee of Nine Persons be appointed to take into consideration whether any, and if any, what Legislative aid may be necessary for the better regulation of this Town in respect to a Market and other matters not now provided for by any existing Law, and to Report to a special or to the next annual Town meeting for the consideration of such meeting—and that Wm. S. Pennington, Caleb S. Riggs, Theodore Frelinghuysen, John Taylor, Robert B. Campfield, Moses Smith, Joseph C. Hornblower, Ephraim Bolles and Charles T. Shipman be the Committee to carry the foregoing resolution into effect.

Resolved, That the next Annual Election for Members of the

Legislature, Sheriff, &c., be held at the House of Stephen Roff, and that the Poll open and close there.

Resolved, That the next Annual Town Meeting be held in the Session House of the first Presbyterian Church, to commence at one o'clock P. M. in this Town.

Ordered, that Mr. Munn be Paid Two Dollars for cleaning the Session House.

Meeting adjourned.

JOS C. HORNBLOWER, Moderator.

Attested by
ARCH'D WOODRUFF, Clerk.

Newark Annual TOWN MEETING, for the Township of Newark, held in the Session House of the 1st Presbyterian Church, on Monday, *April* 11th, 1825,

When Joseph C. Hornblower, Esq., was Chosen Moderator, and Archibald Woodruff, Town Clerk.

Agreeable to the requisition of the Law, the Clerk was instructed to read the Seventh section of the Act required to be read at every Annual Town Meeting and the Riot Act.

The Minutes of the last Annual Town Meeting being called for and read.

The Committee appointed at the last Annual Town Meeting on the subject of the old Town Dock being called upon to Report, It appeared by the Statement of the Chairman of that Committee, that nothing had been done by them in relation to the object of their appointment. Thereupon it was, on motion,

Resolved, that said Committee be discharged, and a Committee of Three appointed with the same powers and instructions as were given to the former Committee, on the subject of the said Dock—Whereupon Samuel Pennington, Stephen Hayes and John Alling were appointed on said Committee.

The Committee of Nine, appointed at the last Annual Town Meeting to take into consideration what Legislative aid might be necessary to enable the Town to establish and regulate a market, &c., was discharged, and the subject dismissed.

The following Resolution was moved and Seconded, viz:

Resolved, that it is expedient and proper to take measures to erect a Town House, on the Lot belonging to the Town, on the West side of Broad Street, and after some discussion, the further consideration thereof was indefinately Postponed.

A memorial from a number of the Inhabitants of this Town was presented and read, Praying leave to erect a new Market on the sight of the old one, in Market Street Upon Certain Terms &c.

On motion Resolv'd that the consideration thereof, be postponed, and that the subject of said memorial, and also the subject of Building a Town House, be referred to a Committee of

Five, with instructions to Report thereon, to a special Town meeting, should they deem it necessary, and Expedient to call one for that purpose, or to the next annual Town Meeting.

Whereupon Wm. S. Pennington, Smith Burnet, Luther Goble, James Vanderpool and Jabez Harrison were appointed on that Committee.

The annual Report of the Town Committee was call'd for and read, and in connection therewith, the Report from the Male Free School Committee, and the managers of the Female Free School, and on motion, the same were accepted, and ordered to be filed.

Whereupon on motion Resolv'd that the sum of Four Hundred Dollars, be raised for the use of the Male Free School, and the like sum for the use of the Female Free School for the present year.

The Town Committee, layed before the meeting the Report made to that Comittee by the Trustees of the lower Town Dock, by which it appeared, that the Trustees, had agreed, to lease the same to Nehemiah Tunis, for Ten Years, at Ninety Dollars a year, and the Trustees to Expend thereon, Three Hundred Dollars, in repair if necessary. It was thereupon moved and Seconded, that it is inexpedient, and improper for the Trustees, to proceed to Execute, any lease of the said Dock,—and after a considerable discussion, the further consideration thereof, was indefinately postponed.

It was moved and Seconded, that the Roads be worked this year by Labour, as the same had been done before the system of raising money by taxes, for making and repairing the same, was introduced, and after, a considerable discussion, the motion was negatived by a very large majority.

On Motion Resolved, that the sum of Two Thousand Dollars be raised for the support of the Poor this Year.

On Motion Resolved that the sum of Two Thousand Dollars be raised this Year, for the purpose of making and repairing the Roads.

On Motion Resolved that the meeting now proceed to the Election of Township Officers.

Constables, Benjamin S. Jarvis, Joseph Sayres, Jacob Osborn, David Ball and John Searing.

Collector, Abraham K. Ward.

Chosen Freeholders, James Vanderpool and Robert B. Campfield.

Commissioners of Appeal, James Vanderpool, Stephen Hayes and Joseph W. Camp.

Surveyors of Highways, Moses Faitoute and Ezra Baldwin.

Overseers of the Poor, David Nichols and David Hayes.

Street Commissioners, William S. Pennington, Caleb S. Riggs and Silas Condit.

Town Committee, Stephen Hayes, Joseph W. Camp, Ephraim Bolles, Wm. Tuttle and Stephen Dod.

Judge of Election, Col. Stephen Hayes.

Committee of the Male Free School, Jas. Tichenor, Ellison Conger, Joseph Wilbur, Silas Condit, David Hayes, Wm. Tuttle, James Bruen and Stephen Dod.

Overseers of the Roads in the Town Platt, Moses Faitoute, Stephen Hayes and Johnson Nichols.

Overseers of the Outer Districts, Hugh K. Toler, Joseph W. Camp and Caleb H. Camp.

Pound Masters, John I. Plume, Upper; Elihu Pierson, Center; and Robert Hayes, Lower.

On motion Resolved that the Committee of the Male Free School, be and they are hereby instructed, to introduce the Lancasterian System of Teaching, in that School if practicable under existing circumstances.

Resolved that Hogs found running at large shall be liable to be impounded, and that the Driver be paid, and is Entitled to receive with the Pound Master the same Compensation—respectively, as was agreed upon at the last annual Town Meeting.

Resolved that the next annual Election be opened held and Closed, at the House of Stephen Roff Innkeeper in this Town.

Resolved that the Town Clerk be Paid Five Dollars for his Service in Keeping the Minutes and Records of the Town last Year, and that he receive the same sum annually, hereafter, untill otherwise ordered.

Resolved that the Sexton of the 1st Presbyterian Church be paid Two Dollars for Cleaning out this House after Town Meeting is over.

Resolved that this Meeting Adjourn to meet in this Place, at Two O'Clock P. M. on the Second Monday in April next.

JOS. C. HORNBLOWER, Mod'r.

Attested by Arch'd Woodruff, Town Clerk.

Special Town Meeting Held at the House of Enoch Bolles *October* 1st 1825.

When Mr. Silas Condit was chosen Moderator and Arch'd Woodruff acted as Clerk. The Seventh Section of the Act relating to Town meetings was by the Moderator ordered to be read as also the Notice for calling this meeting.

The memorial which was read at the last annual Town meeting was again read—which relates to the granting to a Company upon certain terms the lease of the Lot of Ground in Market Street where the old Market now stands for the purpose of Erecting a new One thereon.

The Minutes of the last Annual Town Meeting in relation to the Market and also the subject of Building a Town House being also called for and Read both of which were referred to a Committee with powers to report thereon. Whereupon said Committee now Report, Recommending the leasing of said Lot to a Company for the Building of a new Market. As also that application be made at the next sitting of the Legislature for a Law authorizing the raising of money to Build a Town House.

On motion, Resolved, that the first part of the Report in relation to the Building a Market, be accepted.

Resolved, that the Town Committee be, and they are hereby authorized and instructed to make and execute a Lease to such Persons as shall be appointed by the Market Street Market Association of the Ground whereon the Old Market House stands, which lease shall be upon the principles contained in the Report of the Committee appointed at the last Town Meeting upon this subject—provided that such lease shall contain a provision that at least Fourteen feet of the Market Lot next to the premises of Mr. Jabez Harrison shall be left open for a Street in connection with the Fourteen feet of Vacant Land Adjoining the same, belonging to the said Jabez Harrison. And such lease is only to be made, upon condition that the said Jabez Harrison will in some legal and binding way dedicate his said vacant strip of Fourteen feet to the use of a Public Street.

Resolved, that the Report of the Committee in regard to the Town House be accepted.

Resolved, that a Committee of Three be appointed to make application to the next sitting of the Legislature for a Law authorizing the Town to raise money for the purpose of Building a Town House; and that Caleb S. Riggs, William S. Pennington and Smith Burnet, Esquires, be and they are hereby appointed on that Committee.

Meeting Adjourned.

SILAS CONDIT, Moderator.

Attested by ARCH'D WOODRUFF, Town Clerk.

Annual TOWN MEETING For the Township of Newark, Held in the Session House of the first Presbyterian Church, on Monday, the Tenth day of *April*, One Thousand Eight Hundred and Twenty Six, at Two o'clo'k P. M.

Aaron Munn, Esqr., was chosen Moderator, and Archibald Woodruff, Town Clerk.

The 7th Section of the Law relating to Town Meeting was read, as also the Riot Act.

The minutes of the last Annual Town Meeting as well as of the last Special Town Meeting were called for and read.

The Report of the Town Committee was call'd for and read by their Clerk, (together with an appendix, No. 1 Report of the

Trustees of the new Town Dock, No. 2 Committee of the Male Free School, and No. 4 A communication from Aaron Marsh, on his having encroached upon vacant land belonging to the Town) when, on motion, it was

Resolved, to accept the Report of said Committee so far as to exclude the appendix.

Resolved, that the Trustees of the new Town Dock take such Legal measures to secure the rights of the Town in said Dock as they in their wisdom may deem necessary.

The Committee on the subject of encroachments made by Aaron Ward on the old Town Dock, Report that after several interviews with Mr. Ward, he has made the following proposition, viz: that he will relinquish to the Town Twenty five feet of the North part of his Dock for the Twenty five feet of the South part of the Dock, claimed by the Town, and occupied by him, provided the Town will give him One Hundred Dollars in the exchange, and which the Committee would respectfully recommend.

The proposition of Mr. Ward was rejected, and 2 Resolutions were offered by Mr. S. Pennington, the first of which was to make an even exchange with Mr. Ward, which was afterwards amended, by Instructing the Com'ttee to offer Mr. Ward Ninety Nine Dollars for the difference. And the 2d Resolution was to continue the old Committee, with powers to effect the exchange agreeable to the foregoing Resolution, or take legal measures to recover the Town Claims in the said Dock, and the Com'ittee to draw on the Township Collector for any sum not exceeding One Hundred Dollars not otherwise appropriated.

Resolved, that the Report of the Committee of the Male Free School be accepted, and the Town Meeting coincide with the views of the Committee as recommended in their Report of altering said School from a free to a Pay School, and on the Lancasterian Plan. And said Committee were authorized to hire a Room sufficiently large to hold from 2 to 300 Children.

Resolved, that it be recommended to the Managers of the Female Free School to Adopt a similar course as that recommended by the Com'ittee of the Male Free School, viz: that of receiving pay by gradation instead of its being an entire Free School, should they deem it practicable.

Resolved, That the amount of the Judgment and Cost obtained against Mr. Bolles in the suit instituted against him by Mr. Morehouse, before Justice Munn, in relation to the manure removed to the Poor Farm by said Bolle's order, while acting as one of the Town Com'ittee, be paid.

Resolved, that the Resolution passed in 1823, in relation to collecting the manure in the Street, for the benefit of the Poor Farm, be Repealed.

A Report of the Committee of the Watch (which was kept up during the last Winter) after having been read, was ordered to be filed.

The Report of the Managers of the Female Free School was read, accepted, and ordered to be filed.

APPROPRIATIONS.

Resolved, that the sum of Two Thousand Dollars be raised for the purpose of making and Repairing the Roads this Year.

Resolved, that the sum of Sixteen Hundred Dollars be raised for the support of the Poor this Year.

Resolved, That the sum of Four Hundred Dollars be raised for the use of the Male Free School, and the like sum of Four Hundred Dollars for the use of the Female Free School this Year.

Resolved, that Silas Condit, Esq., be appointed to fill the vacancy in the Trustees of the New Town Dock, occasioned by the removal of Mr. Lewis Thibou to New York.

Election of Township Officers:

Constables—Benjamin S. Jarvis, Joseph Sayrs, Jacob Osborn, David Ball and John Searing.

Assessor—Isaac Nichols.

Collector—Abraham K. Ward.

Chosen Freeholders—James Vanderpool, Robert B. Campfield.

Commissioners of Appeal—James Vanderpool, Stephen Hayes, Robert B. Campfield.

Surveyors of Highways—Moses Faitoute and Jabez Cook.

Overseers of the Poor—David Nichols and Caleb Carter.

Street Commissioners—Silas Condit, Caleb S. Riggs and Wm. S. Pennington.

Town Committee—John Alling, Joseph W. Camp, Wm. Tuttle, Luther Goble and Stephen Hayes.

Judge of Election—Stephen Hayes.

Committee of the Male Free School—Ellison Conger, James Tichenor, Silas Condit, Wm. Tuttle, Joseph Wilbur, David Hayes, James Bruen, Stephen Dodd. Two new ones appointed, viz:—Luther Goble and Caleb H. Shipman.

Overseers of the Road in Town Plott—David Doremus, Stephen Hayes and Johnson J. Nichols.

Overseers do. of Outer Districts—Joseph W. Camp, Caleb H. Camp and David Earl.

Resolved, that when this meeting Adjourn it shall be to meet at Eleven o'clock A. M.—the next Annual Town Meeting.

Pound Masters—Hugh Cammack, Robt. Hays and David J. Baldwin.

Resolved, that the next Annual Election be opened, held and closed at the House of Mr. Stephen Roff, Inn-keeper in this Town.

Resolved, that Hogs runing at large be liable to be impounded, and that the Driver be entitled to receive 25 Cts., and the Pound Masters 25 Cts. for each Hog.

Resolved, That Two Dollars be paid the Sexton for Cleaning this House.

The Town Meeting referred the application of Mr. Aaron Marsh in relation to his having in possession and now occupying some of the Public or Vacant Town Lands, to the Town Committee.

Resolved, that the Dog tax be 50 Cts. this year.

Resolved, that this meeting now Adjourn, to meet in this Place at their next Annual Town Meeting at the time before agreed upon.

AARON MUNN, Moderator.

ARCHIBALD WOODRUFF, Town Clerk.

Annual TOWN MEETING For the Township of Newark, held in the Session House of the first Presbyterian Church, on Monday, the Ninth Day of *April*, A. D. 1827, at 11 o'clock A. M.

Aaron Munn, Esqr., was chosen Moderator, and Archibald Woodruff, Town Clerk.

After having read the Riot Act and the Seventh Section of the Act of Assembly required to be read at Town Meetings, The Town Committee were called upon to make their Report, when it was read by their Clerk and accepted.

The Report of the Trustees of the New Town Dock was made, Stating a Ballance in the Hands of their Treasurer of the sum of $337 23-100ths, which was accepted.

The Report of the Committee on the old Town Dock was read, in which it was stated they had not effected an exchange with Mr. Ward, as recommended at the last Annual Town Meeting, and asked to be discharged, which was granted.

Resolved, that the subject of the Old Town Dock be referred to the Town Committee, with powers to compromise with Mr. Ward, or to take legal measures to recover the same.

Provided they be not authorized to Pay Mr. Ward any money in the exchange.

Reports of the Male and Female Free Schools was read and accepted.

Appropriations for the current year:

Resolved, that the sum of Two Thousand Dollars be raised for the working of the Public Highways.

Resolved, that the sum of Seventeen Hundred Dollars be raised for the maintainance and support of the Poor.

Resolved, that the sum of Four Hundred Dollars be raised for the support of the Male Free School, and the same sum of Four Hundred Dollars for the Female Free School.

Col. Isaac Andruss made application to the Town Meeting to have refunded to the Trustees of the New Market in Market Street the stipulated amount for the last year's Rent, which was rejected.

Resolved, that this meeting now proceed to the choice of Township Officers for the ensuing year.

Constables—Benjamin S. Jarvis, Joseph Sayres, David Ball, Jacob Osborn and John Searing.

Assessor—Isaac Nichols.

Collector—Abm. K. Ward.

Chosen Freeholders—Robt. B. Campfield and James Vanderpool.

Surveyors of Highways—Moses Faitoute and Jabez Cook.

Over Seers of the Poor—Caleb Carter and David Nichols.

Judge of Election—Luther Goble.

Overseers of the Road for the Town Plott—John Alling, Robert B. Campfield & Samuel Pennington.

Overseers of the Outer Districts—Joseph W. Camp, Caleb H. Camp, Abm Johnson and James Eaton.

Street Commissioners—John Taylor, James Vanderpool and Samuel Pennington.

Town Committee—Silas Condit, Luther Goble, William Tuttle, Stephen Hays and Ephraim Bolles.

Committee of the Male Free School—Silas Condit, James Bruen, James Tichenor, David Hayes, Joseph Wilbur, Luther Goble, C. H. Shipman, Stephen Dod, Ellison Conger and Wm. Tuttle.

Commissioners of Appeal—James Vanderpool, Robert B. Campfield and Stephen Hayes.

Pound Masters—Hugh Cammack, Robert Hayes and David J. Baldwin.

Resolved, that the next fall election be opened and Closed at the House of Stephen Roff.

Resolved, that Hogs be impounded, and that the Poundage be Fifty cents, Twenty five of which will be for the Pound Master and Twenty five Cents for the Driver.

Resolved, that the Sexton be paid Two Dollars for Cleaning this House.

Resolved, that this meeting now Adjourn to meet in this Place at the next Annual Town Meeting at 1 o'clock P. M.

AARON MUNN, Moderator.

Attested by Arch'd Woodruff, Town Clerk.

A Special Town Meeting For the Township of Newark was held agreeably to previous Notice, at the House of J. A. Britten on Tuesday, the Second day of *October*, A. D. 1827.

Col'nl Isaac Andruss was chosen Chairman and Arch'd Woodruff acted as Clerk.

The Notice for calling said Meeting was read. Also the 15th and 11th Sections of the act relating to Town Meetings.

Resolved, that it is expedient for the Township of Newark to procure a Lott or Lotts of Ground for a Public Burying Ground for the use of the said Township of Newark.

Resolved, that the Township Committee be instructed to apply to the Legislature of this State at their next sitting for a Law authorizing the raising by taxation, a sum not to exceed One Thousand Dollars for the above object.

Resolved, that the aforesaid Town Committee be instructed to procure an Act of the Legislature at the same time for power to raise money for the support of a regular Night Watch, the expense of which to be Assessed on the Inhabitants of the Town and on such property only as is contained within the following prescribed Boundary, viz: to commence at the North End of the Town of Newark at Mill Brook, running along the Passaic River to the extent of the Commercial Dock, thence including Mulberry street and down Broad street to the forks of the Road by David Hays' at the South end of the Town, thence along each side of High street to the place of Beginning.

ISAAC ANDRUSS, Moderator.

ARCHIBALD WOODRUFF, Town Clerk.

Special TOWN MEETING for the Township of Newark was held at the House of Mr. Brittain, on Teusday, the 1st *Jan'y*, 1828.

Robert B. Campfield, Esqr., was Chosen Chairman, and Arch'd Woodruff acted as Clerk.

After the notice for calling the meeting was read. The Town Committee made their report as follows:

One Bill for an application to the Legislature for a Law authorizing the raising of money to purchase a Burrying Ground.

And a Bill authorizing the maintenance of a Night Watch, with certain prescribed powers.

While these Bills were under consideration, A motion was made to have another Bill read, the intention of which was to make application to the Legislature for certain Corporate powers, for the benefit of the Inhabitants of the Town of Newark.

After the reading of said Bill, it was, on motion, referred to a Committee of Eleven, whose duty it should be to examine and consider on the merits of said Bill, and make Report to an Adjourned meeting to be held on the eleventh Jan'y Instant at 3 o'clock P. M. Also to publish such parts of said Bill as they may deem expedient for the Information of the Inhabitants of the Town generally.

Resolved, that the Chairman appoint the aforesaid Committee.

When the following Gentlemen were duly appointed by him, Viz: Silas Condit, J. C. Hornblower, Isaac Andruss, Wm. Tuttle, Luther Goble, Isaac Nichols, Jabez Harrison, David Nichols, Charles T. Shipman, Wm. Pennington and James Vanderpool.

Resolved, that the Bill just read for an application to the Leg·lature for authority to purchase a Burying Ground be approved of as presented by the Town Committee.

Meeting Adjourned.

ROBERT B. CAMPFIELD, Chairman of said Meeting.

Attested by ARCHIBALD WOODRUFF, Town Clerk.

An Adjourned Special TOWN MEETING, held *Jan'y* 11th, 1828, at the House of Mr. Brittain.

Smith Burnet, Esq., was Chosen Chairman, and Archibald Woodruff acted as Clerk.

The Report of the Committee to whom was refered the Bill for certain Corporate powers for the Town of Newark was made with amendments by Silas Condit, Esqr., Chairman of that Committee. And recommended that it should not go into operation untill fairly considered by the Inhabitants and an Election specially held for its adoption or rejection.

The Bill was called for and read as amended, and after Some time spent in the discussion of different subjects which said Bill embraced. It was on motion rejected entirely by a large majority. And the Meeting Adjourned.

SMITH BURNET, Chairman of the Meeting.

Attested by ARCH'D WOODRUFF, Town Clerk.

Annual TOWN MEETING for the Township of Newark, held in the Session House of the First Presbyterian Church, on Monday, the fourteenth day of *April*, at 1 o'clock P. M. In the Year of our Lord 1828.

Coln'l Isaac Andruss was Chosen Moderator, and Archibald Woodruff, Town Clerk.

The 7th Section of the Act required to be read at the opening of Town Meetings was read. As also the Minutes of the last Annual Town Meeting, and of the subsequent Special Town Meetings held during the last year.

The 9th Section of the Act relating to Free Schools—Also an Act of the Legislature passed at their last sitting, in relation to the same subject were read.

The Street Commissioners made a Report, stating that they had entered into an Agreement with Ellison Congar, And had received the sum of Fifty Dollars from him as an acknowledgement for having violated the Law in Building beyond the line of the Street, on Market street—and stipulating to remove the encroachment at a future day—which Report was accepted and ordered to be filed.

It was stated that Moses Ward had built beyond the line of the Street on Market street, which was on motion refered to the Street Commissioners.

The Report of the Town Committee was read, stating a Ballance of $1868 10·100 in the Hands of the Township Collector and 72 Cts. in the Hands of the Clerk of the Committee.

The Report of the Trustees of the New Town Dock was received from which it appear'd that there was a Ballance in the Hands of their Treasurer of $413 69-100.

The Report of the Male and Female Free Schools were made and accepted.

An application was made by Abraham and John King, Two Colour'd Men, for assistance towards the education of Poor Coloured Children in the Town, amounting to the number of Fifty.

Resolved, that the money that has been paid by individuals and expended on the Road at the Bridge over the Branch Brook occasioned by the Canal being constructed across the Road, be refunded by the Overseers of the Highway (to be hereafter appointed) amounting to the sum of One Hundred and Sixty Dollars, $160.

Resolved, that the Town Committee be instructed to tender to Aaron Ward the sum of $100 by way of compromising the controversy as respects the Old Town Dock, $100.

The following Resolutions in relation to the Building of a Town House were introduced and passed:

1st. Resolved, that it is expedient to erect a Town House for the more convenient transaction of Town business.

2d. Resolved, that the Town Committee be authorized to borrow any sum not exceeding Ten Thousand Dollars, on the Credit of the Town, and to apply and expend the same from time to time, in the erection of a Town House upon the Town Lot adjoining Stephen Roff Inn, after such a plan, and in such a manner, as shall be prescribed to them by a Committee, to be appointed by the Town Meeting for that purpose.

3d. Resolved, that the Town Committee be authorized to Pay the first Year's Interest on the sum or sums by them borrowed, for the aforementioned purpose, out of any unappropriated funds belonging to the Town.

The following persons, consisting of Five, were appointed a Committee to prepare a plan for the Town House, agreeably to the second Resolution on that subject, Viz: Robert B. Campfield, William Halsey, Isaac Andruss, Smith Burnet and Moses Dod.

Resolved, that the Town Committee be instructed to purchase one or more places for a Burying Ground.

The following appropriations were made for the ensuing year:

Resolved, that the sum of Two Thousand Dollars be raised for the support of the Poor.

Resolved, that the sum of Two Thousand Dollars be raised for working the Public Highways.

Resolved, that the sum of Five Hundred Dollars be raised for the purchasing a Burying Lot or Lots of Ground.

Resolved, that the sum of Four hundred Dollars be raised for the Male Free School, and the same sum of Four Hundred Dollars for the Female Free School in the Town.

Resolved, that the sum of One Hundred Dollars be raised for the instruction of Female Children in the outer districts of the Township.

Resolved, that the sum of One Hundred Dollars be raised for the Poor Coloured Children's Instruction in the Township, to be paid out at the discretion of the Town Committee.

Resolved, that this meeting now proceed to the choice of Township Officers for the ensuing year.

Constables—Benjamin S. Jarvis, Joseph Sayres, David Ball, John Searing, Isaac Beach, David Jones.

Assessor—Isaac Nichols.

Collector—Abraham K. Ward.

Chosen Freeholders—Robert B. Campfield, James Vanderpool.

Surveyors of Highways—Moses Faitoute, Jabez Cook.

Overseers of the Poor—David Nichols, Caleb Carter.

Judge of Election—Luther Goble.

Overseers of the Road in the Town Plott—Robert B. Campfield, Stephen Hayes, Johnson Nichols.

Overseers of the Road in the Outer Districts—Abraham Johnson, Caleb H. Camp, James Vanhouten.

Street Commissioners—Samuel Pennington, James Vanderpool, John Taylor.

Town Committee—Silas Condit, Luther Goble, William Tuttle, Ephraim Bolles, Moses Smith.

Committee of the Male Free School—Silas Condit, James Bruen, James Tichenor, David Hayes, Joseph Wilbur, Luther Goble, C. H. Shipman, Stephen Dod, Ellison Congar, William Tuttle.

Commissioners of Appeal—James Vanderpool, Robt. B. Campfield, Stephen Hayes.

Pound Masters—Robert Hayes, Hugh Cammack, David J. Baldwin, John Griffith, Elihu Pierson.

Resolved, that Hogs be impounded, and that the Poundage be Fifty Cents, one half for the Driver and the other half for the Pound Master.

Resolved, that the Elections for next fall be held at the House of Stephen Roff, and to be opened and closed there.

Resolved, that the Sexton be Paid Five Dollars for Cleaning this House.

Resolved, that the meeting now adjourn to meet in this Place at the next Annual Town Meeting at One o'clock P. M.

ISAAC ANDRUSS, Moderator.

Attested by ARCH'D WOODRUFF, Town Clerk.

Special TOWN MEETING For the Township of Newark was held at the House of J. A. Brittain, Agreeable to previous Notice on Wednesday *July* 16th, 1828.

Robert B. Campfield Esq'r was chosen Moderator. And Archibald Woodruff acted as Clerk. A motion was made to ascertain the sense of the meeting, wether they would proceed to the business for which they had convened, or Adjourn. When it was agreed to proceed. And the Town Committee made their Report, which was read by their Clerk, And is as follows:

In obedience to the vote of the last Annual Town Meeting instructing the Township Committee to purchase one or more Lots for a Town Burying Ground, the Committee gave it Early attention, and after considerably Enquiry and deliberation, purchased Two Lots of the Mrs. McWhorters, situated on the South Side of the Old Ferry Road, adjoining the land of Widow Aaron Harrison, as best adapted to answer the purposes of the Town both as to location and as to the Price required for the same.

The first Lot having a front of 250 feet on the old Ferry Road, Containing 8 Acres and 66-100, and Cost, at the rate of $90 an Acre. The other directly in the rear, and Adjoining the first Lot contains 5 Acres and 64-100, and was purchased at the sum of 80 Dollars per Acre. On the latter lot is a verry fine young apple Orchard now in bearing order. The aggregate sum paid for the Two Lots amounts to $1230 60-100 for the 14 Acres and 30-100 of an Acre. The same has been Deeded to an individual of the Committee untill the whole might be partitioned into a Square Lot, suited to accomplish the wishes of the Town. And here the Committee would beg leave to remark, that if our constituents are dissatisfied with the location, or the price Paid for the land, The Committee will cheerfully Exonerate the Town from the purchase, and take the same upon themselves.

As before remarked there are 250 feet front on the Old Ferry Road, as a matter of Economy to the Town, the Committee Resolved after throwing out 20 feet for a road on the East boundary of the first lot, to sell the remaining 230 feet for Building lots, which have accordingly been sold at about One Dollar a foot producing $230 for 17-100 of an Acre, Mr. Harris who ownes on the same line has also contributed 20 feet towards a road, so that a Street 40 feet wide will be opened sufficiently spacious for all purposes of communication with the lot designed for the Public Burying Ground.

The Committee further remark that by drawing parallel lines from North to South in Order to make the lot Square, there will be a projection or strip of land on the Two sides of the Premises, which they propose to sell, still reducing the price of the original purchase.

The first is the marsh or low land west of Widow Harrison's House, containing 2 Acres and 48-100 of an Acre, which is not esteemed verry valuable. The other projection is in the rear of Wm. Harris lot, and contains 2 Acres 18-100 of thrifty orchard. The two together the Committee Estimate will bring not less than $300. So that the 8 Acres and 87-100 of an Acre, designed for a Burying Ground, (as may be seen by the Map herewith presented), will cost the Township about $700—after deducting the Building Lots sold, and the skirts of land still to be sold.

Signed By Order of the Township Committee.

WM. TUTTLE, Clerk.

Newark, July 16, 1828.

Resolved that this Town Meeting approve of the proceedings of the Town Committee, in procuring a lot for a Public Burying Ground, and of the purchase which they have made for that purpose, and that they be authorized and requested, to dispose of such part of the premises, as they may not deem necessary for the use of the Town for the above purpose—

Provided however that at least the Square containing Eight Acres 87-100 of an Acre, as designated on the Map submitted by the Committee be retained for the use of the Town.

Meeting adjourned.

ROB'T B. CAMPFIELD, Moderator.

Attested by Arch'd Woodruff, Town Clerk.

Special Town Meeting For the Township of Newark, was held at the House of Mr. Brittain, Agreeable to previous notice on Monday the 10 day of *Nov'r* 1828.

Mr. Moses Smith was chosen Moderator and Archibald Woodruff acted as Clerk.

The 7th Section of the Act was read relating to the opening of Town Meeting.

Also the Notice for calling this meeting was read stating the objects of calling said meeting.

Resolved that the Township Committee be and they are hereby instructed, to apply to the Legislature, to obtain authority by Law, to appropriate any part of the funds, that may arise by way of income, from Town Property in the Town Plott of Newark, for the purpose of purchasing or repairing Fire Engines, procuring Hooks, ladders, and fire buckets, or other Expenses connected with the object of Extinguishing Fires.

Resolved that the Township Committee be instructed to apply to the Legislature, for a Law authorizing the vesting of the New Town Dock in the County of Essex in the Inhabitants of the Township of Newark.

Resolved that the Township Committee be authorized to sell a part of the new Burying Ground, to such Persons as may apply for the purpose of interments.

Meeting Adjourned.

M. SMITH, Moderator.

Attested by ARCHIBALD WOODRUFF, Town Clerk.

Annual TOWN MEETING For the Township of Newark, was held at the Session House of the 1st Presbyterian Church on Monday *April* 13th, 1829, 1 O'Clock P. M.

Isaac Andruss Esq'r was chosen Moderator and Archibald Woodruff Town Clerk.

The 7th Section of the Act relating to the opening of Town Meetings, was read, and the acts in relation to Education.

The Minutes of the last Annual Town Meeting, and of the Special Town Meetings, held within the last Year, was also read.

The Town Committee made their Report, which was read by their Clerk, and accepted, Stating a Ballance in the Hands of the Township Collector of $1175 15-100 and $2,56 in their Clerks Hands.

The late Act of the Legislature directing the new Town Dock to be taken under the care of the Township Committee, and the appropriating all monies arising from Town Property, to the purchase and repairs of Fire Engines, and for purposes of Extinguishing Fires—as also the authorizing the raising or borrowing of money for Building a Town House, was read.

In consequence of the management of the New Town Dock having by a recent law been placed under the direction of the Town Committee, The Old Trustees of the same reported that the sum of $495 76-100 remained in their hands, and asked leave to pay the same over, to the Township Committee, Whereupon it was

Resolved That the Trustees of the New Town Dock be instructed to hand over all monies, Securities, and papers, in their hands, in relation to said Dock, to the Township Committee, and that said Trustees, for such performance be indemnify'd and saved harmless.

The Subject of Building a Town House was called up, and a motion was made and Seconded, to Build a Town House, on the

Old Town Lot in Broad Street—when after a full and fair discussion of the subject, it was on motion,

Resolved to postpone the further consideration of the subject for the present.

Upon a motion being made and Seconded, it was Resolved that a Committee be appointed to consult the feelings and wishes of the Inhabitants of the Township, whose friends and relations had been intered in the old Burying Ground, on the subject of changing the use of said Burying Ground, and having their remains reintered in some other place at the Town's Expense, with suitable mementoes.

The following Persons were appointed a Committee for that purpose, with instructions to make a report at a future Town Meeting, viz: David D. Crane, Robert B. Campfield, Jesse Baldwin, Moses Roberts, Samuel Pennington, Isaac Nichols, and Henry L. Parkhurst.

Resolved that the Town Committee apply to the Legislature for a Law giving them authority to sell the old Town Lot on Broad Street, if thought Expedient and purchase another Lot of Ground for the purpose of Building a Town House thereon.

Resolved that the Town Committee be instructed to improve, the new Burying Ground, and to lay out the same in small Lots and dispose of them to any Persons who may apply for them.

Resolved that the sum of $250 be appropriated to fencing and improving said Burying Ground.

Resolved That in future there be no more interments made in the Old Burying Ground, and that Notice be given thereof, by the Town Committee in the Newspapers printed in the Town.

Resolved that the Town Committee be instructed to take such legal measures in relation to the Controversy with Aaron Ward respecting the Old Town Dock, as they may judge necessary to obtain the rights of the Town.

Report of the Male Free School was read.

Resolved that the School Committee be instructed to make Reports annually to the Town Meeting of the different free Schools in the Township.

APPROPRIATIONS.

Resolved that the sum of Four Hundred Dollars be raised for the Male Free School.

Resolved that the Sum of Four Hundred Dollars be raised for the Female Free School.

Resolved that the sum of One Hundred Dollars be raised for the Education of Coloured Children in the Town.

Resolved that the Sum of One Hundred Dollars be raised for the Education of Poor Children in the Outer Districts.

Resolved that the sum of Two Thousand Dollars be raised for the support of the Poor.

Resolved that the Sum of Two Thousand Dollars be raised for the working of the Public Highways.

Resolved, that the Roads be worked by Tax—and that it be recommended to the Town Committee to make six districts in the Town Plott, extending North as far as the Township extends.

Township Officers Chosen for the ensuing year:

Constables—Benjamin S. Jarvis, Joseph Sayres, David Ball, John Searing, Isaac Beach, David Jones, Daniel S. Moore, Henry D. Hedden.

Assessor—Isaac Nichols.

Collector—Abraham K. Ward.

Chosen Freeholders—Robert B. Campfield, James Vanderpool.

Surveyors of Highways—Jabez Cook, James Searing.

Overseers of the Poor—David Nichols, Caleb Carter.

Judge of Election—Luther Goble.

Overseers of the Road in the Town Plott—Robert Baldwin, Edward Jones, Jabez Cook, J. Johnson Nichols, James Black, Moses Roberts.

Overseers of the Road in the Outer Districts—Abraham Johnson, Caleb H. Camp, James Vanhouten, Stephen Baker.

Street Commissioners—James Vanderpool, John Taylor, Samuel Pennington.

Township Committee—Silas Condit, Moses Smith, David Doremus, William Tuttle, Samuel Pennington.

Committee of the Male Free School—Silas Condit, James Bruen, James Tichenor, David Hayes, Joseph Wilbur, Luther Goble, Stephen Dod, William Tuttle, Ellison Conger, C. H. Shipman.

Commissioners of Appeal—James Vanderpool, Robert B. Campfield, Stephen Hayes.

Pound Masters—Zadok Meeker, Robert Hayes, Aaron Camp, Hugh Cammack, Elihu Pierson, Daniel Clearman, David J. Baldwin.

Resolved, that there be a Committee of 5 to act under the late law relating to the School fund appropriation of this State 2nd that said Committee be appointed by the Moderator from the School Committee—Whereupon Messrs. Condit, Goble, Bruen, Dod and Tuttle were appointed.

A communication was made by A. Gifford from inhabitants living in the upper part of the Town, asking remuneration for money layed out, in repairing the road leading to Orange—when, after some time had been spent in making statements and explanations, the subject matter was refered to the Town Committee.

Resolved, That the Poundage of Hogs be the same this year as it was last—That is, Twenty five Cents for the Driver, and Twenty five Cents for the Pound Master.

Resolved, that the Annual Election for next fall be held at the House of Stephen Roff, and to be opened and closed there.

Resolved, that there be paid to Mr. Francisco for Cleaning this House Five Dollars.

Resolved, that the next annual Town Meeting be held at this Place, at One o'clock P. M.

Town Meeting Adjourned.

ISAAC ANDRUSS, Moderator.

Attested by Archibald Woodruff, Town Clerk.

The following resolutions were omitted to be recorded in their proper place at the Annual Meeting, April 13, 1829, having been regularly adopted at said meeting, and are as follows:

Resolved, that the Trustees of the New Town Dock of Newark, be and they are hereby requested to pay over, to the Township Committee, any monies in their hands, that may have arrisen, by way of rent, or otherwise, from said Dock, and also all documents of any kind, and for so doing the Township is hereby pledged, to indemnify and save harmless the said Trustees.

Resolved, that the Township Committee be, and they are hereby directed, to set apart and preserve, as a distinct fund, "Any monies belonging to the Township, and arising from Town property, and lying within the Town Plott, by way of rent or otherwise," and which said fund, as to receipts and disbursements therefrom, shall by the said Committee be specifically reported at the annual meeting of the Township.

Resolved further, that the Township Committee be and they are hereby authorized to expend from the aforementioned fund, so much as they may from time to time deem expedient, for objects connected with the business of extinguishing fires, as is provided by the Sixth Section of an Act of the Legislature, entitled an Act concerning the new Town Dock, and other matters in the Township of Newark, in the County of Essex.

ISAAC ANDRUSS, Moderator.

Archibald Woodruff, Town Clerk.

Annual Town Meeting for 1830 for the Township of Newark, convened by the Session room of the 1st Presbyterian Church, One o'clock P. M., *Ap'l* 12th.

Samuel Pennington was chosen Moderator, and Stephen H. Pierson, Clerk.

Resolved, To Adjourn to the Lecture room of the Third Pres'n church.

The 7th Section of the act in relation to the opening of Town Meetings, and the Act in relation to education were read.

The Report of the Township Committee was read and approved.

The subject of the Docks in possession of Aaron Ward, and claimed by the Town, was discussed, and the next Town Committee authorized to settle with Mr. Ward at their discretion.

Resolved, That the Town Committee be instructed hereafter to settle with the Collector and Assessor agreeable to the written opinion of C. S. Riggs, E. Vanarsdale and Theo. Frelinghuysen, on file.

The Reports of the Male and female free Schools, Infant School and Coloured do. were read.

Resolved, That One Thousand dollars be raised for the education of poor Children, to be distributed in the different districts in the same proportions as the State funds.

Resolved, That One Hundred and fifty Dollars of the above sum be appropriated to the Coloured School.

Resolved, That the road districts remain the same as the last year, and the Overseers of the different districts be recommended, as far as it can be done consistent with other duties, to Macadamize in their Districts.

Resolved, That Two Thousand dollars be raised for the support of the Poor.

Resolved, That Two Thousand dollars be raised for making and repairing the roads.

Constables—David Jones, David Ball, Dan'l S. Moore, Benj'n S. Jarvis, Joseph Sayres.

Assessor—Joseph L. Wheeler.

Collector—James Whitamore.

Chosen Freeholders—Robt. B. Canfield, James Vanderpool.

Surveyors of Highways—John W. Baldwin, Capt. E. Beach.

Overseers of the Poor—Caleb Carter, David J. Hayes.

Judge of Election—Stephen Dodd.

Overseers of the Road for Town Plott—Robert Baldwin, Joel W. Condit, Edward Jones, Lewis Nichols, James Tichenor, William H. Earl.

Street Commissioners—Sheldon Smith, Jabez Harrison, Samuel Pennington.

Overseers of the Outer Districts—Caleb H. Camp, James Vanhouten, Abm. Johnson, Stephen Baker.

Town Committee—Silas Condit, Moses Smith, David Doremus, William Tuttle, Samuel Pennington.

Commissioners of Appeal—James Vanderpool, Robt. B. Canfield, Stephen Hays.

Pound Masters—E. E. Boudinot, David J. Baldwin, Wm. H. Wolf, Hugh Cammack, Joseph L. Camp, Wm. Crane, Jun'r.

School Committee—Silas Condit, James Bruen, James Tichenor, David Hays, Luther Goble, Stephen Dodd, William Tuttle, Ellison Congar, C. H. Shipman.

Resolved, That the above Committee take charge of the money and Superintend the coloured school.

Resolved, That hogs be impounded, and that the driver have fifty cents and pound master fifty cents.

Resolved, That the annual election for next fall be opened and closed at Stephen Roff's.

The Town Committee laid before the Town Meeting a communication addressed to the said Town Committee by Nicholas Longworth, Esq., in behalf of the surviving sisters and Brothers and other heirs of Jabez Longworth, deceased, in relation to the supposed will of the said Jabez Longworth, deceased, of which communication the following is a copy, to wit:

To the Town Committee of the Township of Newark:

Gentlemen—The surviving Sisters and Brothers and other heirs of Jabez Longworth, Dec'd, (some of whom not only deserve to inherit his estate but are in limited circumstances) cannot but deeply feel interested in the result of the controversies likely to take place, between the Township of Newark and themselves, in relation to the validity and legal effect of the instrument of writing purporting to be his will. They verily believe that their deceased Brother and relative was not in such a state of mind, as to be capable of making a legal disposition of his property, and they feel confident that the inhabitants of Newark, if they knew the real circumstances of the case would not be willing, under the forms of law, even if it were certainly in their power to avail themselves of the supposed will, and thereby divert the property of the deceased, from a deserving widowed sister, and other near and dependent relatives, to the uncertain and indefinite objects of charity named or refered to in that writing.

But our Council, after a full and I believe an impartial investigation of the facts connected with that instrument, and the points of law arising in the case, have come to the conclusion,

1st. That were it possible to sustain the Instrument as a will, that the bequest to the Town cannot be sustained.

2nd. That if sustained and enforced the estate is so situated that The Town could derive no eventual benefit from it.

The bequest is limited in its object, and is so devised that many years must elapse before the Town could possibly (if at all) derive any benefit from it.

But they apprise me, that the nature and variety of the grounds of objection, and the numerous suits to which they would give rise—if the instrument purporting to be a will be proven, would subject us to endless Litigation in various Courts, where the expenses are great, and Litigation mutually inconvenient to all parties, and which we should have no reasonable prospect of seeing closed in our day.

The citizens will readily perceive, that with the view the heirs have of the case, it would become the duty of such of the heirs as are able, to support the interest of the rest and maintain their rights, by seeking protection in every fair and legal way in every Court of the State and of the United States, that could be re sorted to.

It would afford the heirs great satisfaction could an amicable arrangement take place to accomplish so desirable an object, and give satisfaction to the citizens, they would cheerfully pay something to be applied in the manner named in the bequest.

If the Town Meeting approve the measure and will appoint a Special Committee of intelligent citizens, I will lay before them such vouchers and papers of the estate as they may request, with such evidence of facts, in my power, as they may deem usefull and request, whether for or against our interests, to enable them to come to a fair and Just conclusion, the submission to be without prejudice to either party, should a compromise not take place.

The Committee to be vested with power to make a final settlement, or merely to report the terms agreed on, to a subsequent Town Meeting, for acceptance or rejection, as the Citizens may deem most advisable.

Very Respect'ly,
N. LONGWORTH.

Whereupon the said communication being read to the meeting it was, on motion,

Resolved, That a Committee of Seven be appointed by this meeting to confer with the heirs of said Jabez Longworth, deceased, upon the subject of the bequest contained in said will in favor of poor Orphan children of the Township of Newark.

Resolved, That it shall be the duty of the Town Committee upon the request of the Committee above appointed, to call a special Town Meeting in the manner directed by Law, for the purpose of receiving and acting upon their report, and that they do then make report to such special Town Meeting.

Resolved, That Isaac Andruss, James Tichenor, David Doremus, Amzi Dodd, Silas Condit, Asa Whitehead, Samuel Pennington do compose said Committee.

Resolved, That the Sexton be paid Ten Dollars for cleaning this House.

Resolved, That the election for Town Officers at the next annual Town Meeting shall be by ballot.

Resolved, That Isaac Andruss, C. T. Shipman, Rodney Wilbur, Geo. W. Campbell and David Doremus, be a Committee to select a more suitable spot than that next to S. Roff's, for a Town House, and report to a Special Town Meeting.

Resolved, That the next Annual Town Meeting be held in this place at (10) ten o'clock A. M.

Adjourned.

SAM'L PENNINGTON, Chairman.

Attest—STEPHEN H. PIERSON, Town Clerk.

To Stephen H. Pierson, Town Clerk of Newark:

Sir, you are hereby directed to give notice of a Special Town Meeting of the inhabitants of the Township of Newark, to be held on Monday, the third day of May next, at three o'clock P. M., at the session room of the first Presbyterian Church, to receive and Act upon the report of the Committee appointed at the last Annual Town Meeting to confer with the heirs of Jabez Longworth, deceased, relative to the bequest in the last will and testament of said dec'd in favour of the Poor Orphan children of the Township of Newark.

By order of the Township Committee.

SAMUEL PENNINGTON, Chairman.

WM. TUTTLE, Clerk.

April 24, 1830.

SPECIAL TOWN MEETING.

Public Notice is hereby given, that a Special Town Meeting of the inhabitants of the Township of Newark, in the County of Essex, will be held at the Session Room of the first Presbyterian church in said Township of Newark, on Monday, the third day of May next, at three o'clock in the afternoon of said day, for the purpose of receiving and acting upon the report of the Committee appointed at the last annual Town Meeting to confer with the heirs of Nicholas Longworth, deceased, in relation to the bequest contained in the last will and testament of said deceased, in favour of poor Orphan children of said Township.

By Order of the Town Committee.

STEPHEN H. PIERSON, Town Clerk.

April 24, 1830.

Copies of the above were put up at the Court House, at J. O'Donnel's, Z. Drake's and Mansion House Hotels.

At a Special TOWN MEETING of the Inhabitants of the Township of Newark in the County of Essex, holden at the Session room of the first presbyterian Church in the said Township of Newark, on Monday, the third day of *May*, in the year of our Lord One thousand eight Hundred and thirty, at three o'clock in the afternoon of said day, in pursuance of due and legal notice given of the time and place and purpose of said meeting, for the purpose of receiving and acting upon the report of the Committee appointed at the last Annual Town Meeting of said Township, to confer with the heirs of Mr. Jabez Longworth, deceased, in relation to the bequest contained in the last will and testament of said Jabez Longworth, deceased, in favour of poor Orphan children of said Township.

General Thomas Ward was appointed Moderator.

The Committee above mentioned having made their report, and the same being read, the following preamble and resolutions were unanimously adopted—

The Committee to whom was referred by a resolution of the last Annual Town Meeting of this Township, the subject of the devise or bequest in the supposed will of Jabez Longworth, deceased, for the benefit of poor Orphan children of this Township having reported to this meeting,

It is ordered, that the said report be accepted and agreed to, and that the Clerk do file the same in his office, and make a record thereof at length in the minutes.

Whereupon, on motion, it was further resolved, that this meeting do approve of, consent to and accept the terms of compromise offered by the heirs next of kin of the said Jabez Longworth, dec'd.

Resolved, that upon payment of the said sum of Five Thousand Dollars by the said heirs and next of kin, or any of them, to James Vanderpool, Theodore Frelinghuysen and Luther Goble, or upon the execution and delivery by the said heirs and next of kin or any of them to the said James Vanderpool and Luther Goble of a good and sufficient bond and mortgage, securing to them the payment of the said Sum of Five Thousand Dollars in one year from the third day of May instant with interest, this Township do relinquish all further claim and demand on the representatives of the said Jabez Longworth, deceased, for and on account of any devise, bequest or clause contained in the said supposed will.

Resolved, That the money when received by the said James Vanderpool, Theodore Frelinghuysen and Luther Goble, or the security to be given to them therefor, shall be taken and held by them and their Survivors and Survivor of them in trust for the Inhabitants of the Township of Newark, in the County of Essex, until an Act of the Legislature of this State shall be obtained creating Trustees for the said fund, and providing for the use and application of it as near as may be, according to the true intent and meaning of the said Jabez Longworth, as expressed in his said supposed will and the report of the aforesaid Committee.

Resolved, That the Township Committee be and they are hereby instructed at the expense of the Township to procure an Act of the Legislature of this State at their next session, making permanent provision for the appointment and succession of suitable trustees for the said fund, and the application of the Interest and income thereof forever, towards the support and education of poor Orphan children of this Township in the manner aforesaid.

Resolved, That the meeting recommend the said James Vander Pool, Theodore Frelinghuysen and Luther Goble to accept the bond of Nicholas Longworth, Esq., secured by a mortgage upon Lands in the Town of Cincinnati and its vicinity in the State of Ohio, as security for the payment of the said sum of Five Thousand Dollars with interest as aforesaid, provided the Hon. Jacob Burnet and Nathaniel Wright, Counsellor at Law, shall certify that the mortgaged premises are unincumbered and of sufficient value, and the mortgage duly executed and recorded.

The Committee appointed at the last Annual Meeting of the inhabitants of the Township of Newark, for the purpose of confering with the heirs of the late Mr. Jabez Longworth, upon the subject of a bequest in his last will and testament for the benefit of poor Orphan children of said Township,

Respectfully Report, That they have met several times upon the subject, and have been attended by Nicholas Longworth, Esquire, in behalf of himself and the heirs of the Testator, who has made before the Committee, as far as they are able to Judge, a full and fair exposition of the circumstances and situation of the estate of the Testator, your Committee have also had stated before them the various objections raised against sustaining the bequest in question, which are too numerous and complicated to be discussed in this report.

The Committee, after a full consideration of the subject, with a view to promote the best interests of the Township, to save expensive and tedious litigation and to effect a compromise upon Terms which they think Just and equitable between the parties agreed to propose to Mr. Nicholas Longworth that they would recomend to the Township to receive the sum of five thousand Dollars in lieu of the bequest in question, which proposition was agreed to by Mr. Nicholas Longworth in behalf of himself and the other heirs of the Testator, And the same is now submitted for the consideration of the Town Meeting. The Committee think but Just to mention that the intercourse between them and Mr. Nicholas Longworth has been of the most satisfactory character, that on his part it has been distinguished by a gentlemanly candour and frankness which has greatly facilitated the Committee in the discharge of the duties assigned them.

And your Committee would further beg leave to recommend that should the Township accept the terms proposed, That the five Thousand Dollars be set apart as a distinct fund, and be loaned out upon Bond and Mortgage, and the Interest of the same be appropriated in accordance with the will and intention of the Testator, viz: for the support and education of poor Orphan Children of the Township of Newark, to be Selected by the Township Committee yearly. And that a special report be made to the Annual Town Meeting by the Township Committee of the situation of this fund, the amount of interest received and the names of the Orphans selected, and the amount expended upon each individual, and that the said yearly report be entered at large upon the Town book, by the Clerk yearly, as a perpetual memorial of the liberality and beneficence of Mr. Jabez Longworth, deceased, a native citizen of the Town of Newark. All which is respectfully submitted.

Newark, May 3d, 1830.

Isaac Andruss, David Doremus,
Samuel Pennington, Silas Condit,
James Tichenor, Asa Whitehead,
Amzi Dodd.

Resolved That this Town Meeting Entertain a high opinion of the frank open and honourable conduct of Nicholas Longworth Esq'r in the negotiation and settlement of the matter of the bequest in the will of Jabez Longworth dec'd in favor of poor Orphan Children in the Town of Newark and that the Clerk of the Township be directed to furnish to Mr. Longworth a Copy of this resolution and also a Copy of the report of the Committee and also of the resolutions of this Town Meeting in relation thereto duly certified by the Moderator and Clerk of this Meeting.

Adjourned.

THOMAS WARD.

Attest STEPHEN H. PIERSON, Clerk.
May 3, 1830.

Special TOWN MEETING.—Agreeable to Notice given, a Special TOWN MEETING was held in the Session Room of the first presbyterian Church The 29th day of *June* 1830, for the purpose of adopting measures, if Expedient for removing a Collection of Water in the old burying ground lot. Also to remove a Collection of Water in the North part of the Town and similar public nuisances in other parts of the Town—if necessary—and to Elect an Overseer of the Poor in the room of D. J. Hays.

James Vanderpool was chosen Moderator.

Resolved that a Committee of five be appointed to Examine into the Evils complained of by the Inhabitants of different Sections of the Town arrising from stagnant waters, and advise with and recommend to the Overseers of the highway in the respective districts in which such Evils exist as to the best mode of removing them, and that Rob't B. Canfield, Capt. Ephraim Beach, Samuel Pennington, A. W. Kinney, David Doremus, be that Committee.

Resolved That the Town Committee be authorized to appropriate Two Hundred Dollars out of any monies in their hands not already appropriated to any specific object and which may legally be used for this object to assist the Overseers of the high ways in Effecting the removal of the Evils above Complained of provided the same shall be deemed necessary by the Examining Committee appointed in the foregoing resolution.

Resolved That this Committee Examine the law, authorizing the draining the low grounds in the Town of Newark passed Nov. 25, 1822—and also the Supplement passed Nov. 20, 1823—and also other acts on the subject, and advise whether any thing further can be done under the same Acts to remove the nuisances complained of.

Resolved That David Nichols be Overseer of the poor in room of David J. Hays.

Resolved, That David Doremus, C. T. Day and Isaac Andruss be appointed to fill the vacancies in the School Committee.

Adjourned.

JAMES VANDERPOOL, Moderator.

STEPHEN H. PIERSON, Town Clerk.

Special TOWN MEETING, *August* 10th.—Agreeable to notice given a Special Town Meeting was held at the Session room of the first Presbyterian Church on the Tenth day of June 1830 to receive the report of the Committee appointed at a recent Special Town Meeting to Examine Stagnant Waters Considered public nuisances in said Town and other purposes.

Asa Whitehead was chosen Moderator.

The report of the Committee being read, It was Resolved that the water now running into the Old burying ground, be continued down Broad Street the entire length, from the Cannal to S. B. Browns.

Resolved That a Committee of Three be appointed to carry this resolution into Effect and that the Overseers of highways of districts in which the work is to be done be requested to perform the work according to the direction of the Committee—and that Rob't B. Canfield, A. W. Kinney and Capt. E. Beach be that Committee.

Resolved, That this Committee recommend that the road running from Obadiah Woodruffs to plane Street, be raised by filling in gravel so as to Cast the water into its old course and that the same plan be adopted in Bank, Harrison and Acadimy Streets.

Resolved that Rob't B. Canfield, Theodore Frelinghuysen, David Doremus, John Alling and Silas Condit be a Committee to confer with the Managers of the Morris Cannal their Agents or Engineers respecting the best mode of constructing bridges over Said Cannal where it crosses any of the Streets in Town and all other matters of interest to the Inhabitants arising out of the Erection of said Cannal through the Town of Newark.

Adjourned.

ASA WHITEHEAD, Moderator.

STEPHEN H. PIERSON, Cl'k.

The annual TOWN MEETING was held in the Lecture Room of the third presbyterian Church, The Eleventh of *April* One Thousand Eight hundred and Thirty one—At Ten O'Clock A. M.

Gen'l Thomas Ward chosen Moderator and Abraham Beach Town Clerk.

The 7th Section of the act in relation to the opening of Town Meeting was read.

It was moved that the minutes of the last annual and special Town Meetings so far as respects the Settlement with the Heirs of Jabez Longworth Dec'd be read.

Which was finally posponed untill after the Town Committee made their annual report.

On motion Resolved That the resolution of the last Annual Town Meeting respecting the Voting by Ballot for Town Officers be rescinded.

Resolved That the standing resolution of a former Town Meeting, That all those objects which require the appropriation of money to be acted upon and disposed of previous to the Election of Town Officers be rescinded.

Resolved That we now proceed to the Election of Town Officers.

Resolved That Seven Constables be appointed for the ensuing year.

Constables—David Ball, Daniel S. Moore, Isaac Beach, David M. Fitzgerald, Benjamin S. Jarvis, Joseph Sayre, David Jones.

Assessor—Stephen Dod.

Collector—Caleb Carter.

Chosen Freeholders—James Vanderpool, Robert B. Campfield.

Surveyors of the Highways—Robert Baldwin, Jabez Cook.

Overseers of the poor—Aaron Nichols, Abraham K. Ward.

Judge of Election—Isaac Nichols.

Overseers of the roads for the Town Plott districts—No. 1 David C. Brown, 2 Enoch Bolles, 3 Charles Grant, 4 Aaron Camp, 5 Joseph Magie, 6 James Tichenor.

Overseers for the Outer districts—Stephen Baker, James Van Houten, John Hayes, Elias Roberts.

Street Commissioners—William Lee, Abraham W. Kinney, Samuel Pennington.

Town Committee—Luther Goble, Ephraim Bolles, Isaac Baldwin, David Doremus, William Tuttle.

Commissioners of Appeal—Stephen Hays, Isaac Nichols, James Vanderpool.

Pound Masters—Jabez Cook, Elias E. Boudinot, Hugh Cammack, William Crane Jun'r, David J. Baldwin.

School Committee—Luther Goble, Richard M. Crane, George W. Campbell, Caleb H. Shipman, David Doremus, Isaac Andruss, Ashbell W. Cory, Ellison Congar, Stephen Dod.

Town Meeting adjourned untill Two O'Clock P. M.

At Two O'Clock P. M. met agreeable to adjournment.

Called to Order and proceeded to Business.

It was moved and seconded to re-consider the appointments made previous to Adjournment. And after discussion it was decided by the Moderator to be out of Order.

The annual report of the Township Committee was then read by their Clerk. On motion Resolved That it be accepted and Filed.

The following Statement in relation to the settlement with the Heirs of Jabez Longworth Dec'd, from the Hon'le Theodore Frelinghuysen, made a part of the Town Committees report:

Nicholas Longworth
To
Luther Goble,
Theodore Frelinghuysen
and James Vanderpool. } Sealed bill for $5000, dated Ohio, May 3rd, 1830,

payable with legal Interest from date at six per cent. till paid and secured by a Mortgage of same date on lots of land in Cincinati, Ohio. Certified by Jacob Burnet and Nathaniel Wright, Esq'rs to be free from incumbrances and sufficient security for said sum. The said sealed bill and mortgage are in the possession of the Subscriber.

Signed THEODORE FRELINGHUYSEN.

Newark, March 31st, 1831.

Resolved, That Two thousand dollars be raised for the support of the Poor.

The subject of working the roads was taken up. And after considerable discussion and the reading of an estimate of the cost of McAdamizing the streets in the Town Plott, It was, on motion, Resolved, That the sum of Five Hundred Dollars be raised for working the roads in the Town Plott.

Resolved, That the sums levied in the several districts to make out the above mentioned sum of Five Hundred Dollars, be expended in the districts where levied.

The meeting were informed by Amzi Dodd, Esqr., the prosecuting Attorney on the part of the State for the County of Essex, That the Township of Newark had been indicted for a nuisance in suffering the water to stagnate and become offensive in the old burying ground.

On motion, Resolved, That the sum of Two hundred dollars be raised, and if necessary expended to remove said nuisance.

Several Overseers of the Highways having informed the meeting that they had expended more money than they had received from the Town to work the Highways in the Town Plott districts, On motion, Resolved, That the Township Committee be authorized to pay each and every Overseer of the Highways all the money they have expended in their districts beyond what they have received from the Town funds, Out of any monies not otherwise appropriated.

The School Committee, in pursuance of the Act to establish Common Schools, made their annual report.

Resolved, That the same be accepted and Filed. The report of the Managers of the School for educating the poor children of Colour in the Town was read.

Resolved, That the same be accepted and Filed.

Several sections of the Law respecting Common Schools having been read—It was, on motion, Resolved, That the money received from the State fund for the support of Common Schools, Together with the money raised by the Town for the same purpose, be appropriated to the schooling of poor children in the districts where they reside.

Resolved, That the sum of One Thousand Dollars be raised for the support of Common Schools.

Resolved, That One Hundred and fifty Dollars be appropriated to the education of the poor children of colour, Out of the money raised for the support of Common Schools.

A motion to raise the sum of Three hundred Dollars to aid the Female Union School was negatived.

On motion, Resolved, That the Township Committee be authorized to remove all Buildings and all other incumbrances from the Town Lott on Broad street.

The motion to instruct the Town Committee to lease the Town Lott on Broad street was on motion posponed untill the next Annual Township Meeting.

Resolved, That hogs running at large be subject to poundage, with the same penalties as last year, Viz: Fifty cents to the driver and Fifty cents to the pound master.

Resolved, That the Annual Election for members of the State Legislature, Sheriff and Coroners be opened and closed at the House of Stephen Roff, Inn Keeper.

Resolved, That the Town Committee be authorized to pay Mr.

Ephraim Beach, the Sexton of the third presbyterian church, the sum of Ten Dollars for cleaning this room.

Resolved, That the next Annual Township Meeting be held in this place at Ten o'clock A. M.

Town Meeting Adjourned.

THOMAS WARD, Moderator.

Attest—ABRAHAM BEACH, Town Clerk.

NEWARK TOWNSHIP MEETING FOR 1832.

The annual TOWN MEETING for the Township of Newark Was held in the Lecture Room of the third Presbyterian Church, Monday, the ninth of *April*, One Thousand Eight hundred and Thirty-two, at 10 o'clock A. M.

When Asa Whitehead, Esq., was chosen Moderator.

The 7th Section of the Law relating to Town Meetings was read by the Moderator.

Abraham Beach was Chosen Town Clerk.

The minutes of the last Annual Town Meeting was read.

It was, on motion, Resolved, That we now proceed to the election of Township Officers for the ensuing Year.

The following Officers were chosen:

Assessor—Moses Dodd.

Collector—James Whittemore.

Commissioners of Appeal in cases of Taxation—Joseph W. Camp, William Lee, William Grummon.

Chosen Freeholders—John Alling, Samuel Pennington.

Surveyors of the Highways—John W. Baldwin, Matthias Plum.

Overseers of the Poor—Abraham K. Ward, Aaron Nichols.

On motion, Resolved, that seven Constables be appointed for the ensuing Year.

Nominations for the Constables having been made, A motion to reconsider the above Resolution prevailed.

It was, on motion, Resolved, That nine Constables be appointed for the ensuing year.

When the following were chosen—David M. Fitzgerald, David Jones, Daniel S. Moore, David Shuart, David Ball, Ambrose Bruen, Joseph Sayre, William Johnson, Samuel Beach.

Meeting adjourned untill half Past Two o'clock P. M.

Town Meeting again assembled at ½ past Two o'clock, and the following Officers were chosen:

Overseers of the road for the Town Plott districts—District No. 1. David S. Osborne; 2. Asa Torry; 3. Matthias Plum; 4. William H. Earle; 5. Jediah J. Nichols; 6. Abner Pierson.

Overseers of the road for the out districts—Abraham Johnson, Stephen Baker, James Van Houten, Josiah Meeker.

Resolved, That five pound Masters be appointed for the ensuing year.

Pound Masters—Thomas J. Philips, Enoch Bolles, Elihu Pierson, William H. Ross, William Crane, Jun'r.

Resolved, That Hogs running at large be subject to poundage, with the same penalties as the Two last years, Viz: Fifty cents to the driver and Fifty Cents to the pound Master.

A motion to impound Cattle running at large without a driver was decided in the negative.

Judge of Election—Elias E. Boudinot.

Town Committee—David Doremus, Luther Goble, William Tuttle, Elias E. Boudinot, Pruden Alling.

Street Commissioners—John H. Stephens, Pruden Alling, William Lee.

School Committee—David Doremus, Isaac Andruss, Luther Goble Ashbell W. Cory, William Grummon.

The Town Committee made their Annual Report, which was read by their Clerk and accepted.

The Annual report of the School Committee was read and accepted.

The subject of working the Highways was taken up, and on motion,

Resolved, That the sum of Five hundred dollars be raised for working the roads the ensuing year in the Township.

Resolved, That the Town Committee shall as soon as practicable apportion to each Overseer of the road for the Township the sums of money they are severally to receive out of the Five hundred Dollars raised for working the roads in said Township.

Resolved, That the Town Committee be authorized to pay Mr. Aaron Camp, one of the Overseers of the road, for the last year district, No. 4, the expence of a plough and drag purchased by him for the use of the Town out of any monies belonging to the Town not otherwise appropriated.

A motion to authorize the Town Committee to pay Mr. James Tichenor, one of the Overseers of the road for the last year, district No. 8, his monies advanced in working his district, was decided in the negative.

Resolved, That the sum of Two thousand five hundred Dollars be raised for the support of the poor for the ensuing year.

Resolved, That the sum of One Thousand five hundred Dollars be raised for the support of Common Schools for the ensuing year.

Resolved, That the sum of Two Hundred dollars be appropriated for the education of the poor Children of Colour out of the sum raised for the support of Common Schools.

Resolved, That the money received from the State fund for the support of Common Schools, Together with the money raised by the Town for the same purpose, be appropriated to the Schooling of poor Children in the districts where they reside.

Resolved, That the Chairman of the School Committee be allowed the sum of Ten Dollars per year for his services untill otherwise ordered.

Resolved, that the Town Clerk be allowed the yearly sum of Twenty five dollars for his services.

Resolved, That the Town Committee be authorized to pay to Ephraim Beach Ten Dollars for cleaning the Lecture Room of the third Presbyterian Church.

The Report of James Bruen, Robert B. Campfield and Stephen Hays, Commissioners appointed by the Legislature of the State to superintend the cutting a ditch to drain the low grounds in the vicinity of Washington street having been read and accepted, It was, on motion,

Resolved, That the Town Committee be authorized to pay the said Commissioners the sum of Two hundred dollars towards paying the expences of making said ditch and keeping the same in repair out of any monies belonging to the Township not otherwise appropriated.

Resolved, That a town house be built on the Town Lott on broad street.

When after considerable discussion, it was, on motion,

Resolved, that the further consideration of the subject of building a town house be postponed until a Special Town Meeting be called whenever the Town Committee shall think proper to call the same.

Resolved, That the next Annual Election for a member of the Legislative Council, Members of the General Assembly, Sheriff and Coroners, Together with the election for Electors of President and Vice President and representatives in Congress be oppened and closed at the house of Zephaniah Drake, Inn Keeper of this Town.

Resolved, That the Town Committee be authorized to make such a disposition of the Town Dock as they may think proper.

The following preamble and Resolution was introduced by Gen'l Isaac Andruss, and adopted by the meeting:

Whereas, The Township of Newark has become so populous that it is impracticable to procure a room adequate for the accommodation of the Inhabitants of the Township, when in Town Meeting assembled for the transaction of the annual business of the Township,

Be it Therefore Resolved, That a Committee be appointed to digest a plan for the division of the Township into two or more Wards, with a system for the transaction of the Township business upon equitable principles, by the Two, or more separate Wards, and that the Committee report to a special Town Meeting to be called for that purpose. That time may be afforded to obtain Legislative aid in the premises, before the next annual

Town Meeting, should the measure be approved of by the Township, in Town Meeting assembled,

Resolved, That the Moderator of this meeting appoint a Committee of five in accordance with the foregoing Resolution, and the following persons were appointed, Viz: Isaac Andruss, Joseph C. Hornblower, Stephen Dod, William H. Earle, Archer Gifford.

Resolved, That the next Annual Township Meeting be held at the Lower point of the Military Common, at Ten o'clock in the forenoon.

Town Meeting Adjourned.

ASA WHITEHEAD, Moderator.

Attest—Abraham Beach, Town Clerk.

COPY OF NOTICE FOR SPECIAL TOWN MEETING.

Notice is hereby given, that in accordance with a request made to the Township Committee, signed by a number of respectable freeholders of the Township of Newark, the Town Committee have directed that a Special Town Meeting be held at the Session Room of the first presbyterian Church on Saturday the 2nd day of June next at 2 O'Clock P. M. for the purpose of taking into consideration certain Encroachments alleged to be made on a portion of the public lands belonging to the Town in the Neighborhood of the Commercial Dock. Also to hear the report of the Committee appointed at the last annual Town Meeting on the subject of dividing the Township into Wards for the transaction of Town Business, provided said Committee are prepared to report. And Also to consult on the propriety of providing for the Town a new place of interment instead of that now occupied in Newark neck.

By Order of the Township Committee.

ABRAHAM BEACH, Town Clerk.

May 23rd, 1832.

Copies of the above notice was put up at Isaac C. Winans Store, at the Eagle Tavern (Z. Drakes), at the Mansion House (Hinchmans), at John Remers Store near the Canal Broad Street and at the Northern liberties Hotel Kept by John Agens—published in Sentinel and Chronicle Two Weeks.

Special Town Meeting, *June* 2nd, 1832.—Publick notice having been given according to Law a special Township Meeting was held in the Lecture room of the first presbyterian Church Saturday June the Second, One Thousand Eight Hundred and Thirty Two at Two O'Clock P. M.

The Meeting being Called to Order

Asa Whitehead Esq'r was chosen Moderator.

Abraham Beach acted as Clerk.

The Notice calling a Special Town Meeting at this time was then read by the Clerk.

The first business in said Notice being certain Encroachments alledged to have been made on the public lands belonging to the Town in the neighbourhood of the Commercial Dock—The Township Committee were called upon to give the Meeting all the information in their possession on the subject.

Mr. William Tuttle Clerk of the Township Committee stated that the Committee had no special information to communicate. A petition having been presented to the Committee signed by a number of respectable freeholders requesting a Special Township Meeting to be called upon that subject—The Town Committee has seen fit to call such meeting accordingly.

Whereupon after discusion It was on motion Resolved That a Special Committee to consist of five be appointed by the Moderator of this Meeting whose duty it shall be to obtain all the information they can upon the subject of the Encroachments alledged to be made upon the Township lands in the Neighbourhood of the Commercial Dock and report the same to a future Town Meeting.

The following persons were appointed accordingly, Viz: Edward Jones, James Vanderpool, John W. Baldwin, Stephen Dod, John P. Jackson.

The Committee to divide the Township into Wards or districts for the transaction of Town business made the following report:

The Committee appointed at the last annual Town Meeting To investigate the subject of dividing the Township of Newark into two, or more *Wards* and make report thereon—

Beg leave to make the following Report: Your Committee after deliberating upon the Subject referred to them are of the opinion that owing to the numerous population of the Town and its rapid increase that a division of the Township into two or more districts for the transaction of the Township business would be a great public convenience by affording an opportunity to a greater proportion of the Inhabitants to assemble and take a part in the Township business. The measure contemplated could not be carried into effect without Legislative aid.

Your Committee would therefore premise—That should the plan meet the views of the Township, It would be advisable and they would recommend that a Committee be appointed to draft a Law to be presented to the next Legislature for Enactment, embracing the objects contemplated. And that the said draft be presented to a future Town Meeting for their sanction or rejection. All Which is respectfully submitted.

ISAAC ANDRUSS, Cha'n of said Committee.

Newark, June 2nd, 1832.

It was on Motion Resolved that the report above be accepted.

Resolved That a Special Committee to consist of three be appointed by the Moderator to draft a Law to divide the township into two or more districts and report the same to a future Town meeting and also to publish the same in one or more of the public newspapers printed in the Town previous to any Township Meeting to act upon the same.

The following persons were appointed said Committee, Viz: Joseph C. Hornblower, Isaac Andruss, Amzi Dodd.

On Motion Resolved That it shall be the duty of the Township Committee to order a Special Town Meeting whenever the above Committee shall request the same.

The subject of the burying Ground in Newark neck was taken up and after discussion It was on motion

Resolved as the opinion of this meeting that as few interments ought to be made in the burying lot lately purchased by the Town as possible and that the Town Committee be instructed to apply to the Legislature for an act to vest the said lot in the Inhabitants of the Township of Newark with power to sell the same in lots or otherwise as the public Interest may require. And further that the Town Committee should be authorized to purchase one or more lot or lots in the neighbourhood of the Town for the purpose of burying the dead.

No further business, Adjourned.

ASA WHITEHEAD, Moderator.

Attest ABRAHAM BEACH, Town Clerk.

COPY OF NOTICE FOR SPECIAL TOWN MEETING.

Notice is hereby given, that a Special Town Meeting of the Inhabitants of the Township of Newark, will be held in the Session Room of the First Church, on Thursday, the third day of January, 1833, at 2 o'clock P. M., to receive the Report of the Committee appointed to draft a Bill for dividing the Town into Wards or Districts, agreeable to the Vote of the last Special Town Meeting, and also to take into consideration such other measures relative to a Corporation of the Town as respects the better regulation and municipal government of the same as may then be brought before the meeting. Also to hear the report of the Committee appointed to select a new Burying Ground for the use of the Town, if that Committee is prepared to report.

By order of the Township Committee.

ABRAHAM BEACH, Town Clerk.

Newark, December 25th, 1832.

Copies of the above were put up at John O'Donnel's Tavern, at Z. Drake's Eagle Tavern, at the Mansion House kept by Hinchman, and at G. D. Small's Cadet Hall.

Also advertized in the Sentinel of Freedom, Newark Eagle and Newark Daily Advertiser.

In accordance with a Public Notice given according to law, A Special Town Meeting was held in the Lecture Room of the first Presbyterian Church, on Thursday, the third day of *January*, One Thousand Eight hundred and Thirty three, at 2 o'clock P. M.

The meeting being called to order, Stephen Dod, Esq., was chosen Moderator. Abraham Beach acted as Clerk.

The notice calling said meeting was then read by the Clerk.

The first business in said Notice being to hear the report of the Committee appointed at a Special Town Meeting, held on the 2nd of June last, on the subject of dividing the Township into Wards for the Transaction of Town business.

When Gen'l Isaac Andruss, Chairman of the said Committee, presented the General features of a Bill for dividing the Township into four Wards, which Bill is now on file, marked A.

The Bill having been read by the Chairman of the Committee, it was, on motion,

Resolved, That the said Bill be read and considered by Sections.

The first Section of the Bill was amended as follows, by altering the division of the Wards, viz:

All that part of the Township of Newark lying North of a line drawn in the middle of New and Centre streets, untill it strikes the Township of Orange West and the Passaick River East, be called the North Ward.

All that part of the Township lying South of a line drawn in the centre of Fair street running parallel east and of a line drawn in the centre of William, Running parallel West, untill it strikes the Township of Orange, be called the South Ward.

All that part of the Township lying East of Broad street in the Centre and South of the middle of Centre street and North of the middle of Fair street, be called the East Ward.

All that part of the Township lying West of Broad street in the Centre and lying South of the Centre of New street and North of the Centre of William street, be called the West Ward.

Section 2nd was adopted without any alteration.

Section 3rd Amended in the following manner: The officers to be chosen by Ballot, except Moderator and Ward Clerk, who are to be chosen Viva Voce. Also one Fire Warden, not less than two or more than five Constables, not less than two or more than five Overseers of the Highways to be chosen in each Ward. Also Two Chosen Freeholders, Two Surveyors of the Highways to be chosen by General Ticket by the four Wards. The Votes to be Canvassed by the Town Committee, And the Overseers to work the roads as directed by the Street Commissioners.

Section 4 Amended as follows: The Annual report of the Township Committee, to be published at least two weeks previous to the Annual Ward Meetings, and In addition to have power to raise money by tax for the extinguishment of fires.

Section 5 Amended as follows:

The Chosen Freeholders of the Township, The Surveyors of the highways for the Township and the Street Commissioners appointed by the several Wards shall constitute a board of Commissioners, and shall have power to lay out and vacate and alter the public Streets and Highways in the Township.

Section 6 superseaded by other provisions.

Section 7 adopted.

Section 8 adopted.

Section 9 adopted.

Section 10 Amended as follows: A majority of the Wards necessary to change the use of any Public burying ground in the Township.

On motion, Resolved, That a Committee of two from each Ward be appointed by this meeting to prepare a bill according to the foregoing plan, to be presented to the Legislature of this State for enactment.

When the following Gentlemen were appointed:

North Ward—James Vanderpool, Archer Gifford, Esqrs.

South Ward—Asa Whitehead, Amzi Armstrong, Esqrs.

East Ward—Joel W. Condit, Joseph C. Hornblower, Esqrs.

West Ward—Isaac Andruss, William Pennington, Esqrs.

Resolved, That the Sexton of the first Presbyterian Church have Three dollars paid by the Town Committee for cleaning the Lecture room of said Church out of any monies belonging to the Town not otherwise appropriated.

On motion, Town Meeting Adjourned.

STEPHEN DOD, Moderator.

Attest—Abraham Beach, Town Clerk.

[Note.]—The Committee appointed for that purpose prepared a Draft of a Law, dividing the Township into 4 *Wards*: and the same was enacted by the next Legislature and became a Law. And the Ward system was organized and carried into effect in April, 1833, and opperated 3 Years.

1836—The Township obtained a Charter making Newark a City, which Charter was received by a public vote in April, 1836.

[ABRAHAM BEACH, Town Clerk.]

APPENDIX.

OFFICE HOLDERS,

FROM THE SETTLEMENT OF THE TOWN UNTIL ITS INCORPORATION IN 1713.

*** A dash between the dates indicates that the person appears to have deen re-elected annually during the intervening period, but it is evident that re-elections must frequently have taken place without any record having been made of the fact.

Some of the offices were of a temporary character, and others seem to bave been created, suspended, revived or abolished, as the circumstances of the town required, without any official entry being made of the change. This will account for the want of continuity that will be observed in several offices.

The manner of spelling many of the names differed at different periods.

DEPUTIES TO PROVINCIAL ASSEMBLY.

Jasper Crane, Sen'r, 1669–'73.
Robert Treat, 1669–'72.
Stephen Bond, 1673.
John Ward, 1675–'76.
Thomas Johnson, 1675–'78, '80–'84.
Thomas Richards, 1677, '79, '86, '93.
Samuel Swain, 1678.
John Curtis, 1679–'88.
Thomas Huntington, 1685.
Daniel Dod, 1693.
John Treat, 1694, '95, '99–1702.
Azariah Crane, 1694, '95.
Jasper Crane, 1697, 1702.
Joseph Harrison, 1712.
John Cooper, 1712.

ALTERNATE DEPUTIES, OR "THIRD MEN."

Samuel Swain, 1666, '71–'73, '76, '79.
John Ward, 1680, '81.

MAGISTRATES.

Jasper Crane, Sen'r, 1669–'74.
Robert Treat, 1669–'72.
Matthew Camfield, 1670, '72.
Samuel Swain, 1671, '74.
John Ward, 1674.
Stephen Bond, 1674.
(Mr.) Kitchell, 1674.
Thomas Johnson, 1680.

ASSISTANT MAGISTRATES.

Samuel Swain, 1669, '70, '71, '73, '76, '79.
Matthew Camfield, 1669, '71, '73.
Stephen Bond, 1673.
Thomas Johnson, 1677.

PRESIDENT OF TOWN COURT.

Jasper Crane, Sen'r, 1671.

JUSTICES OF MONTHLY COURT.

Stephen Bond, 1675.
John Curtis, 1691.
Thomas Johnson, 1675, '78, '79, '80.
Samuel Swain, 1678–'80.
John Ward, 1675, '78–'80.

MESSENGERS.

Edward Ball, 1675, '77.
David Ogden, 1678, '79.
Joseph Harrison, 1680.

CLERK.

John Brown, Jr., 1676–'80.

TOWN ATTORNIES.

John Catlin, 1677, '78.
Edward Ball, 1679, '80, '86.
Joseph Harrison, 1686.

CONSTABLES.

Benjamin Baldwin, Jr., 1694.
John Baldwin, Sen'r, 1692.
Edward Ball, 1683, '89.
Thomas Brown, 1696.
William Camp, 1684.
John Cooper, 1697.
Azariah Crane. 1682.
Jasper Crane, 1690.
John Curtis, 1676.
Thomas Davis, 1695.
Samuel Dod, 1702.
Samuel Freeman, 1701.
George Harrison, 1687.
Thomas Huntington, 1678.
Thomas Johnson, 1669–'73.
Samuel Kitchell, 1677.
John Lindley, 1700.
Anthony Oliff (Deputy), 1684.
James Nottman, 1703.
Thomas Pierson, Sen'r, 1679.
Theophilus Pierson, 1692.
Samuel Pierson, 1699.
Samuel Plum, 1682.
Thomas Richards, 1688.
Jabez Rogers, 1681.
John Ward, '*Turner*,' 1670.
Nathaniel Wheeler, 1682.

GRAND JURY MEN.

Samuel Kitchell, 1676.
John Baldwin, Jr., 1676.
Stephen Davis, 1676.
Joseph Walters, 1677.
John Ward, *Turner*, 1677.
Ephraim Pennington, 1677.
John Crane, 1678.
Wm. Camp, 1678.
Richard Harrison, 1678.
Sam'l Plum, 1679.
George Day, 1679.
Azariah Crane, 1679.
Thomas Pierson, Sen'r, 1680.
Thomas Pierson, Jun., 1680.
Stephen Bond, Jun., 1680.

RECORDER, OR TOWN CLERK.

Robert Treat, 1669, '70–'72.
John Brown, 1672, '73, '76–'80, '82–'85, '88.
John Curtis, 1692.
Nathaniel Ward, 1696.
John Cooper, 1706.

ASSESSORS AND RATE MAKERS.

John Curtis, 1685–'88, '90.
John Brown, 1685–'88, '90, '95, '96.

Zophar Beach, 1695, '97, '99.
Nath'l Ward, 1691-'98, 1701, '2, '6, '7, '9-'11.
Joseph Harrison, 1696-'98.
Joseph Johnson, 1696.
Theophilus Pierson, 1697.
Robert Young, 1697.
Seth Tompkins, 1697.
Thomas Hays, 1697, '99, 1701.
John Cooper, 1698, 1702, '6, '7, '9, '10, '11.
Thomas Richards, 1698.
Samuel Harrison, 1699, 1702.
Daniel Dod, 1701.
John Morris, 1702.
Eliphalet Johnson, 1702.
John Richards, 1712.
Samuel Cooper, 1712.

COLLECTORS.

Thomas Johnson, 1668.
Thomas Davis, 1694, '95.
Nath'l Ward, 1699, 1706.

TREASURERS.

Henry Lyon, 1668-'73.
Thomas Johnson, 1676-'82, '83.
John Curtis, 1677-'81, '85, '86, '87-'89.

OVERSEERS OF THE POOR.

Edward Ball, 1692.
Joseph Baldwin, 1712.
William Camp, 1692.
Azariah Crane, 1692.
Jasper Crane, 1703.
John Dalglesh, 1712.
Thomas Davis, 1706.
Joseph Harrison, 1699.
Samuel Harrison, 1692, 1701.
Thomas Hayes, 1701.
John Morris, 1706.
Theophilus Pierson, 1699.
Samuel Pierson, 1703.
Caleb Ward, 1709.
Nathaniel Wheeler, 1709.

TOWN'S MEN.

John Baldwin, Sen'r, 1697, '88.
John Baldwin, Jun'r, 1677, '78, '83, '84, '87, '88.
Edward Ball, 1679, '80, '85, '91.
Zophar Beach, 1691, '93.
Stephen Bond, 1679.
John Brown, Sen'r, 1674.
John Brown, Jun'r, 1682, '96.
Thomas Brown, 1691.
Ephraim Burwell, 1678, '79, '87.
William Camp, 1696, '77, '81, '82.
Matthew Campfield, 1677, '79.
John Catlin, 1677-'79, '81, '82.
Azariah Crane, 1676, '78, '83, '84, '87, '95.
Jasper Crane, 1681, '87, '88, '93,' 97.
John Crane, 1683, '84.
John Curtis, 1674, '75.
George Day, 1677, '78.
Stephen Davis, 1674, '78, '80-'82, '86, '87.
Thomas Davis, 1694.
Robert Denison, 1669.
Daniel Dod, 1691, '95.
Stephen Freeman, 1674, '75.
Richard Harrison, 1669, '74.
Samuel Harrison, 1682, '83, '88, '93, '94.
Joseph Harrison, 1684-'86, '93, '94.
Thomas Huntingron, 1675, '76, '83, '84.
Thomas Johnson, 1674, '75.
Joseph Johnson, 1679, '80, '85, '86, '91, '93.
Samuel Kitchell, 1675, '76, '86, '87.
Richard Lawrence, 1667.
Thomas Ludington, 1680, '81.
Samuel Lyon, 1693, '84.
John Morris, 1694, '95.
David Ogden, 1680, '81.
Anthony Oliff, 1688.
Thomas Pierson, Sen'r, 1677, '78.
Thomas Pierson, Jun'r, 1677, '78, '85, '86.
Theophilus Pierson, 1674, '75.
Samuel Plum, Sen'r, 1675, '76, '88.
Thomas Richards, 1687, '88,
Edward Riggs, Sen'r, 1669,

Joseph Riggs, 1682, '83.
Jabez Rogers, 1685, '86.
Samuel Rose, 1679.
Jonathan Sargeant, 1601.
Samuel Swain, 1667, '74.
Michael Tompkins, 1667.
Seth Tompkins, 1687, '88, '93.
Robert Treat, 1667.
John Treat, 1681, '85, '91, '92, '96.
Joseph Walters, 1667, '76, '82, '83.
John Ward, 1667, '69.
John Ward, "Turner," 1675, '76.
Nathaniel Ward, 1693, '94.
Nathaniel Wheeler, 1684.

TOWN COMMITTEES.

1674.

Richard Harrison,
Stephen Freeman,
Stephen Davis,
Richard Lawrence,
Thos. Richards,
John Ward,
(Mr.) Kitchell,
Abraham Pierson,
Michael Tompkins.

1696.

John Browne,
Joseph Harrison,
Samuel Harrison,
Thomas Hays,
Thomas Ludington,
Eliphalet Johnson,
Jasper Crane.

FENCE VIEWERS.

Hans Albers, 1677.
Benjamin Baldwin, 1680.
Daniel Baldwin, 1703.
John Baldwin, 1695.
John Baldwin, Jr., 1675.
Joseph Ball, 1701, '5.
John Brown, Sen'r, 1673.
Samuel Baldwin, 1703, '19.
Daniel Brown, 1701.
Joseph Brown, 1702.
Eleazer Bruen, 1700.
Zechariah Burwell, 1672, '91.
Ephraim Burwell, 1691.
Samuel Camp, 1697.
William Camp, 1670, '92.
Matthew Canfield, 1698.
James Clisbe, 1696.
John Crane, 1671.
Jasper Crane, 1683.
John Dalglish, 1701.
George Day, 1672.
Paul Day, 1700.
Stephen Davis, 1673.
Daniel Dod, 1676.
Richard Fletcher, 1684.
Samuel Freeman, 1695, 1709.
John Gardner, 1694.
Samuel Harrison, 1692.
Daniel Harrison, 1705.
Thomas Huntington, 1680.
John Johnson, 1686.
Joseph Johnson, 1688.
Eliphalet Johnson, 1696, 1708.
John Lindley, 1697.
Ebenezer Lindley, 1698.
Thomas Lyon, 1681.
Henry Lyon, 1706.
Samuel Lyon, 1680, 1705.
John Morris, 1701.
Anthony Oliff, 1684.
Ephraim Pennington, 1677.
Judah Pennington, 1712.
Thomas Pierson, Sen'r, 1678.
Thomas Pierson, Jun'r, 1679.
Abraham Pierson, 1702.
Samuel Potter, 1683.
Samuel Plum, 1675.
Edward Riggs, 1669.
Joseph Riggs, 1682.
Hugh Robards, 1697, 1706.
John Rogers, 1706.
Samuel Rose, 1671.
Eleazer Lampson, 1694.
Jonathan Sargeant, 1674.
Daniel Tichenor, 1688, '89.
Micah Tompkins, 1669.
Seth Tompkins, 1676, '99.
Eleazer Tompkins, 1699.
Joseph Walters, 1674.
John Ward, "Turner," 1678.
John Ward, Jun'r, 1686.
Nath'l Wheeler, 1670, '79, '81, 1705.
Wm. Wilson, 1706.

BURNERS OF WOODS AND MEADOWS.

Jasper Crane, 1672.
John Curtis, 1669.
Stephen Davis, 1670, '2, '3.
Stephen Freeman, 1673.
Thomas Johnson, 1673.
Henry Lyon, 1673.
Samuel Swain, 1673.
John Ward, 1673.
Nathaniel Wheeler, 1669, '70, '72.

SURVEYORS AND LAYERS-OUT OF HIGHWAYS.

Edward Ball, 1674–'78.
John Baldwin, Sen'r, 1684–'86.
Zachariah Burwell, 1686.
Wm. Camp, 1671, '72, '78, '86.
Azariah Crane, 1684, '86, '88.
Jasper Crane, 1684–'86, '99.
John Curtis, 1668, '89.
George Day, 1674–'78.
Stephen Davis, 1670–'2, '4–'8, '84, '86, '88.
Thomas Johnson, 1674, '77, '86.
Richard Harrison, 1670.
Samuel Harrison, 1686, '88, '99.
(Mr.) Kitchell, 1671, '2, '4–'8.
Richard Lawrence, 1671, '2, '4–'8.
Francis Lindley, 1686.
Thomas Luddington, 1684.
Anthony Oliff, 1684.
Samuel Plum, 1686.
Edward Riggs, 1686.
Joseph Riggs, 1685.
Jabez Rogers, 1685.
Samuel Swain, 1670.
John Treat, 1684, '99.
Joseph Walters, 1685.
John Ward, 1668, '70–'72.
Josiah Ward, 1671, '2.

WARNERS OF TOWN MEETING.

Hans Albers, 1679.
Benjamin Baldwin, 1682, '85.
Aaron Blatchly, 1669.
Stephen Bond, 1677.
John Brown, Sen'r, 1676.
John Brown, Jun'r, 1683.
Joseph Brown, 1681.
Ephraim Burwell, 1674.
Zachariah Burwell, 1678.
Wm. Camp, 1672.
John Crane, 1674.
George Day, 1670.
John Davis, 1683.
Stephen Davis, 1673.
John Harrison, 1672.
Thomas Luddington, 1674.
Samuel Lyon, 1679.
Samuel Plum, 1674.
Thomas Pierson, Jun'r, 1680.
Thomas Richards, 1671.
——— Riggs, 1671.
Edward Riggs, 1682.
Samuel Rose, 1677.
Jonathan Sargeant, 1680.
Martin Tichenor, 1673.
John Tichenor, 1684.
Seth Tompkins, 1685.
John Ward "Turner," 1676, '84.
Josiah Ward, 1670.
Nathaniel Wheeler, 1669.

POUNDERS AND POUND KEEPERS.

John Baldwin, Sen'r, 1696.
Edward Ball, 1691.
Joseph Ball, 1701.
John Brown, Sen'r, 1676.
Daniel Brown, 1697.
Obadiah Bruen, 1698.
Zechariah Burwell, 1703.
Azariah Crane, 1678, '83.
Azariah Crane, Jun'r, 1703.
Robert Dalglish, 1697, 1712.
Paul Day, 1696, '97, 1700.
Robert Denison, 1669.
Richard Fletcher, 1677.
Samuel Freeman, 1693, '98.
John Gardner, 1692, '95, '99.
Samuel Harrison, 1682.
Benjamin Harrison, 1689.
Samuel Huntington, 1702.

Thomas Johnson, 1670.
John Johnson, 1689.
Samuel Lyon, 1682.
Thomas Lyon, 1684, '87.
Eleazer Lampson, 1692.
John Morris, 1689, '92.
David Ogden, 1678, '86.
Anthony Oliff, 1688.
Thomas Pierson, 1699.
Jabez Rogers, 1684, '86, '87, '94, '86.
Daniel Tichenor, 1691, '98.
Nath'l Ward, 1699.
Wm. Wilson, 1702.
Thomas Williams, 1703.
Robert Young, 1680.

SEALERS OF LEATHER.

Richard Lawrence, 1676.
John Curtis, 1676, '79, '80.
John Baldwin, Sen'r, 1676, '79, '80.

SEALERS OF MEASURES.

John Brown, Sen'r, 1676, '79.
Joseph Walters, 1671, '78, '79, '87.
John Brown, Jun'r, 1678, '87.

PACKER OF MEAT.

Joseph Walters, 1676-'80.

HAY-WARDS.

Robert Denison, 1671.
John Catling, 1671.
Wm. Camp, 1672.
Jabez Rogers, 1672.
Stephen Davis, 1673.
Martin Tichenor, 1673.

BRANDERS.

Stephen Bond, 166, '77.
John Ward, "Turner," 1660, '77.

TOWN DRUMMER.

Joseph Johnson, 1668-'71.

GRAVE DIGGERS.

Edward Ball, 1679.
Richard Fletcher, 1679, '80.

MILITARY OFFICERS—1673.

Captains—Samuel Swain, Thomas Johnson.
Lieutenants—John Ward, Joseph Ward.
Ensigns—Richard Harrison, Samuel Harrison.

THE INDIAN BILL OF SALE TO THE NEWARKE MEN.

Entered 2d March, 1676-7. [E. J. Records, Lib. 1, fol. 69.]

Know all men By these presents, that WEE, Wapamuck the Sakamaker, and Wamesane, Peter, Captamin, Wecaprokikan, Napeam, Perawae, Sessom, Mamustome, Cacanakque, and Hairish, Indians belonging now to Hakinsack, the known acknowledged proprietors of a certain tract of Land Lying on the West of Pesayak river being parties on the one Side, and Mr. Obediah Bruen, Mr. Samuel Kitchell, Michael Tomkins, John Browne, and Robert Denison, with the consent and advice of Capt'n Philip Carteret Governeur of the Province of New Jersey, and in the behalf of ye Inhabitants now being or to be ye possessors of the Tract of

Land Inserted in this Deed of Sale the other parties, Doe make this Indenture the eleventh day of July in the year of our Lord 1667 (being the enlarging and perfecting of a deed of Sale made With the Indians the year before the present) in manner and form following, viz:

THAT WEE, the said Wapamuck the Sakamaker, and Wamesane, Peter, Captamin, Wecaprokikan, Napeam, Perawae, Sessom, Mamustome, Cacanakque, and Harish, doe, for ourselves and With Consent of the Indians, Bargain, sell and deliver, a Certain tract of Land, Upland, and Meadows of all sorts, Wether Swamps, Rivers, Brooks, Springs, fishings, Trees of all sorts, Quaries and Mines, or Metals of what sort soever, With full liberty of hunting and fouling upon the same, Excepting Liberty of hunting for the above said proprietors that were uppon the upper commons, and of fishing in the above said Pesayak River; which said tract of Land is bounded and Limited with the bay Eastward, and the great River Pesayak Northward, the great Creke or River in the meadow running to the head of the Cove, and from thence bareing a West Line for the South bounds, wh. said Great Creke is Commonly Called and known by the name Weequachick, on the West Line backwards in the Country to the foot of the great mountaine called Watchung, being as is Judged about seven or Eight miles from Pesayak towne; the said Mountaine as Wee are Informed hath one branch of Elizabeth towne River running near the above said foot of the mountaine; the bounds northerly, viz. Pesayak River reaches to the Third River above the towne, ye River is called Yauntakah, and from thence upon a northwest line to the aforesaid mountaine; all which before mentioned Lands for the several kinds of them, and all the singular benefits and Priviledges belonging to them, with ye several bounds affixed and expressed herein, as also free liberty and range for Cattle, horses, hoggs, and that though they Range beyond any of the bounds in this deed Expressed, to feed and pasture Without Molestation of or damage to the owners of the cattle &c. above said. WEE the above said Indians, Wapamuk, &c. doe sell, Alienate, make over and Confirm all our Right, Title and Interest of us, our heires, and Successors forever Unto the said Lands, &c. as above mentioned to Mr. Obediah Bruen, Mr. Samuel Kitchell, Michael Tomkins, John Browne and Robert Denison, townsmen and Agents for ye English Inhabitants of Pesayak, to them, their heires and associates for Ever, to have, hold, and dispose of, Without Claim, Let, or Molestation from ourselves or any other Whatsoever. These Lands, &c. are thus solde and delivered for and in consideration of fifty double-hands of powder, one hundred barrs of lead, twenty Axes, twenty Coates, ten Guns, twenty pistolls, ten kettles, ten Swords, four blankets, four barrells of beere, ten paire of breeches, fifty knives, twenty howes, eight hundred and fifty fathem of wampem, two Ankors of Licquers or something Equivolent, and three troopers Coates; these things are received, only a small remainder Engaged to them by bill. To the true and just performance according to ye true intent of our Bargain, WEE ye said Obediah Bruen, and the rest above said, doe for ourselves and heires, Ex'tors, Adm'n'tors or Assigns, to the said Wapamuk, &c., the true proprietors of the said Lands doe bind and Covenant. WEE the said Wapamuk and the rest of the Indians above said doe fully surrender, pas over and Yeild up all our Right, privilege and power in the same, and to free the above said Lands from Claim, Incumbrances, of What kind soever; all the above mentioned purchasse Wee doe Grant and deliver to Obediah Bruen and ye rest above said, to them, their associates, heires, and all the lawfull possessors. And for the full Ratiffication and testification of the above said bargain and agrements about the aforesaid tract and parcells of Land so bounded, Wee, the said parties above mentioned have hereunto Enterchangeably sett our hands and seales, the day and year above said, in the presence of Us Witnessing. Moreover Wee doe grant them free liberty to take what timber and stones they please in any of our Lands, where Wee the above said Indians have yet propriety.

OBEDIAH BRUEN,
MICHAEL TOMKINS,
SAMUEL KITCHELL,
JOHN BROWNE,
ROBERT DENISON.

WAPAMUK, his marke.

HARISH, his marke.

CAPTAMIN, his marke.

MAMUSTOME, his marke.

PETER, his marke.

WAMESANE, his marke.

WEKAPROKIKAN, his marke.

CACANAKRUE, his marke.

SESSOM, his marke.

PERAWAE, his marke.

Signed, sealed and delivered in presence of
SAMUEL EDSSALL,
PIERWIM, ye Sachum of Pau, ⋈ his marke.
EDWARD BURROWES,
mark of **R** RICHARD FLETCHER,
CLASSE ⋈ his marke.

{ SIGIL. }

INDIAN DEED OF SALE AND CONFIRMATION TO THE TOWNE OF NEWARK.

Entered 18th March. [E. J. Records, Lib. 1, fol. 107.]

WEREAS in the original deed of sale make by the Indians to the inhabitants of the town of Newark, bareing date the ellevent day of

July, 1667, it is said to the foot of the Great Mountaine, called Watchung, alias Atchunck, WEE Winocksop and Shenocktos, Indians and owners of the said Great Mountaine, for and in consideration of two Guns, three Coates, and thirteen kans of Rum, to us in hand paid the receipt Wereof wee doe hereby acknowledge, doe Covenant and declare to and with Mr. John Ward and Mr. Thomas Johnson, Justices of the peace of the said towne of Newark, before the Right Hon'ble Phillip Carteret, Esq., Governeur of the Province of New Jersey, and the other witnesses here under written, that it is meant, agreed, and intended that their bounds shall reach or goe to the top of the said Great Mountaine, and that WEE the said Indians will marke out the same to remaine to them the said inhabitants of Newark, their heires or Assignes for Ever. In Witness hereof WEE the s'd Indians have hereunto sett our hands and Scales the 13th of March, 1677-8.

WINOCKSOP, his marke. [SIGIL.]

SHENOCKTOS, his marke. [SIGIL.]

Signed, sealed and Delivered in the presence of
JAMES BOLLEN, Secretary,
HENDRICK DROGESTRADT,
SAMUEL HARISSON.

This acknowledged before me the day and yeare above written.

PH. CARTARETT.

DEED FROM THE PROPRIETORS.

[E. J. Records, Lib. F, fol. 166-168.]

THE PROPRIETORS of the Province of EAST NEW JERSEY, To all persones to whome these presents shall come GREETING. Know ye, that WEE the sayd Proprietors for and in consideration of the Rents and services herein After Reserved and for severall other good causes and considerationes us hereunto moving, HAVE Given, granted, bargained and sold, And by these presents Do give, grant, bargaine and sell unto John Curtis, John Treat, Theophelus Peirson and Robert Yong, all of the Towne of Newark in the Countie of Essex and Province afore sayd, ALL those severall Tracts of Land and meadow hereafter Expressed, scituate, Lyeing and being within the sayd Towneship of Newark:

1st. A Home Lott, In Length tenn chaines, in breadth at the east and middle three chaines Lack six foot And att the west end foure chaine and three quarters of A Chaine; bounded North by John Johnson, south by Daniel Browne, east and west by high wayes.

ALSO A tract Lyeing Above Daniell Dods Home lott BEGINING at Daniel Dodd's South-west corner, thence runing North at the East End twenty Eight chaines to the highway; thence as the highway runes twentie six chaines to the branch of the Mill Brooke; thence Along the Brooke seaven chaines at the west End to Samuell Huntington's line; bounded west by the sayd branch, North by the highway, East by Hance Alberts, Samuel and Daniel Dod, and by the other Lotts South.

Another tract beyond the Mill brooke branch BEGINING At A Chestnut tree markt on foure sides which is John Ward's corner; thence runing north west Seaventeene chaines to a maple tree markt as before at the swamp side; thence south and by west seventy to another tree markt as before; thence East and by south twentie chaines to Mr. Crane's corner, bounded North by Land unsurveyed, East by other Lotts, west by the Swamp and fresh meadows, south by other Lotts.

ALSO a peece of meadow at the Lower tide pond, in Length seaventeene chaines, In breadth seaven chaines, bounded east by the creeke that runs into the tide pond, south by Hugh Roberts and Thomas Staples', north by the Pond, west by Oyster Creeke.

ALSO a peece of swamp Lying at the Great Swamp in the Neck, begining at the Bogg [*bridge*, in the survey,] and running in Length twentie chaines north, and at the south end fifteen chaines, bounded south by the bridge, east by the boggs, west by other Lotts.

ALSO another peece of meadow at the head of the Great Meadow, BEGINING at Samuel Potter's South west corner And running North twentie chaines in breadth to Aaron Blackley's line, in length twenty chains, bounded east by Samuel Potter, north by Aaron Blackley and John Johnson, west by the swamp, south by Eliezer Lampson and unsurveyed Land; containing in all the above said tracts of upland and meadow (after allowances for barrens, highways, &c.) two hundred acres, being alotted for the parsonage.

2dly. All that small tract alotted for the bureing place, takeing in the Pond and meeting house, being seaven chaines in Length and foure chaines in breadth, bounded west by John Treat, south by John Johnson, North and East by Highways.

3dly. A triangle peece aloted for a Markett place, six chaines wide at the south end, on the west side nine chaines in length, and on the east side eleven chaines in length, bounded on all sides by highways.

4thly. Another triangle peece alotted for a training place, in length on the west side seaventeen chaines, on the south-east side fifteen chaines, and on the east end seaven chaines and a halfe, bounded on all sides by Highways.

5thly. Another triangle peece Alotted for a watering place for cattle, Begining at John Plum's corner and running up the brooke west seaven chaines, thence east and by north seaven chaines to the highway, and at the east end one chaine three rodes; bounded south by John Plum, and Robert Daglish, North and East by highways.

And lastly, the streets of the sayd towne of Newarke, as they are now layed out, viz: the high street to remaine about two chaines more or less in breadth, and in length from Hugh Roberts' brooke to the mill brooke thorow the Middle of the Towne; and the rest of the streetes to bee as they are now in breadth; TOGETHER with all and all manner of rivers, rivolets, springs, runes, streames, Dams, feedings, Pastures, woodes, under woodes, trees, waters, water courses, water falls, ponds, poolls, pitts, meadowes, easements, profits, commodities, liberties, advantages, Emoluments and Appurtenances whatever to the same belonging or any manner of ways appertaining; To HAVE AND TO HOLD the said several tracts of upland, meadowes and premises with theire and every of theire appurtenances to them the sayd John Curtis, John Treat, Theophelus Peirson and Robert Yong their heires and Assignes forever; to the only proper use, benefit and behoof of the Old Setlers of the towne of Newark aforesaid, their heires and Assignes forever, In Com'on; granted to bee and Remaine to and for the several uses herein particularly expressed, and to be appropriated for no other use or uses whatsoever; To bee Holden in free and com'on soccage of us the sayd Proprietors, our heires and Assignes forever As of the seignorie of East Greenwitch; YEELDING and paying therefor unto us the Proprietors, our heires and Assignes forever, sixpence sterling monie of England, for the aforesaid several tracts of Land on every five and twentieth day of March forever hereafter, in Leiu and instead of all other services and demands whatsoever.

IN WITNESS whereof WEE HAVE caused the seale of our sayd Province to be hereunto affixed, and the same to be signed by our Governour and the Major part of his Council for the time being this tenth day of December, Anno Dom. 1696, and in the eight yeare of the Raigne of our soveraigne Lord, William the Third, over England, &c., KING.

{ L. S. }

AND. HAMILTON,
JOHN INIANS,
SAMUEL DENNIS,
JOHN BISHOP,
JAMES DUNDAS,
JOHN ROYSE.

"TOWN PATTENT OR CHARTER."

[E. J. Records, Lib. A. A. A., fol. 145.]

ANNE, by the Grace of God Queen of Great Brittain, ffrance and Ireland, Defender of ye faith &c. To all to whome These Presents Shall Come or may in any wise Concern Sendeth Greeting. Whereas, our Loveing Subjects John Treat, Joseph Harison, Eliphelet Johnson, John Cooper, and John Morris, freeholders and Inhabitants of ye Town of Newark in ye County of Essex in our Province of New Jersey, on behalf of themselves and the Rest of ye freeholders of ye said Town and by their order, by their Humble Petition Presented to our Trusty and well Beloved Robert Hunter Esq'r Captain General and Governour in Cheife of our Said Province, have Sett forth, that their Ancestors and Predecessors, freeholders of ye said Town, by Licence from ye Proprietors Governour, in ye Month of July one Thousand Six Hundered Sixty Seven, had Purchased from ye Indians, all that Tract of Land now Known by ye Name of Newarke, Bounded Easterly by a Great Creek that Runs from Hackingsack Bay through ye Salt Meadow Called by the Indians Wequahick, and now Known by ye Name of bound Creek: and Continuing from the head of ye Said Creek to the head of a Cove to a Markt Tree, from thence it Extended Westerly upon a Straight Line, by Computation Seven Miles be the Same more or Less to the End or foot of the Great Mountain and to the Ridge thereof Called by the Indians Wacchung, Near where Runs a branch of Raway River, from thence Extending on a Northerly Course along the Ridge of the Said Mountain to a heap of Stones, Erected to Asertain the Boundary between the s'd Town of Newark and the Town of Achquickatnuck, from thence Runing a South East Course by Achquickatnuck Bound Line, to where the brook or Rivolet Called by the Indians Yantokah, but now Known by the Name of the Third River, Emtieth itself into Pasayack River and from thence Continuing Down along by the said Pasaiack River and Hackingsack Bay to the mouth of the said Bound Creek: and that for want of a

Charter or Pattent of Incorporation they are under Sundry Inconviences and Disorders, which to prevent for yᵉ future they have therefore Prayed our Charter or Pattent of Privilidges accordingly: which Request we being willing to Grant. KNOW YEE, that of our Especiall Grace, Certain Knowledge, and Mear Motion, WE have Given, Granted, Rattified, and Confirmed, and Do by these Presents, for us, our heires, and Successors for Ever, Give, Grant, Ratifie, and Confirm unto John Treat, Joseph Harison, James Notman, Eliphelet Johnson, John Cooper, John Morris, Joseph Crane, Thomas Davis, Nathaniel Wheeler, and George Harison, in Trust to and for themselves and yᵉ Rest of yᵉ freeholders and Inhabitants of yᵉ said Town and their Successors for Ever, within the Limits and Bounds aforesaid, the free Liberty and Privillidge of being a Town Ship, and They and their Successors for Ever hereafter are and Shall be a Comunity or Township, in Deed and in Name, in the said County of Essex, within our Said Province of New Jersey, by the Name of the Trustees of the freeholders and Inhabitants of the Township of Newark, AND that they and their Successors for Ever hereafter Shall have a Perpetuall Succession of the Number of Ten, Principle freeholders and Inhabitants of the s'd Township of Newark, who shall be the Trustees of the Freeholders and Inhabitants of the Township of Newark for Ever, (That is to say) that upon yᵉ Death of any one or more of the said Trustees, it Shall and may be Lawful for the freeholders of the said Township for the Time being, being therunto Sumoned or Warned by the Constable or Constables of the said Town for the Time being, by order of the Surviving Trustees of the said Township of Newark for the time being, or the Major part of them, and by other Publick wayes and Meanes, to Assemble and meet together, at Such time and Publick Place within yᵉ said Township as the s'd Surviveing Trustees for the time being, or the Major part of them from time to time as Need shall be shall think fitt to Nominate and appoint, and there by Majority of votes of the said freeholders, to Elect and Choose so many of yᵉ Principle freeholders of the said Township Resideing within yᵉ Bounds of the said Township as may fill up the Number of the s'd Trustees to be Ten, which Trustees so Chosen and Elected as aforesaid, together with the Surviving Trustees for the time being, Shall be Trustees of the Said Township to all Intents and Purposes as Much as if they had been particularly Nominated and Expressed in this our Said Grant. AND WE Do further Give and Grant unto the said Trustees and their Successors for Ever, that it shall and may be Lawful to and for yᵉ said Trustees and their Successors for Ever, by yᵉ Name of the Trustees of the freeholders and Inhabitants of yᵉ Township of Newark, In any of our Courts within Said Province of New Jersey to Sue and be Sued, Answer and be Answered unto, Defend and be Defended. AND WE Do further Give and Grant unto the said Trustees and their Succsssors for Ever hereafter, and to the Major part of them, full Power and Lawful Authority once in Every Year at their Discretion, to Summons and Call together the freeholders of the said Township, and for the said freeholders and their Successors so Summoned and Called together, to assemble and meet on Such Certain Day and at such place as the said Trustees for yᵉ time being or the Major part of them shall appoint, to Elect and Choose by Plurallity of Votes of the said freeholders and their Successors, Such Number of the Said freeholders and their Successors as they shall think fit, Not Exceeding five, to be Overseers for appointing what Improvement Shall be Made for the Ensuing Year upon a Certain Neck of Land within the Bounds of the said Township, which by Reason of its Scituation and Natural advantages is or May be Easily Encloseed by a Generall fence, and for apportionateing to Each of the said freeholders Interested in the Said Neck, and their Successors for the time being, their Share of ye Charge of the Said Generall fence for the Common Good, which s'd apportionateing So made as afores'd shall be of force against Each of ye Said freeholders and their Successors for the time being for their Respective Shares or Portions of the said Charge their Executors, administrators or assigns, for so Long time as the said Trustees and their Successors or ye Majority of them shall think fitt and no Longer, and in Case of Refusall or Neglect to Pay ye Same, it shall and may be Levied by ye Constables of the said Town or any one of them, by warrant from a Justice of the Peace within the said Township by Distress, and by the said Constables or Constable to be paid into the said overseers for ye time being, for the use aforesaid and no other use whatsoever. AND WE Do further Give and Grant to the said Trustees and their Successors for Ever, that it shall and may be Lawful for ye freeholders and Inhabitants of ye said Town, Annually and once in Every Year, to Assemble and meet together and to Choose Two Constables, one overseer of ye Poor, and one overseer of ye highwaies, by Majority of the Votes of the ffreeholders and Inhabitants of the s'd town of Newark, which Constable and overseer so Chosen as aforesaid Shall Serve in the said Respective Offices in the said Town untill the Next Anuall Election, if they so Long Live, or Pay the Sum of five Pounds for the use of the poor of the Said Town, AND that in Case of the Death or Refusall of any of the said Officers to serve in any of the said Offices as often as the Same Shall Happen out of the Useuall Anniversary time of Election, that it shall and may be Lawful for the said freeholders and Inhabitants to assemble, and meet together to Choose others in their Room and place, and it shall and may be Lawful for a Justice of the peace within the said Township to administer an Oath to the Said Officers of the said Town, for the faithfull Discharge of their Respective Offices. AND WE Do further Give and Grant to the said Trustees and their Successors all other Privillidges, Rights, Liberties and Immunities that the Township of AMWELL or any other Township within our s'd Province of New Jersey Doth or may of Right Enjoy, To HAVE, HOLD AND ENJOY all and Singular the Privilidges, Rights, Liberties, and Immunities aforesaid, unto the said John Treat, Joseph Harison, James Notman, Eliphelet Johnson, John Cooper, John Morris, Joseph Crane, Thomas Davis, Nathaniel Wheeller, and George Harison, Trustees of the freeholders and Inhabitants of the Township of Newark and their Successors for Ever; they ye s'd Trustees and their Successors for Ever Yeilding, Rendering, and Paying unto us, our heires and Successores, Yearly and Every Year, on the feast Day of the ANNUNCIATION of the Blessed Virgin Mary, as an acknowledgment for the Said Privilidges, the ANNUAL Rent of five Shilings, In Leiu and Stead of all other Rents, Services, and Demands whatsoever for the Same.

In Testimony whereof, we have Caused these our Letters To be made Pattent, and ye Seall of our Province of New Jersey to be affixed. Wittness our said Right Trusty and well beloved Robert Hunter Esqr, Captain General and Governour In Cheiffe of the Provinces of New Jersey and New York, and the Teritories and Tracts of Land Depending thereon in America, and Vice Admirall of the Same &c. at fort ANNE In New York, this Twenty Seventh Day of Apreill, in the Twelfth Year of our Reign, ANNOQE DOM, 1713.

J. BASSE, Secretary.

[L. S.]

"BOUNDARIES OF YE TOWNSHIP OF NEWARKE."

[E. J. Records, Lib. A. A. A., fol. 155.]

By Warrant from his Excelencie yᵉ Governour, to me Directed, bearing Date yᵉ 7th Day of November, 1713.

Sirveyed, Marked out, & Acertained yᵉ Lines and Boundaries of yᵉ Township of Newarke, According to their Pattent or Charter, which bears Date yᵉ 27th Day of Apreill 1713: begining where Bound Creek Emtieth itself into Hackingsack Bay and Runing up yᵉ s'd Creek to yᵉ head thereof, where a black Cherry tree Markd with yᵉ Letters N on the one Side & E on the other Stands under a Steep hill, thence South Twenty one Degrees West Twenty five Chaines forty Three Links to a Dead Black oak Tree, Standing in Joseph Lyons feild, thence North Sixty Degrees fifteen Minutes West four Hundered and five Chain or five Mile & five Chains along Markd Trees, many of them being Markd with yᵉ Letters N & E as aforesd (because tis yᵉ Partition Line betwen Sd Newark & Elizabeth Town) to a Black oak tree & a Small Red oak Tree by it, both Markd on four Sides Standing on yᵉ Riscing Ground of yᵉ South End of yᵉ Mountain Call'd Watchung, & about forty or fifty Rod North Easterly from yᵉ Westmost of yᵉ Two branches of Raway River which Comes Down on Each Side of yᵉ s'd Mountain, Thence Extending on a Northerly Course along yᵉ Ridge of yᵉ s'd Mountain to a heap of Stones, Erected to Ascertain yᵉ Boundaries between s'd Town of Newark & the Town of Acquackanong, Thence on a South East Course to yᵉ brook or Rivollet Called yᵉ Third River, Where it falls into Pasayack River, Thence Continuing Down yᵉ s'd Pasayack River & Hackingsack Bay to where it began.

By JOHN REID, Sirveyor.

A True Copy of yᵉ Return of yᵉ Sirvey of yᵉ Township of Newark, Entered pr me.

JOHN COOPER, Town Clerk.

FROM PROPRIETORS' RECORD OF WARRANTS AND SURVEYS.

Lib. 2, fol. 36.

Anno 1676. A WARRANT to Lay out for Benefit & Use of the Town of Newarke So much Land as shall be Convenient for Landing places within the said Towne, Land for a School House, for a Town house, a Meeting house, a Market Place or Market places; and two hundred Acres of Upland and Meadow in proportion for a parsonage, PROVIDED that none of the said Land be Already Surveyed and Appropriated by any particular person & to return &c. Dated 31 Octob.

INDEX.

*** References to the pages on which appointments to the regular town offices are recorded, have not been inserted in this Index. The names of those holding office prior to the obtainment of the Town Charter in 1713 are given in the Appendix. Office appointments after that time it was thought unnecessary to refer to particularly, as they were made annually with great regularity, and the recapitulation of so large a number of names would have unnecessarily increased the size of the volume.

A dash between the figures indicates that the name or subject is mentioned on each of the intervening pages.

Differences in the mode of spelling a name have sometimes been pointed out.

Abett, Daniel, 93.
Acquackanong, (Hackquocánung) Bounds with, 94. Line renewed, 128.
Advertiser (newspaper), 270.
Agens, John, 267.
Agreement, between people of Milford, Guilford and Branford, relative to settlement, 1; by inhabitants of Branford, 2; with John Catlin and Edward Ball about Neck, 57; those not signing fundamental, to be called upon, 97; with heirs of Jabez Longworth, 257.
Alarm, Signal of, 78.
Albers, Hans, 3, 8, 9, 14, 16, 24—26, 28, 30, 31, 37, 49, 55, 70, 73, 85, 102.
Alling, John, 228, 235, 260.
Joseph, 157.
Samuel, 116, 121—125, 133, 137, 138.
Ammunition, to be procured, 63.
Andros, Governor, answer to, 78.
Andros, Nathaniel, 131, 132.
Andruss, Isaac, 200, 202, 210, 211, 242—244, 255, 256, 259, 266, 267, 269, 271.
Arent, Dr. Jacob, 128.
Arentsen, Lawrence, 127.
Arms, Inhabitants to be provided with, 51.
Armstrong, Amzi, 271.
Ashton, J., 199.

Baldwin, [Bauldwin] Benjamin, 8, 9, 12, 24, 36, 37, 49, 55, 70, 85, 100, 107, 127.
Daniel, 125.
Ebenezer, 150.
Elias, 166.
Elijah, 142, 145.
Eluathan, 125.
Jesse, 190, 250.
Baldwin, [Bauldwin], John, Sen'r, 3, 5, 8, 9, 17, 28, 32, 34, 37, 49, 54, 57, 70, 84, 85, 90, 93, 98, 102, 120.
[Bauldwin], John, Jun'r, 35, 7—9, 24, 26, 28, 33, 36, 37, 49, 53, 61, 70, 85, 93, 102, 125.
John W., 268.
John Y., 190, 228.
Jonathan, 193.
Joseph, 125, 127, 128.
Joseph T., 200, 215.
Jotham, 207.
Moses, 154.
Nehemiah, 148.
Phineas, 193.
Samuel, 125.
Thomas, 178.
Timothy, 125.
Ball, Edward, 2, 8, 9, 24, 26, 28, 36, 37, 44, 48, 49, 54, 56—59, 63, 65, 68, 70, 71, 74, 85, 89, 90, 92—94, 97—102, 104—106.
Hannah, 199.
Joseph, 127, 128.
Moses, 128.
Thomas, 127.
Banks, David, 165, 166.
James, 183, 139.
Bayard, Nicholas, Committee authorized to arrest him, 57, 59; to be sued, 62.
Beach, Ephraim, 260, 264, 266.
Joseph, 195.
Nathaniel, 192.
Zophar, 94, 107, 122.
Bears, 80, 88.
Beckly, Richard, 1.
Beech, Azariah, 19, 21.
Widow, Martha, 127.

Bergen, Deputies sent to, to hear the Governor's warrant, 56.
Blatchly, [Blacthly], Aaron, 3, 7—9, 24, 26, 28, 33, 39, 45, 49, 69, 70, 84, 86.
Thomas, 1, 2.
Bloomfield, Dividing lines between, and Newark and Orange, 198.
Boatman's Lot, 15, 18, 24, 31, 32.
Bollen, Capt., Letter of, referred to a Committee, 17.
Bolles, Ephraim, 225, 234, 239.
Bond, Mrs. Mary, 85.
Robert, 10, 23, 49.
Stephen, 3, 8, 9, 24, 26, 31, 36, 37, 49, 50, 51, 59, 60, 70, 85, 93, 105, 106.
Bostick, John, 8, 9, 21, 23, 24, 26, 37, 70.
Bonnel, Joseph, 134.
Boudinot, Elias E., 230.
Bowers, Mr. Nath'l, to be minister for one year, 121; called permanently, 122, 124; dies, 127.
Bradbury, John, 125.
Branford, Agreements with settlers from, 1, 2, 5.
Brant, William, 100, 107.
Brooks, John, 3, 8, 9, 24, 26, 36, 37, 70.
Browne, [Brown] Daniel, 125.
James, 123, 125, 128.
John, 3, 8, 9, 11, 17, 18, 20, 24, 26, 28, 31, 32, 34—37, 45, 49, 53, 54, 64, 70, 71, 85, 93, 97, 102—104, 107, 113.
John, Jun'r, 3, 8, 14, 21, 24, 28, 35—37, 41, 43—46, 49, 51, 55, 56, 58—61, 63—65, 68—70, 72—74, 78—80, 82, 84, 86, 87, 89, 90, 92—97, 99—102.
Joseph, 85, 93, 99, 102.
S. B., 260.
Thomas, 85, 93, 97, 99, 102, 104, 106, 125.
Bruen, David, 138.
Elijah, 143.
James, 251, 266.
John, 15, 23, 53, 70, 85, 93, 102.
Joseph, 123, 128.
Obadiah, 3, 7, 8, 9, 15, 23, 24, 28, 32, 37, 41, 49, 50, 64, 70, 76.
Burnet, James W., 230.
Smith, 202, 215, 225, 236, 238.
Burr, Aaron, a candidate for the ministry, 132, 133.
Burwell, Ephraim, 3, 8, 9, 24, 26, 28, 36, 37, 40, 49, 70, 78, 85, 86, 89, 90, 92, 93, 95, 99, 101, 102, 106, 107.
John, 85, 93.
Joseph, 125.
Theophilus, 143.
Zachariah, 3, 8, 9, 17, 24, 26, 28, 34, 35, 37, 49, 70, 85, 89, 93, 96, 102, 106.
Burying Place, let out for pasture 132, (and thereafter annually for some years); to be fenced, 140, 211; right of inhabitants thereto not to be abandoned, 200; leasing for pasture prohibited, 211; put in charge of Town Committee, 314; nuisances removed from it, &c., 220; passage into it from Broad street, 220; removal of remains from proposed and no more interments to be made therein, 250.
Burying Place, New, to be procured, 220, 223; subject indefinitely postponed, 224; proposition revived, 225, 267; proposition for application to Legislature for authority to raise money for, lost, 226; again authorized, 243, and approved, 244; expedient that lots should be purchased therefor, 243, 269; land procured, 247, 248; part to be sold, 249; to be improved 250; stagnant water in, 259, 260; burials in, to be discontinued, 269.

Cadmus, Thomas, 136.
Camell [Campbell?] Robert, 127.
Camfield, Ebenezer, 2, 85, 93, 102.
[Canfield] Matthew, 3, 7—10, 13, 14, 17, 24, 26, 33, 37, 49, 70, 84, 86, 102, 105, 111.
Samuel, 8, 24, 25, 37.
Camp, Aaron, 265.
Caleb, 149, 151, 152, 155, 158, 165, 166. 183, 186, 200, 207.
Nathaniel, 136, 139, 141.
Samuel, 127.
[Campe] William, 3, 5, 8, 9, 20, 24, 26, 28, 29, 33, 36—38, 42, 43, 59, 68, 70, 74, 77, 82, 84—90, 92—95, 97—101, 104, 105, 107, 112, 118, 154, 157. 158.
Campbell, George W., 255.
Campfield [Canfield] Robert B., 195, 202. 207, 211, 234, 250, 260, 266.
Canfield, Jonathan, 85.
John, 127.
Candfield, Thomas, 157.
Carteret, Governor, letter from, rec'd and answer'd, 29.
Catling [Catlin] John, 3, 8, 9, 15, 18, 24, 26. 28, 35—38, 42, 44, 49, 51, 54, 57, 58. 68, 69, 70, 78, 80, 85, 93.
"Centinel of Freedom," 192, 209.
Chapman (Mr.) 159.
Chronicle (newspaper), 267.
Church of England, to share in Parsonage Lands, 145, 150.
Clark Daniel, 127.
Clizbe, James, 107.
Cockburn, John, 101, 102.
Cocker, Emanuel, 137, 138.
Coe, Benjamin, 161, 189.
Cole, "Goodman," 9, 15.
Colours of the Town, 43.
Colve, Anthony, letter to, about Neck, 71.
Collectors to give bonds, 179, 182, 183, 188.
Committee, to instruct and advise with Deputies to Assembly, 90, 111; to devise measures of protection, &c.. 104, 114; to divide Parsonage lands, 145; Report of, on Parsonage lands disagreed to, 146, 147; to look after the privileges of the town, 154, 166, 183, 186; to inspect the poor, 155; to lay out land for school house, 157; in dispute with Joseph Riggs, 158; to instruct members of legislature, 159; to nominate members of Legislature and Congress, 181, 182; Report of, upon encroachments on Highways, 185; Report of, on poor of Orange and Newark, 195, 199; to superintend schools for Poor, 208, 210; relative to Burying Ground, 200, 247; to enclose Commons, 205; to adopt measures for erecting Town house, 220, 225, 236; to provide a new Burying Ground, 225; Report of, on vacant lands, 233; relative to a Market, &c., 234—236; on Docks, 235, 267, 268; to frame Act of Incorporation, 243, 244; on Longworth Legacy, 255; report of on Longworth Legacy, 257;

on Canal bridges, 260; on division of township into wards, 266—278.
Commons, 26, 157; two to be enclosed, 205; trespasses upon to be prosecuted, 228.
Conch, John, 94.
Condit [Condict, Cundit] John, 137, 145, 146, 165, 166; to have charge of Town Charter, 159.
Joel W., 271.
Moses, 199.
[Condict] Silas, 200—207, 210, 211, 220, 230, 231, 244, 245, 251, 255, 259, 260.
Congar, Ellison, 244.
John, 199.
Congregational Churches, members of, only admitted as freemen, 2.
Constables, to give security, 180, 181, 183.
Connor, James, 214.
Cooper, John, 114, 120, 123, 127, 128, 132.
Samuel, 124.
Cornbury, Lord, to be petitioned relative to a minister, 118.
Corn Mill on Bound Creek, 82. (See Mill.)
Courts established, 14, 45, 61.
Court-yards to houses prohibited, 153.
Crane, Azariah, 3, 49, 85, 87, 93, 94, 99, 101, 102, 104—106, 111, 119—122, 127, 128.
Daniel, 127.
David, 137, 138.
David D., 199, 215, 224, 225, 226, 250.
Delivered [Deliverance], 3, 8, 9, 16, 22, 24, 26, 28, 37, 49, 70.
Elihu, 156.
Jasper, 2, 8—10, 20, 21, 22, 24, 26, 28, 32, 33, 37, 40, 43—45, 48—52, 54, 55, 70, 74, 75, 85.
Jasper, Jun'r, 86, 91, 98, 102, 105, 106, 108, 110—113, 119—123, 127.
John, 2, 8, 9, 24, 26, 28, 29, 36, 37, 49, 53, 70, 75, 85, 102, 129, 131—133, 137, 139, 142, 145, 166.
Jonathan, 124, 125, 129, 132, 134.
Joseph, 127.
Josiah, 142.
Nathaniel, 127.
William, 136.
Cumming, John N., 205.
Currency, Issuing of tickets as, in 1814 rejected, 209.
Curtis, John, 5, 8, 9, 24, 28, 29, 35, 37, 38, 41, 44, 45, 49—52, 54, 61, 68—72, 77, 79, 80, 84—87, 90, 92—103, 105, 106, 109, 111, 113, 115—117, 144.

Daglesh [Dalgleish, Dalglish] Robert, 3, 8, 9, 24, 25, 26, 28, 36, 37, 45, 49, 53, 55, 70, 75, 78, 85, 93, 95, 102, 124.
Dalglish, John, 124, 125, 127.
Davis, John, 69, 74, 86.
Jonathan, 100.
Robert, 199.
Thomas, 100, 108, 114, 127.
Widow, Law suit with, about Wessells, 160.
Davies [Davis] Stephen, 8, 9, 14, 16, 24, 26, 28—31, 35, 37, 38, 42—44, 46, 47, 49, 51—55, 69—71, 74, 78, 83, 85, 86, 88, 90, 93, 94, 97, 98, 100—102.
Day, George, 3, 5, 8, 9, 17, 24, 26, 28, 36, 37, 49, 70, 76, 82, 85, 89, 127.
Joseph, 1, 11.
Samuel, 127.
Stephen D., 109.
Delepierre [Deleprary] Mr., 76, 80; enquiry of, relative to the recording of the Town bounds, 67; third Division of land laid out by, 91.
Delevall, Mr., 50.
Denison, Robert, 3, 8, 9, 24, 25, 26, 30, 31, 35—37, 49, 69, 70, 85.
Denison's Wife, Robert, 5.
Denison, Widow, 43.
Deputies, Pay of, 1697, 110; thanks to, for not consenting to a certain act, 118.
Dey, Anthony, 205.
Divident Hill, 10.
Docks, Town, 190, 324, 227, 230, 233, 235, 236, 239, 241, 249, 250, 252, 253, 266, —268.
Dock, Commercial, encroachments at, 267—268.
Dodd, Amzi, 255, 259, 253, 269.
John, 181, 200.
Dod [Dodd] Daniel, 8, 14, 16, 30, 37, 44, 49, 71, 73, 85, 86, 88, 101, 103, 116, 127.
Ebenezer, 53, 54.
Martha, Widow, 127.
Samuel, 86, 103, 129.
Stephen, 251, 267, 268.
Dogs, First regulation for killing, 140.
Doremus, David, 255, 259, 260.
Doud, Widow, her claim against the town, 19.
Dow, John, 200.
William, 159.
Drake, Zephaniah, 256, 266, 267, 269.
Drummer for the town, 11, 34, 85.
Dutch Authorities at New Orange, application to, for a privileged county, 50; negotiations with, about Neck, 50, 51; about confirmation of purchase of lands, 55; authorities in Holland to be written to about Neck, 71.

Eagle Newspaper, 270.
Earle, Wm. H., 267.
Education, Measures relative to, 65, 67.
Elder's Lot, 9, 15, 21, 24, 41, 65, 74, 75.
Elections for member of Legislature, where to be held, 177.
Elizabethtown Bounds, 10, 23, 112, 123, 134, 141.
Elizabethtown, Consultations with, 10, 43, 60, 77, 82, 97, 99, 112, 123, 134, 137, 141, 153; laws relating to the affairs of the two towns to be obtained, 68.
Episcopal Church, 205.

Falconer, Mr., 104.
Falconer, Mrs., 106.
Farrand, Samuel, 132, 134.
Fen, Benjamin, 9.
Fences, Regulations respecting, 6, 18, 25, 35, 42, 46, 47, 78, 81, 82, 84, 86, 89, 97, 125, 134.
Fire Engine, application to Legislature for authority to appropriate money for, 249; expenditures authorized therefor, 252.
Firemen, Proposed exemptions for, 229.
Fish Market, authorized to to be built on the Common, 199.
Fletcher, Richard, 55, 64, 67, 85, 93.
Fortifications to be erected, 61.
Ford, John, authorized to erect mill, 124.
Fordham Stephen, 183, 186.
Foster Nathan, 127.
Francisco, Abraham, 136.
Mr., 252.

Freeholder, admitted, on his promising to learn to read, 39.
Freeholders, Chosen, first elected, 1715, 125; disputed election of, 151.
Frelinghuysen, Theodore, 230, 234, 260, 262.
Freeman, Amos, 158.
Samuel, 85, 102, 125.
Stephen, 1, 3, 5, 8, 9, 20, 22, 24, 26, 28, 33, 36—38, 44, 46—50, 52, 54—57, 70, 79.
Frog Pond, pound by side of, 18; land about, to remain common, 26; John Johnson's appropriation of part of land objected to, 67, 74.

Gardner, John, 69, 86, 94, 104, 106, 120,
Thomas, 127.
Garretson, Harmanus, 127.
Gate, Large swinging, on the road to salt meadow, 162.
Gifford, John, (Capt.) 204.
Archer, 231, 267, 271.
Goble, Luther, 236, 245, 251.
Godden, Elizabeth, 156.
Goden, John, 127.
Goodrich, Bartholomew, 49.
Grant, William, 144.
Gregory, John, 5, 9, 11, 22.
Guard to be kept, and where stationed, 60, 75, 83.
Guilford, Agreement with settlers from, 1, 5.

Halsey, William, 195, 233, 205, 225.
Halstead, John, 139.
Harmanusen, Garret, 128.
Harris, Mr., 247.
Harrison, Amos, 148, 155.
Aaron, 199.
Benjamin, 104, 127.
Daniel, 127, 131.
George, 91, 102, 112, 117, 136.
Ichabod, 148.
Jabez, 236, 238, 244.
Japhia, 215.
John, 2, 7—9, 11, 24, 28, 36, 37, 48, 49, 70, 78.
Joseph, 58, 91, 93, 101, 102, 108, 110—113, 117—123, 127, 129.
Nathaniel, 141.
Richard, 1, 3, 8—12, 15, 20, 24, 26, 28, 31, 33, 34, 36, 42, 49, 50, 54—56, 60, 63, 70, 73, 74, 77, 79, 85, 86, 90, 91.
Samuel, 49, 50, 55, 71, 78, 84, 86, 89—94, 97—102, 105, 106, 108, 114, 117, 118, 127, 129.
Thomas, 9.
Widow, 248.
Haven [Havens] Ebenezer, 216, 225.
Hay, Augustus M., 246.
Hays, Thomas, 110, 111, 114, 117.
Hayes [Hays] Daniel, 210, 243.
[Hays] Samuel, 157, 166, 183, 186.
Robert, 127, 128.
[Hays] Stephen, 202, 211, 215, 235, 206.
Health Committee appointed, 73.
Hedden, Joseph, 157; permitted to build a boat, 156; to transcribe the old Town book, 157.
Widow, 157.
Henderson, Hendrick, 107.
Hendrickson, Hans, 107.
Hester, The ship, act relative to, 113, 114.
Highways, Regulations respecting, 4, 8, 15, 19, 20, 39, 52, 53, 86, 95, 96, 98, 178; encroachments on, 184, 185, 219; overseers of, first appointed, 1754, 141

Hinchman, ——, 169.
Hinsdale, Epaphras, 200.
Hockquecanung. [See Acquackanong.]
Hore, Richard, 94, 104, 105.
Hornblower, Joseph C., 203, 205, 210, 216, 234, 244, 267, 269, 271.
Josiah, 159.
William, 176.
Hopkins, Mr., 52.
Horses, Remonstrance against act suppressing the running of, in woods, 94.
Horton, Joseph, 9, 31.
Humes, James, 199.
Susannah, 199.
Huntington, Samuel, 155, 156.
Widow, Sarah, 127.
Thomas, 3, 8, 9, 24, 28, 36, 37, 39, 46, 49, 61, 67, 70, 77, 78, 85, 95.

Incorporation, Bill proposed and referred to Committee, 243; reported on and rejected, 244.
Indians, Proposal to send men to them to demand robbers, 51; to treat with them about land, 55; bill of sale from, to be recorded, 67; to be treated with for land to top of mountain, 71; north and west lines with, to be run, 71; threatened rising of, 75.

Jackson, John P., 268.
acobs, Peter, 79, 80, 81.
unnings, Patience, 182.
oanes, Jeffery, 10.
Jones, Edward, 210, 268.
Joseph, 127.
Johnson, Aaron, 211, 215, 216, 217.
Eliphalet, 111, 112, 115, 117, 119, 120—125, 127, 156, 157, 158.
Hezekiah, 127.
John, 3, 10, 18, 48, 67, 74, 75, 80, 86, 93, 119, 127, 134, 187.
Joseph, 85, 93, 95, 102, 140, 142.
Nathaniel, 134, 136, 139.
Robert, 159.
Thomas, 1, 3, 5, 8, 9, 11, 13—15, 17, 23 24, 26—28, 30, 34—38, 41, 44—46, 49, 50, 52, 54—56, 59—63, 65, 67, 71, 73, 76, 85, 86, 87, 88, 89, 90, 93, 94, 95, 97, 98, 99, 101. 102, 104, 105, 106, 114, 127.
Tunis, 107.

King, Abraham, 245,
John, 245.
Thomas, 153.
Kingsland, Major, 57.
Kinney, A. W., 200.
Kiper, Johannes, 136.
Kitchell Abraham, 127, 128.
Robert, 8, 9, 24, 26, 28, 37, 70.
Samuel, 1, 3, 8, 9, 11, 15, 19, 24, 25, 26, 27, 28, 32, 36, 37, 45, 46, 49, 50, 56, 59, 60, 62, 68, 70, 71, 76, 85, 93, 95, 102.
Mrs., 44, 49.

Lancasterian system of teaching, to be introduced into the schools for the poor, 237.
Landing-place to be laid out, 63; gate to, 65.
Lands not to be sold until two years after settlement, 6; bought of Indians, how to be paid for, 7; how to be designated, 15; manner of laying out recorded, 22; in common, not to be given away without unani-

mous consent, 26; divisions of, 27, 29, 32, 59; declaration as to how held, 29; no Patent of, to be for more than 100 acres, 48; Patents of, reduced to 40 acres, 59; up the river to be bought, 61; beyond Second river, 69; to top of mountain, 71; on Rahway river, 80; not to be parted with to strangers, 83; west of Town bounds to be purchased, 114; rights to, bought of the heathen, to be upheld, 95; irregularly laid out, 117; common, to be dug for mines, 129, 131, 132; vacant, to be vested in Township, 231; law obtained relative to vacant, 233.
Lampson, Eleazer, 107.
Laurance (Lawrance), Richard, 3, 7—9, 24, 26, 28, 37, 45, 49, 50, 56, 59, 70, 70, 73, 76, 85, 93—95, 102.
Laydicker, Garret, 107.
Leet, Mr., 9, 21—24, 26, 34, 37, 44.
Linle (Lindly), Francis, 3, 8, 9, 24, 26, 28, 33, 37, 42, 44, 47, 49, 70, 85, 93, 98, 102.
Lindsley, Ebenezer, 127.
John, 127.
Jonathan, 127.
Joseph, 127, 138, 139, 171.
Longworth, Jabez, resolutions, &c., relative to will of, 254—257, 261, 262.
Nicholas, 254, 255, 258, 259.
Thomas, 150.
Ludington, Thomas, 8, 9, 17, 24, 26, 37, 44, 49, 55, 64, 70, 73, 74, 82, 85, 86, 88, 89, 93, 96, 102 105, 106.
Lovelace, Col., Governor of N. Y., to be consulted about relations with that colony, 21.
Lymens (Limon), Robert, 3, 8, 24, 26, 37, 49, 70.
Lyon, Abraham, 221.
Benjamin, 127.
Henry, 3, 9, 11—13, 15, 17, 22, 24, 26—28, 30, 32—34, 37, 38, 43—47, 49, 50, 70, 76, 79, 85, 93, 127.
Isaac, 133, 134, 142.
Joseph, 159, 162.
Samuel, 3, 8, 45, 94, 96, 97, 100—102.
Thomas, 3, 8, 80, 85, 90, 93, 107.
Zophar, 134.

Manure, to be gathered in the streets for Poor house farm, 239.
Map of Town, to be copied, 213.
Market house, permission to build one in Broad street, 162.
Market House lot, inquiry into rights of property in, 221.
Market, Committee on securing a better, 234; discharged, 235; another Committee appointed, 236; proposal to erect a new, 235, 237, 238.
Marsh, Aaron, 239, 241.
McWhorter, Rev. Alex'r, 159.
Mrs., 247.
Meadows, provision for laying out, 15, 21, 22, 24, 29, 37; for burning, 16, 119, 157, 159, 172.
Measures and Weights, how regulated, 100, 101.
Medles, John, 116.
Meeker, William, releases the town from all claims, 65.
Mekeny, John, 80, 85.
Meeting House, to be built, 11, 12; where placed, 17; nails for it, 18; the townsmen to attend to completion of, 19; the flooring of, 34; to be lathed, 60; to be protected by a guard, 60; to be seated, 73, 75, 94; irreverent behavior therein to be rebuked, 77, 80, 132; seats in, regulated, 77, 79, 88; how congregation to sit in, 94, 108; shingles for, 106; north gallery in, 117; floor of, to be transferred to the school house, 124; those who seated the congregation in, to be themselves provided for, 127; charge of, 132, 138; hovel to be built near, 134.
Metfield, Matthew, 134.
Milford, Agreement with people of, 1, 5.
Mill, Grist, measures for erection of, 16; agreement for, 30, 91; rate for, 35; grinding days at, 39; on Bound Creek, authorized, 82.
Mill Lot, 24, 26.
Mines, common lands to be let to dig for, 129, 131, 132.
Ming, John, 198.
Ministry, provisions for obtaining and supporting, 4, 10, 22, 32, 41, 62, 66, 69, 72, 76, 101, 102, 106, 107, 112, 113, 116, 118—121, 127, 128, 132—136.
Molyns [Molynes, Melyne], Jacob, 52, 58.
Montgomery, Robert, 297.
Moore, Mr., (of Woodbridge), 62.
Morehouse, ———, 239.
Morris, Mr., [Morrish], 1, 8, 9, 24, 26, 36, 37, 70.
John, 112, 114, 117, 120, 123, 124, 125, 127—129.
Thomas, 3.
Mrs. Elizabeth, 76, 85.
Philip, 104.
Stephen, 136.
Mountain Society (Orange) to share in Parsonage Lands, 145, 150.
Munn, Aaron, 202, 215, 223, 239.
Joseph, 148, 156.
Samuel, 177, 183, 188, 191, 193.
Munrow, Alex., 8, 28, 37, 49, 70.

Neck, The, arrangements for procuring, 50, 51, 52, 54, 57, 62, 63, 70, 71, 80, 87; regulating use of, 109, 111, 114, 115, 119, 125, 126.
Newark, agreement between people of Milford, Guilford and Branford as to mode of settlement, 1; none but members of Congregational churches to be admitted, 2; dividing line between Elizabethtown and, 10; enquiry to be made if the bounds are recorded, 67; a Charter from Proprietors applied for, 71; application for settlement of bounds, 78; dividing line with Second River, as to domicils of the Poor, 136; Charter deposited with Justice Cundit, 159; dividing between and Bloomfield and Orange, 193; receipts and expenditures of, in 1815–'16, 214; N. and Mt. Pleasant Turnpike Co., letter from received, 225; proposed division into wards, 268—271; law passed by the Legislature, 271; chartered as a city, 271.
Newark Mutual Fire Ins. Co., 216.
Newbury Port, application for relief from, 202.
New Haven, agreements with settlers from, 5.

New Orange. (See Dutch.)
New York, relations with, 21, 22; small pox there, 73.
Nicholls, Col., letter to be sent to, 22.
David. 244.
Isaac, 211, 220, 225, 244, 250.
Robert, 136.
Night Watch, application to legislature to be made to raise money for, 243.
Nottman [Nuttman] James, 122, 124, 127, 129, 132, 142, 145, 146, 148, 150.

O'Donnell, John, 256, 269.
Ogden, Abraham, 150.
David, 76, 84, 89, 93, 102, 125, 127, 139, 146.
Isaac, 154, 157.
John, 10, 28, 43, 52, 155.
Josiah, 127, 134.
Lewis, 157, 159.
Samuel, 195.
Oleff, Anthony, 74, 86, 93, 102.
Orange (Mountain Society) Church to share in Parsonage Lands, 145, 150; dividing lines between Newark and Bloomfield, 193; Poor of Orange and Newark referred to Committee, 195, 198; road to, 251.
Ordinary, for the entertainment of Travellers, to be established, 13.
Osborne, Abner, 199.
Joel, 156, 199.
Overseers of Highways, first appointed 1754, 141; restricted to three within Newark Town Plot, 231.
Owens, Widow Moses, 199.

Paper Currency in 1787, 163.
Parkhurst [Parkas], Benjamin, 87.
Caleb, 181.
Henry L., 250.
Parratt Samuel, 199.
Parsonage Land to be run out, 128, 136; Fines for cutting wood from, 136, 137, 139, 141; put in charge of a Committee, 138, 139; deed for, to be obtained from David Young, 144; division of, among the three congregations, 145; division of, disagreed to, 147; division again authorized, 150.
Parsonage Meadow, bounds settled, 139; rented, 141 (and thereafter annually for several years;) the three ministers to participate in the rent, 142, 148.
Patent for Town, to be obtained, 52; negotiations relative to, 59, 123; published, 124.
Pease, not to be sown, 73.
Peck [Pecke], Jeremiah, 3, 5, 8, 9, 24, 26, 31, 36, 37, 46, 47, 49, 57, 60.
Joseph, 128, 138, 139,
John, 154, 165, 166.
Pennington, Ephraim, 3, 8, 9, 24, 26, 28, 36, 57, 49, 61, 70, 85.
Judah, 125.
Samuel, 150, 192, 200, 207, 225, 227, 230, 235, 239, 250, 255, 259, 260.
William, 271.
Wm. S., 183, 186, 200, 202, 220, 227, 230, 231, 234, 236, 238, 244.
Peshine, Jacob, 216.
Pierson [Peirson, Person], Abraham, 2, 7—11, 17, 22, 24—26, 28, 30, 32, 33, 36, 37, 40—42, 49, 52, 59, 62, 70, 71, 76, 85, 89, 91, 105, 112.
Abraham, Jun'r, 8, 37, 49, 55, 59, 70; called as assistant minister, 22, 43.
Bethuel, 145, 146, 150, 153, 154, 181, 184, 189.
Daniel, 145, 146.
Elisha, 193.
Dr. Isaac, 181, 183.
Jonathan, 183.
Joseph, 214.
Samuel, 100, 102, 127.
Theophilus, 98, 102, 104, 108—115, 117—123.
Thomas, 3, 8, 9, 17, 24, 26, 37, 49, 55, 85, 98, 102, 125.
Thomas, Jun'r, 49, 76, 77, 85.
Zenas, 164, 171.
Pigot, Dr., 136.
Plum, Jacob, 204.
John, 5, 111.
Samuel, 3, 8, 9, 24, 26, 28, 44, 45, 49, 61, 70, 74, 77, 79, 86, 88, 89, 93, 98, 102, 138, 139, 142.
Poinier, John, 225.
Pool, Albion, 216.
Poor, Overseers of, appointed, 105, 111, (thereafter annually); dividing line of, between Newark and Second River, 136; of Second River again included in Newark, 176; first specific sum appropriated for support of, in 1763, 147 (thereafter, with some exceptions, annually); to be let out, 1765, 148 (thereafter, with some exceptions, annually for many years); children of, to receive schooling from those who take the families, 151, 155, 170, 171; to be inspected monthly, 155; to be taken to church, 155; divided into classes, 171; children of, to be bound out, 172; children of, to be let out, 189; questions respecting those of Orange and Newark referred, 195, 198; provision for education of children of, 210, 214; report on state of, in 1816, 213, 214.
Poor-house, to be built or hired, 144, 147; to be built, 190; place to be obtained 200; one for the county to be tried for, 206; site to be selected, 207; site fixed upon in Mulberry st., 207; site rejected, 208; one to be hired, 208; hiring one found ineffectual, 209; authority given to buy as well, 209; purchase made, 210; report thereon, 211; meadow added to, 217; to be enlarged, 232.
Potter, Samuel, [Goodman], 69, 75, 77, 79, 81, 86, 93, 104.
Pounds established, 13, 138, 156, 162, 164, 177, 181, 198; regulations of, 19, 64, 126, 158, 175, 178, and generally annually; number reduced to one, 200.
Powder and Lead to be procured for town's use, 63.
Presbyterian Church, Trustees of, to obtain deed from David Young for Parsonage lands, 144; they protest against division of Parsonage lands, 150; called upon to surrender all the town lands, 203.
Preston, Eliafaph, 36, 37.
Price, Benjamin, Sen'r, 87, 98.
Ephraim, 125.
Hannah, Widow, 199.

Thomas, 134.
Prices of Produce in payment of rates, 30, 31, 74, 119.
Privateers, Address against arming, in 1798, 178.
Proprietors, relations with, 29, 30, 34, 35, 40, 41, 43, 44, 50, 52, 56, 59, 60, 62, 64, 71, 78, 90, 95, 97, 100, 102, 106, 112, 114, 118, 123, 144, 185.
Potter, Samuel, [Goodman] 69, 75, 77, 79, 81, 86, 93, 104.
Provost, Dr. James, 127.
Pruden, John, to be called to be minister, 105; arrangements for his accommodation, 106—113; a successor to be looked for, 113, 118, 119, 127.
———, Margaret, (Widow), 127.
Public Securities, holders of, to have like privileges with holders of Real Estate in borrowing under the Loan Act of 1787, 183.

Quinby, Josiah, 148.
Quit-Rents, 118.

Receipts and Expenditures, 1815-16, 214.
Religion, subverters of, to depart, 4.
Remer, John, 267.
Reves, Isaac, 159.
Richards, John, 127.
Martin, 193.
Thomas, 6, 9, 24, 26, 34, 36, 37, 44, 47, 49, 54—56, 59, 60, 63, 65, 69—71, 78—80, 85, 90, 93, 96, 97, 100—102, 106, 111—113, 115, 118—120.
Riggs, Caleb S., 205, 224, 225, 227, 230, 231, 233, 234, 238.
Edward, 1, 5, 9, 11—13, 15, 20, 24, 26, 30, 42, 49.
Edward, Jr., 77, 80, 85, 97, 98, 102, 127.
Elizabeth (Widow), 28, 33, 36, 37, 70.
Joseph, 3, 34, 49, 78, 80, 83—85, 93, 94, 102, 132, 140, 144, 154—156, 158, 159.
Robards, Amos, 137.
Joseph, 134.
Samuel, 116, 118.
Sayres, 170.
Robarts, [Robards] John, 139, 169.
Roberts, Hugh, 3, 8, 9, 20, 24, 26—28, 36, 37, 70, 125, 139.
Moses, 214, 250.
Rockwell, John, 9, 17, 28, 31.
Rod-pole, Length of, used in measuring fence, 85.
Roff, Moses, 201, 204, 206—208, 211, 212, 216, 218, 219, 224.
Stephen, 202, 204, 206, 211, 214, 219, 224, 226, 229, 232, 235, 237, 240, 246, 252, 255, 263.
Rogers, David, 216.
Eleazer, 9, 14, 19, 21, 24, 36.
Jabez, 49, 82, 85, 93, 107.
John, 8, 9, 19, 24, 26, 28, 36, 37, 70, 127.
Rose, [Ross] Samuel, 3, 8, 9, 24—26, 29, 37, 49, 55, 70, 85, 93, 98, 102, 105.
Rutgers, Anthony, 157.
Ryon, James, 199.

Sabbath, regulations for guard duty on, 39.
Salt, to be bought of Mr. Windor, 56.
Sandford, William, to be treated with for the Neck, 40.
Savage, Mrs., 227.
Saw-Mill, Thomas Davis authorized to erect one, 108.
Sayer, Jonathan, 127.
Sayrs, Caleb, 215.
Schools, Free, Committee to superintend, appointed in 1814, 206 [thereafter annually); room in upper part of market appropriated for use of, 222; Female, in Union School-house, 231; Lancasterian system of teaching to be introduced in, 237, 239; recommendation to turn them into pay schools, 239; first appropriation for, for colored children, 250.
School-house, to be floored with floor of meeting house, 124; to be built on common land, 155; an acre and a half on North commons appropriated for, 157; permission given to remove it, 175.
School-master, Equiries respecting a, 65; an engagement with one authorized, 67, 109, 111.
Seaman's Lot, 9, 15, 24, 53.
Seargeant, [Sargent, Sargeant] Jonathan, 3, 8, 14, 16, 28, 30, 31, 34, 36, 37, 49, 52, 70, 93, 102, 127, 137, 138, 142.
Second River, Lands beyond, 69; land between it and Newark as regarded the poor, 136.
"Sentinel of Freedom," (newspaper) 267, 270.
Sheep, measures for preservation of, 195.
Shepherd for the town, 117.
Sherman, Mr. Samuel, to preach on probation, 118; to be settled, 119.
Shingleton, Hannah, to sweep the meeting-house, 133.
Shipman, Charles T., 234, 244, 255.
Sidman, Thomas, 172.
Small, George D., 269.
Small-pox in 1760, 145.
Smith, Moses, 234.
Soldiers, to be paid their wages, 104.
Squier, [Squire] Henry, 156, 167.
Squire, Elijah, 166.
Stagg, Thomas, 128.
Staples, Thomas, 8, 24, 26, 36, 49, 61, 70, 85.
Staves, to be gathered and sold to pay the debt for Neck, 70.
Stites, John, 139.
Strangers, regulations for admitting, 83.
Streets, Commissioners of, first appointed, 1809, 197; to be regulated, 198, 213; encroachments on, to be removed, 219.
Stockman, William, 162, 171.
Swain, Samuel, 1, 2, 7—10, 15—17, 24—26, 28, 33, 37, 43, 44, 48—50, 52, 54—56, 61, 63, 70, 73, 85.

Tan-yard, allowed to A. Crane out of common, 111.
Taylor, John, 234.
Nathan, 172,
"Taylor's lot," 9, 15, 24, 44, 45.
Thibou, Lewis, 207, 216, 220, 225, 228, 240.
Tichenor, Daniel, 82, 96, 107, 116, 139.
James, 255, 259, 265.
Jonathan, 107.
John, 74, 95, 102.
Josiah, 172.
Martin, 3, 5, 8, 9, 24, 25, 30, 36, 37, 42—44, 49, 51, 70, 127.
Samuel, 93.
Timber to be cut and sold only for the town, 30.
Tompkins, Ebenezer, 127.
Eleazer, 101, 125.
John, 125.
Jonathan, 3, 8, 9, 24, 36, 37, 44,

49, 102.
Michael [Micah], 1, 3, 5—9, 11, 18, 20, 24, 26, 32, 33, 36, 37, 40, 46, 49, 62, 65, 70, 71, 78, 84, 88, 102.
Obadiah, 162.
Samuel, 127.
Seth, 12, 49, 86, 90, 102, 107, 115, 125.
Town-book, to be transcribed, 157.
Commons, what declared to be, 26.
docks, 90, 224, 227, 230, 233, 235, 236, 239, 241, 249, 250, 252, 253, 266.
house, erection of proposed, 202, 211, 213, 217; to be placed on town lot in Broad street, 220, 235, 236; authorized to be built in 1821, 225; proposition to apply to legislature to raise money for, lost, 226, 230; subject of, revived in 1829, and rejected, 250; more suitable lot than town lot to be selected, 255.
lot, selected as the site for town-house, 220, 235, 236; to be leased for five years, 221; not to be built on if leased, 221; authority to be applied for to sell, 250; incumbrances on, to be removed, 263; to be leased, 263.
map to be copied —
meetings, attendance at, regulated, 11, 38, 45, 52, 62, 71, 81, 91, 93, 98.
Town's men appointed, 54. (See list of officers in Appendix.)
Town patent (Incorporation) obtained, 124; deposited with Justice Condit, 159. (See Appendix.)
plot, surveyed, 200.
Township divided into three districts, 192; proposed division of, into wards, 266; Report of Committee thereon, 268; Committee to draft law relating thereto, 268; proposed law respecting, 270; passed by legislature, 271.
Training days established, 78.
Treasurer's accounts to be examined, 1685, 96.
Treat [Treatt], John, 49, 54, 71, 85, 86, 89, 93, 97, 102, 107—109, 111—113, 117, 118, 122, 123, 125.
Robert, 1—3, 5, 7, 8, 10, 13—17, 21, 22, 24—28, 30, 32—34, 37, 42, 43, 46, 49, 70, 91.
Trees, old, to be cut down, 53; preservation of, 66.
Trustees of Town, authorized to let out the common lands for mining, 131, 132.
Tunis Nehemiah, 228, 236.
Turner, William, 135.
Turkey Eagle Rock, 193.
Tuttle, Johnson, 178.
William, 210, 244, 251, 268.

Uriansen, Thomas, 128.

Van Arsdale, Elias, 230.
Vanderpool, James, 200, 202, 220, 225, 236, 244, 262, 268, 271.
John, 143.
Van Geise, Bostyan, 107.
Van Siles, Stephen, 136.
Vincent, Levi, 136.
Vraeman, Jacob, 127.
Vreelandt Abraham, 127.
Johannes, 127.
Michael, 128.
Wakeman, Rev. Jabez, 112, 114—118.
Walters, [Waters] Joseph, 3, 7, 9, 24, 33, 36, 37, 43, 49, 52, 55, 70, 76, 78, 80, 85, 89, 90, 93, 95, 99.
Ward, Aaron, 230, 233, 239, 241, 250, 252, 253.
Caleb, 107.
Ebenezer, 166.
Elizabeth, widow, 28, 35—37, 42, 70.
Isaac, 201.
Jacob, 195, 200.
John, Sen'r, 2, 3, 8, 9, 11, 12, 14, 16, 24, 26—28, 32, 35—38, 41, 45, 46, 49—52, 54—59, 63, 65, 67, 70, 71, 73, 75, 78, 89, 90, 93—95, 101, 102, 104—106.
John, Jun'r, 8, 37, 84, 86, 93, 127.
John, "Turner," 9, 24, 26, 28, 36, 49, 51, 52, 62, 63, 69, 70, 74—76, 82, 85, 93.
John, "Turner," Jun'r, 86.
Josiah, 3, 8, 24, 26, 28, 36, 37, 46, 49, 50, 70, 139.
Laurance [Lawrence], 2, 7, 8, 11, 12, 16, 17, 22, 24, 25, 26.
Nathaniel, 69, 93, 102, 106, 108, 110—112, 114, 116, 120.
Samuel, 93.
Samuel, Jun'r, 127.
William, 210.
Washington street, low grounds in vicinity of, 260.
Watchmen, 60, 75, 83.
Water courses, regulations respecting, 5.
Watering Place, 154, 156, 158, 186, 191, 192, 198, 200, 202.
Waters, stagnant, measures to remove, 259, 260.
Watson, Luke, 10.
Webb, Mr., to be minister for three-fourths of a year, 128; continued with Mr. Burr, 132.
Webster, Mr., 9, 15, 21, 24.
Weights and Measures, how regulated, 100, 101.
Welford, John, 16.
Wheeler, Caleb, 143, 150, 154.
Joseph, 127.
Nathaniel, 3, 5, 8, 9, 26, 28, 30, 35—37, 43, 49, 54, 57, 70, 80, 85, 96, 124, 127, 136, 139, 142.
Whitehead, Asa, 255, 259, 271.
Isaac, Sen'r, 87.
Samuel, 79.
Whittlesey, Mr. Sam'l, to be minister, 120, 121.
Wilkins, John, 91, 93.
Wilkison, Alling, 127.
Wilson, Mr., 57.
Wilbur, Rodney, 255.
Williams, David, 142.
Joannah, 199.
Matthew, 80, 86, 127.
Moses, 178.
Winans, Isaac C., 267.
Windor, Mr., to furnish salt, 56.
Wolves, 6, 76, 80, 88, 96, 103, 111, 117.
Wood, Joseph, 107.
Woodruff, Obadiah, 214, 260.
Seth, 195, 202, 208, 211.
Wool, Premiums for best shearings of, 166.
Wright, Nathaniel, 258, 262.

Young, David, of Hanover, presumed heir to Parsonage Patents, 143, 144; deed from, 144, 145.
People, regulated, 77, 80, 84, 88, 90, 107.
Robert, 107, 112, 114, 117, 119, 121, 127, 144.